BLOODLINES OF ATMOS

THE STORY OF JACE
BOOK 2 - SAVIOR

J. P. EDGAR

BLOODLINES OF ATMOS
THE STORY OF JACE, BOOK 2 — SAVIOR

Copyright © 2020 by J. P. Edgar

ISBN: 978-1-68046-903-5

Melange Books, LLC
White Bear Lake, MN 55110
www.melange-books.com

Published in the United States of America.

Cover Design by Ashley Redbird Designs

Copyright Page

ISBN: 978-1-68046-903-5 Print

ISBN: 978-1-68046-904-2 eBook

✿ Created with Vellum

A special thanks to Leslie, who convinced me to start writing in the first place, and to Nakia, who supported me in this strange adventure. Step one would never have happened without you two.

PROLOGUE

Drill Sergeant Shepard stood motionless in the desert sun waiting for his new recruits. With his hands behind his back and sweat dripping down his face, he stared off at the distant bus that kicked up dust, thinking back to when he first rode to the isolated boot camp. He remembered the stench of the body odor from dozens of recruits, the miserable heat, and listening to nothing but the squeaking of the bus joints because of the no-talking rule. One of the hottest days on record and the recruits were riding in an old, cramped, and stuffy bus. As soon as they agreed to climb the stairs in to find their seat, they were going to be tested on everything. Even the ride to the camp tested them, simulating a prison in all but shackles to let them know their old lives were over.

Sand pelted his face from the breeze when the bus pulled up. It was time to go to work. It was time to break down these kids and stripping them of their old habits of civilian life and rebuild them into tough, hardcore soldiers.

The doors opened with a creek, and the recruits started to walk out. They seemed to be a healthy mix of rookies—boys and girls, short and tall. Every single one of them would be fine examples of discipline and valor when he was through with them.

Shepard blew hard on his whistle, catching the attention of the kids who poured out of the bus. "Line up!"

One by one, the children stood side by side, each of them standing with their backs straight. Or as straight as they could. He quickly looked them over, then started to pace in front of the line. He looked for the weak link. An example to help break down the spirit of these kids and to turn them into figures of discipline and respect. "My name is Drill Sergeant Shepard. When you address me, you will call me Drill Sergeant." When he reached the end of the line, he turned around and walked back down the row. "There are only four words you will tell me. And unless I tell you otherwise, I don't want to hear you say anything BUT those words. Those words are 'yes,' 'no,' and 'Drill Sergeant!'"

He stopped at the shortest recruit in the line. The boy couldn't have been more than five and a half feet tall. Worst of all, his features gave him a feeling of uncaring and lack of discipline, like he stared off in the distance and ignoring the world around him. He had found his first example. "Do you understand, recruit?"

The kid nodded.

"What the shit!" Shepard stepped up and got close to his face. "What did you say?"

The kid shrugged. "Nothing."

"Was 'nothing' something I said you could say?"

"No, sir!"

Though the reply was better than the last, Shepard had a feeling this kid was going to be a problem. "What's your name, boy?"

"Jace."

"Not anymore, Tiny. Drop and do push-ups until I tell you to stop!"

Without skipping a beat, Tiny leaped back, dropped to the ground and began his punishment. Shepard knelt, getting closer to Tiny's ear. "Yes, Drill Sergeant! No, Drill Sergeant! I don't want you to say anything else. Is that understood, Tiny?"

"Yes, Drill Sergeant!"

"Good!" Shepard stood up, still watching Tiny while he pumped out one push-up after another. "Seems there is hope for you after all." He continued his pacing in front of the row of would-be soldiers.

"Now, you are NOT to speak unless I tell you to. You are not going to sleep unless I tell you. You will not shit! You will not piss!" He spun around and looked a recruit in the eye, a rather chubby-faced kid with a large gut. He would have to work on this kid to get him in shape. "If I see you wipe your ass without permission, I'm going to kick it!" He leaned in closer. "Then you will clean my boot with your tongue!" Shepard spotted a grin at the corner of Chubby's lip. He had found another that needed a severe ass-kicking. "You find that funny?"

"No, Drill Sergeant!"

"I bet you're undressing me with your pretty little eyes. I bet you wish I were a rack of ribs you could bite into."

"No, Drill Sergeant!"

"Bullshit, Chubby! Drop and give me twenty!"

On command, Chubby fell to the ground and started doing push-ups. Before Shepard continued his pacing in front of his line, Chubby spoke, "The concrete is hot, Drill Sergeant."

Shepard glared at Chubby, who looked up from his push-up position. "What did you say?"

Chubby's voice gave a painful quiver. "N-Nothing, Drill Sergeant."

Shepard watched Chubby for a moment while he struggled to pull himself off the ground, then took a step back to look over the recruits. "Everything you think you know, forget it! You are mine! And until I tell you otherwise, you're nothing but maggots. Is that understood?"

The battalion answered in unison, "Yes, Drill Sergeant!"

The single reply from a mass of people always sounded so good to his ears. Then a whimper sounded from Chubby, who visibly trembled. "You're not done, Maggot?" He knelt and put his face close to his ear. "How many have you done, Maggot?"

His reply came after a struggling gasp. "S... Six!"

"Six? Holy shit! You're no longer a maggot. You're a piece of shit!"

Chubby's reply was barely audible. "Yes, Drill Sergeant."

"What did you say?"

"Yes, Drill Sergeant!"

"Better. Now get back up, you piece of shit, and get back in line!"

Chubby pushed himself to his hands and knees, then struggled to get to his feet. Tears ran down his red cheeks, and he panted heavily.

3

Shepard looked at him once more, noting the shaking hands. The pavement was hot, and he should probably dismiss the line soon to get some ice on his palms.

Shepard turned to continue his pacing. "From this moment on, if one of you gets in trouble, all of you get in trouble. There is no 'you.' There is only your unit." Shepard paused when he noticed Tiny, who still did push-ups. His back was straight, and he continued at a good pace. Still, he had a schedule to keep, and he needed to get Chubby something to put on his burns. "Get up, maggot!"

Tiny quickly got to his feet and stood up straight. Though he breathed deeply, he still seemed to have his breath. Sweat poured down his face, and his soaked shirt. His hands weren't trembling, regardless of the apparent burn marks on his palms. At first, Shepard was pleased with the potential of Tiny, but the kid's gaze—uncaring and uninterested—started to make him angry, as if nothing had happened. This kid was going to be trouble.

Shepard paused for a few heartbeats. "You rested up, Tiny?" He didn't care about the reply. Shepard blew on his whistle and announced to the line, "Let's go for a run, Maggots. Grab your shit and keep up!" He turned and started jogging toward the dunes to the base.

———

The following week, Shepard went to check on his recruits. More importantly, to check on Tiny. His attitude and his passive-aggressive defiance was something Shepard couldn't stand. It constantly undermined his authority, making his recruits less like soldiers every day. So every time Shepard saw Tiny doing the smallest thing, he would make Tiny an example.

When he walked in the door to the barracks, he saw Tiny doing sit-ups. "What the hell are you doing, Tiny?"

Tiny quickly got to his feet and stood straight.

"Did I say you could exercise?"

"No, Drill Sergeant."

His arrogance was aggravating. The discipline he tried to teach this child went over his head, and that would put him and his unit at risk.

He couldn't allow that to happen. "Then it's your turn to clean the bathroom. I want to see my face in the porcelain. I want the floor so clean I can eat off it. Is that understood?"

"Yes, Drill Sergeant."

Tiny marched off, but Shepard decided to give him a bit of motivation. "Move, move, move!" After Tiny was out of sight, Shepard turned to the rest of the recruits. "As for the rest of you..." He eyed each of them for a moment, especially locking his gaze at Chubby. "I told you to keep an eye on him. The next time he does something, I'm going to make you all clean the shit tank! Now drop and give me twenty!"

In unison, everyone in the room fell to the floor for their push-ups. Discipline. Synchronization. Perfect harmony once more. He calmed down almost instantly, then turned and left the recruits to their punishment.

———

Training recruits hand-to-hand combat was always Shepard's favorite time in boot camp. The last strands of defiance were beaten out of the recruits, and it marked when the kids could be turned into soldiers.

The third recruit fell on the mat with a loud thud. Shepard stood victorious, staring at the three who rolled and moaned on the floor mat. He started to pace as he continued the introduction to his next lesson.

"Being faced against a powerful force is something you all will have to deal with in your lives. Your opponent on the battlefield won't care if you're down or not. They won't care if you're a mother or a father. A son or a daughter. If your enemy overpowers you, you need to find a way to win, or go down fighting!" He turned to Tiny, eager to finally break the last defiant member of his crew. "Tiny, get up here." As Tiny stood and approached, Shepard continued, "Next, I want you maggots to see how to block and counter any given attack. It doesn't matter if it's against a human or those magical creatures who call themselves 'Evolved' or whatever. Urban combat will have a high chance of hand-to-hand combat. So you must be prepared for anything." He turned to face Tiny. "Okay, Tiny. Try to hit me. Do whatever you want. Just try to—"

A sudden, sharp pulse of pain shot through his entire body. His head violently jerked back. Before he knew it, he felt himself swept off his feet and crashing hard on the mat. Then, he knew nothing.

———

Shepard leaned heavily on his crutch all while trying to keep the pressure off his torso. The uncomfortable neck brace made his skin itchy in places he couldn't scratch, and the bandages around his chest made the hot days hotter. Though no official medical released had been signed, Shepard insisted on getting back to his battalion to teach that little bastard a lesson. He had never been so embarrassed, and the damage to the recruit's discipline, as well as to his own reputation, was severe.

Tiny sat in an awkwardly shaped chair cleaning and polishing every boot in the base. The sun turned his skin red, and polish covered his hands. Still, the pain that bastard went through was nowhere close to being enough.

When Lieutenant Westmen's special forces recruits marched by, Tiny looked up, his head turning as he stared at the progression.

Shepard hobbled up to the table and picked up a boot, carefully scrutinizing the leather. Not a scuff mark on it. "You missed a spot!" Shepard threw the boot back in the dirty pile, then tipped the table over. Though the movement stung his chest and shoulder, his anger overrode the pain. "Do it again. Do it all again and do it right this time!"

Tiny stared hard at him.

"You eyeballing me, boy?" Shepard leaned forward, challenging Tiny's stare.

Finally, the undisciplined recruit replied in a quiet, humbled tone, "No, Drill Sergeant."

Shepard stared hard at Tiny, closely looking over the red skin that already started to peel. Though he wanted this punk to pay, he knew if the captain saw Tiny in such a poor state, a possible court-martial would be in order. "Take a few minutes and put some lotion on your skin, maggot. Be back in ten, then get back to work." He turned and slowly made his way toward the barracks. When he turned back, he saw Tiny staring at the Westmen's group. Shepard scoffed, then entered the air-conditioned building, getting out of the intense desert heat.

———

Unable to run with his squad, Shepard sat in the back of an ATV, watching the recruits jog up and down the sand dunes. It was especially pleasing because the sun beat on Tiny's sunburnt skin, and knowing wind blew sand into his wounds. And if he couldn't teach Tiny respect and discipline, then turning the group against him would.

Shepard called out, "Come on, maggots! Don't make me come to you."

Chubby had improved quite a bit over the many weeks they have been in his care, and the weight had gotten more manageable. Still, his lagging behind was inexcusable.

Shepard had the ATV slow and pulled up beside Chubby. "Move it. Keep up, shit head!"

The amount of moisture Chubby had dripping down his face and neck made it look like he just got out of the pool. He put everything he had into his training. Shepard silently commended his commitment and dedication. Still, he was out of breath and was barely able to reply.

"Y-Yes, Drill… Sergeant."

"Thank Tiny for your wonderful run in this cold afternoon. You should have checked to see if there were any spots in the bathrooms!"

Though recruits groaned, no one protested.

A glance at Chubby showed that he was about to collapse. Shepard decided it was time for a break, but not before reaching the top of the dune. "Okay, maggots. That's enough." He stopped the ATV, then hobbled out of his seat. "Line up! It's time to hydrate." The driver got out and carried a large ice chest, staying a step behind Shepard. He reached down and grabbed water bottles from the cooler, handing them to each of his recruits. He took an extra moment when he got to Chubby. After nodding his approval, he gave him the bottle. Chubby gave a slight smile, grabbed the bottle, and put it on the back of his neck.

When he got to Tiny, he paused, staring the little shit in the eyes. That cocky bastard hardly seemed out of breath, unlike everyone else. Shepard took a swig from the bottle, swished the cold water in his dry and sandy mouth, then spat it back into the bottle.

"Hydrate!" Shepard ordered as he shoved the slosh in Tiny's chest. He paced down the line of recruits as they drank. After a couple of minutes, the break was over. "Present bottles!"

Each recruit held their arm out, showing empty bottles. All except Tiny, who hadn't touched his water.

"I said hydrate, maggot."

The disgust in Tiny's eyes made the day in the heat worth it. When he brought the bottle to his mouth, each gulp was a forced swallow.

"That's right, boy. Stay hydrated."

After Tiny finished the disgusting slosh, he presented the near-empty bottle. Only a thin part of spit and sand remained.

Shepard grabbed the bottle, then showed it to the group. "Bad news, maggots!" He tilted it upside down, showing everyone the water that poured out. "Tiny here didn't do as ordered." He tossed the bottle on the ground, then returned to the ATV. "No more breaks until we're done! Move, maggots!"

After some glances toward Tiny from the squad, Shepard knew his plan was working. He can't punish Tiny, but the team will.

———

When the squad finally returned to the base, the sun almost reached the horizon. Everyone looked exhausted and angry. That pleased Shepard. Tiny's squad hazing would be soon, and then he would be ready to be turned into a soldier.

"That's enough, maggots! Line up!" Shepard stopped the ATV as Westmen's squad marched past. Probably to do the Hell's Bells obstacle course. Shepard smirked. The course itself was made ridiculously difficult. Almost impossible to complete in the time the base officers wanted.

As his squad started to line up, many of them struggling to stay standing straight while gasping for breath, Shepard got up and began to pace. "Get your smelly hides cleaned up!" He noticed Tiny staring at the obstacle course. That was exactly what he was talking about—an evident lack of respect to superior officers. "Tiny!" That snapped the attention of the daydreamer. "Time to clean the bathroom floors. And this time, don't miss a spot, or you and your squad will go for another stroll in the desert." The two stared at each other for a long moment, Shepard seeing the deep red on his face and neck. "I can't hear you."

"Yes, Drill Sergeant."

"You're damn right." He took a step back to address the rest of his squad. "Same time tomorrow, maggots. Dismissed!" He turned and started to make his way into the cooled barracks, but not before hearing someone from his squad say, "Thanks, asshole." Knowing that remark was directed toward Tiny, Shepard smiled.

Before he went inside, he turned to see Tiny approaching Lieutenant Westman. That smug bastard was given an order to clean the bathrooms. Shepard grinned. This was the opportunity he needed to discipline the troublemaker properly.

Just as Shepard started to make his way toward Westmen, Tiny took off toward the monstrous obstacle course.

"Lieutenant," Shepard said when he stood beside Westman.

"Sergeant," Westman replied. "One of yours?"

"Yes, sir. A stubborn troublemaker. Even now, he's disobeying a direct order."

The two watched Tiny as he made his way through the running tires and past the monkey bars. Tiny conquered one obstacle after another.

"Didn't you just come in from a run in the dunes?"

"Yes, sir."

"Seems kind of cruel to have your crew run like that."

"Necessary, sir.

Tiny virtually leaped up the climbing wall and raced through the pitch-black crawlspace. Moments later, he popped out of the top from the climbing rope.

Westmen rubbed his chin. "He's making good time."

Shepard didn't answer.

Tiny passed people in front of him as he made his way through the course. Finally, he leaped down from the wall, then sprinted back, finishing with him standing attention before Shepard.

Westmen didn't say anything. And though Shepard was impressed, he still hoped Westmen would permit a proper disciplinary action against Tiny.

"Fall in!" Westmen called out. Immediately, the recruits from the obstacle course stopped what they were doing and made their way to line up in front of them. "Some of you are still having problems with Hell's Bells. Remember, it's supposed to be hard. It's designed to test you both physically and mentally. Tomorrow, we do the second half. O-six hundred. Dismissed!"

Westmen turned and started to make his way back to the officer's barracks. When he figured Tiny wasn't going to be disciplined, Shepard turned and walked beside him.

"Did you need something, Sergeant?"

It was apparent that Westmen wasn't going to punish Tiny. It would have to be up to him. "No, sir."

"Meet me in the lineup tomorrow morning. I'll need a second pair of eyes on the wall."

It was a good sign to get a remark like that from Westmen. "Yes, sir. I'll be there."

A recruit ran past the two, catching Westmen's eye. "Private Marshall, a word."

Shepard went inside the officer's barracks, smiling. Tomorrow would be a good day.

———

Sergeant Shepard walked out toward the obstacle course at the requested time to meet with Lieutenant Westmen. The sun wasn't quite above the horizon, giving the desert a dark blue hue. Even so early in the morning, without a wakeup call, it looked as if Westmen's squad lined up in front of the course. Westmen approached from behind, and the two reached the squad at the same time.

"Attention! Fall in."

Like a well-oiled machine, the squad lined up in front of him.

Westmen started to walk the line as he addressed his recruits. "Today, we do part two of Hell's Bells!" He stopped and looked at someone as if something was out of place.

Shepard leaned to try to get a better idea of what was happening. There stood Tiny in line with the rest of the recruits.

"Son, you do know that this is the special forces unit?"

"Yes, sir!" Tiny answered with enthusiasm.

Westmen glanced back to Shepard. Who did this punk think he was?

After a brief pause, Westmen looked back to Tiny. "So be it. Fifty push-ups. Go!"

The line went to their faces and started their warm-ups.

Westmen approached Shepard. "Start his transfer."

Shepard was taken back but knew better than to question Westman. "Yes, sir."

CHAPTER ONE

AN EXPLOSION, THEN THE STING OF FLYING DIRT AND PEBBLES. A high-pitched ringing sounded in Jace's ears as he peered through the protective shield that was his arms. When the dust settled to let the intense light from the desert sun come through, he noticed the rock and sand wall in front of him was gone.

With the ringing drowning out all of the noise around him, Jace gripped his rifle, reflecting on the decisions that led him to this point. His goal was to save humanity from The Evolved. Humanity. To him, that meant never taking the life of a human. Out of all of his missions months after graduating from bootcamp, this one may have him break his promise. That was something he felt he couldn't do.

When he regained his senses, Jace pushed his back against the building he used for cover. The wall that had been in front of him couldn't have been destroyed by a grenade or artillery. The reports read the militia didn't have that kind of firepower. There must be Evolved somewhere, attacking with their uncanny abilities.

He looked over to the rest of his small squad across the street. They too were huddled in a thin alley, taking cover from the militia fire. Unlike Jace, the alley they hid in had no escape.

With his radio broken, Williams, the commanding officer of the squad, communicated to Jace via hand signals. "You cover fire. We move."

Jace nodded, then broke cover, staying low. Three easy targets presented themselves as he lifted his rifle. Human targets. Or at least human-looking. Until he was sure, he couldn't kill them.

He fired a short burst just as one of the targets took cover. He aimed at a second, who used a bullet hole-riddled car to protect him. Before Jace could take the shot, the second target fired back. The small section of the wall inches away from Jace's face burst into pieces. A sharp sting came from his cheek, but he stayed focused. He returned fire, a three-shot burst, with each shot just close enough to scare the second target into hiding. He then shot up at the third, who hid behind a building.

The suppressive fire was enough for his squadmates to make their move. One by one, they started to break cover to get to the other side of the street. Each of them fired wildly toward their attackers.

Jackson, the last of his squadmates, fell to the ground. He didn't trip, but the pavement suddenly melted, turning to some sort of thick liquid. Even though he was only buried hand and foot deep, Jackson visibly struggled to get up. Slowly, he was being consumed by the now slush concrete.

It was confirmed. Jace turned to call out at his commanding officer. "Evolved!"

Williams turned around but was forced to take cover after some bullets blasted away at his surroundings. "Pennington, call in the rain!"

"Yes, sir!" Pennington started to fiddle with his gear to grab his radio.

Jackson's wrist and ankles were buried. There was no more time to waste.

Jace sprang from his cover while taking off his rucksack. Before he reached the edge of the tar-like substance, he leaped up, threw his backpack beneath him, and landed on his gear with a crunch. He gripped the collar of Jackson and pulled, his hands finally getting free from the trap.

Williams shouted from Jace's left, "Cover fire!"

Jace reached a hand out, crouching down to avoid getting shot. "Give me your bag." He turned to look around, visually scanning the slightest nook and cranny for the familiar signs of the unnatural. He stopped his search when he felt the weight of Jackson's rucksack in his hand. Like his bag, Jace tossed it behind him into the liquid pavement. "Stepping stones." Jace grabbed Jackson's extended hand and yanked him back to his feet. "Come on." Leading the way, he and Jackson escaped the trap and made it behind cover.

Before they could reach the alley, the area behind Jace exploded. He was launched to the side and on the ground, his cheek bouncing off the pavement.

The muffled sounds of Jackson shouting were heard while Jace lay sprawled on the ground. "Man down!"

After a moment, Jace looked up at the hostile militia. There were a lot of people coming. "I'm alright." He gripped his rifle, then scuttled to a building doorway for cover. When he looked back to his squad, his heart sank. Jackson didn't mean him.

Pennington lay on his side, splashes of blood pooling under him. His chest heaved up and down. He was still alive.

Tims reached Pennington and drug him behind cover.

Jace brought his rifle to his chest. "You got him?"

Tims looked up and nodded. "Yeah!"

Jace briefly wondered if the rain was called in, then peeked his head around the corner. More militia moved in. At this rate, he and his squad would be overrun. Once again, it was time for him to act.

Jace broke cover and started his suppressive fire. "Get out of here! I'll draw them off!" When his clip clicked empty, he kicked the door open and stumbled in the house.

A distant yell from Williams sounded while Jace started to make his way through the house. "Negative, soldier! Get back here!"

Jace slapped a fresh clip into his rifle as he made his way up the stairs. The roof should provide him with ample cover while he warded off the militia and distract them enough for his squad to finish their retreat.

Up the third flight of stairs he went to the top floor. His eyes were locked on the ceiling as he moved around the halls—no ceiling access. Jace bashed through a door that he figured would be a room that faced the road, then paused when he spotted a woman cowering in the corner of the sparse bedroom with her children—two girls.

They visibly shook, the children whimpering and trying to stifle their tears.

Jace put out a hand to try to calm the unfortunate family. "Shh, it's okay." With that simple gesture, they huddled closer together. They were too scared. They didn't understand, and he didn't have the time to calm the family.

He went to the window to scan the area. To his left at the center of the village where a huge well was, a dark plume of smoke covered the area. A smoke grenade. Good. They must be going to the safe zone. He looked up the street toward the enemy lines. More armed people were running toward him. One looked up at him and pointed, shouting something in a language he didn't understand. Three men ran into the building.

Well, he did offer to be the distraction.

Jace rushed to the door and put his back against the wall, holding his rifle to his chest. He closed his eyes and focused on his surroundings. The civilians cowered in fear, and their breaths were heavy. More gunfire sounded from the outside. No explosions. No artillery, just like he suspected. Footsteps came from the stairway. He wouldn't have long before the three armed men were going to capture or kill him.

He clenched his rifle and whispered to himself after an exhale, "Never kill a human." Again, his resolve would be tested. This time though, it was close-quarter combat—Jace's favorite.

The footsteps approached the room, and Jace opened his eyes. He swatted downward, using his rifle as a club, knocking the gun from the lead assailant's hands. He stepped forward and grabbed the attacker's shirt to block the entry into the room and to prevent him from running away. The attacker responded with his fists—a right cross, and a left hook. Both were slow and clumsy.

Jace bobbed and pivoted, his body effortlessly swerving out of the way from the awkward punches while keeping his arm extended to block any possibility of a ground grapple. Each movement threw the attacker off balance. After a dodge of an uppercut, Jace looked behind his attacker at the other two. They each had their weapons up but didn't fire. His plan went smoothly. They wouldn't shoot so long as he had his body shield.

The other two started to approach with an arm extended, intending to break the grapple to get a clear shot. Jace let go of the shirt, then kicked the first guy hard in the abdomen. The attacker stumbled back, arms flailing, smacking into the others.

Jace made his move. After shouldering his rifle, he sprinted down the hallway, kicking the guns out of the attackers' hands. One guy tried to grab Jace's leg, but Jace replied with a boot to his jaw. His head bounced off the wall, and then he laid motionless on the floor.

When he turned around, he stared at the other two who flanked him. The guy to the left drew a knife. He would have to go first. And with a weapon, he would have more confidence to lead the attack.

Jace brought up his hands, keeping his thumbs close to his rifle strap. As predicted, the knife started the fight. It came in low and toward Jace's gut. Jace pivoted his waist, the blade slightly cutting his uniform. He spun around and used the rifle strap to entangle the man's wrist, then gave a quick backhand to the nose.

Arms from behind wrapped around Jace. The lurching made the first guy stumble. Because of that additional weight, the guy who held Jace fell forward, and all three fell to the ground with Jace's elbow leading the way.

Jace, landing in a crouch, grabbed the wrist that held him, and he elbowed the second attacker in the face, then reached back to wrap his arm around the neck. He twisted, flipping the back attacker to his side. Jace proceeded to smash his knuckle into the unprotected face. Finally, he released his lock and stood up to assess the three. That's when he noticed the mangled shoulder and arm of the one who held the knife.

Jace slowly rotated his left shoulder, feeling a deep and dull pain in the socket. That fall hurt a lot more than he thought it would. Still, no one died, and he stood victorious.

He ran back into the room where the small family still cowered in fear in the corner and shut the door behind him. He hardly paid them any mind as he ran toward the window. Jace looked down at the hostile militia and the flood of armed men running into his building. He was trapped.

Jace knew he couldn't handle the dozen or so men that came into the building. He looked around the room, trying to think of a way out. The longer he stayed in that confined space, the more in danger the small family would be.

His eyes went back up to the window, and at the ledge that led to the rooftops. It was out of his reach, but if he jumped, he might be able to grab it. Or he could fall three stories into a group of angry armed men.

Feeling he had no other choice, he leaped into the open space. He reached his hand up just as the armed militia kicked open the door. The windowsill burst from gunfire. Then, his fingertips caught the lip of the ledge. After swinging his other arm up to get a better grip, he pulled himself up, getting a leg onto the roof. Just as he rolled over onto the roof, gunfire came from below, and small pieces of the ledge exploded.

After getting to his feet, he looked around for options, running to the far end of the building. When he reached the back ledge, he looked for a fire escape he could use. Nothing but another thin alleyway. He sighed, wondering what his next step should be. Then an idea came to mind. The buildings were close together. Maybe close enough to leap across. He turned and looked at the surface he stood on, then to the building across the way, judging his running distance versus the jump. After a nod, Jace took a few steps back, then ran as hard as he could toward the three-story cliff. He leaped off, waving his arms in the air, landing on the opposite side with an "umph" in a less-than-graceful roll. He got back to his feet, taking a moment to feel the racing of his heart.

Seeing the next building was about the same distance, he lined himself up and leaped once more, this time landing with a little more grace. Behind him, the militia shouted, but they couldn't get to the roof to follow. Jace figured there might be something to this climbing and jumping thing. He would have to look into it later. For now, he needed to get out of sight.

———

The village remained on alert, even late into the night. Jace stayed on the roof, keeping low until he could better escape. Armed guards were commonly spotted throughout the streets, and one wrong step would give away his position. Only when he didn't see an armed militiaman would he move to a different building.

Jace leaped to another rooftop, rolling to absorb the fall. When he peered over the far ledge, he saw the large well. The space was circular and open so that he could get a clear view of the area A stage with a long post in the middle was erected for announcements or parties or whatever. It was where a lot of traffic ran, as it also served as a meeting place for the citizens.

He cursed to himself when he realized he had returned to the center of the settlement. Jace couldn't spend much time wondering how he got turned around like that as excited commotion came from below. Lights in various houses turned on, and people poked their heads outside. A lot of the village started to leave their homes to meet up at the well.

Jace looked through his night vision binoculars to try to get a better idea of what was going on. He gasped. "Williams…" He was bound and beaten, and the people were dragging him toward the stage next to the well. After a few hits from his captors, they tied Williams to the post.

Jace put the binoculars down to try to think of a way out of the mess. Options were limited. There were too many people, and he still didn't know who was human and who wasn't.

A deep quiet hum in the far distance gave him hope. Pennington pulled through.

"Here comes the rain." An idea started to form in his head, and Jace grinned. He brought up his rifle, then he waited. Waited for the right time.

The people looked up at the night sky in confusion as the hum grew louder, and slowly growing in pitch. Then the hum went to a low roar as the unseen aircraft flew by. Moments later, on a clear night sky, what seemed like rain showered the area.

The people looked baffled and started to talk amongst themselves. Some of them stared at their hands. Others covered their heads. Some even screamed in horror.

Just as the water evaporated, the hum from the aircraft started to grow louder once more. Then, brilliant flashes shot out from the sides of the aircraft, momentarily giving its position away. Slowly, the flares started to fall toward the ground.

Jace gripped his rifle, paying close attention to the people. Then one man started to glow blue.

Demon.

Jace aimed and pulled the trigger. Headshot. The figure fell to the ground, and the blue faded away.

The people screamed and started to flee. But one by one, people began to glow. As the telltale glow appeared, Jace aimed and fired, killing as many as he could before his rifle clicked empty. He took cover on the roof and reloaded. Before he broke cover to shoot more demons, a small but bright light from the corner of his eye caught his attention. It was the size of a coin, rich and intense, and very and reminiscent of something that seemed so long ago. It got more substantial, and it got warmer.

Jace's eyes widened, and he leaped forward, rolling over his shoulders and down a ledge just as the strange light struck. Flames blew out in every direction, and intense heat surrounded the area. But only for a second. Then, the air returned to its frigid temperatures as dust and sand fell from the sky. His position was compromised. He needed to move. First things first, that damn fire-throwing demon needed to be taken care of.

After a moment to regain his senses, Jace ran hard toward where the strange attack came from. As he approached the edge of the rooftop, he noticed a window across the way having a faint blue light in the shape of a man. Just as Jace leaped off the rooftop, another bright orb appeared. He twisted his body in the air, the sphere singing his arm as it flew by. The area behind him flashed brightly as the roof exploded.

He crashed hard through the window, landing on his side on the floor before hitting and smacking his head against a wall.

The fuzzy shape of a blue person stood before him. Before the disguised monster made any of its unnatural attacks, Jace fired wildly at the shape. It dove to the side into a hall, allowing Jace to get to his feet.

The creature shouted in its native language while footsteps ran down a hall. "Krim del seramun! Krim del seramun!"

When he could see once more, Jace peered around the corner and shot the glowing demon in the back as it ran away. It fell forward, and the blue faded as the creature died.

As he started to make his way down the hallway, Jace got a sense of familiarity. He paused and looked at a broken door, and some splotches of blood barely visible on the floor. Then Jace realized it was the house he climbed up to make his escape. Just as he reached the stairs, something caught his eye. He stopped, then peered into the room. Once again, the mother and two daughters huddled in the same damn corner; they hadn't moved. One thing was noticeably different though—the small girl-shaped figure glowed blue.

Jace approached the family, took out his pistol, and pulled the trigger.

The mother shouted and cried as the blue light faded. "Tiki! Tiki impo tex louseid!"

No one else glowed. The other two were human.

He put the pistol away, turned, and left. Another demon killed. Another life saved. He felt pretty good about that.

He exited the building with his back against the wall. With their cover blown, it was time to free his commander and escape. And with the sun slowly brightening the sky, it would be that much harder to escape.

After a few steps down the road, bullets smashed into the walls to his left, the plaster blowing debris on him. He ducked into an alleyway and waited for the gunfire to stop. When it did, he peeked his head around the corner for a moment to try to see where the attacker was. Instead of a single person, a small group of people formed. They were regrouping much faster than last time. He was running out of time.

He broke from his cover and skid behind the broken down car. Bullets hit the vehicle, punching even more holes in the frame. Jace stayed low, patiently waiting for his opportunity to move.

Bullets stopped hitting the car, possibly indicating they had to reload.

Jace sprinted toward another building and crashed through a window. He bounced off a couch and landed on a coffee table, his rifle slipping from his grasp and smacking against a wall. Unable to reach his gun, Jace rolled over, grabbing the lip of the table just as he fell to the floor. Gunfire came through the broken window. Bullets blew holes in the couch, the wall, and the table. When the shooting stopped once more, Jace took that opportunity to move. He rolled back behind another sofa, getting a glance at two figures at the window. Neither of them glowed.

More gunfire. Holes were blown into the second couch with fluff and stuffing floating in the air. He crawled to cover behind a wall, then around a corner to enter a kitchen. He took a quick moment to look for a way out, seeing a door on the opposite side of the room. Jace ran through the kitchen and through the door that led into the back alley, bullets chasing him as he made his escape with a bullet grazing his leg.

He ran down the alleyway and ducked behind some boxes. Someone ran past him. Then a second, and a third, who glowed blue.

Jace shot the demon, making two holes in its back. It flopped lifelessly to the ground.

Just as the two men turned around, Jace held the gun up and took a few steps forward. They paused, staring hard at Jace.

Jace gestured to the ground. "Drop it!" He didn't know if they understood him, but it was better than nothing. Even if they had no idea what he said, the message came across loud and clear. The two dropped their guns.

Footsteps from behind, and a suspicious whisper. Jace glanced back at a blue figure, then he went into a forward roll just as some dark ball flew above him.

Before he could stand, someone kicked Jace's gun from his grasp. Jace lifted an arm, blocking a punch. He rushed toward the attacker, wrapping his arms around the man's waist. While hugging his hips, Jace lurched back, swinging the grasped man's legs out toward the second guy. His boots landed cleanly into the second guy's chest.

Perfect. Someone between him and the demon.

The second guy leaned over to grab the dropped gun. Jace kicked dirt in his face, then lunged back to pick the first up off the ground. Jace tried to take a couple of steps to the side to make space between his attackers and the weapons on the ground.

It didn't work.

The squirming from the first guy made Jace stop two paces short from the second guy.

The demon took a couple of steps forward, probably to get into a better position to use those unnatural attacks. Jace let go of the first guy and pushed him forward into the demon. They collided and stumbled back. The second guy stood up, pistol in hand. Jace grabbed the barrel and swatted it aside just as it fired a round. He kicked the guy in the stomach, then landed a hard punch across the jaw just as he bounced off the wall. The second guy fell to the ground.

With his sidearm back in his hands, Jace turned toward the other two. The human charged forward with a knife, shouting a battle cry. Even with the weapon, he was still human.

Jace casually tossed the gun to the guy, who stumbled and dropped the knife to catch the pistol. The confused delay gave Jace more than enough time to act. He closed the distance in a single leap, then gave a one-two blow to the abdomen and kidney. Slowly, he fell to the ground. Jace grabbed the pistol as if it were handed to him.

Now it was just him and the demon.

Before he could move, the demon had his hands forward, palms down and fingers spread. After a murmur, darts of flame shot out of the fingertips. Jace rolled forward to try to close the gap between the two and to avoid that strange attack. He stood just as another barrage of darts flew by, feeling a sharp sting on his left arm shortly after.

Jace grabbed the demon by the throat and pushed him against the wall. He glared hard at the creature as he lifted his pistol, the blue glow slowly fading away. The flares from the aircraft were probably burning out. No matter. He still had this one in his grasp.

The demon looked pathetic. How could something so weak have so much power?

It spoke in broken speech. "P... Please don't—"

Jace squeezed the trigger. The recoil brought the gun up, and the demon's head jerked back. Blood splashed on Jace's face. The creature fell to the ground.

Jace lowered the gun and looked down the alleyway. No one came.

His shoulder burned. Jace looked down at one of those darts in his upper arm. He swatted it away, then watched in surprise as it turned into mist before it even hit the ground. Before he knew it, his arm went numb. Every time he tried to move it deep pains shot through the bones—a very nerve-wracking feeling.

He approached the corner that led to the road. Surprisingly enough, everyone's shouts came from a distance. Could it be the rest of the squad? Either way, it was a blessing, and he couldn't waste it. But with the rain no longer working, he had to resort to non-lethal means to take out his enemies.

Jace made his move, sneaking his way out of the alleyway and toward the stage. He stayed low, moving from one hiding spot to another until he reached the open area. There Williams was, beaten, blindfolded, and gagged with a dirty cloth. And he had a guard with him.

Sneaking up on the stage, Jace slowly made his way toward the guard. The wood beneath him creaked. The guard turned, and Jace gave a steel-toed boot kick to the groin. The guard yelped and hunched forward, dropping his gun to guard his goods, allowing Jace to pistol whip the side of the head. The guard fell back off the stage to the ground.

Jace looked down to make sure the guard, who whimpered and moaned on the dirt, was incapacitated. Then Jace scanned the area for any other threats. No one was around.

He holstered the pistol and turned around, taking the opportunity to inspect the deep cuts and bruises all over William's face and body. He was in bad shape. Jace knelt and took out a boot knife, then cut the gag so Williams could speak once more.

Williams gagged once Jace removed the cloth from his mouth. "Is that you, corporal?"

"Yes, sir." Jace removed the blindfold, then started to cut the rope. "We don't have a lot of time."

The bindings fell to the floor. Williams tried to lift his hands to rub his wrists, but his limbs seemed to flop down. He winced in pain from the sudden movement of broken bones.

Jace put the knife away and put Williams' weight on his shoulders. "Something is going on over there." Jace gestured to his right with a nod. "We should go that way."

CHAPTER TWO

SIMPLE OFFICES ALWAYS REMINDED JACE OF DR. CRISP'S
interrogation rooms—two places to sit with some table in between,
and some ridiculous item or object around the room to make things
seem relaxed and natural. Very minimal in their designs.

Jace sat in one of those very offices. A wall calendar to his left. A
picture of a man in uniform saluting on the right. The tick tick tick of
the wall clock behind him. If this were supposed to make his
debriefing more relaxing, then those designers would have to look for
another job.

Finally, the door opened. A one-star general with a long face and
short hair entered the office, a folder in one hand and a briefcase in the
other. Apparently, Captain Williams getting injured was a big deal,
and Jace would have to tread carefully to make sure his report wasn't
going to be misunderstood.

Jace stood to salute.

The general kept his nose in a file, moving around the desk and
sitting in the chair without looking up. "At ease."

When the general sat, Jace returned to his chair.

The two sat in silence for a long moment. Jace grew nervous. His
heart started to pump harder with each passing second.

The general turned a page, then a second as if only skimming through the file. "You have an interesting record, corporal." The general turned back a page. "One of the youngest to ever get accepted into special ops. Graduated at the top of your class in tactical training, hand-to-hand, and urban combat strategies. You did well in the airborne training, despite apparent motion sickness, and you did well on general surveillance." He flipped the page. "But you fell short on general technology and engineering courses. In fact..." He turned another page. "Anything that involved computers for that matter."

Jace never had this kind of evaluation before. He wondered if the problems from the last mission were going to have him kicked out of the military. What would he do then? He needed to get his side of the story in. "Sir, about the mission..."

"Says here you came from a 'Sanctuary of Orphaned Children.' Started there at the age of six. Did rather poorly in school. But then you brought your grades up and graduated. But just barely."

"Sir, about the mission..."

The general looked up from the file. "What do you mean?"

Jace grew even more nervous. "I, uh... Isn't this a debriefing?"

After a long moment, the general put the folder down, put his hands together, and placed them on the desk. "Alright, then. Proceed."

As Jace started his moment-by-moment recap on what happened, he couldn't help but notice the feigned interest coming from the general. At least until he began to discuss when the airplane flew overhead. "And when the hospital released me, I got a letter requesting my presence."

"Is that it?"

"Yes, sir."

"Good." The general picked the folder back up from the desk and leaned back in his chair. "You have transferred between four squads all over the world in the last six months of service."

This had to be the most unusual debriefing he had ever had. It seemed as if the general didn't even care about the mission.

The general flipped the page. "In those six months, you have taken on quite a few perilous missions. Some would have even called them suicide missions. Yet here you sit—unharmed and yet successful."

It was still unclear what this guy wanted. Apparently, it had nothing to do with the mission. Otherwise, he wouldn't be asking about his history.

"Tell me, corporal, what are your goals here?"

"Goals?" Jace took a moment. He never really thought about a future beyond the military. He figured it was his only option in his life. "No goals, sir."

"Have you considered schooling?"

Jace couldn't contain the frown. That thought made him sick to his stomach.

"You need a degree to get to a respectable officer rank."

Jace shook his head. "No, sir. Not my style."

"Then what?"

What was with these strange questions? Why was it when he sat in one of these stupid offices, people wanted to know about him? Still, he couldn't think of a good, solid answer. After a few heartbeats, he finally replied with, "To survive. Survive and succeed."

"Survive and succeed..." The general put the folder in his lap and stared hard at Jace for a long moment. "Tell me, corporal, what do you think about these 'Evolved' people?"

The fact that the general put those monsters in the same category as people made Jace's blood boil. Still, he took a breath to steady his nerves.

"I see," replied the general, apparently reading Jace's body movement. He tossed the folder on the desk. "I read a report on the casualty count of that village."

He knew it! It was about that damn village.

"Twenty-six dead. Some of them women and children. All deceased were positive on blood tests."

Jace stammered for a moment to reply. "I—"

"Multiple injuries from others. However, all of these people tested negative." The general leaned forward, putting his elbows on the desk. "In an intense fight like that, with the gunfire and the explosions and running around, you managed to pull out a zero human casualty count. Zero. So tell me, corporal. What do you think about them? These 'evolved'?"

"I, uh... I'm not fond of them... sir."

"I asked you to tell me what you thought about them, corporal."

It didn't take long for Jace to think about an answer. "I hate them, sir. I will kill every last one of them if I can. Without mercy."

"That's what I wanted to hear." The general stared hard at Jace as if to figure out what he wanted to say or do next. "What if I told you that you could hunt those monsters down?"

That threw Jace for a loop. He stared, silent and confused.

"It would require more training, but what if I could offer you a position that would have you destroy these vermin. What would you say?"

"General, I don't think the—"

"General?" The 'general' looked at his uniform. "Oh, yes. I thought I was a colonel today. No matter." The 'general' stood and pulled a card from an inside pocket.

Jace stood in alarm. "You're not a general?"

The 'general' ignored the question. "You're being transferred."

"Wait. What? Transferred?"

"Consider this a reward for your hard work." The 'general' slid the card on the table, then swapped the folder on the desk with one from his briefcase.

"Wait, who are you?"

"Get your things packed up. And don't tell anyone about our conversation, or your destination." He handed the other folder to Jace. "Here are your approved transfer files."

Jace grabbed the folder and stared blankly at it, then looked up at the imposter general while he opened the door. "Wait..."

"You heard me. That's an order." He shut the door behind him.

Jace's gaze went from the door to the folder, then picked up the card. It was a beautiful card: fancy and pressed designs with an unusually soft feel. Strangely enough, there were no words on it. Only intricate designs.

Was this even real?

He opened the folder to look for answers. A plane ticket and a prepaid taxi service voucher to the airport, and all of the proper transfer paperwork apparently signed by the appropriate people. Jace snapped the folder shut and looked back at the door. "What the hell is going on?"

The chill surprised Jace as he stepped off the plane. Being in the desert for so long, he wasn't used to icy weather, nor did he have any clothes to help him keep warm. Even though it was cold, it was good to stand and stretch from a long trip. The only thing worse than the cramped muscles and the hours of boredom was the turbulence. and the lack of barf bags within arm's reach. Oh well. That's what they get for not properly keeping those things stocked.

He started to walk off the tarmac, his backpack on his back and a duffle bag in his hand, before a black stretched limo stopped in front of him. The driver got out and walked around the car toward the back door with a thin plastic-looking device tucked under his arm. He stood expressionless, like a statue in a museum.

Jace looked around, wondering if the limo was for anyone else. No one was near him. He stared back to the driver, seeing his dark suit fluttering in the cold breeze. The man looked totally unphased. "Are you here for me?"

The chauffeur held out his hand. "Card, sir."

"Card?" Jace looked at the white-gloved hand for a moment. Then his eyes went wide. "Oh, the card." He put the duffle bag on the ground and started to pat himself down. Remembering where he put it, Jace reached in his jacket and took out the fancy card that the 'general' gave to him. "Is this what you're looking for?"

The chauffeur took the card, then ran his gloved fingers over it, all while keeping his eye on Jace. A few moments later, the chauffeur grabbed the plastic device under his arm and held it in front of him. It lit up, and a light flashed. A beep and the chauffeur put the device back under his arm. "You are expected." He opened the door and stepped aside.

Jace eyed the man suspiciously. He had never heard of any military transfer that wound up like this—a private plane, a fancy limo with a creepy driver, and flat plastic device flash. Something was going on.

The chauffeur cleared his throat. "Would you like for me to grab your bag, sir?"

Jace looked down to his duffle bag. "Uh, no. I got it." There was no way he would let that out of his sight. "What's going on?"

"I am your ride, sir."

"And where are we going?"

"I am not at liberty to say, sir."

That made Jace that much more suspicious. He eyed the man once more, but the emotionless bastard gave him no insight. "Fine." He grabbed his duffle bag and tossed it in the back of the limo, took off his backpack and climbed in. The chauffeur shut the door behind him, leaving him alone in the surprisingly open and comfortable space. A mini-bar and a snack stand, bottles of water, and a view screen for shows and movies. Very fancy.

However, the comfort and luxury immediately left him as the limo started its bumpy ride up the mountainside. It didn't take long before Jace began to feel his stomach churn, and a burp gave a telltale sign of vomit.

With no bag in sight, he knocked on the window to the front of the car. "Pull over!"

The car came to a halt. Just as the chauffeur opened the door, Jace pushed it wide open and collapsed on a thin layer of snow. His body heaved, and the pristine snow gave way to the contents of his stomach. Finally, he stood up. "Carrots. Why are there always carrots?" He brushed himself off, then turned to see the chauffeur standing next to the door, presenting a cloth. Jace took it with a grateful nod, then got back into the car. "I didn't even eat carrots."

———

What seemed like hours passed in the rocky and bumpy ride. He couldn't tell how long it was as he did his best to contain his motion sickness.

When he looked out the window, a steep drop-off possibly hundreds of feet down awaited him. No guardrail was present to protect the vehicle from slipping and sliding from the ice and snow off the mountainside. He scooted to the other side but was greeted with a wall of rock and snow so close he could touch it if he reached out the window.

His stomach growled after a particularly large bump. He couldn't tell if it was because he was hungry, or if his gut wanted to give another donation to nature.

He sat back in his seat, holding his backpack to his chest.

————

The car finally stopped, which was good because the smell started to get to him. The chauffeur opened the door and Jace, exhausted from the long trip, climbed out.

Plumes of steam visibly escaped Jace's mouth and nose with each exhale. His boots crunched in the ankle-deep snow, with more falling from above. A cobblestone pathway, apparently untouched by snow, led to a bridge and curved behind the mountainside.

Jace, feeling his energy drained from the long trip, slung his backpack over his shoulder and grabbed his duffle bag. Then he looked at the chauffeur, who stood like a statue holding the door. "Sorry about the mess."

That rose a reaction from the porcelain driver. Just as he looked inside, Jace started to walk away, leaving the stinky prison behind him.

The bridge was decorated and well kept, with a fresh coat of paint and no visible damage. A potted fern sat on the rails every five or so paces. Jace found it odd that there was a thin layer of snow on the bridge, but none on the plants. The bridge went over a frozen river, where a large waterfall to his left supplied the water, then fell off the cliffside through a thick line of pine trees to his right.

Jace turned around, seeing the limo drive back down the mountainside. Either throwing up in the back of the car upset the chauffeur so much that he would leave Jace to die, or he was in the right place.

Feeling his energy weakening with each passing moment, Jace continued down the curved path. He paused and stared at a circular garden with spruce trees, junipers, and many other plants he couldn't name, all in a beautiful and organized fashion. Behind the circular garden was a blast from his past—the orphanage where he grew up but build inside the mountain. It was a three-story tall building with two wings on each side. In the middle of the structure were stairs that led up to a large awning, and double doors that led into the building.

On top of the stairs stood a man, very tall, and dressed in fur and leathers. Even as the chilling winds picked up, Jace noticed the long but well-trimmed mustache, and the straight and smooth neck length dark hair. The man stood motionless, seemingly unphased by the cold that ate at Jace's bones.

While the lack of food, water, and sleep wore Jace out, the battle against the blowing winds and the biting cold took its toll on him. Every step around the massive garden grew harder and harder.

With struggling steps up the stairway, Jace finally reached the top. Sharp pains from the cold ran all up and down his body. He visibly shivered but stood in front of the large man. The duffle bag slipped from his grasp, and his attempt to salute failed when his arm turned out to be too heavy for him to lift.

The mustached man didn't say a word.

After a long moment, Jace decided to go first. "I—"

"Silence!" Moustache snapped. "You are not authorized to speak lest I ask you to."

Jace couldn't hide his surprise. He wasn't in the mood for any shit while standing in the cold, but he reminded himself why he was there.

Another long moment of silence with only the sound of Jace's chattering teeth and the howling wind to occupy the ears.

"You are Corporal Jace?"

Jace's reply came through chattered teeth. "Y-Y-Yes, sir."

"You are no longer Corporal Jace."

Jace gasped in surprise. He tried to clench a fist, but he didn't even know if his fingers moved.

"I shall give you the rank of Squire."

Squire? That wasn't in the military ranks. Was this a demotion? "A wh-what?"

"Do you deny this honor?"

"A s-s-squire?"

"A Squire of The Order."

Jace knew that if he had been more surprised, his eyes would have fallen out of their sockets. The Order. Something he heard about a long time ago. Something he only dreamed of being a part of. So it was true.

"Kneel." Moustache brought back his arm, pushing his cloak aside to reveal a sheathed sword.

A sword? Really? If his face wasn't so numb, he might have bust out laughing. But as ridiculous as a sword seemed to him, the belt this guy wore was what really caught Jace's eye. It was thick, made of leather, and was by far the most decorated item this guy had on him. It seemed like some writing or pattern was etched in gold all the way around, and for a moment, it looked as if it pulsed with power.

Still, the transfer, The Order; If everything was true, then this was an interesting and exciting opportunity. Jace went to a knee, which was a bad idea because his wet pants started to freeze from the ground, and he didn't know if he had the energy to stand.

Moustache brought the sword over his head. "By order of the measure..." The flat of the blade came down and tapped Jace's head. "I bestow upon you the title of Squire. By deed and by duty, you shall..."

Moustache started on some rant of nobility, but Jace stopped paying attention. Instead, he thought about his life and wondered if this was the right move. His goal was to join the military and be a part of special forces. He achieved that goal, and now he could be throwing it all away. How would he get Maya back if he lost his job?

"Rise, Squire."

With a struggled groan, he finally got back to his feet, ice cracking and his knee aching from the frigid ground.

Moustache took a step back and sheathed his sword. "And enter our halls." He turned and pushed against the double doors. The hinges creaked, blinding light and a blast of warmth hit Jace's face.

The door slammed shut behind Jace while Moustache walked to a table. There he removed his cloak and put it down. "Welcome, Squire, to the entry halls of The Order."

Deja vu. The entryway was tiled with a room straight ahead of him, and halls going to the left and right. The orphanage and this place, this couldn't just be a coincidence.

Jace put down his duffel bag and his backpack, then crossed his arms to rub them trying to warm them up. "This p-place looks f-f-familiar."

Moustache took his sword off his belt and placed it on top of the folded cloak. "Yes. Your Sanctuary for Orphaned Children, as well as many other orphanages, are modeled after this structure."

Jace couldn't help but lower his arms. "Sanc... But why?"

"Now isn't the time for questions." Moustache turned and approached Jace. "It is the time... for pain!"

Moustache's mighty boot slammed into Jace's stomach. He slammed hard into the double doors, knocking the wind from his lungs. He fell to his hands and knees.

"Do you really believe you belong here, boy?" Moustache kicked Jace in the stomach, lifting him off the floor, hitting the door again. He crumpled to the ground. Moustache stepped on Jace's back, crushing Jace on the tile. "I have heard great things about you." Moustache stomped on Jace's back. "Tell me I heard right."

Jace gasped for breath. He had been hit many times in his career, but this was different. These hits were the hardest he had ever felt. At least from a human. At that moment, he wondered if this man was a demon.

Moustache knelt to put his face next to Jace's. "I am told you are the great fighter who landed hits on Sir Xin." He got to his feet and started to walk away. "You are worthless."

With the moment of reprieve, Jace got back to his knees and put his back against the door. The sharp pain that coursed through his back and side escalated when he gave a single cough—the familiar pang of broken ribs. A metallic taste and a bit of dribble escaped his lips. He saw blood drip down on his hand, and he knew he was in bad shape.

Moustache turned back toward Jace, swinging his arms side to side as if relaxing his shoulders. "And I'm through dealing with nothing."

Broken ribs or not, Jace wasn't going to sit and get his ass kicked. It was time to fight back.

CHAPTER THREE

THE OPEN, GRASSY FIELDS AND THICK BORDERING TREES DIDN'T catch Jace's attention. Nor did the orphanage behind him—the place of pain and suffering he was stuck at for most of his life. It was the back of a young woman that stood in front of him who laughed a familiar laugh. A laugh from a distant memory. She spun around, her hair twirling around her neck and face. She smiled, her big brown eyes staring deep into his soul.

Jace couldn't breathe. It seemed as if he was underwater, and he gasped for each breath. Finally, he gulped, catching a hint of air in his lungs as the woman gave her usual half-smile. He whispered, "Jessica..."

Just one look at her made his heart beat wildly. Her voice instantly soothed Jace's anxiety. "Hey, fuckhead."

"Jessica. What happened?"

She scoffed and shrugged. When she opened her mouth to talk, a blinding flash took over the entire world.

Jace woke up with a single watery cough. He stared up at a white ceiling and bright lights, and a machine rhythmically beeped next to him.

Another damn hospital.

He tried to sit up, but the aches in his body made him pause in his movements. They didn't feel like the pains from a fight, but the sore muscles from a workout.

Heels clicked against the floor, and the scent of vanilla wafted into Jace's nose. A woman's voice spoke from behind him. "Welcome back, Squire."

Jace collapsed on his back, groaning with the effort. Next to him, a dark tan woman his age, maybe a little older, stood tapping her fingers against a piece of rectangular glass in her hand. When she looked up, he gazed into her blue eyes. She seemed as if she was continuously stressed, with her short blonde hair with black roots tied back in a tight ponytail. Though the buttoned-up white coat hid her physical features, Jace figured she was taller than him. Then he remembered the heels. Maybe shorter, but just by an inch. Jace's throat was dry, regardless of his spitting up water, and his voice came out hoarse and labored. "Where am—"

"The infirmary." The woman took the stethoscope from a coat pocket and started to examine Jace. "You've been out for a few days, which is a lot less than usual."

Jace flinched a little when the chill of the metal hit his skin. "Who are—"

"Dr. Erica Patel. I'm in charge here. You can call me Erica." She removed the stethoscope and put it around her neck. "All done. Your broken ribs are healed." She tapped on the glass screen. "Are you feeling any different?"

That comment took Jace by surprise. Even more than being out for a few days. "My what?"

"Sir Dunmore. He broke three of your ribs near the spine. And I must say, I've never seen him come in that beat up before. Impressive. Now, are you feeling any different?"

Again with that question. "Uh, no."

"Hmm. Maybe a little longer." She turned and seemed to wander off in thought. Jace barely heard her mumble, "Normally recruits are submerged for at least a week..." With that, she turned to leave.

Jace couldn't remember what had happened. The last thing he knew, he stood face-to-face against Moustache. He lifted an arm. "Wait!"

Erica turned and paused, a look of annoyance in her eye.

"How—"

"A full subversive hyper-metabolic chamber with white cell infusion via epidermis absorption with genetic fixing and enhancements."

Jace's jaw hung ajar, and he blinked slowly. "Uh, what?"

She turned and called over her shoulder, "Let me know if something happens. And go get some food. I know you'll be hungry."

"Something?"

She closed the door behind her, leaving Jace and the lingering scent of vanilla behind.

———

The biggest thing Jace found different between his military training and this facility was how informal it was. The only exception was when it came to people's titles, which was presentable from gems in jewelry everyone carried with themselves one way or another. Not Jace's style. Aside from that, people looked and dressed however they wanted. He resorted to his usual attire: steel-toed combat boots, jeans, a simple shirt under his dark leather jacket, and fingerless gloves. Because he didn't need to keep his hair shaved, he started to grow it out once more.

Jace spent every day inside the mountainside facility. During that time, he got to know the place: a kitchen, personal quarters for everyone, elevators to efficiently get to one of the available sublevels, vast open areas for whatever. The entire site was self-sufficient.

He also noticed that there were very few people around, and the only time he ever saw the outside was when someone came through the main doors. Even then, all he saw was snow and the same amount of light from the sun. Or was it the moon?

The training proved to be an interesting experience for Jace, from memorizing codes of honor to watching videos and hearing horror stories of women and children throughout the ages. He was taught how to dance, cook, read people's faces, tactical maneuvers while driving, and more. His training went on all day, every day. A lot of the things taught to him he already learned when he went through special forces training. And even then, those lessons bored him. It reminded him of when he was in school at the orphanage. When he did get sleep in his private quarters, he discovered that the lessons would appear in his dreams. He knew it was a convenient tool for drilling propaganda into recruits, and he wasn't going to fall for that. Much like he had done during his stay in the orphanage, he'd play along.

Some courses did catch his attention: the history of the demon's invasion, their unnatural abilities, how to fight and counter their supernatural advantages, and how they can hide in human form. It didn't matter to Jace. A demon was a demon, whether or not they were in human form or how old they appeared.

The lessons took an unusual turn when he was told to go to a subfloor of the facility he never had access to. The only thing he was told was to "be prepared," whatever that meant.

Jace stood in front of the elevator, ready to face whatever challenge they had in store. When the door finally slid open, Jace leaped back, smacking against the wall.

Moustache stood tall, still wearing that ridiculous cape and probably the stupid sword too. He looked the same as the day that seemed so long ago. The day he got his ass handed to him in the entryway.

"Well met, Squire."

Jace noticed the red gem embedded in the belt buckle. Before he could stop himself, he blurted out, "A fucking knight?"

"I am Sir Dunmore, Knight Lieutenant of The Order. You shall address me as Sir Dunmore. Do not dishonor The Order and what it stands for with your childish insolence." Dunmore took a step to the side. "Come. You don't want to be late."

Jace didn't feel comfortable being in such proximity to someone who wasn't afraid to take cheap shots. This time, if this asshole tried something, he would be ready. He entered the elevator and stood opposite of Moustache, keeping his back against the wall to make sure he was in his sight at all times.

While they were standing quietly, Jace considered the name. It sounded familiar. "Dunemore?"

"*Sir* Dunemore, boy."

That's when he remembered—Erica mentioned he came in all beat up, but the guy didn't have a mark on him. He then wondered about Erica. He hadn't seen her ever since he woke up in the infirmary.

"Today, you will be meeting with Sir Xin."

Though Jace didn't initially care what Dunemore had to say, he said that name before. But who was he?

The doors slid open to reveal a dark room with only a single spotlight maybe fifty feet away. Jace could barely make out the shape of a man sitting on the floor in the middle of the lit area. No one moved or said anything for a long moment.

"Go. Don't keep him waiting." Dunmore pushed Jace out into the darkness, and the doors closed behind him.

Jace cautiously approached the circle. As soon as he breached the light, the man stood up and turned to face him. Jace's heart skipped a beat as he remembered the man. "You!"

The man stood as tall as Jace. He wore a white coat with a black shirt underneath, black pants, and white shoes. Those key details paled in comparison to what was on the tan man's face—sunglasses.

"I understand you have improved your techniques." Glasses approached Jace, stopping a few paces away.

"I won't lose to you again!"

Glasses smiled. "You believe you are the best because you seek combat. Beware. Those who are truly the best know how to fight, and how *not* to fight."

Jace chanced a glance around at the darkness. "Who are you? What am I doing here?"

"I am Sir Xin, Paladin Commander of The Order. You are here for two reasons."

Jace cycled through the ranks in his mind, remembering each rank had three sub-ranks: Squire, Sergeant, Knight, Knight Lieutenant, Knight Commander, Grand Marshal. If this guy was indeed a commander, he was a pretty high rank. Still, paladin wasn't in that list. He shook his head. "That isn't a rank."

"Ah, but it is. I am glad you have paid attention to your studies."

Jace stared hard at Xin, waiting for an explanation

"It is another path in The Order. Those who follow the path of knight are those who fight for humanity. The path of paladin is a bit more... I suppose you could say 'specialized.'"

Jace believed he started to understand, but he wondered why it was never brought up. "Like special forces?"

After a moment, Xin nodded. "I suppose you could say that. Every candidate is evaluated to see which path they are to follow. This is your test."

"Another test?" Jace shook his head. "Haven't I proven myself enough?"

"Do you believe your past deeds have proven yourself? In that case, if you are the same as when we first met, then you do not belong on this path."

Xin was right. When they first met, Jace was too frenzied to think correctly. Then he thought about the fight in the arena altogether, and how unusual it was. At that moment, he remembered that drink. That strange drink.

"I see you are starting to understand what I mean."

"Okay, then. What's reason number two?"

"Number two?" Xin's head slowly nodded, as if checking Jace out. "I was requested to evaluate your change."

Jace stomped his foot and clenched his fists. "Bring it on. This time, I'll win."

Xin smiled. "Then, you may begin." He sat down, crossed his legs, and rested his arms on his knees.

That baffled Jace. "Wait. What?" His confusion was replaced by alarm after a low growl echoed from the darkness. He turned and faced the black wall. "Who's there?" After a moment of nothing, Jace turned to Xin for answers. He still sat on his ass, not moving or saying anything. He wasn't going to be any help.

Another growl.

Jace snapped his attention back to the dark. He spotted two glowing red dots from above, then a loud stomp boomed in the unseen. "Uh, Xin..." Jace slowly walked back toward the middle of the circle as the stomping came again and again. "What's that?"

Just before the two dots made it to the light, a puff of smoke burst from the wall of darkness. Then horns broke the black barrier as a seven-foot-tall bipedal creature stepped into the light. It had a head of a bull, with a large mane that traced the back of its spine. Around its neck was some metal guard or brace. Its huge upper body was muscular, with bracers that covered its massive forearms. Its hands, only having two fingers and a thumb, were so large that Jace's head could be crushed inside them with a single squeeze. A tattered cloth covered its crotch, and a tail flared behind its body. The muscled legs stomped forward, showing the giant hooves it had.

Jace fought something that size back in The Pit. Back then, he had two massive handguns, that body armor Brian got him, and a considerable amount of luck. Now, he faced off against something similar with no weapons at all. And that Xin guy just stayed sitting and doing nothing like an asshole!

The creature clanked its bracers together, creating a shower of sparks. It huffed and stomped the ground with a hoof.

Jace's breaths came in short gasps. Sweat built up in his palms, and his mouth went dry.

The creature let out a roar, then went to all fours and charged, horns leading the way.

In near panic, Jace leaped head-first to the side, his cheek bouncing off the ground. Hearing the stomps go by, he rolled over and got to his feet. Jace chanced a glance back to Xin.

Yep. Still the asshole.

Jace leaped to the side, dodging another fatal gouging. When the creature stopped and turned around, it let out another roar, smashing its hands on the ground and flailing about, as if throwing a hissy fit.

Using the moment to take control of the situation, Jace took a deep breath, getting a grip on the fear that built up in his chest. With the panic fading away, Jace started to think clearly on the situation around him.

Treat the circle of light like the ring. Asshole to his left in the middle of the arena. Big, dumb creature near the edge. Slow movements. Conserve strength. Keep dumb creature off of asshole.

Another stomp of a hoof, and a charge. This time, Jace kept his composure. The creature was slow. Very slow. For a moment, that struck Jace as odd, but he didn't have time to worry about that.

He leaped to the side, staying on his feet this time as the sharp horn breezed by. It stopped short of its usual charge and swung a clumsy fist toward Jace. He ducked under the blow, then backed up to dodge a stomping fist.

Was the beast getting tired already? Its movements kept getting slower.

It stood up, reaching to the sky and roaring in frustration. Very human-like. At that moment, Jace started to consider his opponent. Not like a monster but a living creature. Soft spots near the neck and collarbone, and critical points under the ribs. Those would be his targets. That's how he would win.

Jace clenched his fists and whispered to himself for reassurance. "I can do this." He took a step back, waiting for another charge to start his offensive.

The charge didn't come. Instead, the creature turned and faced Xin, who, like the asshole he was, still sat motionless in the middle of the light.

"Look out!"

The monster went back to all fours, then charged.

The asshole still didn't move.

Out of options, Jace rushed toward the beast and leaped into the legs. A hoof smashed into his side, and he went flying up and out of the ring of light. He slid and rolled uncontrollably for a few moments, finally coming to a rest on his side facing Xin.

The creature got up, apparently tripped by Jace's stupid idea, and charged Xin once more. After a single step, the metal on the beast lit up. Its arms went to the floor, then its legs, followed by its neck.

Xin stood up and approached Jace, the spotlight following his every movement. "Why did you do that?"

The metallic taste of blood filled Jace's mouth. He spat red on the ground, then collapsed to his back. The ribs in his chest grinded and poked into his skin. There he was, lying on the ground with broken ribs, and who knows what else, and this asshole wondered why? "W-What?"

Xin leaned forward. "Why did you do that?"

The pain started to grow with each passing breath. "It..." He coughed, blood escaping his lips. "It seemed like a good idea at the time."

"Is that so?" Xin straightened his posture. "I thought you would see me beaten. So, why? Why did you not let it beat me?"

Jace took a moment to try to answer this asshole's questions.

Never mind that he was in a lot of pain. "I don't know. I guess... I guess it's because it was going to kill you."

Xin nodded.

"Besides..." Jace coughed up more blood but tried to keep a straight face. "If anyone is going to kick your ass, it's going to be me."

Xin gave a single chuckle. "Come. Allow me to assist you."

When Jace finally sat up, he thought he was going to pass out. "Where... Where are we going?"

"To the tank."

CHAPTER FOUR

THE TANK COULDN'T BE MORE APPARENT THAN WHAT IT WAS—A big, empty glass tube that he laid in, connected by pipes, machines, and all sorts of random crap. It was cramped, with hardly any room to even move.

Unable to lift his arm, Jace awkwardly yet painfully knocked on the glass at Xin, who stood staring at him with his silly sunglasses still on. "What am I supposed to be doing in here?"

No answer. Xin turned and walked away with his hands clasped behind his back.

A strange green light illuminated the capsule, then the light narrowed and focused on various parts of Jace's body. A hiss sounded. A few seconds later, Jace felt the back of his shirt get wet. He tried to sit up to see what was going on, but the pain in his chest, as well as the limited space, stopped him.

The tank continued to fill with strangely dense liquid. With each inch it rose, Jace's fear built, going to borderline panic.

He pressed his face against the glass, desperately trying to take a full, deep breath before the water took over. After a final gasp, the pocket of air was gone.

Jace pounded on the glass again, doing his best to ignore the agony in his torso. The glass was too thick.

He patted his hands around, searching for anything he could use as a weapon. Everything around him was smooth.

Dizziness started to take over from the lack of oxygen in his burning lungs. After a final attempt to break the glass, Jace's body forced out an exhale, then took in a reflexive breath.

The watery substance consumed him, and he felt the liquid go into his lungs. He coughed and choked. Then coughed again. And again. At that moment, Jace realized he was breathing.

The panic and fear whittled down to confusion.

His chest tingled, then went numb. Soon after, various other parts of his body shivered and dulled.

At the corner of his eye, he saw someone looking down at him. Jace tried to talk, but no voice came from his throat. The figure left.

Paralyzed and helpless, Jace had no choice but to wait in the water-filled tank.

———

After what seemed like hours, or even days, the watery substance started to drain from the tank. White smoke filled the capsule, heating it to desert-like temperatures. Jace coughed. At first, it was a wet cough, but it quickly dried up. Jace felt the tank move, and it rotated upright. The glass opened, and the white smoke poured out.

Jace almost fell forward, his legs catching his stumbled step. He stood up straight, his muscles achy and sore, but his chest didn't hurt. It reminded him of when he first woke up in the infirmary. Jace caught the scent of vanilla as he looked at his hands and clothes. Everything was dry.

A woman's voice sounded from behind him. "I see you stayed awake this time." Jace turned around to face the darker-skinned woman once more. Erica held the rectangular glass thing in her arm, visually looking him over. "How are you feeling?"

"I, uh…" Jace looked down and patted his torso, amazed at the recovery from severely broken bones. "Sore, but good."

Erica tapped on the glass device. "You have a knack for breaking ribs." She leaned forward and poked Jace in the chest as if physically inspecting him. "Quickly too. So… Did you experience anything?"

"Did I exp…" Jace's eyes bulged, and he gestured to himself. "I experienced a monster kicking me across a damn room."

"Is that it?"

Jace was taken back at that comment. "What else was I supposed to experience?"

She sighed, then started to tap on the glass device, looking disappointed. "Fine." She turned and started to leave the room.

"Wait!" Jace reached to grab her arm but paused just inches away.

Erica turned around, noticing the extended hand.

When Jace noticed his arm, he recoiled it, using it to instead gesture to the tank. "What is that?"

"I already told you—the full subversive chamber."

Jace blinked, not understanding.

Erica put her arm down in frustration and spoke in a mocking tone, "Goo is good." She rolled her eyes as she turned and continued to walk out. "Go get some food. You'll be hungry."

She was right. Jace's stomach grumbled, and the hunger pains came almost instantly. He looked up at her as she turned a corner. How did she know?

———

After the ordeal with that monster, Jace's training took a huge turn for several months, going from stupid propaganda techniques to more hands-on lessons. After fighting with various demons and monsters the facility had stored somewhere for whatever reason, Jace would visit Erica to be dipped in the goo. Broken bones, punctures, and scratches ripped and burned skin—all would be healed in hours or days, not the weeks or months if in a regular hospital. Apparently, he would always take his hands-on training just a touch too far. He also got better and more confident in his fights. He wondered why this hyper-whatever goo wasn't readily available to the general public. He also noticed that Erica would always ask if something felt different with each visit. And she was always disappointed when he answered "no." When he questioned why she always asked, she explained support and assisted equipment couldn't be assigned until she gets the answer she wanted.

And every time he asked what she meant, she never explained. He also noticed he was always painfully hungry after he got out of the goo, even if he was submerged for an hour.

He had seen many people come in to look at the holographic board on the first floor and leave shortly after. Jace stood in front of that board, staring at the holographic screen with job postings from around the world. Assassinations, settlement purges, investigations, and other contracts filled a list to his left. Next to each were financial rewards and rank requirement. Some of the missions paid very well. Far more than he made in the military. For a moment, he wondered where the jobs and the money came from. He reached to tap an assignment like he had seen many people do. The job turned red, with an error reading, "Unauthorized to accept jobs." He only saw general info—no real details.

Jace was startled when he saw Xin standing next to him, his hands behind his back.

"Come," he said, then he turned and walked away.

Jace followed him into the elevator, where Xin pushed a button to the lower levels. Jace looked at his hands. "Hey, why do I always have to fight barehanded?"

Xin looked straight at the door, never making eye contact through his sunglasses. "I never said you had to fight unarmed."

"What?" Jace stomped on the floor. The elevator shook. "You mean this entire time I could have had a fucking weapon?"

"You showed up with no weapon. I figured you were your own weapon." Before Jace could explode in anger, Xin continued, "However, when you know your enemy up close and personal, there is nothing they can do to stop you."

That wasn't something Jace had considered before. After a while, he did see that he could predict some of the movements from demons they put him up against. Because he knew a lot of their abilities and attacks, they seemed slower and much easier to defend against. "So you're saying that if I keep fighting with my bare hands, I'll be better than if I used some sort of weapon?"

"To a point."

The elevator stopped, and the doors opened, showing another dark space with a circle of light. Another dark room. It seemed as if the place was made of dark, ominous rooms, and everything else was built around it.

Xin exited with Jace following behind. "Indeed, knowledge is power in this world. If you know your opponent well enough, you can use anything you wish to defeat them."

Jace lifted his arm to look at his hand in the shadow, then clenched a fist. "In that case, I'll keep using my fists. I'm going to be the best."

"I have never seen someone come as far as you have." Xin reached the light. "Perhaps it is time for another test."

"Did you tell Erica to get that healing goo ready?"

"Healing goo?" A smile broke the side of Xin's lips. "I believe you misunderstand the purpose of the formula. You believe it is just for healing. Instead, it can unleash your potential."

That kind of shocked Jace. "What? Like magic?"

Xin turned to face him. "Not at all. The doctor's formula is all-natural and scientific."

More fancy talk. But at least it wasn't magic. "So, what's the test?"

Xin put a fist in his palm and gave a slight bow.

Jace had seen Xin make that move before. So when he did a backhand, Jace was able to block it. He blocked a second punch, ducked a swing, then shielded his chest from a kick. Jace rolled backward to get some distance between him and Xin.

The two stood facing off for a moment.

Jace always enjoyed facing off against tough opponents. "You're slower than last time."

Xin paused for a moment. "Am I? Interesting."

"Are you going easy on me? Or perhaps it's your age."

Xin didn't answer. Instead, he stepped forward to continue his assault. Jace, all the while enjoying every hit he took, knowing Xin wasn't going to get out of this match unscathed.

———

Jace woke up in the tank after another ass beating. Shortly after, the tank drained, and the capsule opened. There stood Erica, tablet in hand.

"How are you feeling?"

Jace smiled, like seeing Erica in that situation became a common thing. "How long this time?"

"Not long. Maybe twenty minutes." She tapped on the glass screen. "Did you actually get a hit on Sir Xin?"

Jace stepped out of the tank, brushing himself off. "Yeah, quite a few. Apparently, he was testing me again."

Erica's tone didn't sound sarcastic for once. "A few? Very impressive. Any changes?"

"I still don't know what you mean."

After a few taps on the screen, she turned around. "You're clear. Until next time."

Though the constant questioning of changes bothered him, Jace brushed a hand through his hair, thinking about the first duel he had with Xin, and how quick he was. This time, he was actually able to keep up. Jace rubbed his lip with his thumb, remembering a particularly painful kick. Well, almost.

He walked out of the infirmary and went to his private quarters. After a moment to reflect on what Xin had told him earlier about fighting barehanded, Jace reached under his bed and grabbed the large duffle bag he had with him when he first arrived in the mountains. He shuffled through the various gear, taking out some of the contents and putting them on the bed: a large case and a smaller container. Inside the smaller container, two large custom desert eagles sat in a cushioned material.

He thought about when he found them in the crate in the SOC-G house, and his first demon kill. These guns had a history with him, and they were the weapons he was most comfortable with.

Jace fingered the chrome plating, and at the intricate golden design engraved in the polished metal. He paid a lot of money to have these guns look and feel the way they did. The design webbed down the barrel to the intricate grip. Individually, the designs didn't look like anything particular. When put side by side, the engraved skull was very apparent.

He picked one up, remembering how heavy they were relative to the sidearm the military gave him. These were his babies. His tools of destruction. He put the gun back in the case and opened the bottom drawer showing rows and rows of organized bullets. A few were missing, remembering he forgot to make more ammo to refill his stock.

When he opened the second box, he grabbed the custom-made holster he and Brian had constructed. Having to carry a pair of large guns in public, the two spent a lot of time making sure he could adequately hide them when he walked around. After making some minor adjustments, he put on the harness, then grabbed the two guns from the box. He slapped a clip in each, then put them in their respective holsters on his back. Next, he grabbed the jacket from his bag and put it on. It felt a little tight, but it fit, nonetheless. He stood in front of the mirror, turning side to side while looking at his reflection. Nothing was visible. Non-descript. Perfect. He brushed off the jacket with his hand, then smiled.

———

When Jace met with Xin in the elevator, he knew it would be different. He had his guns, and no demon they put him up against that would survive.

At first, Xin didn't seem to notice Jace's change in attire. At least, until he said, "That jacket is a little tight on you."

Jace rotated his shoulders. "Yeah. It's an old one."

"Today is the last day you will be a squire."

He couldn't believe his ears. After all these months, he was almost done!

"When you are finished, you will meet with the Emperor and his council for your ultimate mission."

Jace had only heard about the Emperor and the council. Even then, he didn't hear any details about them.

The door opened to the standard dark room with a single light in the middle. "In the meantime, your duty is to destroy the monsters and protect the innocent by any means necessary. Do you understand?"

Jace made a point to focus on the "any means necessary" part. He nodded. "Yes."

"Excellent." Xin gestured to the darkness.

Hesitatingly, Jace exited the elevator. The doors closed behind him, and he started to make his way toward the circle of light. When he reached the middle of the ring, the light went off, leaving him in the pitch black.

Jace's heart started to beat faster, and he widened his eyes to get a glimpse of something, anything, in the void beyond.

A muffled noise had Jace whip to the side in alarm. Slowly, he went down to a crouch. He stared hard but saw nothing.

The entire room slowly lit up, revealing a massive circular room that had three support pillars evenly spaced apart. A person was bound, gagged and blindfolded to each pillar—two men and a woman. Jace was surprised at the sight of people used for this test. He briefly wondered how The Order could hold people hostage like that.

The thought was interrupted when he saw a flash of light from the corner of his eye. He turned to see a partially armored creature sitting on a huge stone chair. He could hardly make out the dark blue-purple of its skin. Its two long horns burst into flame, and its eyes glowed red. It opened its maw showing sharp, jagged yellow teeth. Its long, white hair, apparently fireproof, went down its muscular neck to huge, spiked pauldrons. Two large chains dangled down from the pauldrons, which connected to a piece of armor that wrapped around the demon's abdomen. The armor was a dark blue but had golden trim that accentuated each spike and razor it had.

The creature leaned over and stood up to stand well over nine feet tall. It lifted its spiked gloved arms and flexed its claw-like hands. It took a deep breath, then let out a booming roar. Bat-like wings with armored talons shot out from the monster's back, and a tail with a glowing red tip waved behind the beast. The creature had cloth attached to the abdomen armor that hung toward its knees. Its exposed legs were vast and powerful, going down to a three-toed hoof. As it finished its roar, the tail whipped around and smashed into the chair, cleaving it into two. The chair flew into the air and crashed into the wall.

Jace didn't move for a long moment. He watched the creature in cautious fear, glad he had his guns with him. Because he figured there would be no way he'd win against that thing if he were barehanded.

He slowly stood up as the creature advanced. It took long strides, and it's maw hung open. Drool poured from its lips while it reached a claw toward Jace. He leaped back. The creature roared in anger, apparently expecting Jace not to resist.

The attempted grab turned into a vicious swipe. Jace leaped back again, barely getting back far enough to dodge the attack. He needed information about the creature. Knowledge would be his key to victory, so he stayed purely on the defensive.

The demon lifted its arms and slammed its fists into the ground. The room lightly shook. Each breath it took, smoke blew out from the nose and mouth. Then it turned its attention toward the helpless people.

Of course the damn thing would go for the helpless.

Jace couldn't delay any longer. He pulled out one of his pistols, letting the harness automatically bring the slide back for quicker draws. He shot the monster in the back of the skull. It bobbed its head on impact and paused in its tracks. Then it turned to face Jace, seeming angrier than injured, and gave a flap of its mighty wings. Dirt and dust gushed from the floor and into Jace's eyes.

Not wanting to remain motionless, Jace leaped to the side. A crash came from behind him, and the ground again shook. He rolled to his feet and moved back a few steps, while only being able to see blurry shapes. Feeling he was far enough away, he turned and shot at the beast once more. A loud clang. He must have hit something metal.

The creature roared and began its chase. Jace turned and ran. After a few steps, he noticed he was near the helpless woman bound to one of the supports. He looked behind him as he started to redirect his path. The creature reached its arm back, its clawed fist bursting into flames, and it threw a massive ball of fire.

Jace's eyes went wide, then he dove to the woman, shielding her from the uncomfortable warmth that instantly built up. An explosion and intense heat. Smoke filled the area.

With practiced precision, Jace put the pistol back in its holster strapped to his back in a fluid motion, then started to remove the blindfold from the woman. "Are you okay?"

The woman stared back in wide-eyed horror.

Jace looked back at the demon, who was still blurry from the smoke. It started to advance.

He grabbed the right boot knife and cut the binds on her hands, then handed her the knife. "Take this and hide." He stood and grabbed one of his handguns.

The creature swiped. Jace leaped to the side, then ducked another claw that would have easily decapitated him. The claw dug deep into the pillar the woman was bound to. Jace hoped she took cover.

Jace took another shot, this time at the foot. Like the rest, it seemed to do nothing.

The creature spun, whipping it's glowing red tail around, leaving a visible streak in the dark of the smoke. The attack was a little too high and struck the pillar, cleaving it in two. Slowly, the support started to crumble over itself.

He looked over to see the silhouette of the woman behind the broken pillar, cutting the rest of her bindings. She survived the attack.

The creature reared back with its three-toed foot and stomped with a mighty roar. The floor cracked and split. To Jace's surprise, the cracks started to glow. Not taking any chance, he turned and sprinted toward the next pillar.

Red glowing liquid shot up from the ground higher than Jace, splashing all over the place and sizzling upon impact. Jace leaped over a large pool of glowing ooze, feeling the heat emanating from the puddle, making it to the next helpless person.

He took out his left boot knife, cut the binds on the wrists and handed it to the bound guy. "Here. Cut yourself free and hide." Jace stood up and stepped to the side to make sure the creature's attention was still on him. The shape loomed in the steam and smoke; it's glowing eyes and tail told Jace he still had its focus.

Before Jace ran to the last pillar, he looked at the man next to him. The man stared, jaw agape, in horror at the menacing shadow. Jace kicked a fist-sized piece of rubble, hitting the man in the leg. That seemed to snap him out of his terrified trance. "Don't just sit there. Hide!"

Jace pulled out the second gun and ran toward the last pillar. The creature charged as Jace fired. No visible effect.

The creature lurched back and roared. Its horns blew out fire from the tips, and its tail glowed even brighter. It spun around and tail slashed. Jace ducked but was taken by surprise by an attack from its wing. The talon cut Jace, leaving a gash from his chest to his shoulder.

Jace skid to the pillar, doing his best to ignore the pulsing pain in his chest. Since both of his boot knives were gone, he shot the bindings from the next captive, hoping the bullet impact wouldn't blow his hand or any fingers off. The man flinched, but his hands were free, all limbs attached.

When Jace looked back to the demon, it covered itself with its wings. Then the wings unfolded, and a massive wave of flames shot out.

Jace grabbed the guy and yanked him behind the pillar. The red tide hit the support, and the flames started to engulf it. His skin immediately began to sweat from the intense heat.

The clanging of chains warned Jace that the monster was just behind the pillar. Jace grabbed the helpless guy and leaped back just as the pillar exploded from some physical attack. Rocks showered the area, bruising Jace's arms and face. The prisoner was alive though, and he was frantically unbinding his legs.

Blood dripped down from his chest. It wasn't too bad. Nothing that strange goo in the tank couldn't handle.

Jace stood and stepped to the side, putting distance between himself and the hostages. The creature's gaze followed. He stared for a long moment, thinking about his next step. His eyes locked on the pauldrons, and he had an idea.

After putting the guns away, he took two quick breaths, then charged at the demon. It flexed its claw and smashed downward as if to squash a pesky insect. Jace leaped forward, going into a roll underneath the monster's legs. When he got to his feet, he jumped onto the demon's back, grabbing on to where the wings met its back shoulder.

The beast flailed wildly. Jace reached for the chain that dangled from its right pauldron, catching himself just as he lost his grip.

The creature jumped toward a wall, then leaped off of it as it spread its wings to take flight. Jace grabbed the chain that dangled from the left to get a better grip. The monster swerved back and forth, trying to get Jace to lose his grip. Then the beast slammed into a wall. Jace smacked against the side but held onto the chains.

He needed to ground this thing.

Jace gripped the chains tight and pulled himself up, just enough so he could wrap an arm around a chain. Then he grabbed one of his guns and aimed the wing joint. A bullet bounced off, as did a second. The slide came back after the third, but that round didn't ricochet. The bullet dug in, punching into the monster's hide. The beast howled as blood sprayed all over Jace's legs and chest.

With the wing not functioning correctly, the creature dipped to the right and started its trajectory to the ground. It corkscrewed and shifted, crashing headfirst into the last of the pillars. The impact made Jace lose his grip on the gun, as well as the hold on the chain, and he crashed on the ground, finally coming to a rest on his back.

He took a moment to catch his breath, but the dust made that simple task difficult. When he tried to roll over, he collapsed after his right arm gave out—pain shot through his shoulder and chest.

The loud groan of the demon told Jace he had to get to his feet, with or without his arm working. He rolled over again and looked around the room. The creature was under a bunch of rubble from the destroyed pillar and a partial cave in from the ceiling. Now was his chance.

Jace got to his feet and grabbed the second handgun from the back holster and ran toward the rubble that covered the demon. Rubble shifted, and its head emerged from the debris. It looked bloodied and broken. Not broken enough.

Jace put the barrel of his desert eagle against a bleeding part of the head and pulled the trigger. Glowing hot liquid shot out of the skull, then oozed down its face. Jace stared hard into the demon's eyes and watched the glow dim, then fade away.

His arm dropped to his side, and he surveyed the room once more. The hostages were relatively unscathed, and the demon was killed. All he wanted at that moment was a dip in the tank to soothe his pains.

After retrieving his dropped gun, he reloaded the weapons, just in case the demon wasn't quite dead, and met with the three prisoners in the middle of the room. But before he could put the gun away, a chill mist came from above. The cold was nice in contrast to the high heat the demon blew out, and they felt soothing against his burns. Surprisingly, one of the men started to glow blue.

The man looked in horror, but the telltale blue glow was all Jace needed. He pointed the desert eagle at the glowing demon's chest and pulled the trigger, blowing a hole through its torso. It flew back a few feet, and the glow faded from its skin. Jace put the gun away and started his way toward the elevator.

Just what the hell was going on?

CHAPTER FIVE

When the elevator doors opened, Xin stood in the small space as if waiting for Jace, hands behind his back, his gaze going from the floor to eye-level.

Jace cradled his right arm in his left hand. "Why the hell were there hostages?"

"Hostages?"

"That fucking demon could have killed them!"

"But you saved them." Xin stepped to the side and gestured invitingly in the elevator.

"That's not an answer!" Jace almost swept his arm to the side in frustration but was given a painful reminder on his physical condition.

The two stood in silence for a long moment. "The woman is a black widow. She kills her husband for money, then seeks out another wealthy man. The man killed his brother and his brother's wife, then kidnapped their son and daughter. When he was caught, he killed the son and held the daughter as a hostage."

Those were very gruesome crimes. After a moment's thought, Jace shook his head. "We're here to save humanity, not play executioners."

"Sometimes, the two cross paths." Xin gestured to the elevator again. "Come. You have to recover. We have lots to do."

Hesitantly, Jace stepped in the elevator. The door closed, and the elevator started to move.

———

The water drained from the tank, and the capsule opened. Erica stood with her clear rectangular glass thing tapping away at it.

"How are you feeling?"

Jace sighed, a little bummed about what Xin had told him. "Fine."

"Any changes to report?"

"None."

It was Erica's turn to sigh. She rested her arms to her sides and stared at Jace for a moment. "So, you use guns?"

"Guns?" Jace looked down to the harness he still had on. "Oh, yeah. I picked these up when..." His mind started to wander off to when he infiltrated the SOC-G hideout. Then his thoughts went to Maya. When would he be able to see her again? Would this place allow him to adopt her? Was he even allowed to have a family?

"When what?"

That broke Jace out of his trance. "Nothing. It's was just something that happened when I was younger."

"That's an interesting thing you have to hold them in." Erica gestured to the harness that Jace pieced together. "I didn't even know you had those on you."

"Yeah. Took a long time to get these right." Jace lifted an arm to show the strange contraption.

Erica looked as if her interest was only feigned. "I see. Anyways, I found something a little strange in a blood test."

He lowered his arm and looked concerned at Erica.

"The samples I took..." She brought up the plastic computer thing and started to tap on it. "You seem to be absorbing a lot of the DNA restructuring material. Far more than anyone I've worked with."

That alarmed Jace. "What does that even mean?"

Erica tapped a few more times, then lowered her arms to her sides once more. "The goo."

Jace turned toward the tank, then went back to Erica. He still didn't understand.

"Just let me know if there are any changes." She turned and walked away.

Xin entered the room just as Erica left. "It is time."

Jace raised an eyebrow. "Time? Time for what?"

"For your briefing."

———

The elevator door opened to another black room with a spotlight in the middle. Jace sighed. It was as if this place had a serious hardon for these kinds of rooms. Xin walked into the darkness. Jace shook his head, following shortly after. Somewhere in the dark, he lost track of Xin, and he entered the circle of light alone.

The sound of a man's voice called from the darkness all around him, "You have faced many trials, and you have conquered them all."

A second voice, a woman's, said, "You have an impressive record. You slew the devil while saving everyone you thought was human. And when the time came, you showed no hesitation."

A third voice, another man. "You have shown us you have a true desire to save humanity."

The first voice, "It is now time for you to know your ultimate mission."

The area around him lit up. Holographic screens and images appeared all around him. Jace turned around, lost in the sea of shapes.

The first voice continued, "The Emperor demands all members of The Order to seek out the source of the demon's power—an entity known as Atmos."

That word, or name, sounded familiar to Jace. Then he remembered. Brian spoke of it a long time ago, and of the images of mass destruction. He felt his resolve strengthen at that moment.

The woman spoke, "Find the ancestor of this heritage and report it immediately so it may be brought to us alive."

Jace's eyes went from one floating image to another, noticing a long timeline of sightings and incidents. He stopped at the most recent event—a hidden town in a forest that was swallowed up by an earthquake during a massive and sudden storm. It surprised Jace that it happened about fifty miles from the orphanage where he grew up, and it was only about eight years ago.

Xin approached and stood next to Jace. "We have a long history with them." He reached out and touched the last entry. The window expanded, and a massive block a text appeared to the side. "This is the day my friend, the great Sir Blu Huntsmen, died." He paused for a long moment as if to steady his nerves. "Witnesses have reported that he fought against a pack of these creatures to get to Atmos. A child screamed, then the earthquake happened. The child screamed again, and the storm formed, with lightning shooting from the sky."

Jace was disgusted at the thought that single child was capable of so much death and destruction. "All of that from just screaming?"

Xin nodded. "Many of us died that day. And many others, including everyone in your orphanage, would have died if Sir Blu had not fearlessly charged the child to put a stop to it."

He had no idea how close he was to death. It scared him a little. "So, what happened? Did Blu kill the monster?"

"Perhaps." Xin pushed another holographic window. "This volcano erupted on the opposite side of the world around that time. The Emperor believes that if the creature is killed, its power is transferred to another source. This event may be its location. We have people on that island looking for Atmos as we speak, but we fear that it escaped."

"So, what is Atmos? How can I find this monster?"

Xin tapped the window, closing the image of the erupting volcano. "The Emperor believes that Atmos is the source of the Evolved. If we can stop Atmos, we can end these attacks." He gestured toward the elevator. "Come."

Jace's gaze followed Xin's hand, and the two started to walk in the darkness toward the elevators.

"Capturing Atmos is the ultimate goal to end this war. Many have gone their entire careers never seeing that monster."

They entered the elevator. Xin pushed the main level.

"So," Jace said after digesting the story. "Find and bring back this Atmos. Got it."

Xin nodded. "If you find Atmos, you must report in as soon as possible. Do not take that creature lightly." He handed Jace a latched wooden box.

"What's this?"

"Your training is over. Congratulations, Paladin."

Jace opened the box. Inside was a silver chain necklace with a large red gem of some kind set in it. He was excited when he realized he could finally take on missions. He smiled, trailing his fingertips over the metal. "My rank..." He looked up at Xin in surprise. "Wait, paladin?"

Xin nodded. "From what I have seen, I believe you will do well on this path." The elevator door opened. "Come."

Xin led Jace down to the job board in the front room. He had stared at the board many times in the past couple of months but was never able to get any access. When he stood in front of it, images and posts appearing all around him.

"Each job is yours to do with as you please. You use your resources and build your teams. That includes transportation. When you finish the job, you get paid." Xin swiped the screen, cycling through jobs and their details. It was amazing how many jobs were available. "From time to time, specific jobs will be assigned to certain people. In those cases, we will get a hold of you."

A job caught Jace's eye. His heart skipped a beat when he saw the pay. "Hey, look at this."

Xin pointed at the suggested rank and indicator.

Jace frowned. "So I can't take the job?"

"You can take the job. Be warned. Once you take a job, you will be responsible for its completion within the job requirements."

Jace sighed.

Xin swiped to another job. Then another. Each of them looked the same—too high level. "Do not worry about law enforcement. All government agencies have been instructed to leave us be, so long as you do not cause too much trouble." He stopped swiping at a job and turned to face Jace. "This one shall do. All you have to do is go to this location and plant devices on a rooftop."

Jace looked over the details. The words "hostile" and "gang" caught his attention.

"Accept the job, get the file and the hardware from the cage, and return when it is completed." Xin indicated the criteria. "It seems that this job needs to be done in six days before noon." He turned and started to walk away, hands behind his back.

"Wait."

Xin turned around.

"How do I... Uh, accept a job? And where is the cage?"

Xin approached. Jace noticed him ever so slightly shaking his head. "Open your hand with your palm down in the white window."

Jace noticed the area and put his hand in. The skin on his fingers and palms felt warm for a moment, then Jace's information popped up in the window with "In Progress" visible on the screen. The window vanished. Jace rubbed his fingers and palms, wondering what that feeling was.

"Come." Xin gestured toward the elevators.

They rode the elevators down until they reached a floor that led to a small room with a man in blue overalls and a red hat behind some semi-transparent glass sitting behind a desk. The man leaned back in his chair, feet up on the desk, face buried in a dirty magazine. In front of the counter was a glass screen.

Jace approached, leaving Xin in the elevator, noticing the small space this guy was locked in. For a brief moment, he wondered if the guy was trapped behind the semi-transparent glass. The casual flip of a page told Jace the guy was doing alright.

Without looking up from his naughty publication, the man said, "Put your hand on the pad."

Jace stared at the glass pane for a moment before putting his palm on it. The glass lit up for a second, then dimmed. A blue and green handprint remained when Jace removed his hand.

"You want your stuff with you, or delivered?" The man's eyes never left the magazine.

"Uh, I don't know."

Finally, the man looked up at Jace.

"What is it?"

The man glanced to the side at something Jace couldn't see, then he went back to his reading. "Small. You can carry it with you." He reached over and touched something. A compartment to the side of Jace opened up. There, a box that could fit in his backpack lay on an extended platform.

Jace assumed this was the equipment he would need for the job. He took the box and put it in his backpack.

"Okay." He put his backpack on and walked toward the elevator. "Let's do this."

The man behind the desk cleared his throat. "Forgetting something?"

Jace turned around. A folder and an envelope lay on the desk. Must be the mission details.

"Oh. Yes, of course." Jace grabbed the folder. When he looked inside to confirm that it was mission details, his eyes widened in surprise—money. Jace was pleased when he realized that he was getting paid for his training. A strange detail on the payment details caught his attention. "Bounty," "3 star x1," and a nice chunk of change. Interesting how the more he killed, the more money he would make. That would make paying for his trip a little bit easier. He put everything in his backpack and started on his very first mission as an agent of The Order.

———

Being properly clothed, the cold trek down the mountainside wasn't Jace's problem, nor was it the long walk to the airport. It wasn't asking someone to get him a plane ticket because he hardly understood the kiosk's directions. And though the sickening flight was a pain, as was the taxi ride that took him to the general area he needed to get to, those obstacles were relatively simple. It was the maze of streets and houses in rundown suburbia that gave him the biggest problems. He stayed out of sight, mostly going from one alleyway to another. No matter where he turned, he wound up in a new and unexpected area. And with the trip to the mission site taking days longer than he originally expected, Jace was running out of time.

Midmorning of the sixth day of his mission, Jace hid in an alleyway and brought out the mission folder, taking a moment to scratch his back and slightly adjusting a holster that poked particularly hard in his spine. The details were rather vague: the territory and city of the mission, an address, the job description, the time frame, and directions on how to set up the device. But no map.

Jace slapped the folder shut and returned it in his backpack, swapping it out for a water bottle and an apple. A long sigh followed a juicy bite. If the notes in the folder were accurate, he couldn't just ask someone where the address was. He didn't want his first mission to be a failure. But why couldn't he ask for directions? He decided to ask, regardless of the folder's information.

After stuffing the provisions back in his bag, Jace went to the street. Very few people walked on the sidewalk. That meant no witnesses.

After waiting nearly a half an hour, a trio of guys with facial tattoos finally walked toward him. Each had a dirty t-shirt, torn jeans, and worn sneakers, telling Jace they didn't come from any form of money. But if his countless encounters with the gang from the orphanage taught him anything, it was how to spot a gang member from a mile away. And this trio of clones was no exception.

Jace figured he had to lure them away from the streets to avoid any witnesses. That way he could have a talk with them and not draw any unwanted attention.

He set a trap to lure them away from the open. He put down a little bit of cash visible from the sidewalk, and another a few paces inside the alleyway. Then he waited.

"Yo, man. Check this shit." The sound of some footsteps came from the alley. "Aw, snap."

The gang members stepped into view into the alleyway. Jace stood from his hiding spot. "I'll let you guys keep that for some information."

The guys leaped back startled. One guy put his fists up, the second pulled out a knife, and the third put his hand behind his back as if to reach for a weapon. Probably a gun.

"Step back, fool!" The guy with his fists up said.

His first human confrontation in months. If he had to take these guys out, it would be a nice change of pace from the massive creatures and magic he was put up against during his training. "Look, I just have a simple question—where is Acron West Drive?"

The front guy grinned, showing a gold tooth, and gestured to the sidewalk. "You put the ched there?"

What was with people like them making up their own words?

The front guy approached Jace, nodding to his backpack. "I bet you have more. So how about you give us all you got, and we'll let you leave."

Deep down, Jace knew it was going to end up like this. He sighed and looked up at the sky. "What time is it?"

"What?"

Noticing the sunlight slowly crawling into the alleyway, Jace's gaze went back to the trio. "What time is it? Maybe ten?"

The front guy grinned again and shook his head as if baffled at the question. "Didn't you hear me? I said give me your bag, fool!"

If it was ten in the morning, he only had two hours left.

The front guy seemed to have had enough, and he took a step and reached for the backpack. "I said give me—"

Jace cut him off by grabbing the extended wrist and pulled him forward with his left hand and giving a hard backhand with his right. The guy's nose crunched under his knuckle. He kept his right guard up, expecting some sort of counter-attack before his next move. None came.

Not taking the opportunity for granted, Jace finished his combo by kicking the guy in the exposed side. The impact from his boot pushed the guy toward the potential gun holder. They collided before he could even raise any possible gun he held, and they crashed to the ground.

A slow slash came from the knife. Pathetically slow, as if he weren't even trying to land his attack. Jace caught the wrist in mid-swing and twisted it, forcing the knife holder to hunch over reflexively with some nasty sounding pops. After grabbing the back of the guy's head, Jace brought his knee up to intercept his nose. The impact loosened the grip on the knife. Jace tossed him over the laid out duo just as they started to get on their feet. All three of them toppled over one another.

Jace was pleased with himself. He had never dispatched three guys like that so quickly and effortlessly before.

He approached the trio, who looked up at him in shock.

The guy who had the pistol tried to crawl backward. "What are you? One of them Evolved or something?"

That angered Jace more than he expected. Before he knew it, he reached behind him and pulled out one of his chrome hand cannons.

His jaw locked, his muscles tensed with rage, and his finger hovered over the trigger. "Say that again."

No one moved for many heartbeats.

Jace took a few breaths and blinked a few times in an effort to control his anger. He removed his finger off the trigger and lowered his arm. "Now I'll ask again—Acorn West Drive. Where is it?"

———

1406 Acorn West Drive. The address in the folder led Jace to a dilapidated corner building four stories high—the tallest on the block. With broken windows and missing paneling, the structure looked like it hadn't been occupied in many years.

Jace wondered if he would make it on time since he had to stay out of sight the entire job. His first mission and he was on the brink of failing because he got lost in gang-infested suburbia. On top of that, the directions from the three gang members weren't exactly accurate. And because he couldn't risk the three running off and getting help and compromising the mission, he had to bind them in duct tape. And that took a bit longer than he wanted. He didn't expect them to wiggle and resist as much as they did. Apparently, staring down a barrel of a fifty caliber handgun wasn't enough to shut them up or have them sit still.

When no one was visible, he approached the building, the rotted stairway creaking with each step. Jace caught the scent of a sickening smell. When he opened the door, it partially fell as the bottom hinge broke apart. The putrid odor hit Jace hard. The bottom level contained trash so thick, he couldn't even see the floor. Flies buzzed all around and through the many holes in the artistically altered walls. At least the light from the sun allowed Jace to look at the rats as they scurried away.

Jace took a step to the side to take a breath of fresher air, holding back the urge to vomit with the experience of a motion sickness veteran. When he regained his composure, he looked back in the room. It reminded him of when he infiltrated the SOC-G hideout, and the piles of trash they had in the house. This instance smelled worse. Much worse.

Voices came from around the corner. A lot of them.

He didn't have any more time to hesitate. After another deep breath, Jace went into the stench filled room and got out of sight. From his hiding spot, he could see at least six people walk by the doorway. None of which noticed, or cared, that the front door was open.

Already in neck deep of the stink, Jace waded his way through the trash, eventually finding a stairway up to higher floors.

When Jace got to the roof, he went to the middle and took out the scanning device and its directions from his backpack. After putting down the base of the telescoping pole, he brought out six smaller nodes that attached to a cable. He lined them up with laser guides that shot out of the center post, making a circular perimeter around the pillar.

It didn't take long to set up. Once he finished, a small light blinked. According to the instructions, the device was set up, and he could go home.

He stood at the perimeter of the device and stared at his work. He looked up at the sky, seeing the sun was almost straight above him. Hopefully, he made it before noon, and his mission was a success. His eyes went back to the device, and he shook his head, not understanding any of it. "What the hell was the point of this?" Not caring for an answer, he picked up his gear and left, hoping to find his way back to the airport.

CHAPTER SIX

EVEN THOUGH THE HIKE BACK UP THE SNOWY MOUNTAINSIDE was cold and exhausting, Jace found it a nice, relaxing trip, and an efficient way to reflect on his mission. The fact that getting lost almost made his mission fail concerned him. That was something he couldn't let happen again.

He walked up the stairs and opened the grand double doors. Uncomfortable heat blew on his face. Was it always so hot inside?

The doors closed behind him, and Jace let the warmth melt the snow from his clothes as he considered where he might find Xin. Deciding his quarters would be as good a place as any to start his search, Jace ran his fingers through his wet hair, patted himself down, then went for the elevators, taking it to the lower levels.

He knocked on Xin's door with no reply. Just as he lifted a hand to knock again, he heard Xin respond, "Come" from the other side.

Exotic smelling smoke poured out of the room when Jace opened the door. Xin sat cross-legged in front of a statue of a smiling fat man with incense burning on either side.

Xin always sounded so calm and confident, like his tone set the mood of the room. "What can I do for you, Paladin?"

Of course Xin knew it was him. "I'm here to report and debrief."

"Why?"

He was unsure of his answer. "Bec... Because that's what you do?"

"Your mission was a success. There is no need to report to me unless you have something important to tell."

"How do you know my mission was a success?"

"We know. Just like we count your bounty."

Cryptic as always.

"Unless there is anything else you need, you may leave."

Jace thought to himself for a couple of seconds, then shook his head. "Uh, what about the pay?"

"The cage."

"Of course." After another moment to think to himself, Jace shut the door behind him to visit the cage.

———

Getting paid was easy enough. Just like getting the hardware for missions, a simple press of his hand on glass would get him the cash the job promised. As the elevator doors closed, the doors opened after a petite hand stopped their closure, and the subtle scent of vanilla entered the space. It was a welcome smell, considering the stench he ran through the day before. He stood up straight and proud.

Erica walked up to and stood beside Jace, silly glass thing in hand. "Hi there. Hit three. You need a shower."

Did he still smell? He sniffed his shoulder. Apparently, one shower wasn't enough to get the stench off. "Just got back from my first mission."

"Oh? And did the mission involve you to smell like that?"

Jace's shoulders slumped.

"How was your first mission?"

After an ego hit, Jace didn't quite know how to reply.

"Was it a success?"

Jace nodded. "Yes. It ultimately was a success."

"Congratulations." She lifted the glass and started to tap on it. "Any changes?"

There was that question again. Jace turned to face Erica. "Why do you keep asking that?"

"Because that's the primary purpose of that goo I told you about.

And like I said before, I can't assign your support equipment until I know what you need."

Again, Jace was baffled. He didn't know how to reply, or if he had any changes. "I guess not."

"Hmm." She seemed disappointed once more, tapped a few times on the screen, then relaxed her arms at her sides. "Have you always been a fast healer?"

Jace looked at her in a little bit of surprise. "What?"

"I've been wondering if your ability to recover from injuries is what the change is."

"What do you mean? That 'change' thing you keep talking about?"

Erica nodded, but then shook her head and started to mumble to herself. "That can't be possible. I've run every test..."

The two stood quietly for a long moment. Jace's eyes darted around, feeling uncomfortable in the silence. He cleared his throat to change the subject. "I kind of had some problems with the mission." When Erica didn't respond, he added, "I got lost."

After a brief hesitation, she finally turned to look at him, as if trying to mentally catch up to the conversation. "Lost?"

Jace felt embarrassed. "Yeah. I couldn't find the right street. I had to ask some gang bangers. Even then, they gave me shitty directions."

"Didn't you do your research? And where was your support?"

Jace ran his fingers through his hair and diverted his gaze.

"No research and no support." She turned and faced the door again.

"I always work alone."

"Well, maybe you shouldn't. Nobody works alone, you know."

That gave Jace pause. Maybe he should find some people to work with. Build his own team. Then the chubby image of Brian came to mind. He had always helped Jace with jobs in the past. Slowly, Jace started to nod his head. Brian was Jace's support team. All of his hunts and all of his jobs wouldn't have been possible without Brian's intel. He sighed, realizing he didn't know how to get a hold of Brian. When Jace left the orphanage, the little earpieces didn't work, so he threw them away.

After a few moments, Jace realized they were still in the elevator. "This is a long elevator ride."

"Yeah. It wouldn't be as long if you just hit three as I asked."

Jace's eyes went wide when he realized he didn't press anything. He pushed three, then one. The elevator started to move.

He considered his predicament for a moment, concluding that he would need some sort of support. At the very least, so he didn't get lost again. Jace cleared his throat. "Hey, could you help me?"

As if she were prepared for that question, she quickly answered, "I'm not interested in joining your crew."

Jace shook his head. "No, no. I need help finding someone."

Erica gave a slight glance toward Jace. "Oh?"

"Yeah. Someone I used to work with."

"Didn't you say you always worked alone?"

"I do. I mean, I..."

Erica smiled. The elevator door opened. "Okay, soldier boy. Tell you what. You come to my office for some more blood samples, and I'll help you find your work buddy."

More blood work. Jace sighed, realizing he didn't have much choice. "Sure."

Erica started to leave the elevator. "And take a shower before you visit. I don't want that smell in my office."

The doors closed before he could answer.

———

After a shower and having his clothes washed, Jace went into Erica's office. For the first time, she wasn't wearing a lab coat, and her hair was out of that tight ponytail she always had. Erica looked more casual and relaxed. That is, if a buttoned-up blouse, slacks, and heels could be called casual. She sat at her desk with papers in her hands.

Jace knocked on the opened door.

"Come in," Erica answered without looking up from her paperwork.

As Jace walked up to the chair opposite of her to sit, she reached in her desk and produced a needle and tube kit for blood extraction. "Sit and roll up your sleeve." When she looked up to him, she seemed tired. Overworked.

71

Jace sat, rolled up his sleeve, then presented his arm. "How long have you been up?"

Erica rubbed the bridge of her nose. "I don't know. Thirty-two hours, maybe?" She rubbed Jace's arm with a swab, then stuck the needle in. "Maybe more. I lost track." She attached the tube and started to take her sample.

Jace never liked having his blood drawn. Every time the vial started to fill with red, he'd have to look away. "What is this test for?"

"Call it a hunch. You wouldn't understand, even if I told you."

After a few vials were filled, Erica removed the needle and placed a cotton swab on the puncture mark. After she taped the swab on his arm, she stood with a hand on her hip. "So, who do you need help finding?"

———

Brian McGuen. Jace never knew his last name. In fact, he had a bad habit of not getting anyone's last name. Because of that personal hiccup, he never was able to find Jessica. Or Brittaney and Claire, for that matter. He paused for a moment in thought—what was Maya's last name?

Jace hardly contained the excitement during his trip. He had so much to say, and having Brian support him on the missions would make everything so much easier.

After a sigh, Jace snapped the folder shut and looked up at the clean school campus. The pristine sidewalk went between two brick pillars, flanked by well-groomed lawns and gardens. Bushes were sculpted in various shapes, ranging from animals to the likeness of a person. At the end of the pathway, tall multi-story buildings stood. Each of them was old but well maintained, with a seemingly fresh coat of paint on them. The people who walked around and sat in the grass seemed like some picture in a magazine. They wore similar attire—tan top and green slacks for the men, green top and tan skirt for the women. He noticed some of them glancing toward him.

Jace jogged to a group of people who were walking toward the buildings. "Hey, can you help me?"

One guy, a man in a tan coat with swishy black hair, recoiled his arm, his face looking disgusted. "Don't touch me!"

Jace stopped and blinked a couple of times.

Swishy visibly scanned Jace. "Oh my, a beggar."

"A what?" He looked down at his attire. Sure, his jacket and shirt had some dirt on it, and his fingerless gloves were a bit worn out, but that didn't mean he looked like a beggar. He scratched his head and looked back to the group. "No. Listen, I—"

"Begone, filth!" When Swishy turned, the entire group followed.

What a bunch of snobby bitches!

Before he could find someone else to talk to, three law officers approached. Probably security guards.

For a moment, Jace thought about showing him The Order amulet to see if that would ward off this guy. Then again, this was a fancy private school. He probably didn't have any real authority here.

The security guards blocked Jace's path, the middle guy taking the lead. "You can't be here."

"Why not?"

"Private property. No beggars or solicitors allowed on the premises."

Why did everyone think he was a beggar? "Actually..." Jace opened the folder Erica had gotten him.

"No solicitors. Last chance to leave."

Jace eyed the three for a moment. He could just beat the crap out of them, but that wouldn't help him find Brian. Finally, he sighed and turned to leave.

———

Jace sat in a restaurant booth near the school campus. He stared at a picture of Brian just before he left the orphanage—the dirty, chubby kid with thick glasses and short red hair. Brian was one of the few kids who was shorter than Jace. After a while, he put the picture away in an inside pocket of his jacket.

On the far side of the room, a TV hung above a bar with the evening news, showing scenes of a neighborhood destroyed by some strange demon attack. Though the area looked familiar to Jace, he couldn't quite remember where he saw it.

His hand absent-mindedly grabbed a tater tot from his plate while he stared at the screen. Maybe if he were there, he could have stopped the attack and saved the lives of those hundreds lost. Those damn demons.

A shape of tan blocked Jace's view. He looked up to see Swishy and his group standing at the table.

"How dare you assume you can enter our place and eat our food." Swishy grabbed a tater tot from Jace's plate and lifted it above his head so everyone behind him could see what he held. "He's so poor, this is all he could only afford - a plate of tater tots!"

The group laughed.

Jace had other things to think about, and Swishy wasn't making things any easier. He ate the tater tot in his hand and grabbed another.

"Your kind is not welcome here." Swishy swatted the plate. It crashed on the floor, breaking on impact.

Jace took a deep breath to calm himself down. He wondered how he always seemed to get into these kinds of situations. He took a bite out of the last of his tater tots, thinking about the dipping sauce that was suddenly taken from him. "I'm not here to cause any trouble."

Swishy waved his hand back and forth in front of his nose. "You stink, filth. You need a bath." He lifted the glass of water from the table and poured it into Jace's lap.

The room erupted in laughter.

Jace was getting fed up with this guy. He didn't even look up at Swishy as he took the last bite of his tater tot.

"It looks like you're done. Tell you what, I'll even pay for your gourmet meal." Swishy placed some cash on the table. "And since you look like a jovial individual, here's your tip." A larger bill was placed in front of him.

It was a generous tip, but it wouldn't nearly be enough. Jace looked to the floor, seeing the broken plate and trampled tater tots. He reached inside his coat and took out some cash, placing it on the table next to Swishy's money.

That seemed to change the guy's attitude. "What the hell is this?"

Jace scooted out of his booth and stood up, finally looking at Swishy. "That's for the mess."

Swishy looked down at the broken plate, then back to Jace. It seemed as if Swishy didn't quite understand. It didn't matter to Jace. Not anymore, at least.

Jace took out Swishy's leg with a kick to the knee, then grabbed the back of his head and smashed it against the table, grinding his face on the solid surface. A tan-coated arm reached out to grab Jace. While holding on to Swishy's once finely groomed hair to continue grinding Swishy's face on the table, Jace grabbed his empty water glass and casually tossed it at the guy. Reflexively, the reaching guy retracted his grab to catch the glass instead. That provided Jace the moment he needed to finish off Swishy and his groomed face by giving a hard right cross while he still gripped his hair. Like a sack of flour, he flopped to the floor.

Apparently, Swishy's crew was more than just a few tan-coated lackeys. Almost the entire restaurant stood up and approached him.

Great. A mob.

They charged in, throwing punches and reaching out to grab him whenever they could. Slow. Careless. Entirely predictable. Jace swatted and weaved around one blow after another, landing his own hard hits whenever he could. He even saw a bottle fly toward him, thrown from one of Swishy's crew, which also seemed painfully slow. He bent his neck, his eyes locking on the label from the twirling bottle—a beer bottle with 4.2% alcohol, and zero calories. Maybe a diet beer?

Before he could question why he could read the label in such an intense situation, someone cried out from behind him after the sound of glass shattering. Apparently, the bottle hit them instead. Jace gave a back kick, tossing the guy behind him into the wall.

Jace leaped onto a table and put his hands out. "Wait! Hold on!"

In a matter of seconds, everyone stopped what they were doing and stood motionless. Almost comedic.

Jace gestured to the guys who were on the floor. Hopefully, he could talk his way out of this brawl, using the four that were taken out of the fight in the matter of a few seconds to his advantage. "Look at your friends. Do you want to end up like them?"

A few tan-coats looked at one another.

Swishy stood up, blood splashed and smeared all over his face. "What are you waiting for? Get him!"

Jace got a sigh in just in time before the mob charged once more. They tipped the table over. Jace leaped back to another booth.

He thought the tables were bolted to the floor. Testing his theory, he stepped on that tabletop and tried to wobble it. Yep. They were indeed bolted down. So how was his table tipped over? Maybe they ripped it from the floor?

More attacks came at him. Jace defended against a few, taking out one after another with precise and well-timed blows. Regardless of their slow and sluggish attacks, their sheer numbers were starting to overwhelm him. He felt a hit on his side or back from time to time indicating a change in position.

Someone flung a chair at him. He ducked the improvised weapon, taking a punch to the cheek in return. Someone broke through the mob and charged. Reckless and unbalanced. Jace grabbed hold of the tan-coat and tossed him out the window.

Using the broken window as a doorway, Jace leaped out to funnel the mob. A tan-coat jumped out to follow. Jace forced him to take a nap just as he landed. One by one, Jace whittled down the mob.

Finally, the mob stopped their advances. Tan-coats and restaurant staff gathered outside, staring at Jace as he stood over a small pile of bloody and unconscious people.

Thankful for the reprieve in the waves of tan-coated bullies, Jace took a few deep breaths and locked his eyes on Swishy. "Now that I got your attention..." Jace approached Swishy, keeping an eye on the rest of the mob while walking over the bodies of the fallen. Some groaned. Others were still unconscious. "I was wondering if you could help me."

Swishy sneered, then ran at Jace with a knife in his hand.

Jace rolled his eyes and shook his head. Why couldn't Swishy stop doing stupid things? He had enough of this. Jace reached back and pulled out one of his hand cannons. Swishy stopped in his tracks, and the crowd scattered in screams. Besides Swishy's trembling, the two didn't move for many heartbeats. Finally, Swishy dropped the knife.

"Maybe you're not as stupid as I thought." Jace lowered his arm.

"Now, I am looking for someone." He grabbed the picture from his inside pocket and showed it to Swishy.

Swishy's eyes went from the photo to Jace, back to the picture. "That looks like Brian."

Just hearing someone say that name gave Jace hope. He rushed over to Swishy, who recoiled in fear. "You know Brian?"

Swishy dabbed his bloody nose with the back of his hand. "Everyone does."

Jace couldn't contain his smile. "Great! Listen, I need you to give him a message."

Sirens sounded from the distance. Law enforcement was nearby.

"Tell him that his old colleague from S-O-C wants to meet." He put his gun away and took a step back. The sirens were close. He had to think about what to say without the possibility of Swishy telling the police and getting him arrested. "Noon tomorrow. Where we used to meet, but here." Jace turned and ran.

"What does that even mean?" Swishy shouted from behind him.

Jace called over his shoulder, "He'll know!"

———

The local library didn't have a second floor, but Jace hoped that his message would be understood. He sat anxiously, snacking on carrots while he waited. More than a few times, eyes glared at him from behind books.

Noon came and went. Brian didn't show. Finally Jace stood and started to leave. Maybe Swishy didn't send him the message. Maybe Brian didn't understand it. Either way, Jace was disappointed. He would have to go back to that campus and find Swishy again.

When Jace opened the front door, a tall, skinny guy inadvertently blocked his path.

"Oh, excuse me," the man said and stepped aside.

Just as Jace walked by, something struck him as odd. He paused and turned around to look at the guy, who he swore he recognized. He stood a foot or so taller than Jace, with a light stubble around his face and short, well-groomed red-brown hair.

The guy stared at him. He looked just as confused under his brown thin-framed glasses. "Is that you, Jace?"

Again, Jace couldn't contain his smile. "Holy shit! Brian!"

"Hey, it is you!" Jace didn't expect Brian to hug him. When the hug broke, Brian said, "Holy smokes, I thought you were dead."

"Dead? What made you think that?"

"I don't know. Something about a mission going bad or something."

At that moment, Jace understood. "No, I just needed to disappear."

"Oh?" Brian smiled and gave Jace another hug. "Holy smokes, man! It's great to see you!" The hug broke, and Brian gestured toward the street. "Come on. Let's get something to eat, and we can talk. I know of this killer pizza place near campus."

"Uh, about that..."

"Oh yeah." Brian nodded. "Right. I heard about what happened. Holy smokes, Jace. If there was anyone I knew that could do something like that, it was you."

The two walked down the street away from the campus, talking about what happened after they left the orphanage. Jace still couldn't believe he found Brian, or how tall and thin he had gotten.

"And after college," Brian continued. "I got hired at a design company. I've been their lead designer and head technician ever since."

"You always were the smart one."

Brian smiled. "I don't think I ever thanked you for helping pay for college. I know you had to get into those fights to get that money. You didn't have to do that."

Jace shrugged. "It was the least I could do."

"Enough about me. What about you?"

"Well..." Jace thought to himself for a moment, wondering where to begin. Then he thought about how Brian heard he was dead. "How did you know I joined the military?"

"After everything we've done, and saving those girls..." His words trailed off for a moment. "I don't know. I was talking to a college buddy of mine, and the topic of Sanctuary somehow came up. It got me thinking about those times."

Jace noticed Brian's eyes wandered, and he had a subtle smile on his lips.

"So," Brian continued. "I looked you up. So, wait a minute." Brian stopped walking and turned to Jace. "What happened? Why did your file read 'killed in action'?"

Jace wondered if he could honestly reply. He took a moment, thinking about Brian's gaze while I spoke. "Before I answer that, let me ask you something."

"Yeah, okay."

"Do you miss it?"

Brian didn't immediately answer. After a long moment of him staring at nothing, he eventually nodded. "Yeah. I mean, we were doing something right. We were like heroes." Brian pointed between Jace and himself. "If it weren't for us, those girls would have been sold into slavery. We stopped it! We saved them, and we ended the SOC-G!"

Jace couldn't help but smile. He felt good about himself and his path after that day. "We made a good team."

"Yeah." Brian turned around and continued the walk.

"I have a job offer for you. You want to team up again?"

Brian stumbled as if he tripped over an invisible root on the sidewalk. When he regained his balance, he turned and stared at Jace. "What?"

"Do you want to team up again?" Jace approached Brian. "It has to do with why you thought I was dead." When Brian didn't answer, Jace added, "and we would be saving more people. A lot more people."

It wasn't every day that Jace could baffle Brian on an intellectual level. So when Brian's face contorted, as if trying to understand or digest what he had just heard, Jace felt a bit of satisfaction.

"What do you mean?" Brian finally was able to ask.

A hologram on a building caught Jace's attention. An illusionary form of a woman talked about that attack on a city. Jace remembered it was the same story that was on the TV above the bar the other night.

Brian turned to see what Jace stared at. "Yeah, that. The death toll is reaching 800. They say one of those giant rock demons did it. They've been appearing randomly out of nowhere."

When a map of the area came up, Jace recognized it. His heart sank, and all sense of happiness at being reunited with Brian vanished. "I was just there."

"What?"

Jace pointed at the hologram. "There. I was just there on a mission."

Brian's eyes went back to the image.

Jace's arm flopped to his side. "I could have saved them. If I had stayed a night, I could have stopped it."

Brian put his hand on Jace's shoulder.

"Why didn't that radar thing work?" Jace looked down at the ground in thought. Did he screw up the mission? Was that post thing not set up correctly?

"According to that story, the rock monster was over three stories tall. How could you have stopped it?"

Jace shook his head. "I don't know. But I should have been there." He looked up sternly at Brian. "I have work to do, so I need to know - are you in or out?"

Brian's gaze went to the hologram for a long moment. He nodded and looked back to Jace. "If you think we can really do something to stop something like that from happening again, I'm in."

CHAPTER SEVEN

IT DIDN'T TAKE LONG FOR JACE AND BRIAN TO FIND THEIR groove once more. Like a well-oiled machine, Jace took on one job after another, many of which were considered out of his rank and capabilities. Regardless of their difficulty rankings, Jace accepted and ultimately completed the tasks, significantly increasing his confirmed kill count. All the while, Brian, in between working his regular job, developed various gadgets and hardware for Jace to use to make his job easier and safer.

Jace exited the limo and stood in front of the giant mansion. He studied the exterior, mentally confirming it was the location of the job. He brushed the sleeve of his crisp dark tuxedo with his gloved hand. A cold and humid breeze bit at his clean-shaven face, but he knew his growing hair was still styled. It needed to be for what he had in mind.

A chill wind filled the air after the rainfall earlier that day. It was going to rain again later that night. Because of that, he had to hurry.

Jace considered the general layout and his escapes if things went poorly. Rich, exotic cars of all make and models, both ground and flying vehicles, were parked by the valet in the back of the building. Men dressed in tuxedos walked next to women who wore fancy dresses and jewelry, usually wearing some form of thick coat around them to protect them from the cold. The butler treated them like royalty, greeting every guest with the highest amount of respect they could muster.

Jace approached the door while producing an envelope from into his inner coat pocket to hand to the butler.

The butler greeted Jace with a slight bow. "Good evening, sir." He opened the envelope and read the letter to himself. "Excellent, Sir Philmore. Please, follow me." The butler opened the door and showed Jace into the building.

Jace stood at the bottom of a couple of stairs that led to a large room, then he followed the butler.

"I present to you, Sir Peter Philmore," the butler announced loudly.

Jace took a moment to observe the room. A live band played slow, classical music in the far corner. The spacious room bustled with chatty businesspeople and shifty politicians. Against the opposite wall were stairs that led to the upper balcony. It was there that his eyes locked onto Sonia Grains.

Sonia, a young woman twenty-one years of age, had flawless looking skin. She looked back at him with her blue eyes. Her fine brown hair with curled tips sagged over her right shoulder, showing her long, slender neck. Her earrings dangled low, but her pearl necklace would catch anyone's eye and lead their gaze down to the slit that showed her bosom. She wore a long, purple dress that draped beautifully down to the floor, the pattern broken up by an elegantly designed white sash that wrapped around her chest.

Someone walked next to Sonia and started a conversation with her. Though she talked to the man, her gaze regularly broke away to stare at Jace.

Jace went around the ballroom, talked to a few high-ranking officials, shook hands with a few politicians, and took a drink from the waiter that navigated between the crowd with relative ease.

———

As the night went on, Jace and Sonia regularly stole glances back and forth. A visual game of cat and mouse. And with the game, it was all a matter of waiting for the opportune time before the pounce.

She sipped at her glass of wine, her fourth glass in the hour by Jace's count, while talking to a couple of older women. When the older women walked away, laughing at whatever their previous conversation was about, Jace decided to make his move. He broke away from his discussion, set down his drink—the same glass he had picked up at the beginning of the party—and slowly walked up to the purple dressed maiden. She had a subtle scent of lavender, and her glow demanded the attention of all of those around her.

Jace gave a confident smile and held out his hand "Might I ask a lady to dance?"

Sonia returned the smile. "Most certainly." She put her drink down on a table beside a potted plant and took his hand. Slowly, the two went to the dance floor.

They stayed quiet throughout the entire song, and they held each other, shifting back and forth in the motions to the music. He took in the scent of lavender, and the touch of the silky smoothness of her soft hair against his cheek when they were close. And when he dipped her during their dance, they just stared into each other's eyes, speaking to one another in an unspoken language. When the song ended, Jace extended his hand and escorted her away from the dance floor.

"Pardon my rudeness, but I must be off," Jace said, holding her hand in his. "I have a flight to catch tomorrow."

Sonia nodded, but a look of subtle disappointment glinted in her eye. After a moment of silence, Jace turned around and started toward the main door.

———

Jace tightened his gloves as he stood outside, waiting for the limo to pull up. He then caught the scent of lavender in the air. Before he could turn around, Sonia walked up beside him with another glass of wine in her hand, a thin shawl around her shoulders to keep her warm.

She pulled out a pack of cigarettes. "You don't really have a flight, do you, Mr. Philmore?"

Jace smiled. "No, not really. I normally find that these events are a publicity stunt. And please, call me Peter."

"Okay, Peter. Sonia Grains." Sonia lit a cigarette and took a deep drag. "Dull and boring, right?" She exhaled the smoke. After a moment, she offered one to Jace, who politely accepted. The two stood silently for a moment, smoking their cigarettes, as Jace's limo pulled up. She turned to face Jace. "Do you want to go somewhere?"

Jace again smiled. "What do you have in mind?"

The chauffeur opened the back door. Sonia walked up beside the chauffeur and whispered something in his ear. The chauffeur looked at Jace as if seeking permission. Sonia finished her wine, put the glass on the ground, then climbed in the back of the limo. Jace walked up to the chauffeur, nodded, then went inside.

The door closed behind Jace as he sat down. Sonia looked at assorted alcoholic beverages.

Jace leaned over, his face getting close to hers, and grabbed a bottle. "It was red wine if I'm not mistaken. Will a pinot noir do for the lady?" He took a couple of glasses then leaned back into his seat.

Sonia gave a coy, mischievous smile, nodded, then grabbed a glass.

Jace popped open the bottle and poured the wine into the glasses. He put the bottle down, then held the glass up while looking into her eyes. She stared back for a long moment, then the two clinked their glasses, and drank their wine. After they both finished their glasses, Jace grabbed the bottle.

"More?"

"I know I shouldn't." After a moment of hesitation, she put up her empty glass. "I'll have one more."

———

The two drank the entire bottle before the limo finally pulled up to a tall building in the city. Jace got out of the limo, smoke pouring out from the opened door, then reached in to help Sonia out of the back seat. Her cheeks were flushed, and her movements were sluggish and uncoordinated. She fumbled to grab Jace's hand, then climbed out of the limo. She staggered and fell into Jace's arms.

"I—I—I'm okay," she said with a slur. "I'm okay." She stood up straight, then put the thin sash around her shoulders. "I'm okay."

Jace grabbed a briefcase that was in the back of the seat, then the chauffeur closed the door behind them as the woman put her arm around Jace's, and the two started to walk toward the building entrance.

Sonia looked around in obvious confusion. "W-Where is the doorman? He, he is always here." Her legs gave out, and she once again fell into Jace's arms. "I'm okay! I'm okay."

Jace helped Sonia to stand up straight. "Allow me to take you to your residence."

Sonia pulled on her dress to straighten it. "You may, sir." She walked up to the security pad that opened the door. She tried to type in numbers, but her hand-eye coordination seemed to have failed.

"Please, allow me." Jace leaned over, ready to push the buttons.

"Oookay. Twelve, twenty-one, five, zero, five."

Jace typed in the numbers. The door quietly beeped, then popped open. "Come." Jace took her arm.

They walked to an elevator on the far end of the marble lobby. Each footstep echoed throughout the room. When the two approached the elevator, the doors slid open.

Sonia took Jace into the elevator. "Come on up." She turned around and put her hand on a small screen. After her hand was scanned, the doors closed, and the elevator started to move. Moments later, the doors opened to show a massive apartment. It was rich and fancy with luxurious furs and carpets. As she walked in, the fireplace lit up in front of a small step that brought the people closer to the warmth. Jace made out the faint scent of her lavender throughout the area. He looked around at the riches and elegance the apartment had to offer. He slowly walked toward the balcony, slid open the door and looked outside. They were on the top floor with a clear sky view with an extraordinary view. He looked across the street at the only other building that was just as tall. Every other building paled in comparison. Jace put his briefcase down and turned to look at Sonia, who slowly made her way toward Jace.

She grinned, grabbing a fur blanket from the couch. That was something he didn't have to worry about. "You like the view?"

Jace didn't say anything. Instead, he grabbed her and kissed her passionately against the balcony railing. She dropped the thick fur blanket on the balcony floor, and the two slowly made their way down on top of it.

———

Jace laid under the fur blanket, naked, with Sonia in his arm. Her brown hair was a mess, tangled from the whipping and lashing of their passion. They were both sticky and exhausted from their intimate activities.

He flicked the embers from his cigarette over the balcony ledge and stared at the night. More pointedly, at the coming rain clouds from the distance. When the clouds didn't block the moon, it was full and high in the night sky, giving a clear and gentle illuminance over the lands below. So much so that shapes and objects were decently visible. And that was a problem.

Jace's eyes peered down at Sonia after hearing the rhythmic breathing of a deep slumber.

It was about time.

After he tossed the cigarette over the side railing, he slowly and carefully removed his arm from behind Sonia's head, taking great care not to wake her up, then climbed out from under the blanket. The breeze chilled his naked body as he started to gather his clothes quietly. After he got dressed, he grabbed the briefcase he brought with him and popped it open. He began to silently assemble the rifle as he stared at the picture of his target. After the silencer was screwed onto the barrel, he walked to the balcony and laid down on the fur blanket next to the drugged unconscious woman. He positioned his weapon and looked through the scope, scanning the balcony of the tall building right across from him. Then, he waited.

It was late in the evening, but he knew his target's schedule. His mark would get home very soon.

Before long, Jace saw the lights in the room across the way turn on. He continued to wait patiently, staring through the scope.

A man walked in front of the balcony window with a woman behind him shortly after. The man turned around and started to undress the woman. Her dress fell to the floor as the man began to take off his pants. Then, they turned out the lights.

Though Jace continued to wait patiently, time was running out. Finally, the clouds once again covered the moon. As the woman took the man to the floor, Jace took a breath, paused, then exhaled while firing the shot. With a muffled pop from Jace's rifle, the woman lurched back and fell to the floor.

Jace took cover behind the wall and began to disassemble his rifle quickly. When the briefcase was finally closed, he left the apartment, taking the fire escape down that led to a back alley where the limo waited. As Jace approached, the limo driver opened the door for him. Jace nodded to the driver and got in the back.

The chauffeur closed the door, then drove the car away from the scene.

The assassination of the confirmed Evolved, Senator Kelley Wells, had been successful. Due to the requirement that the mission couldn't be traced back to The Order because of the Senator's popularity and the resulting overwhelmingly negative publicity, the amount of security Senator Wells had, and the unknown level of power, the job had been deemed temporarily impossible. No one dared to take responsibility. But when Jace learned precisely where the Senator's living quarters were, he started to form his plan.

Sonia Grains, the daughter of a wealthy real estate mongrel, lived in the only apartment that had a vantage point to get a clear shot to Well's balcony. The theft of a banker's party invitation, the seduction of an alcoholic girl, the removal of the doorman, the drugging of her drink to put her asleep and to alter her memories, and the placement of the blanket—all of it went according to plan. The gloves hid any fingerprints, and no one would be able to recognize him since they left the party separately, and when no one was around. And if someone did see the two leave together, he looked like the banker and used their invitation to the party.

Thanks to Brian's work, the ammo he used in the rifle didn't have a shell casing. The moonlight was bright enough to see the target but also dark enough under the clouds to hide his position. The proceeding rainfall would wash anything left on the balcony, including that disgusting cigarette butt he tossed over the side. Brian turned off all surveillance in the building, and the limo driver was the one used when people went up and down the mountainside facility.

Jace took off the gloves, tossed them on the seat, then leaned back to relax a little bit, satisfied all of the bases were covered. "Easy money." He tapped his ear to turn on the communication device Brian had given him. "Mission accomplished."

Brian replied over the communicator. "Holy smokes, Jace. That was good work. But did you really have to use that poor girl?"

"It couldn't be helped. After the Senator was confirmed to be a demon, who knows what kind of damage it could have caused." Jace grabbed a water bottle and took a swig to help get rid of the cigarette taste he had in his mouth. "Hey, that powder you gave me took longer than you said to work."

"Really? Geez. I'm sorry, Jace. Those things aren't really my field."

"Doesn't matter. She passed out eventually." Jace's eyes went to the briefcase. "That rifle and caseless round you gave me worked like a charm though."

"Awesome! I was working on this new formula that compresses more of the gas to give a better shot. See, I've been thinking about how to produce more accurate rounds with better compression and..."

Though Brian continued his rant over the earpiece, Jace's mind started to drift towards a life he could never have. He wondered what his life would have been like if he still had Jessica and Claire, or Brittaney. Jace smacked his fist on the seat and cursed the SOC. After taking a deep breath to calm himself down, he decided it was time to restart the search for his missing friends.

Brian was still in the middle of his rant when Jace interrupted him.

"Hey Brian, do you remember when I asked you to find my friend Jessica in the orphanage?"

"Yeah, kind of."

"I have some other people I'd like for you to look for." Jace considered his mistake with his search for Jessica and wondered if his not knowing their last names would screw things up this time too. "Keep searching for Jessica, but also find a girl named Claire. She was adopted around the same time Jessica disappeared."

After a brief pause, Brian said in an uncertain tone, "Okay."

"And another friend of mine—Brittaney." Jace paused to consider the timeline. "Remember that hurricane-like storm we had? Maybe a few weeks after that."

"I remember that! I was doing research for you. I had to redo everything after the power went out."

"Yeah." Jace reflected on that messed up day, and the girl he rescued in the library. Perhaps that was the first time he ever felt like he actually saved someone. He rubbed his side near his back, feeling the old scar left from a knife wound. "Let me know if you get something."

"You got it!"

Jace tapped the earpiece, turning off the communicator. He took another drink and stared out the window. Next step, turning in the mission.

———

The long walk up the road was always tiring, but very refreshing. It was either the cold walk, or he would throw up in the back of the limo. And he wasn't going to do that after he hired the chauffeur for a job. Jace wondered why they never got one of those fancy hover vehicles. Obviously, they had enough money.

Night had fallen when Jace arrived at the mountainside facility. Xin stood in front of the thick wooden doors that led inside. He had his hands behind his back, like he always did, and had his sunglasses on. "I have been waiting for you."

"Is there a problem?"

"Senator Wells." Xin gestured toward the courtyard, inviting Jace to follow.

Great. More walking in the snow. No matter. He would hear what Xin had to say. "When that mission was posted, it was an impossible task. When I heard that you accepted the mission, I was worried that you were going to fail."

"You were worried, huh? That's nice."

"You mistake my meaning." Xin stopped and turned to face Jace. "I was not worried of your success in killing the Senator but would fail in keeping the attention off of The Order. With a high-profile job like that, you would be denounced from our ranks, and you would be a Fallen."

The mission flashed in his mind once more. He quickly went over the mental checklist for the job. What could he have missed?

"At this time, no one knows what happened. So your mission was a complete success."

Jace blinked, almost frustrated at the supposedly good news. "Then why are you telling me this?"

Xin held out his hand. "Your mark."

The conversation confused Jace. Was he getting fired? But the mission was a success. He took off the amulet and handed it to Xin, who then proceeded to fiddle with the metalwork with both hands.

"You have been with us for only a short time, but you have an impressive record. Your bounty level has caught the attention of many. You have not taken a single break between missions, and you are making a name for yourself within the halls."

"Oh yeah? What's that?"

"Ghost." Xin handed Jace back the amulet. "They should now call you Paladin Lieutenant Third Class Ghost."

"Lieutenant?" Jace was taken aback from that comment. "What happened to the three ranks of Sergeant?" He immediately regretted asking that question.

"You forget your rankings. You bypassed Sergeant when I acknowledged you as a Paladin."

Jace felt like a fool for not knowing that.

"Do not fail the emperor. He has high expectations from you." Xin turned and walked toward the stairs. "And take some time off. Perhaps a month. You have earned it."

Jace didn't move. Instead, he looked at the amulet, seeing the many markings it had around it, signifying his accomplishments. For a moment, Jace wondered how Xin was able to manipulate the amulet so quickly. The thought faded when he considered his promotion. "Paladin Lieutenant." He smiled, feeling a great sense of pride in his job. Then what Xin said cycled through Jace's mind. "Wait. Time off?" He looked up to Xin, who was no longer visible. "Since when did I get a vacation?"

CHAPTER EIGHT

BRIAN SEEMED EXCITED ABOUT THE TIME OFF. HE TALKED ON and on about a new expansion for his VR game, whatever the hell that meant. And even though he was off the clock, Brian said he was going to continue to work on his gear, search for his friends, and to get a hold of him if Jace ever needed anything. Not that he would since Xin said Jace needed to relax.

Two days into his vacation and Jace was already bored out of his mind. Sitting around in his hotel room watching TV and ordering room service had him feel bottled up. He needed to get out and being in the middle of a busy city would be his release. When he looked in the mirror to double-check the concealment of his guns, Jace noticed his clothes looked old and dirty. Perhaps some new clothes would be in order.

Later, he walked through the bustling streets in his brand new suit —his dirty old backpack to make him a visual contradiction. Still, the clothes felt nice, and his guns were better hidden beneath his coat. The tailor even made some minor adjustments, which had the barrels not poking so hard out of his back when he bent forward. Jace gave him a generous tip for the excellent work.

While he strolled, Jace looked at the surrounding architecture, studying them and thinking about how he would climb up and down the structures—small ledges for handholds, holo-ad platforms for leap spots, places where he could wedge himself, jumping from one wall to the next. His mind wandered to the desert settlement that seemed so long ago when he first really considered urban movement; climbing and scaling drainpipes and windowsills. Oh, how much his life had changed since that day. He wondered how many missions he could have completed with ease if he was better at climbing in urban environments.

Feeling the amulet against his chest under the fresh-smelling clothes, Jace smiled and continued to strut down the sidewalk. He was in a good mood, and he didn't care if he showed it.

The scent of smoked meats diverted Jace's path, and he wound up standing in line for a mobile food truck. Eventually, he got to the vendor and looked at the glass display of smoked turkey legs. They smelled terrific, and they looked delicious. Jace's stomach growled when his eyes locked on a particularly tasty looking one.

He got his order and took a few steps away from the truck, bringing the plate of turkey leg to his nostrils—smoked meats on a bright, sunny day. Yeah, today was going to be a good day. His fingers picked the drumstick from the plate and brought it to his wanting mouth.

Sounds of a muffled explosion made Jace pause in mid-bite. An alarm sounded shortly after. Jace looked around, wondering if he could see what was going on. There it was, across the street from him, Sixth Street Bank and Trust.

Jace shook his head. It couldn't be. What were the odds?

People fled from the concrete building. The front entrance, a wooden door with windows flanking it, shut suddenly, stopping the flow of escapees. The single-story structure was vertically elongated to make it look like it had multiple floors with a vaulted ceiling. Pillars from the ground rose to the overhang that was an intricately designed stone rooftop. Near the top, maybe fifteen feet up, were large windows.

Jace leaned toward the food vendor, who packed up his truck to move. "Is that what I think it is?"

"Yeah. And I'm getting the hell out of here!" The vendor, as well as everyone around him, vacated the area.

A woman in dark-colored business attire ran toward Jace in a panic.

Jace brought his turkey leg up to stop her. "Hey, what's going on?"

Her eyes stared at the drumstick for a moment before meeting Jace's gaze. "There are these people. They held up the bank!"

Jace sighed. It was precisely what he thought it was. "Are they armed?"

"Yes. They had guns, like those machine guns you see on TV and—"

Jace raised his turkey-wielding hand once more to stop her and nodded his head to the side. "Go on. Get to a safe place."

The woman didn't hesitate. She fled as fast as her high heels would let her.

Jace tucked the water bottle under his arm as he shuffled in his inside coat pockets. When he finally found the earpiece, he blew on it to take off a piece of lint and stuck it in his ear. He tapped the communications device. "Hey, can you hear me?"

No answer.

"Hello?" Jace tapped the earpiece. "Brian?"

Brian cut in and out. "Stop turn...thing off... Stop turning it off!"

"Ah, there you are. Hey, I need you to do something for me." Jace took a drink of water.

"Yeah. Hey, what's that noise?"

"It's an alarm. I think a bank is getting robbed."

"Serious? Holy smokes. Where?"

"Sixth Street Bank and Trust."

"You want me to call the cops?"

Jace shook his head. "No need. They're probably on their way."

"Okay, Okay. Hold on."

Jace continued to study the architecture, plotting any handholds he could reach. After a moment with no reply, Jace started to walk up to the building. "I'm going to go say hello."

"What? Wait, wait! Put in the lens camera."

Jace bit down on the turkey leg, securing the deliciousness in his mouth and went into his backpack. When he found the lens case, he put them in his eyes, blinked a few times, then put on his bag. "Done," he said with a stuffed mouth. He approached the closed-off building, finally taking a long-desired bite of his smoked turkey leg. "It's a nice day. What is it, Friday?"

"Yeah."

Jace visibly scanned the area, looking at all of the businesses in the vicinity. The bank was probably loaded at this time of day and week.

"Okay, okay. I got the map and some details of the bank. I'm sending it to you now."

"Didn't bring the wrist-thing. Shouldn't that stuff be a secret?"

"Not to me. Hey, is that smoke coming from the bank?"

Apparently, Brian got the lens cameras up and running. "Yes. Some lady said something about some armed guys." Jace took another bite from his delicious drumstick when he approached the stairs.

"Are you eating something?"

"Yeah. Smoked turkey leg. It's actually a lot better than I thought it was going to be. I'm really surprised." Jace grabbed the front door handle. Locked. He tried to peek inside through a window only to find out they had them covered in thick paper, or that the blinds had been closed. He took a few steps back, drinking the last of his water. His eyes fixated on the glass above the front door. "Where does that window go?"

"The window? Umm, to a small balcony on the inside. It's more of a decoration since I don't see any stairs going up to it."

Jace looked at the decorative bevels in the pillar that were too high up for him to reach. Too bad. They went straight to the top and would have made for perfect handholds. He turned and gazed up at the lip above the door, and then the frame itself. An idea came to mind.

He held the turkey leg in his teeth once more, then jumped toward the door. He kicked off the frame and grabbed the lip from above with the tips of his fingers. After pulling himself up a bit, he planted his feet against the wall, then launched himself at the pillar. His hands gripped the beveled stone, and he hit it in a hugging fashion. After a couple of shimmies upward, Jace was high enough to leap to the balcony. At least he hoped he was high enough.

With his focus on the ledge, Jace adjusted his feet to make sure his boots didn't slip. Then he sprang, reaching out for the balcony. It seemed like the leap took its time; like the world decided to slow down so that he could think about how stupid it was for him to climb maybe twenty-five feet up and jump over solid concrete with a ridiculous leg of smoked turkey in his teeth. It didn't matter though, as his fingertips found the ledge. After steadying himself for a moment, he pulled himself up and onto the ledge and knelt next to the window.

"That window looks like a Riggs and Four window. They're known for their quality."

Even though the loud ringing started to give him a headache, Jace was actually thankful for the alarm. That way, when his elbow smashed through the supposedly good quality window, it was less likely that anyone would hear it. He rubbed his arm, a little bit of pain in his elbow. "You're right. The quality is good." He slid his arm in the opening and unlocked the window so it could slide open enough for him to slip through.

In a kneeling position in what seemed to be a flower box for plastic plants, Jace looked over the lobby from his high vantage point. No stair access to the ground level from where he was at, but he spotted six people that were gagged and bound in a circle toward the middle of the room. Two guards paced around the group, each holding pistols. Not quite the weaponry the woman described to him. One looked anxious and nervous while the second seemed calm and casual.

When the pair were turned away, Jace leaped down into the floor, going to a roll to get behind cover. At that moment, the alarm finally turned off, bringing peace once again to his throbbing head. With the silence came the lights turning off. Probably from the power being shut down. The only light came from the glass dome up on the ceiling. After a couple of moments, sirens from police cars quickly approached.

"Finally," one guy said, who Jace figured was the confident one. "That thing was giving me a headache."

"You sure that kid can open the door?" A second voice questioned.

"Yeah. I've worked with him before. He's solid."

Jace moved around from desk to desk, sneaking closer toward the middle of the chamber.

The anxious guy looked toward the back of the room. "Are you sure six will be enough?"

"Boss said we're good." The confident one stood next to the anxious guard. "Relax. We've done this before."

Jace made his move. He stayed low, making sure the hostages blocked any possibility of the two spotting him. One of the hostages noticed Jace's approach. Jace brought a finger to his lips and gave a silent "shh." When he got to the hostages, he stood with them and took a bite from his turkey leg.

"That kid," the anxious guard said with a quiver in his tone. "He's a little..."

"Don't knock the kid. Doesn't matter if he's a little lost in the head. He knows what he's doing."

A voice called from behind, "We're ready. Bring them back."

The confident man pushed a hostage. "You heard the man." The guard paced, then paused when he got to Jace.

Jace took another bite of his leg.

The confident man looked baffled as if trying to put two-and-two together. After a moment of chewing, it seemed as if the guard had an answer to the strange question of a new hostage who ate a turkey leg. "How did you get loose?"

After a few moments of uncomfortable glares, Jace swallowed his bite, then he threw the drumstick at the guard. It hit the gun, smacking it a little bit to the side. It wasn't knocked out of his hand, but it wasn't pointed at Jace or the hostages either. So it was a win.

Jace quick-stepped forward before the confident guard could figure out what had happened and gave a backhand chop to the guard's throat while grabbing the gun with the other hand. He bent the wrist, bringing the gun up toward the ceiling and pulled him forward, then planted his boot into the guard's side with a kick. When the guard leaned forward from the hits, Jace grabbed the back of his neck and shoved him toward the anxious guy, who looked as if he realized what was going on.

When the anxiety guy caught the confident man, Jace charged, leaping into the air and planting a boot on the first guy's back. The two would-be bank robbers fell to the floor, the second pistol sliding across the tiled floor.

Jace knelt and pressed the barrel of the confident man's pistol against anxious guy's head.

He stared hard at the guy, whose expression was of panic and terror.

Jace put him to sleep with a smack to the temple with the butt of the pistol, then had the confident guy join his fellow guardsman in the pistol-whipped slumber.

Jace stood and approached the group of hostages. He put a finger to his lips in another hush fashion, then ungagged the man. "Quietly free the rest."

When he was unbound, he proceeded to help the other hostages while Jace took out the clip, removed the bullet from the chamber, and tossed the pistol to the side. He stopped and stared at the improvised weapon of delicious destruction. "That was a good turkey leg."

Brian chimed in with his thoughts over the earpiece. "Will you stop messing around!"

Jace turned and looked at the hostages, who were in the final stages of releasing each other from their binds. He picked up the second pistol and proceeded to remove the ammo while whispering, "Get out of here when you're done, and be quiet."

Some of the hostages nodded.

Jace tossed the empty gun to the side and made his way toward the back of the bank.

Between two desks was a small stairway that led to a hallway with insets for some silly looking busts—probably presidents or donors or something Jace didn't care much about. At the end of the hall was a busted open vault door. Jace knelt with his back against the wall, then chanced a quick peek around the corner. Two more guards, one taller and muscular, the second shorter but still muscular, who held larger weapons, stood flanking a small child in the middle of the room.

Jace returned to his cover behind the wall.

"Be careful, Jace," Brian said over the com. "The guy on the left has a shotgun. The guy on the right has a semi-automatic rifle."

Someone gave a huff from inside the vault. "Where are those hostages?"

A second voice came from the vault. "I'll get them.'

Jace took to the shadows of the bust-sized cubby.

The shorter guard walked past Jace, apparently not seeing him in the shadow. "Hey, what's taking so long?"

Jace moved from the shadows and behind the man. He took the guard's knee out with a kick. When he started to fall back, Jace caught him and wrapped his arm around his neck, then flipped him up and over his back. To Jace's misfortune, his rifle went off, blowing holes in the walls and ceiling. Then the bank robber landed on the stairs and tumbled to the bottom.

Plaster fell from the holes in the wall, and glass trickled from the ceiling to the floor. So much for stealth.

Before he could make a move, Jace heard the racking of the shotgun from behind him.

Jace ran up the stairs that led back to the lobby. The railing exploded from the shotgun blast. Jace coughed up the dust from his lungs, then he called from around the corner, "Not even a customary 'freeze'?" With a loud bang, the wall next to him blew apart in reply.

Not wanting to take on a shotgun, Jace leaped over the counter for cover just as another shot made it explode. "Brian, what can you tell me about that gun?"

"Twelve-gauge Maverick 88 pump-action shotgun."

"Capacity?"

"Six."

Staying low, Jace made his way toward the edge of the counter. Then, going as quickly as he could, he broke cover for repositioning.

The bank robber stood on a table with the gun pointed at Jace. The floor beneath Jace blew apart. Jace rolled over his shoulders then jumped over a small island, which was almost cut in half by another shot.

A sting in Jace's shoulder caught his attention. There, a bloodied chunk of wood stuck out of his skin. He reached up and painfully pulled the three-inch spike out with a grimace. "Okay, I need to get back into wearing armor."

"Are you hurt?" Brian asked.

"Nothing serious." Jace held the chunk of red-soaked timber in front of him.

"Yeah, I'll start designing it," Brian replied as Jace threw the chunk to the ground.

Jace looked up over his shoulder. "You give up yet?"

No reply.

After a moment of silence, Jace peeked his head around his cover to see the man slowly walking up toward the island in the middle of the lobby. Jace turned and went to a knee, his fingertips at the lower corners near the floor and whispered, "You'd think the police would have come in by now."

"They're still waiting for reinforcements. SWAT is close though."

"Good." Jace lunged, his fingers gripping the bottom part of the island and launching the wooden pedestal toward the armed man. The shotgun went off, blowing the island into pieces.

Jace stood up and faced the assailant. "Now, do you give up?"

The bank robber pointed the gun and pulled the trigger. It clicked. Empty.

After tossing the shotgun aside, the robber reached behind him to pull out a pistol. Jace intercepted, hitting him with a flying tackle.

Arms gripped Jace's chest and threw him aside. The awkward toss had his head smack against the concrete wall. Dazed, he looked up to see the man rush toward him. Strong hands grabbed his jacket and lifted him from the floor, then smacked him hard against the wall once more.

"Are you going easy on him?" Brian asked.

Jace could only shake his head in reply. In a lazy and slurred tone, Jace looked up to the attacker and said, "Last chance to give up."

The reply Jace got was him being thrown back toward the middle of the room, and he slid across the hardwood floor.

Jace stood up, his vision starting to clear from the hard, dazing hit on the back of his head. Just in time for him to see the man rushing toward him with a crazed look in his eye.

With his focus back, Jace shifted his weight for balance and swatted away a right cross, then took a step back to dodge a surprisingly quick uppercut.

This guy was fast. Probably quicker than most people Jace had faced. But not as fast as Xin.

He ducked a right hook and sidestepped a leaping left cross. The bank robber swiped the contents of the desk next to him toward Jace. Papers blinded him, and he lifted his arms to defend against any incoming punches.

None came.

Instead, his opponent grabbed him, and lifted from the ground, only to be thrown hard to the floor. Clearly, this guy was no stranger to combat. Jace grinned. It's been a while since he's had a challenge.

A flurry of blows came from the attacker. Jace held up his guard to protect his face. The attacker then brought his entire weight down on a left elbow strike. Jace was barely able to keep his arms up to block the powerful attack. Jace felt a painful sting in his side as the man then proceeded to hit him in the ribs.

The robber sat up once more in a full-mounted position. When he threw a brutal right hook, Jace planted his feet and thrust his hips upward. The attacker fell forward. Jace rolled with the fall, nimbly breaking the man's balance to be in the top position.

The robber wrapped his legs around Jace—a strong maneuver from a veteran brawler. Seeing the robber's guard up, Jace decided to shake things up. He used pressure points to weaken the man's strength, and he broke the pin, standing at the feet of his attacker.

With Jace on his feet, he waited for the inevitable kick from the robber. After all, there wasn't much you could do lying on your back with your feet toward your attacker.

The man brought his leg back. There it was—the feeble kick.

Jace caught the leg and dropped down, wrapping the limb in a leglock. The robber resisted, trying to pry his leg from Jace's grasp. The strength of the tugs slowly started to overpower Jace's grip.

Instead of releasing his grip, Jace kicked the robber's hip. He groaned in pain, and his strength waned. That was enough for Jace to make his move, and to overpower the robber's superior strength, securing his leglock.

The robber grimaced in pain, reaching and punching feebly toward Jace. When the robber tried to sit up, Jace stopped him with a kick in the inner-thigh. Finally, the robber moved as expected. He twisted, allowing Jace to bring his leglock to a punishing conclusion. Jace pulled back, and the robber's leg popped. The fight was over.

The robber screamed in pain, reaching to his awkwardly shaped leg.

Jace tossed the limp noodle-leg to the side and stood up, running his fingers through his hair and taking a moment to catch his breath. "You should have given up." He paced a couple of steps, his eyes locked at the vault. Was the kid still in there? A tingle of worry made Jace's hairs stick up. He grabbed the robber by the shirt and sat him up while pointing toward the vaults. "Is that kid a demon? An Evolved?"

The robber's skin seemed pale. Sweat beaded from his skin.

"Is that kid—"

Even though the robber seemed on the verge of passing out, he still took a slow and pathetic swing at Jace.

After releasing the shirt, Jace caught the punch in mid-air and twisted it, feeling the pain from another limb turning into a noodle would be a better interrogation technique. "Don't make me ask again." Jace pulled the arm to its limits.

"Y-Yes!"

That answer was precisely what Jace thought. His gaze returned to the vaults, and he released the robber's arm, who crumbled to the ground. "Perfect." Jace reached behind him and pulled out his handguns. So much for his day off.

CHAPTER NINE

THE BOY, IF JACE COULD CALL IT THAT, STOOD IN THE MIDDLE OF the room staring at the main vault doors. Even with all the gunshots and shouting, the boy didn't move.

The thought of blowing some holes in the "child" crossed Jace's mind. However, he couldn't take the word of some beat-up bank robber. Unless he had a blood sample to send to Erica or that crazy moisture-light mixture that made them glow blue, Jace didn't know if this kid was an Evolved. But what should he do? After a moment's thought, he decided to wing it, making up official phrases on the spot.

Jace slowly approached the child, both guns locked on the back of the kid's head. "By the rights of The Order, and for the sake of humanity, you are hereby under arrest for being a suspected demon."

The boy remained still.

Keeping his guard up, Jace circled to the front of the child, keeping two strides away. "Do you understand?" The kid had a blank expression, his head slumped downward and had unblinking eyes drawn to the floor. Jace took a cautious step forward. "Put your hands in the air, or I'll shoot."

Without diverting his lifeless gaze, the child slowly lifted his arms.

Well, the kid listened and apparently understood. But what now? It's not like Jace could just cuff him. "Turn around and exit the room."

Slowly, the kid turned around but didn't budge.

Jace prodded the back of the kid's head. "Move!"

The kid started to walk out of the vaults with his hands in the air. Jace stayed on his heels, keeping his sights on the back of the head. They walked down the hall and up the stairs. The two robbers started to groan in pain, apparently waking up from their forced slumber.

When they approached the landing, even with a messed up arm and leg, the veteran fighter tried to crawl backward away from Jace, an expression of horror on his face. "N-No!" Then he too started to groan. But Jace heard the pain in his tone.

All of the bank robbers, even the ones tied up from the escapees, started to twitch and convulse.

Jace's eyes went from one robber to another, seeing their skin turn red like they had a rash. Then he knew what it was, and his heart skipped a beat. "Blood magic!" He pointed a gun at the child-demon and pulled the trigger. The bullet stopped in midair.

The demon slowly turned to face Jace, pulsing red-purple veins popping out of pale skin.

Brian spoke over the earpiece with concern in his tone. "Jaaace."

Jace fired another shot, and that bullet floated harmlessly with the other one. His gaze followed the two rounds as they fell to the floor. "Well, that's new."

The demon took a deep breath and screamed. Jace was thrown off his feet while every window on the walls and the dome skylight exploded, sharp glass shards falling to the floor. He skidded across the hardwood floor and down the stairs, rolling head over heels.

"Holy smokes! Jace, are you okay?"

Jace coughed while he rolled over, retrieving his lost gun. "Yeah." He stood up and looked at the demon child. Suddenly, it vanished, and the wall to his left blew apart. The ground shook and the entire ceiling started to collapse on itself.

Jace looked down at the would-be robbers that he laid low. Blood dripped down their face from their eyes, nose, and ears. There would be no saving them.

His gaze returned to the lobby, and at the collapsing structure. Jace turned and ran back toward the vault while the ceiling crashed behind him. He smashed his shoulder against the wall and leaped headfirst into the cover of the vault. Dust filled the room as he skidded on the hard floor.

After a moment, Jace coughed, then slowly got back to his feet.

"Jace, what was that?"

"Blood magic." Jace approached the outer vault doors and started to climb out. "Some advanced shit. They take their power from helpless or dying victims." He crawled through the hole and stood on top of the rubble that used to be the bank lobby. "The amount of power they get from their victims is enormous, but it doesn't last very long."

He stared off through the hole as he considered the amount of power that demon had. Could it be that the Atmos wasn't on that volcano island? The child looked the proper age, and it had a vast amount of magic. Jace nodded, slowly reassuring himself that he had found his primary objective.

"Brian, what's over there?"

"Hold on." Tapping on the earpiece before Brian continued, "It looks like there are some warehouses a couple of blocks down. All but one was destroyed by a fire last year."

"Is that so? Seems a good of a place as any to hide out."

The front doors to the bank slammed opened, and some law enforcement officers entered the lobby. They pointed their rifles at Jace as they started to flood the destroyed building.

"Put down your guns!" They started to shout at him.

Jace looked at each one for a brief moment, almost baffled at why they were acting hostile toward him. Then he remembered the chrome hand cannons he held and mumbled to himself, "Well shit." His gaze went back to the hole in the wall. His hunt would have to wait. First, he had to deal with the conveniently late law enforcement.

———

When Xin told Jace he was exempt from a lot of legal problems, Jace figured maybe a speeding ticket or littering. When he showed the commanding officer of the task force his emblem and explained who he was, Jace was let go with no other problems, save some profanity that they mumbled behind his back. It didn't matter. Jace had his sights on something far more important—an Atmos candidate.

Jace took a moment to feel the gentle breeze on his skin, ignoring the grumbling of his empty stomach. He leaned against a building across the street from the abandoned fenced-off warehouse area. Most of them were black and dilapidated. Like Brian had reported, one still stood.

It was a long, two-story building with a peaking rooftop. Near the far end of the red-brown structure was a section on top of the warehouse that reached two stories high. At the end of the nearby pier was a large crane, rusted and broken down.

Jace nodded his head toward the warehouse. "Do you see what I see?"

"That crane is in bad shape."

"No, not that." Jace pointed at the target structure. "A light in the upstairs office."

"Hey, you're right. Isn't that place supposed to be condemned?"

"That's your department." Jace pushed himself off the wall with his hip and started to walk across the street.

"Hey Jace, have you figured out how you're going to beat that blood magic?"

Jace leaped up and started to scale over the fence. "Wear it down."

"What do you mean?"

"Well..." Jace grabbed a handhold on the side of the warehouse and started his climb. "Remember what I said? Blood magic and sacrifices give a lot of energy for whatever, but only for a short time." He grabbed on a pipe and continued his climb. "They have a small window to do whatever they need to do before they're out of that energy."

"What if that monster drains your energy?"

"Not going to happen." Jace grabbed onto a windowsill and looked inside. It was blocked by something. Maybe plastic or paper. He pulled himself up and over, continuing his climb. "Fear, especially the fear of death. That's the key." Finally, he grabbed the gutter and pulled himself onto the rooftop. He took a knee and looked down at the ground and the wall. After a cautious moment, Jace continued his approach the office space, taking care to make his footfalls as soft and silent as possible.

Jace knelt when he saw a shape move in the window. His heart raced as his fingers tightened around the pistol's grip. He needed to stay hidden. The element of surprise was Jace's biggest advantage in fighting such a powerful opponent, so him being spotted so early in his infiltration would be a disaster. He didn't move, his eyes locked onto the window. Nothing.

"Hey, I have a project for you." Jace stayed low, continuing his trek to the window. "I only have seven rounds per gun. Can you somehow get me more ammo?"

"Protective gear and more ammo?"

Jace arrived at the window. He put his back against the side and put his ear against the wall, hoping to hear something inside that could give him some clue on what was going on inside. He only heard silence. He peeked inside through the window - desk, chair, cabinets, and tables—no living thing.

"How about a reload harness?"

"Maybe. What about something that makes me confirm that someone is a demon?"

"Like what?"

Jace shrugged. "I don't know. Figure it out. If I had known that kid was a demon, I wouldn't be getting my new suit all dirty by climbing up an old run-down warehouse. I would have been able to save those people."

"Like a spray or a water balloon?"

"Whatever you come up with." Jace elbowed the window and reached in to unlock the hinge. After sliding the window up, Jace crawled inside and knelt behind a cabinet. He reached behind him and pulled out his handguns. "It's go-time."

He kept in the shadows, slowly making his way through the office space until he found the stairs that led to the warehouse. When he went down the stairs enough to survey the area, Jace noticed a lot of crates still occupying the space, which was more than unusual considering this was supposed to be a condemned structure.

Before he took another step, Jace paused, thinking he heard

something from below. He scanned the area, slowly taking in the scene. He noticed a small clearing of crates and moved to investigate.

Delaying his movements at each corner, Jace finally arrived at the clearing—a portable whiteboard next to a makeshift table that had some computer or electronic device on it, some duffle bags, and another workspace cleared of any trash or debris beside that.

"A high-tech currency counter," Brian said over the com while Jace slowly made his way into the clearing. "This was probably where they were going to count and split the money."

Jace nodded in reply, coming to the same conclusion. He reached the whiteboard and flipped it over. There it was—detailed plans of the bank heist.

"Why would they go back through the front doors?" Brian asked over the com.

It didn't take long for Jace to answer that question. "By turning invisible."

Just as Jace turned around to scan the room, square shapes from above caught his attention. They arced high, almost hitting the roof, and flew straight at the clearing. Jace dove left, a smaller crate smashing into him. It shattered on impact, and Jace was flat on the floor.

He couldn't move for a few heartbeats as he tried to catch his breath. When he got to his feet, more box-like projectiles made their way to the clearing. Jace took cover from the heavy missiles, taking a moment to regain his senses from that hit. Wood, straw, and broken bags filled with white powder crashed all around him.

Jace peaked over his cover to take a look at his attacker. No one was there. Jace couldn't help but grin. This was going to be a fun hunt, and he was excited at the challenge. He returned to his cover and inspected the white powder. Soap.

"Brian, does this place still have working fire sprinklers?"

"Uhh, hold on." Jace could hear the furious tapping over the earpiece. "It looks like it."

"Can you get them to turn on?"

"Uhh..." Again, more tapping. "I think so."

"Good. Get ready and wait for my signal." Jace started to load the duffle bags full of powdered soap.

While he moved into position for his counterattack, the shadows started to take over as the sun made its way behind the horizon. The darkness didn't matter to Jace. Not since those fancy contact lenses Brian got for him allowed him to see in the dark. And just as the surroundings turned to pitch black, the lenses performed their techno-magic, showing Jace monochromatic shapes of the area around him.

Jace knelt on a crate that gave him a clear vantage point to oversee the warehouse, especially the meeting point. He slowly scanned the area, looking for any signs of the demon's whereabouts. It took nearly an hour before Jace caught sight of some straw moving in the middle of the clearing. But no one was there.

He stared at the space, making sure he saw what he thought he saw. More straw mysteriously moved. It must be the demon, and it must still be invisible.

Jace quietly reached into the duffle bag and pulled out some of the pouches. He eyed the area once more, confirming the demon was still there. The snap of wood established his position, and Jace made his move.

He ripped open the top of the bags and started throwing them in the clearing. Then he tossed two high into the air and shot them with his guns. They exploded, and the area was engulfed by a thick white cloud.

"Hit it!" Jace tossed the dufflebag aside and leaped onto a lower crate tier to get into a better position, taking aim at the fog.

A moment later, the sprinklers turned on, and the cloud quickly vanished. Inside the haze, a vague silhouette of a human shape was visible from the falling water. Footprints pressed on the powder while the demon started to run. Then, like a child in the snow, a human shape formed on the now slippery floor.

With a clear target in sight, Jace repeatedly fired with both of his guns. Some bullets stopped in midair. Others seemed to have hit something. Not flesh, but something.

Just as his guns clicked empty, a bolt of blue light appeared near the soap angel and flew at Jace. The crate under him exploded in a flash of hot yellow and red. Jace leaped down, landing on the floor in a roll, holstering one of the guns while grabbing a clip for the other.

When he dropped the clip from the handgun, another flash of bright light fired from the invisible demon. Jace did a spinning sidestep, loading his weapon in a smooth motion. He shot again and again, trying to break through the demon's shield. Finally, the white soap turned dark in Jace's monochrome vision.

Jace approached the soap angel as it phased into view. A hit in the shoulder. It didn't look life-threatening.

Was this creature really Atmos, the blood demon and the source of the world's problems? It looked like a human child, but Jace knew the power demons like that could wield. He didn't want to take any chances while he continued his approach with his gun trained on his target.

"This might be it, Brian. We're safe."

"Holy smokes, Jace! That was scary. But what are we safe from?"

At that moment, Jace wondered how he would contact The Order. Before he could think of a solution, the demon lifted an arm. Jace took a balanced stance and shook his head. "Don't do it."

A light started to flicker at the demon child's fingertips. Jace pulled the trigger, and the arm fell limp to the ground. Jace lowered his gun and stared hard at the demon. "Fucking thing." He turned and started to walk out of the warehouse, leaving the demon with a large hole in its skull bleeding on the floor.

———

As soon as his adrenaline wore off, Jace's stomach growled. Worse than that, his body started to shoot aches and pains to his brain. In the middle of the night, he spotted a bench on the way back to his car sat down, grimacing from the agony all over his body.

"That damn thing hit me harder than I thought." Jace took off his backpack and laid down in a groan.

Brian's voice came from the earpiece. "You okay, buddy?"

When he went to put his backpack on his chest, he saw the blood that soaked his coat. So much for his new clothes. "Yeah. Maybe."

"You want me to tell you how to get to the hospital?"

Jace relaxed his arms, his hands plopping on his stomach. "Nah. I have to report in." He slowly sat up, the painful torture making him immediately regretting his decision.

"What if that crate wasn't hollow?" Brian asked, his voice growing sternly concerned. "What if it had something solid, like paper or machinery?"

Jace wasn't really in the mood to hear about the what-ifs. He stood and grabbed his backpack. "But it didn't."

"You'd be dead, Jace."

That gave Jace pause. After a moment's thought, Jace sat back on the bench, dropping his backpack to the ground.

"You'd be dead, and there wouldn't be anything I could do about it."

"I'm fine. Relax."

"Don't think I didn't see your coat sleeves. I'm not stupid, Jace."

Jace looked at his hands, and at the soapy red that slicked his skin. He thought about the pulsing wound in his shoulder, feeling the chill of the moisture dripping down his arm. "No, you're far from it. You're the smartest guy I know." He laid back on the bench, focusing on individual pains around his body. Just after a brief moment, Jace realized he was in bad shape. Brian was right. He always was. What if he did die? What about all the promises he made—find Jessica, save the world, be with Maya? The last thought made Jace's heart stop. "Maya."

"What's that?"

Jace grabbed the edge of the bench and pulled himself up, enduring the sharp pains all over his body.

"Promise me something. Promise me you'll be more careful because that fight was scary!"

"Tell you what, Brian." Jace grabbed his backpack and stood up. "When you get that armor done, I'll start taking jobs again."

"Really? You mean it?"

Jace nodded as if Brian could see him. "Yeah. After I report in, tell me how to get back to Sanctuary."

"What?"

Jace slung his backpack over his shoulder. "You heard me. I want to go back to Sanctuary. I have a promise to keep."

"Okay. I uploaded your travel plans to your PPC."

Jace looked at his hand. "I, uh... I took it off. Remember?"

Brian's tone hinted at more than just a little frustration. "Why do I even bother?"

"Okay, okay. I'll put it on. That damn thing itches." He dug in his backpack and took out the bracer and ring. When he opened his hand, the holographic image of his travel plans showed up. "Got it. Let me know when the armor is ready. I'll contact you later."

"I'll be here."

Jace tapped his ear, then laid back down on the bench, the pain making him wince and groan. "Maybe I'll just rest here for the night."

———

The only reason Jace took the limo up the mountainside was that he couldn't make it up himself. Even after a couple of days travel, his pain was still too great. Probably from cracked and bruised bones. Because of that, the motion sickness didn't plague Jace during the trip, regardless of how bumpy the road was. And when the door opened to the snowfields that led to the mountainside structure, Jace was thankful that the chill numbed his pain.

Sir Dunemore stood stoically atop the steps, fur cloak billowing in the breeze. His gaze locked onto Jace while he limped and staggered up the stairway. He spoke to Jace in a condescending and high-almighty tone, as if mocking Jace because of his injuries. "You don't look well, boy."

At first, Jace wanted to pay him no mind. But the comment, him berating Jace about respecting the rank, and the handlebar mustache and his ridiculous hair were too irresistible to pass up. "Better than the pubic hairs you have on your lip."

Dunemore brushed back his cloak, showing the silly sword he had attached to his hip. "You dare insult me?"

"Nah." Jace limped by and put his blood-caked hand on the door. "Your mustache does it for me." He pushed open the door and closed it behind him, leaving Dunemore outside in the cold, and went in the elevator to visit Erica.

When the doors opened, a thin man wearing a coat with a fresh skin-colored facial tattoo of three bars walked by. He eyed Jace as they crossed paths.

Jace pushed open the glass doors that led to her office, the intoxicating scent of vanilla filling his nostrils. With the warmth thawing his wounds, the simple act of talking became a painful task. "Hey Erica, I'm going to need that goo again."

Erica glanced and briefly scanned him, sighed, then started to follow him.

"Who was the guy with the face tattoo?"

"Roberts."

Jace teased, "Your boyfriend?"

"I don't date soldier boys."

"Neither do I." Jace grimaced as he took off his backpack and tossed it on the floor next to the tank.

"I thought you were supposed to be on vacation."

"Yeah, well..." He continued to remove his clothes and gear, laying everything on top of his backpack. "I think I found the Atmos."

Erica stopped in her tracks, almost dropping that glass thing she always held. "You what?"

"Yeah. The kid fit the profile—maybe ten or eleven and really powerful magic." When he finished removing his gun holsters, Jace turned to face Erica stood wide-eyed and seemed a little unhappy.

"I didn't hear a report."

"Yeah, well... I couldn't. Bastard tried to rob a bank and killed a bunch of people in the process." Jace stepped in the tank, leaning against the back to take some of the burdens off of his body. "I tracked it to some warehouse. Fucking thing threw shipping containers at me."

She glared at him. Yep, she was angry. "You should have reported it! If that's Atmos, we can end the war!"

Jace brought a hand forward to try to calm her down. "If I knew how to report, I wouldn't—"

The reply Erica gave was a sudden slap in the face. She glared hard at him, then pressed her hand against Jace's chest. Near-paralyzing agony shot throughout his body. "If you weren't a fucking moron, the war could be over by now!"

Jace fought through the pain. "Well, it doesn't matter now."

Erica removed her hand. "What does that mean? Why doesn't it matter?"

"Killed it. Turned its face into a wind tunnel."

Erica's eye twitched, and her face turned red. She pushed a button on the glass tablet to start the tank-goo procedure, turned around and stormed off.

CHAPTER TEN

Jace didn't stay long at the mountainside establishment. As soon as Erica released him from the tank, he got dressed in his usual attire, making sure he had the earpiece in just in case Brian called, then started his trip to the nightmares of his past.

It had been three years since Jace in stood front of the three-story building he grew up in. It looked a little cleaner than he remembered, but the memories would always stain over what the sign read—The Sanctuary of Orphaned Children. He stared up at the office window where he, Jessica, and Claire would hide. He couldn't help but smile, thinking about the hours they sat, talking and playing around. The smile faded when some movement came from behind the window. A staff member occupied that sacred space.

When he went through the front door, his mind started to once again drift back to the past once more. He stared at the door that led to Dr. Crisp's office, and the hours of torture he would get from the "therapist." The trance didn't last long when a kid screamed from the Common Room. Jace walked up to investigate to discover two kids playing some sort of video game. Apparently, the screaming child lost.

Jace turned to his left and started to walk down the hall and stopped in front of Miss Stevens' office. He took a deep breath to steady his nerves, then ran his fingers through his hair as he prepared to meet with the woman he'd loathed all his life. He knocked.

Miss Stevens called from inside the office. "Come in."

Jace opened the door and stepped in. Memories and emotions swarmed inside him as he tried to control his raging heart.

The woman looked a little older, and her red hair had a couple strands of white. She looked up at him through her thin-rimmed glasses. "Well, I'll be." Her face beamed, and she pushed back her chair to stand. She started her way around her desk, her arms out as if to go in for a hug. "It's so good to see—"

Jace lifted his hand, stopping her from getting any closer. "I'm here for Maya."

Miss Stevens looked both hurt and confused. "I-I'm sorry. What?"

"Maya. Where is she?" Jace scanned the room, looking for any clue of her location. "It's Saturday. I know she's here."

She stared hard at him for a long moment, then gestured to the chair. Her tone changed from happy and joyous to serious and stern. "Have a seat."

Deja vu. Jace always stood defiantly against Miss Stevens, making sure he resisted everything she told him to do. After a sigh, Jace decided to try to make his visit professional and courteous. He took his backpack off, and the two sat down in their relative seats.

"Well, now." Miss Stevens started to shuffle paperwork around to get her desk organized. "Normally, this stage of the adoption process is done remotely. And as you know, this can take some time."

Jace shook his head. "No. I'm here now. I made a promise to her, and I plan on keeping it."

She didn't even look up at him. "How sweet. Then let's start with a few basic questions." She grabbed a folder from the bottom drawer and opened it, a pen in hand for her to write. "One, what do you do?"

Jace hesitated for a moment. "I can't tell you."

She looked up to him in confusion. After a couple of seconds, she went back to the folder. "Alright. Two, where do you live?"

"Nowhere."

"Nowhere?" She looked back to Jace again and took off her glasses. "How do you expect to take care of a little girl when you don't have a place to live?"

"Not your concern."

"You bet it's my concern! The health and well-being of every child here is my concern!" The two sat quiet and still for many heartbeats before Miss Stevens closed the file. "I'm sorry, Jace. I feel you're not in a position to—"

Jace had heard enough. He stood up and grabbed his backpack.

"Hey!"

Without looking back, he left her office, closing the door behind him.

Knowing each floor was broken down into the age groups of the children, Jace considered Maya's age. Perhaps ten or eleven? With that in mind, he went to the second floor.

He walked toward the girl's quarters and picked up the sleeping chart.

Miss Stevens walked up behind Jace. "She's not here."

That alarmed Jace. He turned and glared at the woman. "Where is she?"

"Out back."

Jace tossed the chart on the table, ran downstairs and dashed through the halls until he arrived in the backyard. He slowly walked through the grass while scanning the area. Finally, he saw her. She read a book while sitting under a tree with her hood over her head.

Excitement started to build up in his chest, and he began to run toward her. He slowed his pace to a walk after regaining some of his composure. He almost laughed when he noticed she still wore the hoodie he bought her many years before.

Jace took off his backpack and sat next to her while he uncontrollably smiled.

A huff from behind the book and Maya looked up from her paper fortress. It didn't take long for Maya's gaze to go from annoyed to surprise. Her smile melted Jace's heart. She tossed the book aside and leaped into Jace's arms, her head buried in his shoulder.

"Hey, you." Jace wrapped her in an enormous hug. "I'm sorry it took so long."

She shook her head, her face still buried in his shoulder. She sniffled, and Jace felt his shirt dampen with Maya's tears.

Jace fought back his own tears. He looked down, getting a closer look at the hooded sweater she wore. "You still have this dirty old thing?"

Maya nodded, then finally leaned back to release the hug, her hand tugging at the chain and pulling out the amulet from The Order, seemingly by accident.

"I have a lot to tell you when we get out of here."

Maya pointed to herself, then to Jace, then toward the front entrance.

Jace stood and grabbed his backpack, then pulled Maya to her feet. "Do you need anything from your room?"

She shook her head. Then she shifted her weight and looked behind him.

Jace turned to see Miss Stevens approach with security. "Jace, I can't let you adopt her." The group stopped a couple of paces away.

Jace's eyes narrowed, and he stared hard at Miss Stevens. "You know me. You know who I am and what I can do."

The security guards started to fan out surround him. Jace felt Maya hide behind him.

"If either of your bullshit lackeys lay a hand on Maya, mark my words, bitch. I'm coming for you."

Jace kept his gaze locked on Miss Stevens as the orderlies took a step forward. The five guys wouldn't be enough to stop Jace from rescuing Maya, and he was fully ready to show the devil woman that. And though Jace wanted to shut the place down, or at least fix its corrupt staff, getting Maya out of the orphanage and into his custody was his immediate priority. He scanned each of the orderlies, plotting the fight in his mind—which ones he would take out first, how he would incapacitate each of the opponents, and what he'd do once he finally got his hands on Miss Stevens.

Miss Stevens' expression went from stern authority to curiosity when her eyes went to Jace's chest. She adjusted her glasses, then her eyes bulged. "Wait."

The guards froze.

Miss Stevens looked back to Jace's eyes. "Okay, Jace. I'll let you take her."

The security guards looked baffled at Miss Stevens, then they parted, creating an opening toward the front.

"You never had a say in the matter." Jace grabbed Maya's hand and started to walk between the group of hostiles cautiously.

Jace led Maya to the outside of the hostiles, and they started to walk away.

One guard asked, "Why are you letting him take her?"

He heard Miss Stevens reply, "Because he can."

———

Jace had to censor what he told Maya. He knew that she looked up to him, and he didn't want her to have the violent and dangerous life he had. He wanted her to be happy and carefree, to enjoy life, and not be involved in the war he fought in. However, he wanted her to trust him, and that meant not lying.

They walked through the city, looking at the sites. Jace summarized his time after the orphanage, taking great efforts to avoid a lot of the details his life of blood and death revolved around.

"After I visited the village and saved my friend, I was transferred to a mountain place where it snows all year round. After about a year of training, I... run errands for them."

Maya looked up at Jace and smiled. She seemed genuinely happy, and that warmed his heart.

Her tattered clothes made Jace frown. The hoodie had to be at least five years old, and who knows how old the rest of her clothes were. He flicked the faded hoodie from her head. She glared at him and put the hood back up. "Come on. Let's go get you some new clothes."

———

The following weeks seemed like a dream to Jace. He and Maya stayed in a nice hotel that was more like an apartment with a view of the city. They ate out all the time, went on walks, and just relaxed. It was the vacation Jace thought he'd never get, and probably the vacation Xin told him to take.

Maya stood on the balcony staring off at the scene beyond— distant city lights, the twilight of the stars, and the shine of the moon. The gentle night breeze rustled her clothes and brushed her hair.

Jace walked beside her and leaned against the railing. "Are you mad at me?"

She looked up at him baffled.

"For being away for so long."

Maya shook her head for an answer then turned to face the cityscape once more, even going on her tiptoes to get a better look.

Her not being upset made Jace feel better. He stared at her for a long moment, wondering where she fit in his life—his life of danger and traveling. He wasn't going to drag her into a violent lifestyle. For a moment, Jace regretted adopting Maya. A moment later, he felt even worse than he did before for even thinking that dreadful thought. To shake the sorrow in his heart, Jace looked out to stare at the cityscape with Maya.

———

Like a never-ending vacation, Jace laid on a grassy hill a few days later. And like they used to when they were living together in the orphanage, the two stared up at the clouds, Maya pointing at a cloud and trying to convey what shape she saw with hand gestures. Jace never initially understood the shapes Maya saw, or Jessica when he would play the same game with her when he was a kid.

She jabbed Jace's arm with her elbow and pointed to a cloud, then held up two fingers and bounced her hand up and down.

Jace looked at the hand, then the cloud. It was the hand gestures that gave him the answer. "Aaaa... Turtle?"

Maya's arm went limp, and she glared up at him.

Jace laughed. "A bunny. A bunny."

Her eyes stayed locked for a moment, but Jace saw the signs of a smile at the corner of her lip.

They stayed on the hill, and Jace's eyes started to grow a little heavy. Then he heard a distant voice and the laughing of Jessica. "That looks like a cock!" "Do you see the guy taking a shit?" What Maya saw and what Jessica did were wildly different. Regardless, Jace envied them for seeing things in the first place. Then Jessica walked up and stared down at him. "What will she say about the monsters? How are you going to protect her?"

Jace's eyes went wide, and he quickly sat up. He scanned the area, alert and on guard. No one was there. He wondered if he fell asleep for a moment.

A tug on his coat sleeve snapped him out of his alarmed state. Maya looked up at him with worry.

"I'm okay." He looked around once more, then laid back in the grass.

Jessica's question echoed in his mind. What would she say? Does she even know? The orphanage was either in denial at the dangers from the outside world, or they were hiding it from the kids on the inside. Either way, her not knowing could put her in danger.

"Hey, uh." Jace sat up again and turned to face his little sister. "I want to talk to you about something... serious." He grew nervous. His hands started to moisten with sweat under his fingerless gloves. "So, there are these... people out there. They have these strange, unexplained abilities. I know it's ridiculous, but it's true."

Jace took a moment to assess Maya's reaction. She didn't seem to disbelieve him, but she also didn't seem surprised. Maybe she knew already.

"And there are monsters in the world. Real monsters. These are called Evolved, and they are dangerous."

Maya shrugged then pointed to herself, then quickly between Jace and herself.

"I'll always be here to protect you. I'm not going to let anyone, or anything lay a finger on you."

She smiled and laid back in the grass.

With that conversation apparently over, Jace plopped on the grass next to Maya. He figured since the two were talking earnestly to one another, it was time to discuss his job. "Do you remember me telling you that I travel a lot for work? Well, when my partner gets a hold of me, I'm going to have to go back to work."

Maya sat up and looked at Jace. She pointed to him and her repeatedly.

"Some of the jobs I take may be dangerous, and I don't want to put you in harm's way."

Her shoulders slumped, and she glared at Jace.

"Besides, we still need you to get your school thing taken care of."

Her glare turned more intense.

"What? I thought you liked school." After a moment of glaring, Jace sighed. "Okay, never mind. We can discuss it later." His stomach growled. "Well, I guess that means we need to get back." The two stood up and started to walk back toward the road. "What do you think? Pizza tonight?"

Maya smiled and nodded. He wrapped an arm around her shoulder and hugged her. Maybe he needed to go on more vacations in the future.

———

That night, Jace and Maya stood on the balcony together watching the sunset when the earpiece beeped. Jace put his hand on Maya's shoulder, then walked into the hotel room. After he closed the door behind him, Jace tapped the earpiece. "Hey, Brian."

"Jace! I think I have a prototype of some protective equipment developed. See, I used the concept of kevlar, which is a form of synthetic fiber with high tensile-"

"I know what kevlar is."

"Oh, okay. Anyways, I have the prototype ready."

Jace turned and looked at Maya through the glass door. He again wondered how he could keep his jobs a secret from Maya. Then Jace started to get an idea. "Hey, Brian, how do you feel about teaching?"

"You finally want to learn how to use a computer?"

"No, not for me. For my sister."

"You have a sister? Holy smokes, Jace. I didn't know—"

"Maya! For Maya."

"Maya? Is that the girl you always talked about but never wanted me to meet?"

"Yes. Remember I said I had business at Sanctuary?"

"Oh yeah. Hey, that's great! I'm so happy for you! But what are you going to do with her and our business?"

"I'm kind of taking it day by day. But I have an idea, and I need your help."

"Yeah, okay. What do you need?"

Jace took a moment to stare out at Maya as a gust of wind blew the hood of her hoodie off her head. "You helped me get through school. Could you help her?"

Brian didn't immediately reply. "I don't know, Jace. You know I got your back and all, but this is asking a lot."

"I know. And I don't ask lightly. It's just..." Jace ran his right thumb over his left hand, feeling the cracked and callous skin on his knuckles. "She deserves so much more than Sanctuary could ever offer, and I don't want her to see the danger and violence my life seems to attract. I need her to have a different path than me, and I'm sure you can make that happen."

After a long moment of silence, Brian sighed. "Okay, Jace. I'll do what I can."

"Thanks, Brian. You're the best."

"Okay, so where do you want to meet?"

Jace sighed and looked over to Maya once more. So much for his vacation.

CHAPTER ELEVEN

WAITING IN THE AGREED PLACE THAT HE AND BRIAN WOULD meet, Jace and Maya sat in a diner booth, him shifting his back a little to adjust a kink the holster dug in his back. Whenever he received new pieces of gear from Brian, he would have to readjust the straps once more to make sure everything fit without being visible. It was always a pain in the ass.

The waitress dropped off their identical meals—grilled cheese and fries. Maya, her hoodie covering her head, dug in, chomping on fries and taking a bite of her sandwich. Before Jace got a taste of toasted bread and cheese, he spotted Brian entering the diner holding a big bag. He waved and approached the table.

"Hey, Jace." Brian presented the bag. "So I got the—"

Jace lifted a hand to stop Brian and gestured with his head toward Maya.

Brian stopped in his tracks, lowered the bag, then knelt and extended his hand in greetings. Maya stopped her chewing and gazed at him suspiciously. "Hello, Maya. I'm Brian. I have heard so much about you."

Maya swallowed, then she looked to Jace as if seeking approval. After a nod from Jace, she smiled and shook Brian's hand.

"Brian is going to help you with your schoolwork so you don't fall behind. And he can keep an eye on you while I go back to work."

"I what?" Brian recoiled and stared at Jace in surprise. "Uh, yeah." He glared at Jace for a second, then turned his attention back to Maya with a nervous smile.

Jace smiled, then finally took a bite of his now-cold grilled cheese, thinking about how things were going. Brian and Maya. This could work.

———

The three sat and talked, save Maya, who communicated with simple gestures, the rest of the day. Jace saw in the general interactions between Brian and Maya that they got along well enough for Jace to go back to work. Finally, they went to the hotel room where Jace put Maya to bed, and he walked into the front room where Brian sat on the couch and waited.

Brian took off his glasses and rubbed the bridge of his nose. "Way to spring that on me at the last minute."

Jace sat opposite of Brian with a coffee table between them and leaned back to relax a little. "What was I supposed to do?"

Brian spoke as if he wanted to raise his voice, but he stayed quiet. "You're the one that adopted her! You should be responsible."

"And I will. I just need your help."

Brian shook his head and leaned back in his chair. After a long moment of silence between the two, Brian let out a deep sigh. "She's a sweet girl." He put his glasses back on and looked to Jace. "Alright, we will do this your way. I will look into online schools tomorrow."

The answer satisfied Jace. He turned his attention to the bag Brian kept with him all day and gestured toward it. "What's that?"

"Oh, this?" Brian's face went from an upset expression to excited as he reached for the bag. "This is a prototype of the protective gear I've been making for you." He unzipped the bag and placed what looked like a loose shirt with clipping straps on the coffee table.

Jace stared at the long-sleeved shirt, studying its size. That's what caught his attention—the bulk. "What the hell is this?"

That got Brian to look up in surprise. "I said this is a prototype.

You told me you want something that can protect you but remains inconspicuous to others." Brian picked up the shirt and held it up against his chest. "This is an adjustable suit of armor that protects against small caliber weapons." He grabbed and tightened a strap. "This can fit around your frame while stopping a nine-millimeter bullet from ten feet." He reached his hand under the shirt and poked at it. The mesh flexed as if it were cotton. "That doesn't mean it won't hurt."

Though Jace was initially disappointed in the general design, he nodded in acceptance in the fact that it could save his life. And he could get back to work. "How much of this do you have?"

"Body, arms, and legs." Brian put the shirt back on the table and pulled out a pair of pants. "You said you want this to be inconspicuous, so I didn't make any neck or head protection."

Jace nodded again, and he reached out to grab the pants. It was heavier than Jace expected but lighter than the kevlar he wore when he was in the military. He bounced the protective pants in his hands, feeling the weight. "Good work, Brian. I think this will work for now."

"I'm not done." Brian went back to the bag and took out a strange metallic contraption. "I wanted to show you the progress on my reload harness." He put it on his shoulders. "See, this fits around the chest and back, and..." Brian looked around, reaching back to attempt to grab something from the contraption, and spinning a full circle in his efforts. He finally got a hold of it and looked at Jace. "And this goes around the shoulder."

The thing appeared bulky and monstrous. Totally noticeable. "And what is this?"

Brian reached behind his other shoulder to grab another piece of the device. "This is a back-strapped reload harness. It'll remove your empty clip and put in a new one. I'm still working out the details, but—"

"That thing is ridiculous." Jace stood, leaned over the table, and tapped on the device. "People will notice this thing sticking out of my side."

Brian didn't reply.

"You're smart, Brian." Jace sat back down. "You're the smartest guy I know. I know you can do better than this."

Brian looked to the device partially strapped to his back. "Well, I guess I can use this as a general proof of concept. Okay, give me a gun."

That surprised Jace. "What? Why?"

"Modifications."

"Modif—" Jace's hand went toward his back to feel the grip of his pistols. He had spent a lot of time and money customizing them—reinforced chrome plating, design engravings, dual-wielding - and now he was asked to give them up. However, he trusted Brian. If there was anyone he trusted who could work on the guns without breaking them, it was Brian. Giving it no more thought, Jace took the pistols out of his back holster and put them on the table.

Brian grabbed one of the handguns and started to inspect it, bring it inches from his face and looking at it from various angles. A gleam in his eye and a smile on his lips. "I just had an idea." He put the gun back on the table, grabbed his bag, and took out a notepad. Without saying anything else, he started scribbling, totally focused on what he was drawing.

Jace's eyes went from his shiny pistols to Brian. When Brian didn't say anything, Jace cleared his throat.

Brian looked up as if surprised at the sound. "Oh, you can put those away. I'll work on them later."

Jace put the guns back in their holsters. "I leave for the mountains tomorrow."

Brian didn't even look up to answer. "Yeah, okay. I'll get your trip set up."

Jace stared blankly at Brian for a long moment, nodded, then left him to his work.

————

After returning to the mountainside facility, Jace was greeted by Erica, who approached him in the hallway.

She held up the glass screen she always carried. "Welcome back. Any changes?"

The elevator doors opened, and they both got in.

Jace shook his head. "Nope."

She seemed frustrated as she put the tablet by her side then started to mumble to herself. "I don't get it."

Even though he'd have no idea how to help, Jace decided to see if he could talk to her. "Don't get what?"

Erica slapped the button that would take the lift to her lab, not answering his question.

Jace sensed either the urgency or the anger in her gesture. His eyes went from the elevator control panel to Erica. He decided to ask once more. "What?"

"Lab. I need samples."

"More blood?"

Erica started to work on her tablet again. "You haven't gone through any changes, and I don't know why. Every test I ran has come back inconclusive."

Jace blinked in confusion for a moment.

"Normally, the epidural bonding agent gives auspicious effects to the human molecular structure. This happens within a few weeks after Sir Dunmore goes through with his initiation.

Initiation? Jace didn't think of beatings as an initiation.

"But you…" She started to nibble on the tip of her thumb. "Over twelve months, you still haven't shown any symptoms."

The doors opened. Erica didn't hesitate and bolted out of the elevator.

Jace didn't move for a moment. "I need to talk to Xin."

"No, you don't!" Erica called from over her shoulder. "Take a job after I'm done with you."

———

Erica always looked as if she enjoyed taking Jace's blood. He rubbed his arm, holding the cotton swab over the many holes she had made in his skin. When the elevator doors opened, he lowered his arm and walked toward the mission board.

The room was a little fuller than usual. Many people went quiet as soon as Jace entered the room. A lot of them began to murmur amongst themselves, while others just sat and stared. Their eyes and whispers followed him as he went to the board.

"Is that the ghost?"

"How did he destroy that village?"

"He's the one that did the senator mission."

"Does he ever stop?"

"What do you think he will get next?"

Jace stared at the board, a little uncomfortable from the unusual attention, and he sifted through one mission after another—plant devices, drop off messages, meet and evaluate a recruit candidate. None of them seemed worth his time. It was as if The Order took down all of their challenging jobs. Remembering he didn't have his equipment, Jace decided that this wasn't a bad thing. He accepted a mission to drop off a couple of packages, then went to go the cage before starting on his way, leaving the mumbling spectators behind him.

———

After dropping off the first package in a coffee shop nearby, Jace returned to the hotel where Brian and Maya sat on the couch eating pizza and watching some sort of animated thing on the TV. As soon as Maya saw him, she smiled and ran up to him for a hug.

"Hey, you. How are you doing?"

She looked up to him, rolled her eyes, and shrugged as if conveying her boredom with her dull babysitter. Behind all that, Jace could see the subtle signs of a grin at the edge of her lip.

"That's good." Jace put his hand on her shoulder and looked through the room. "Pizza and movies?"

"Yeah." Brian put down his food and stood up.

Jace grabbed the envelope from his coat and handed it to Brian.

"What's this?"

"A new job. I don't know where it's at." Jace examined the pizza box. Empty. "You couldn't have saved me one piece?"

Brian and Maya looked at each other, then to their crumb and oil-covered plates.

"I'm sorry, Jace. I didn't know when you'd be back."

Jace waved a hand and started to rifle through the fridge. "Guess it's sandwiches tonight." He grabbed what he needed and shut the door.

Brian started to read the letter inside the envelope. "This isn't too far away."

"Get us directions. Maya and I leave in the morning."

"Sure thing." Brian sat down on the couch and started to tap away on some sort of computer device.

Maya approached Jace and stared questioningly at him.

"Yep. This is the last night we're staying at this hotel. I have work to do."

She stared for a moment longer, then nodded, a hint of disappointment in her expression.

Jace noticed her new hoodie had a tear in it. How come her clothes were always dirty, or had holes in it? "How about we go clothes shopping for you tomorrow."

She turned, smiled and nodded, then hopped over the back of the couch to continue watching her show.

————

Jace and Maya walked through the city to a train station hub. The two stood in a long line at the kiosk to purchase tickets. Slowly but surely, the line shrunk. Finally, he stood in front of his nemesis—technology.

The kiosk spoke in a pleasing woman's voice when Jace stood in front of it. "Welcome. Please select a destination."

Jace read the options, then finally pushed a button.

"Please select time and day."

Jace looked at the screen. To his surprise, the time and day he was looking for weren't there. It was as if they were cut off. "Wh... This doesn't make sense." Upon closer inspection, he noticed the times and days were out of order. Jace took a step back and looked at the oversized departure chart that hung for everyone to see. Confirming the board had the time and day for his planned trip, he stepped back to the kiosk. Again, he looked over the screen and came to the same conclusion. "Where is it?"

Moans and groans sounded from those standing in line behind him.

Once more, Jace took a few steps back to read the schedule. Slowly, he looked at the line which read that a train was to depart in ten minutes toward Jace's location. He returned to the kiosk and stared blankly at the screen. Reading line by line, Jace confirmed, without a doubt, that the kiosk and the giant posted schedules were different.

"You need help, buddy?" a tall, scruffy man asked. "You seem to be holding up the line, here."

Jace turned to look at the man. "Uh, yeah. We're trying to take the 1:14 pm train to—"

The man took a step forward and pushed an arrow on the kiosk. "More than one page, dummy."

Jace stared at the screen in awe and embarrassment. "Damn things make no sense..." After he found the train he was looking for, he read the instructions. "One child, one adult... How many bags?" Jace stared to Maya, who watched him and his kiosk failures one at a time. Considering the bags on their backs, Jace had his answer. "Two. Wait, what is this? Extra charge for bags? That doesn't—"

The scruffy man tapped Jace on the shoulder. "Come on, pal! It don't take more than a minute to get a blasted ticket!"

Even though Jace felt a great deal of embarrassment, he was starting to get fed up with this guy. He confirmed the extra charge, then looked at the screen. "Swipe chip?" He bent down and looked around the screen. "Where do I insert cash?"

The line groaned in frustration.

"This is a fast pay, buddy!" The man said above the protests of the people in line. "You pay cash at the desk."

Jace looked to the man who pointed his finger toward the wall. Following his gesture, Jace saw an extensive line of people standing still. Then, he saw what looked like a desk through the thick line of people. "There?"

"Yeah. Now move! I have a train to catch!"

Jace took a few steps backward as the man walked right by him and to the kiosk. He watched the man operate the machine, then swiped his hand over the screen. After ten or so seconds of operation, the scruffy man walked away with a printed ticket. Jace stared at the man as he walked down the stairs to his train, then sighed. "Come on,

Maya. Let's go stand in line." He grabbed her hand and walked toward the standstill of people that followed the tiny yellow line on the floor.

———

After the embarrassment at the kiosk, Maya handled all of the tickets. She seemed to know exactly what everyone wanted when they needed it. It was the quickest he had ever gotten on the barf-inducing aircraft and the nauseating train ride.

When Maya and Jace stepped off the tram, nighttime had already arrived. Maya rubbed an eye with the back of her hand while she yawned and stretched.

"Yeah, me too." Jace led Maya down the stairs and out of the station into what seemed to be a very questionable neighborhood. He looked around, attempting to get an idea where they were. His stomach growled for an embarrassingly long time. Jace rubbed his empty stomach. "Let's get some dinner, then find a hotel."

Maya grabbed Jace's hand. When he looked down, her eyes were wide open, and she stared off into the night.

Jace followed her gaze to the poorly lit streets and some ominous shadows where a couple of guys lingered from a distance. He knelt, looked into her eyes, and put his hand on her shoulder. "Nothing can hurt you so long as I'm here." He smiled. "Promise."

Maya's gaze met his, and she visibly relaxed.

Jace stood and took Maya's hand as they exited the station with no idea where he was going. As they walked down the street, Jace wondered if he should call up Brian for directions. That's when he heard the echoes of footsteps trailing from behind. He looked down at Maya, worried for a moment that all the trouble he got into may not have her get the happy-go-lucky life he wanted for her.

The footsteps grew closer, and at a pace that told Jace it wasn't just a couple of people walking the same path. No, they were trying to catch up.

In between streetlamps, Jace turned to confront the pursuers. They dressed similarly—white shirts, baggy blue pants, and bandanas. One guy had dreadlocks, while the other sported a tattoo up his neck and face. Gang members. Why was it always gang members?

Dreadlocks flicked his wrist. A knife snapped open, and he took a step closer in a threatening manner. "Hey, you in our turf."

Tattoo followed suit, taking out a knife of his own.

Maya tightly grabbed Jace's arm. Feeling her hands clench in fear made Jace's heart pump with rage. He took a breath to control his emotions.

Dreadlocks took another step. "Give me your bags, or I cut you."

Both held the knives in their right hand, and they stood in similar stances, though Tattoo seemed quiet and a little shaky. Probably new to the gang, or at least robbing people at knifepoint. Dreadlocks had some cuts and scars on his knuckles and eyes. He was no stranger to brawling and apparently had done this many times before.

Tattoo reached for Maya's bag. "Give us your stuff, homes!"

Out of all the stupid things these guys could have done, going after Maya was probably the dumbest.

Jace grabbed Tattoo's wrist and twisted so violently that it popped multiple times before he flipped head over heels to the ground. Tattoo's knife flew into the air and skid harmlessly to the side. Tattoo moaned and grabbed his deformed wrist.

Dreadlocks looked at his friend wide-eyed, then back to Jace. "You gonna get it now!"

As if Dreadlocks wasn't even trying, the knife was thrust slowly and lazily. Jace noticed Dreadlock's other hand, reaching behind his back as if going for another weapon. Most likely a pistol. For a brief moment, Jace wondered why Dreadlocks didn't use the gun in the first place.

Not wanting Maya to be exposed to any more violence, Jace decided to put an end to the ridiculousness. Just as the gleam of dark metal registered in Jace's eye, he reached behind him and pulled out his gun. With the quick draw holsters, Jace's pistol was in position before Dreadlocks', and Jace pressed the barrel against Dreadlocks' forehead. He froze, his eyes crossed to stare at the much larger chrome-plated hand cannon.

Dreadlocks visibly shook in fear. "Y-you... You're one of them!"

Jace gritted his teeth, briefly wondering why people always thought he was some sort of demon. He pulled the hammer back and pressed harder against Dreadlock's forehead. "Don't insult me." He gestured to the knife and gun. "Drop them and kick them to the side."

With trembling hands, the two weapons fell to the concrete and were kicked aside.

Jace stared into Dreadlocks' eyes for a long moment. "Be thankful you didn't go after my sister like your friend did. Your arm would be broken like his." After a few heartbeats, Jace nodded toward Maya. "Do you like her new hoodie?"

Dreadlocks blinked in confusion, but his focus was clearly on the .50 caliber barrel pressed against his skull. "What?"

Jace nodded his head to Maya once more, then spoke slowly with some emphasis to make sure he understood. "Dooo you liiike her hoodie?"

Dreadlocks pried his eyes from the shiny barrel toward Maya. "It, uh... It's nice. Looks warm."

Jace put a little pressure of the barrel against Dreadlocks' forehead, getting his attention once more. "How generous of you." Jace leaned in a little, moving the barrel of the gun from Dreadlocks' forehead to under his jaw. "I don't want my little sister to see any violence, so consider yourselves lucky. She doesn't deserve to see this part of the world." After a moment of glaring, Jace took a step back and holstered his weapon in a single swift movement. "Tend to your friend." Jace grabbed Maya's hand and led her away from the scene.

Maya looked up to him wide-eyed, an expression of fear and shock on her face.

Jace gripped her hand and smiled down at her. He used his gentlest and most calming tone he could think of. "Everything is okay. I'm sorry you had to see that. But like I said, you have nothing to fear so long as I'm around."

She gave a slight nod.

Jace looked down at her and smiled. "Did you hear? He likes your new hoodie."

CHAPTER TWELVE

JACE FELT LIKE AN OVER-PAID POSTAL WORKER. HE MADE A mental note to use the post office to deliver the messages and packages The Order wanted him to send. It would save money and free up his time. Then he wondered why they have these types of missions in the first place.

After dropping off the second package to a dirty apartment building, where every three paces you'd get a different smell coming from the nearby door, Jace again thought about how Maya would fit into the picture of his new life. If Brian weren't able to follow Jace and Maya while they traveled from zone to zone, then Jace would need to figure out a different way for Maya to get her education. And he wasn't smart enough to give her that.

As he exited the multi-scented building, Xin stood out front with his hands behind his back, still wearing those ridiculous sunglasses in the late evening. He wondered why Xin didn't deliver the parcel himself if he was going to spend the time and money getting there.

"I find it rather peculiar that you choose such an easy task."

Jace had a dilemma. If Xin knew about Maya, would that, in turn, affect how The Order would treat him? Was he even allowed to have a family? Deciding keeping Maya a secret was for the best, Jace answered with a shrug. "There wasn't much on the job board."

"Ah, but there was." Xin reached inside his sleeve and produced an envelope.

Jace took the parcel. "What's this?"

"A task."

"You're assigning me a mission?"

Xin shook his head. "Not me. The Order."

Jace started to open the envelope, wondering what job they had in mind. For Xin to find him and deliver the mission personally, it had to be something big. "How much does it pay?"

"Nothing."

That made Jace pause for a moment. Why would he do a job for and not get paid for it, even if it was a request from The Order? After the moment passed, Jace read the short message - investigate and report on a possible Atmos sighting. His eyes bulged in surprise. "A possible Atmos sighting?!" Apparently, the demon he killed in the warehouse wasn't the Atmos.

Jace went to stare up to Xin, who was no longer there. He scanned the area for a moment, then went back to the message, reading the text out loud to himself. "The candidate often frequented a night club. An agent witnessed a young shapeshifter. Investigate and report."

His arms went limp at his sides, and he stared off into the distance. An Atmos sighting. This could be it—the end game. He rushed back to the shitty hotel he and Maya stayed at to pack their things.

———

Getting out of that rundown hotel couldn't have come fast enough. Once Jace and Maya were back on the road toward the potential sighting of the Atmos candidate, Jace wondered how he could get this job done with Maya in tow. The only way he could think of was for Brian to take care of her when he was out on a job. Brian wasn't too keen on the idea since he had his own job to do. Hesitantly though, he agreed to follow for the reason that he could continue his work on Jace's equipment while he worked remotely on his other job. That meant hauling him along as well, which meant paying for his travel expenses.

After dropping Brian and Maya off at a hotel—one much more

luxurious than the roach motel before—Jace started on his reconnaissance for the "job" The Order gave him.

He leaned against a brick building and stared at the nightclub across the street. Even though it was the mid-afternoon, people were already lining up to get into the club. Being that the target was a shapeshifter, Jace had no idea how he could immediately identify the mark.

When the sun fell beyond the horizon, the nightclub finally opened its doors. After tipping the doorman generously, Jace started his recon of the interior. The wide-open space was loud and crowded with a few cages in the corners of the room where ladies danced. A holographic image of a woman whose wardrobe didn't leave much to the imagination lit up the middle of the room as if taking center stage to the brainwashed crowds. Lasers shot around the area, and the bar on the opposite side was packed full of people waiting to get their drinks. Above, an ample square space, which reminded Jace of the owner's box from The Pits, overlooked the entire club. That would be where he had to go once he started his hunt.

Jace tapped his ear, turning on the communications device. "Brian, you read?"

"Loud and clear. It looks like the building has gone through some renovations. The blueprints I have are out of date."

Jace started his way toward the bar, dodging a hip grind from what he hoped was a drunk girl. He ordered a glass of juice and sat at a sticky table near the wall to look around. Or so Brian could look around through the cameras in the contact lenses.

"There is nothing about that space up top, but there seems to be little changes in the fire systems."

"That will be the key." Jace grabbed his drink and started to walk along the walls. "Are you sure you can get that glowing thing to work?"

"If you get me a sample, I'm sure I can reverse engineer it. Or at least modify it."

Jace nodded and stopped at a door. When he turned the handle, it was locked. He grumbled, since picking the lock or breaking down the door would draw too much attention to himself. It didn't matter though as he spotted some sort of keypad with a slot for card swipes, but no physical lock. There went that idea. He released the handle and looked up at the overhead seating area, wondering if he should just go and ask the people in the fancy boxes.

"Don't worry about my end," Brian said. "But are you sure about this? Messing with the fire suppression systems is a serious crime."

"Well, you don't worry about that." Jace continued his walk around the room, avoiding contact with the drunk patrons as best as possible. He spotted a doorway guarded by a single bouncer under the owner's box. Taking the guise as one of the drunken patrons he had been avoiding all night, Jace approached the guard with a stagger. "H-hey, what's over there? Special VIP seats?"

The big buff guy crossed his muscular arms and stared down at him.

Jace decided to push his luck a little. While holding most of his weight on one leg, he reached inside his coat and pulled out a hundred, making sure to spill a bit of his drink on his hand and floor, and handed the money to the bouncer. "Is this enough for VIP seats?"

The bouncer didn't budge. That was enough of an answer for Jace. He put the cash away and lazily blinked. "It's alright. I get it." He turned and walked back toward the bar.

A large hand grasped his shoulder. The bouncer turned him around, shook his head, then pointed to a side door.

Jace looked at the exit, then down to his glass. "Can I at least finish my drink?"

The bouncer took the drink from Jace's hand and escorted him to the door, returning him to the fresh outside air. After the door closed, Jace turned and stared at the club once more. "What about my drink?" After a moment of silence, Jace stood up straight, shook his damp hand, and inspected the structure of the building itself. "Brian, get that light to work."

"You got it," Brian replied.

Jace gave an affirming nod and returned to the main roads. As he walked across the street, he turned around, scanned the area, taking note of the allies and side roads. "This thing can shapeshift. I will need to block off its escape." His eyes went back toward the club, and at the crowd of people lined up to get in. "Maybe draw it out instead of confronting it inside. Too many people at risk. Brian, where is there a nearby space that is wide open and will be alone at night?"

The sound of Brian's tapping before he replied, "there's a park with a small lake less than a quarter-mile northeast of your position. It is closed at sundown."

Jace looked up at the tall buildings and the occasional vehicle that flew by. An idea started to form in his mind. He gave another nod. "Okay, I have a plan. Let me know when the light is ready and tell Maya I will be back as soon as I can. I have to go back to the mountains."

―――――

After a half a day's trip and the hours of walking up the snowy mountainside, Jace walked past the statuesque Sir Dunemore and entered the embedded structure of The Order. With the blast of warmth, he caught the scent of vanilla. Erica stood waiting in the entryway her hair tied tight in a ponytail with the dark roots showing. She needed to dye her hair again.

Erica approached, holding her glass tablet in her arms. "Good, you're back. I need to do some more blood tests."

Her attitude seemed off, almost as if she was happy that he was back. "Well, hello to you too."

"Yes, hello. Come on." She turned toward the elevators.

"Maybe that's just an excuse to see me again."

Erica turned back around and grinned. "Don't flatter yourself, soldier boy. I think there was something wrong with the sample I took last time. I need to retest."

Jace studied her for a long moment wondering what her goal was. Why was it that she needed to draw blood and run tests every time he returned to the mountains? She had always been so meticulous in her work, and for her to mess up now seemed off. He decided there was something else in her motives, and he believed her grin told him what it was. Perhaps his constant visits and his successes caught her attention. Maybe she wanted to play hard to get while learning more about him. That must be it.

He considered that thought for a bit. Erica was smart, beautiful, kind of exotic, and a little shorter than him if she didn't wear her heels. She had the same desires to fight for humanity, and she took care of him during his recovery times. Even on a professional level, she would be a good fit.

Feeling he understood her motives, Jace lowered his guard, letting her play whatever game she had in mind. "Sure. Lead the way."

She turned and led him to the elevators. "Any changes?"

Of course she would ask that question. Jace gave the same answer as he had in the past. "None."

She sighed with a hint of frustration. "How do you compete with higher-ranking officers with no assigned supportive gear?"

Jace didn't quite understand why The Order would supply his equipment. He was under the impression that they only gave him the required hardware for a job. "I seem to be doing alright with my own gear."

The elevator door opened, she walked in, pushed her floor button, and stared at Jace. "True. Which I find amazing, and yet rather unusual."

Jace approached and stood beside her. "What do you mean?"

She didn't answer for a long moment. The doors closed, and the elevator started moving. "You have no enhancements, no support equipment, and no team. You took out that village all by yourself with no explosives or artillery. You even got that senator mission completed before that monster could do lasting damage to the social structure of society."

He knew it. She *was* following his progress.

"The work you do is extraordinary, and you're doing it all so naturally."

The elevator doors opened, and Erica led him to her lab, where he took a seat in his usual spot. The two sat down, and she began drawing a blood sample. "You haven't taken many jobs lately. Old age slowing you down?"

"Not many jobs on the board."

Erica pushed the needle a little tougher than she usually did. Jace winced. "Well, maybe you just need to learn how to use the job board. There are more than enough jobs out there that could use your expertise." When the vial was filled, she withdrew the needle from Jace's vain.

"Doesn't matter right now anyways. I got a special mission to investigate an Atmos sighting."

That caught Erica's attention, and she looked up very interested. "So that monster you killed wasn't Atmos?"

Jace shook his head. "No. At least I don't think so. I'm actually back to get some supplies. I will be heading out soon."

Though Erica didn't reply, her expression told Jace she wanted to know more. However, because of the purpose and importance of the mission, Jace stayed quiet and stood up.

"So what are you going to do?"

Jace grinned, knowing this would be the first time she wanted to talk about something instead of her leaving him behind with unanswered questions. "You'll have to wait and see." He turned and left for the elevator, trying his best to contain the smile on his lips.

When he exited the elevator, Jace approached the cage and wondered if the attendant ever moved from his spot. He always sat in his high-back executive chair with his feet on the desk, looking at a different dirty magazine every time he visited. If he had subscriptions to those magazines, he probably single-handedly kept them in business.

Knowing the cage attendant would never say anything at first, Jace started the conversation. "I need to place an order."

The attendant lifted a finger, telling Jace to hold on. Then he licked his thumb and turned the page. "Mm-hmm."

"A drum of Fenrir and a dozen of those flares."

The attendant glanced up to Jace. "You gonna carry this out like usual?"

"Delivery." Jace reached in his coat pocket and took out a card with the hotel info on it. "Address it to Brian, room 223."

The attendant stared at Jace for a moment, and then his eyes went to the card. But only for a brief moment before leaning back in his chair once more and returning to his magazine.

Jace never knew what he needed to do next. He leaned forward, his hands on the desk. "I said I need a drum of—"

"Hand on the pad."

Jace paused for a moment, then put his hand on the small pad his side.

Without looking up from his magazine, the attendant slid the card from the desktop to some seen shelf. "Be there in six days."

A door to the side opened with his payment for his previous jobs, and a bit extra from his bounties.

Without saying a word, Jace took his pay and left.

Six days. That will be some excellent time with Maya.

CHAPTER THIRTEEN

EVEN OLD CITIES WOULD ABANDON THEIR TRADITIONAL ROOTS and replace them with technology and industry—tall buildings and holo-ads around every corner, cars driving on the streets and progressively popular aero-vehicles that flew on the skyways overhead, and bustling crowds who hardly noticed where they were walking as they mindlessly went toward their desired destinations. Every time Jace found himself in the middle of such a city, he would become alert and aware of everything around him, watching every homeless person who begged for money or the suited man who talked loudly to himself about some business. There were too many moving parts to control. Too many unknowns to manage.

A funky scent came out of the sewer and wafted into Jace's nose. At the corner of his eye, Maya plugged her nostrils, apparently smelling the same foulness he had. She looked up at him and smiled, almost laughing if she ever made a sound. That's when Jace realized his face was twisted and contorted from the stench.

They crossed the street to escape the smell and continued their walk through downtown. Though Maya may have been looking around in intrigue and astonishment, Jace studied his surroundings—critical points in the road to destroy and stop ground traffic, routes of escape for people on foot, climbing points up buildings and imagining shortcuts through the city, structural anchors that he could use, and how to stop the flying cars from getting by. Stopping those flying cars was the key.

While he stared up at the air traffic, Jace felt a tug on his arm. He looked down to Maya, who stared back to him as if asking what was going through his mind.

"Those cars..." Jace's gaze returned to the skyways and the stream of vehicles that zipped by overhead that could be a moment away from crashing down on them. "I was just thinking about how to stop them. And if I could stop them." At that moment, he realized he was telling Maya about his mission. Jace had to make up a reason so Maya didn't ask any questions or learn something she shouldn't know. The more she knew, the more danger she would be in. "I, uh... I guess I feel claustrophobic in big cities like these at times."

Maya lovingly put her hand on Jace's arm. And though it was probably his imagination, Jace felt a calming warmth with her touch. Perhaps it was because he never had anyone in his life which he felt cared for his wellbeing. Then she pointed at one of the oversized lamp posts that rose above regular posts.

He didn't get it at first, but he then realized that the flying vehicles never dipped below those posts. Jace smiled, possibly seeing a possible solution to the flying problem, and maybe to the trafic issue as well. He would have to talk with Brian to see if it would even work.

———

The two walked for hours, stopping by stores and getting small trinkets for Maya. Whatever she wanted, Jace got her. Eventually, they made their way to an open space that the city buildings didn't touch. The grass was a sanctuary from the technology behind him, and the small lake bordered a barrier of trees on the opposite side. The innocent were far enough out of harm's way, and the water would provide a pseudo-wall preventing further escape. This place would be perfect.

Jace sat on a bench next to a playground, satisfied at how his plan was unfolding in his mind. Maya sat beside him, taking a lick of an ice cream cone. Giggles and screams from some children caught Jace's attention.

"Why don't you go play?"

Maya stopped mid-lick and gave an incredulous side glance at him.

Jace chuckled. "What? You're still a kid. Why don't you play with other kids?"

Side pointed to him and shrugged.

"Me? I'm not a kid anymore." His gaze went back to the playground, and he watched the children play.

Jace's mind started to go back to his time in the orphanage, and how he never had the opportunity to go on the swings or climb the monkey bars. He sighed, thinking about how his childhood was stolen from him, then to his friends who had vanished - Jessica, Claire, Brittaney. Maybe Brian or Erica could help him find them. Perhaps he needed to go back to the orphanage to set things straight. Maybe use his new-found authority to save the child prisoners, or possibly even shut the entire place down.

The Sanctuary for Orphaned Children. Jace scoffed and shook his head at the name. What a lie that was.

He blinked, and his mind returned to the present. That's when he realized he subconsciously rubbed the amulet that clung to his chest. Yes, it was time to get back to work, and to think about escape routes.

Jace's eyes went to the lake's borders, noting no paved areas or jogging paths. Just grass and beach. A grin emerged on his lips. His plan was genuinely falling into place.

"Let's head back. I bet you have some school-work to do."

Maya nodded. After taking the last bite of her ice cream cone, she rubbed her hands on her pants and stood up.

Jace wondered why Maya's pants were always dirty. Seeing her use her clothing like napkins, he had his answer. Maybe it was time to carry those pre-moistened cloths he saw at the stores.

———

When Jace and Maya returned to the hotel, he discovered Brian sitting at the table - his hair a mess and with dark circles under his eyes. He stared at papers of drawings and writings strewn all over the place. Jace didn't know if he was hard at work or if he was disappointed or angry.

Though Jace's first thought was to ask what was going on, Maya had a different intent. She approached Brian and presented her leftover banana cream pie. As soon as he saw it, Brian recoiled and gasped in fright. He blinked at Maya as if trying to get his eyes to focus.

"Holy smokes." Brian looked down at the takeout and rubbed an eye with his finger under his glasses. "What's this?" He scanned the area, apparently realizing either it was his mess or the work that Maya was never supposed to see. Or perhaps both.

Seeing Brian was stuck on an explanation, Jace decided to step in. "Hey Maya, can you put my stuff in the fridge?"

Maya turned, took Jace's leftovers, then walked toward the kitchen.

Jace sat at the table while Brian started to gather and organize papers. "You look beat."

"A little. I've been trying to get your armor optimized, and I think I have an idea on a reload harness too. Oh, and that shipment came in." Brian peeked behind Jace's shoulder, then leaned in and whispered, "the barrel and flares."

"Yeah, I know what you mean." Jace pointed at a particular illustration that caught his attention—a ball with buttons. "What's this?"

Brian grabbed the sheet and turned it over to look at it. "Oh, this? This is the Fenrir grenade you asked about a while ago. This is a little tricky, but with that shipment, I think I will be able to refine it." Brian nodded toward Maya, indicating her approach, and he stuffed the stack of papers in a folder. She grabbed the pie and returned to the kitchen.

"Hey, those poles that look like streetlamps…"

"You mean the GRs?"

Jace shrugged.

"GRs. Gravity Rails. They stop hover vehicles from crashing into the ground or a building. You know, they're actually really fascinating devices that—"

Jace lifted his hand. "Yeah, that's great. Listen, does it affect anything below it? Like does it stop something from going up into the skyway?"

Brian put his chin in his hand in thought. "I don't see why not."

"And can these things stop more than just vehicles?"

"Like what? A bird or something?"

Jace shrugged. "Sure."

Brian rubbed the stubble on his chin and stared off in thought. "I suppose if they were programmed at the Central Aero-Traffic Agency to do so, they—"

"So that's a yes?"

Brian paused for a moment, staring hard at Jace. Then he leaned back in his chair, lifting the front legs from the floor and once again rubbing the stubble on his face. "I guess I can adjust one or two without much notice."

"How about, say... Fifty?"

"Fifty?" Brian's eyes popped, and he quickly sat forward to stop himself from falling back.

"Maybe more."

Brian looked over Jace's shoulder, then back to him. "That's asking a lot. I could get in some serious trouble."

"But you can do it?"

"I guess. But—"

"Good." Jace smiled and stood up. "And don't worry about the trouble. I'll handle that." He turned and went to the kitchen to join Maya in the leftover munchies.

"Oh, hey. I got something for you." Brian set aside a single sheet of paper.

Jace returned to the table and grabbed the report. His heart felt like it had stopped. He looked at Brian with his jaw open and in unbelievable surprise. Then he looked back at the document, his eyes going from the picture to the name. "You found her?"

Brian smiled and adjusted his glasses, looking very pleased with himself. "Yep. So, when are you going to visit this girl—Brittaney Webbs?"

———

Jace stood for hours on the street corner of the suburban neighborhood looking at a large two-story house across the street. It was grey with white trim, with the windows being rather broad and clean. The grass was well-tended with a massive shade tree with a swing in front of the house. A spacious garage was attached to the structure at the top of an inclined driveway. A massive deck wrapped around the front door, around the side of the house, and toward the back.

Jace didn't know what to say, or how things would turn out when he saw Brittaney again. He always wondered what had happened. He was worried about her for so many years, but he couldn't do anything about it. Doubts came into his mind. He wondered if she really did get adopted, and he overreacted. Would repressed anger and pain come out upon seeing her? He didn't know.

He watched an aero vehicle fly by, thinking it was his long-lost friend. Just as it went out of sight, a ground car drove by from his peripheral vision, then up the inclined driveway. The vehicle was beautiful and new looking. It hardly made a sound as it passed, and the frame barely shifted after it went over the bump to the driveway. It was a luxury car, that was for sure. The care briefly made Jace think about his next step on his mission.

The garage door opened, but the car didn't enter. Instead, the driver parked the car and opened the door. Out came a woman in a dark suit with a white shirt and a knee-high skirt. She wore heels, and her blonde hair, parted just above her right eye, hung down to her shoulders, slightly curling near the end. She looked empowered and strong-willed. She didn't wear glasses like Jace remembered, which rose a small feeling of doubt in his gut. She pulled out a briefcase from her car, then walked inside the garage.

As she walked away, the car door automatically closed shut, and the vehicle dropped a few inches as if settling in for a long nap.

Jace nervously walked up to the house's front door. He still had no idea what to say. With sweaty palms, he knocked on the door. Loud and deep barking erupted, telling Jace that this woman, whether it was Brittaney or not, had at least two large dogs. A simple muffled command from behind the door had the dogs instantly stop barking. With the sounds of locks being undone, the door opened.

It was her. Without saying a word, he knew it was her. Finally, after years of searching, he found one of his long-lost childhood friends.

Jace couldn't help but smile. "Hello."

"Yes?" Brittaney's eyes went up and down as if inspecting Jace.

At that moment, Jace considered his outward appearance; his longish brown hair, the jacket and shirt that weren't entirely clean, fingerless leather gloves, dirty pants and combat boots, and his old beat-up backpack. Jace's smile slowly faded when he realized he should have thought this reunion through.

Jace nervously cleared his throat. "Uh, Brittaney? Brittaney Webs?"

"Yes…" she replied, skeptical and cautious.

Confirming that it was indeed his long-lost friend, Jace gave a huge smile. "It's me, Jace!" When she didn't react to his proclamation, Jace once again started to grow nervous. "Jace. From the orphanage."

"Who? From where?"

Jace's eyes opened widely at that remark. How could she have no idea who he was, or what the orphanage was? Then he remembered she has some sort of memory thing. Like she remembered everything. He knew something was wrong. "You don't remember me?"

"I'm sorry, I don't. Now please leave." The door shut, and Jace heard the locks on the other side of the door.

Jace felt weak in the knees for a long moment. Her claim was impossible. Not with the history the two had together, and not with her memory. He slowly started to walk off the deck but stopped and sat on the stairway. He tapped his ear. "Brian, are you certain this is the same Brittaney?"

"I'm positive." After a few taps, Brian continued. "Says she was adopted at the age of fifteen from Sanctuary. Went to law school and graduated with highest honors. Now she's an ADA. Pretty impressive if you ask me."

He turned his head toward the house. "She said she didn't remember me."

"Really?" More tapping ensued for a moment. "Yep, that's her."

He looked back up toward the door, then sighed. "How is this possible?"

"I don't know."

Thoughts started to spiral toward the possibilities that Jessica and Claire wouldn't remember him if he found them. He began to feel angry and frustrated. He stood up, jaw clenched, and knocked on the door once more. Again, the dogs barked. With another muffled command, the dogs silenced.

Brittaney shouted from behind the door, "Go away, or I'll call the cops!"

"Look, I just want to talk."

"This is your last warning!"

"How can you not remember me?" Jace shouted through the door. "We practically grew up together! You were in almost every class as me. You helped me pass math. You were going to take me to the zoo..." Jace stood silently for a long, long moment. He heard nothing. Nothing but his heart aching. Finally, with moistened eyes, he gave up. Maybe she didn't want him in her life. "I-I'm sorry to have bothered you." He turned to leave.

Brittaney's voice came from behind, her tone more confused rather than angry or defensive. "Who are you? How do you know me?"

Jace stopped and turned around.

The door was cracked open, and Brittaney peaked outside. "I said, how do you know me?"

Seeing the uncertainty in her eyes, Jace stayed at the bottom of the stairs. "From the orphanage."

"You keep saying that. I didn't grow up in an orphanage."

Once again, that struck Jace as odd.

"I was raised by my parents. I'm sorry, but I think you've got the wrong house." The door shut once more.

"You taught me that I wasn't alone and that I could make friends if I wanted to." Jace took a single step on the stair. "You were the first person I've ever told about my parents. You were...my friend." His words trailed off, feeling hopeless on the matter. Again, he turned around and started to walk away.

The door opened once more. When Jace turned around, he saw Brittaney again peek her head around the corner of the door.

"I was the kid who you always tried to one-up in class. I'm surprised you don't remember me, especially since you told me you have some sort of perfect memory."

She stared blankly at him as if trying to figure out what was going on.

After many heartbeats of uncomfortable and awkward silence, Jace sighed. "You don't remember me. I don't want to bother you." He turned to leave.

"Wait!"

Again, Jace turned around at the woman, who brought an outstretched hand back to her side.

"What else?"

That question puzzled Jace. "We first met when our teacher asked you to teach me the ABC's. We got into a little argument the following day because I already knew them. You called me a jerk."

The door opened wider. "I..." She looked lost and confused. "Remember that..."

"I sat next to you on the bus. You gave me one last chance to not be a jerk. You said I wasn't special because everyone had gone through what I went through. Or something similar."

What looked like recollection continued through her eyes. "I... Wait, you still said I grew up in an orphanage."

Jace nodded.

Brittaney's tone started to turn defensive, and she glared at him. "I remember clearly growing up with my parents."

"Jace," Brian said over the com. "I've been listening, and I have a theory."

Jace almost gasped when he realized he had forgotten to turn off the com. He turned to his side and looked down for a moment, more to hide his embarrassment from Brittaney than anything else. "Go ahead."

"What if she was brainwashed?"

"What?" Jace glanced at Brittaney for a brief moment before returning his gaze to the grass. "How?"

"I don't know. Try to flip the tables. Try to figure out what she remembers."

"How am I going to do that?"

"I don't know. Ask?"

Though Jace was baffled for a moment, Brittaney looked even more baffled.

"Who are you talking to?" Brittaney asked. "You *are* crazy!" She took a step back to close the door once more.

Jace extended his hand. "No. I, uh... had a call."

Brittaney paused. "I didn't see a phone or anything." She started to look at Jace suspiciously once more.

Jace tilted his head to remove the earpiece. "Here..." He presented the miniature device for her to see.

Brittaney lightly leaned forward, trying to get a closer look at the small object.

Jace decided to change the subject and to go with Brian's idea. "You said you remember. What exactly do you remember?"

Her expression turned blank for a moment. "Hardly anything, besides my family."

Again, that struck Jace as odd. He put the piece back in his ear. "How well do you remember your family?"

"Clearly. I have a photographic memory, but I don't remember you or this orphanage you talk about."

Brian chimed in. "Wow, Jace. That's strange how she doesn't remember the school or the orphanage but remembers her family like that. Do you think she had some sort of head trauma?"

Jace cleared his throat. "Okay, you have a photographic memory. You don't remember me, but you remember what I said?"

"I... I don't know." Brittaney started to close in on herself. "It was like remembering a dream or something. It almost feels unreal."

Jace took a step forward but stopped when Brittaney got defensive. He lifted a hand to hopefully calm her down. "May I come up?"

"Jace, something is going on." Brian tapped the plastic for a moment. "Seems like cops are on the way. You have maybe a minute."

Jace looked up at Brittaney, slightly cocking his head to the side. "Did you call the police?"

"There is a creepy, homeless stalker on my property. What did you expect?"

Jace looked behind him for a moment, then back to Brittaney. "I've been looking for you for eight years. I was afraid of what happened when you disappeared. After seeing you well, I'm relieved. I'm also surprised at you not remembering me." Jace peeked his head back and saw a police car turn the corner to her property. He looked back at Brittaney. "Please think about what I said. I'll be right back."

"That did sound rather creepy," Brian teased over the com.

Jace snickered, and he started to walk toward the street with his hands up. "Yeah, I didn't think that through."

Two cops exited their vehicle and approached Jace. "You're going to have to leave, sir."

The other cop gestured at Jace. "What is that?"

"Gun!" The cops pulled out their pistols and pointed it at Jace. "Don't move!"

Jace sighed and whispered, "Brian, the harness isn't concealed enough."

The first cop cautiously approached and started to pat him down. After a moment of searching, they pulled out his hand cannons from the back holsters and tossed them on the grass.

"Officers, if I may..." Jace slowly reached to the chain around his neck and took out the amulet.

The first cop looked back to his support, then back to Jace.

"I assume you know what this is."

"Yes, sir." The first officer lowered his gun. The other cop followed suit shortly after.

Jace lowered his arms. "Now, if you'd be so kind..." He gestured at his firearms.

"Yes. Of course." The first officer holstered his own pistol and reached down to hand Jace his hand cannons.

Jace put them back in their respective holsters. "That'll be all."

"Yes, sir." The two cops returned to their cruiser and drove off.

Jace turned around and walked back up to Brittaney's patio.

She stood there in wide-eyed awe in the doorway. "Wh... Who are you?"

Jace adjusted his coat. "Your friend. Now, may I approach?"

CHAPTER FOURTEEN

JACE COULD ONLY DESCRIBE THE CONVERSATION BETWEEN HIM and Brittaney as awkward and one-sided. She stayed in the doorway of the house, ready to bolt back inside at a moment's notice. In the meantime, he stood at the foot of the porch and talked the entire time. He told her a few stories of their time together, going into detail about their first meeting, his reputation at the SOC, and their planned trip to the zoo. And though she hardly said a word the entire time, Jace could swear he caught a hint of recognition in her eye. And with that hint of recognition came signs of stress and struggle, to which Jace figured it was time for him to leave her be for a while.

On his way back to the hotel where he left Maya and Brian, Jace thought about his mission, and the next step he needed to do before the time came. Mentally going through his checklist, his mind settled on his next task to focus on—the chase.

As Jace walked through the car lot, he considered what he would need—a car with speed and handling. And since the roof of the escape would be closed off, it would have to be a ground car, which didn't bother him since he didn't like flying anyways.

One by one, he looked at the specs of each car by their window sticker. He didn't know what a lot of the terms used in the summary meant, but he figured the more horsepower and torque the car had, the faster it would go. As he looked from one vehicle to another, he found himself going to fancier and sleeker-looking cars, eventually standing over a dark blue sports car with shiny rims and something called "scissor doors"—doors that went up instead of out. He didn't know why he was drawn to that car other than the fact that the doors looked neat and exotic. Regardless of the reason, it was sleek and sexy, and Jace decided he wanted it. He bent over and looked inside, noticing the dark leather seats and the fancy tech-filled dash that Brian would drool over.

Someone approached Jace from behind. "Can I help you?"

Jace stood straight and turned to face at the salesman. He looked similar to the others in the lot; suit and tie, clean-shaven with dark styled hair that appeared suspiciously fake. The expression the salesman gave was one of subtle disgust. That's when Jace remembered he still looked like a dirty hobo.

Jace nodded. "How fast can this thing go?"

"This is a ZTX sports package, top of the line. Unlike the rest of the cars on the road, this model uses a micro-fusion reactor for power, so this costs more than many hover and aero cars you see on and above the streets. And very much out of your price range."

The snobby attitude the salesman gave Jace irritated him. He decided to put the asshole in his place. "Oh." He took off his backpack and pulled out a wad of sorted and organized cash. The salesman's eyes popped wide in surprise. "Oh, I'm sorry. You're right. That isn't enough." He grabbed a couple more stacks, effectively taking out more than the price of the car. When he felt he had the salesman's full and respected attention, he put the cash back into his bag and slung it on his back. "Now stop dicking with me and tell me what I want to know."

The salesman blinked a few times and looked as if he was trying to find his voice. After a few moments, he cleared his throat and adjusted his tie. "Uh, come with me. Let's talk inside."

Jace was led into the main building into a secured office in the back. He sat in one chair, his backpack in his lap, while the salesman sat in another on the opposite side of a table. The room reminded Jace of an interrogation room, and that made him a little concerned.

The salesman sat opposite to Jace. "Our clients usually chip their purchases and not pay for such a fine piece of machinery in bills. I would like to scan the bills for authenticity." He held out his open hand. "If you would, please."

"For authenticity? You mean to see if I stole the money?" Jace glared at the salesman for a long moment, wondering if he could just rip off the fake rug glued on top of his stupid head. Finally, he conceded and took out a couple of bills from his bag. Jace, going great lengths to control his growing frustrations, put the money on the table. "And when you're done insulting me, I want to see your boss."

———

Tires screeched when Jace drove the car off the lot, hoping the management would discuss harassment and discrimination to the salesman. When the salesman returned with the "authorization" to use the money Jace had on him, his attitude totally changed from snobby and uptight to an ass-kissing people-pleaser.

Sharply taking corners and speeding through the countryside made Jace's heart race and his adrenaline pump. It seemed as if the faster he went, the slower the outside world became. Before he knew it, he found himself pulling up to the hotel.

Jace blinked for a moment, wondering how much time had passed and how fast he was going. Brittaney lived two regions away, but he made the trip in good time, and without getting motion sickness, which was the biggest highlight in his opinion. Perhaps keeping the car would work out for him in the end.

A valet approached as Jace opened the door and hopped out. He felt invigorated and excited like he wanted to get back inside and drive some more. He shook off that feeling and closed the car door. "No need to park. I'll be right back."

"Yes sir, Mr. Jace. And welcome back."

Jace gave a nod and walked by while another employee opened the entrance for him.

Wanting to surprise Maya with his return, Jace snuck inside the hotel room. Brian was back at the table, typing away on his strange glass device while Maya doing something he couldn't see. When they didn't look up to acknowledge him, Jace knew he had succeeded in his stealthiness.

Not having a plan beyond sneaking into the room, he slammed the door shut. Brian and Maya jumped in their seats, and both quickly turned their attention to him.

"Holy smokes, Jace!" Brian gave a nervous laugh.

Maya leaped over the couch and rush-hugged Jace. Before he could give Maya a returning hug, she leaned back and smacked him on the arm with a glaring look.

Jace rubbed his arm and laughed at Maya's scowl. "What? You don't like being scared?"

She frantically shook her head in reply and went back to the couch, ignoring Jace like it was his punishment for being a jerk.

Jace sat at the table with Brian and looked at scattered paperwork—more scribbles and notes that Jace hardly understood. He figured it had to do with the job but didn't really bother to ask. He turned his attention back to Maya, who sat nearby writing on some paper while looking at a computer screen.

"She's doing schoolwork," Brian said. "I signed her up for those online classes I told you about."

Jace kept staring at Maya for many seconds. She didn't even turn around to look at Brian when he replied, as his thoughts were on her schoolwork. "She's writing?"

"Yeah. She's a smart girl."

Jace half-stood to get a better look at what she worked on.

Brian answered as if knowing what Jace thought, "A book report. Needs to be handwritten then scanned for the teacher."

"Oh." Jace sat back in his chair but continued to stare at Maya. "Weren't you supposed to be the teacher?"

"Come on, Jace. I have my own job to do."

That caught Jace's attention, and he turned to look at Brian.

"I have a lot of designs to draw, and I'm working on your projects at the same time. I'm here if she has questions though."

Jace's eyes went back to Maya.

"She has a lot of motivation. I don't even have to tell her to work on her schoolwork. As I said, she's a smart girl."

Jace's gaze lingered for a bit longer until he felt satisfied enough with Brian's answer. Then he turned his attention back to Brian. "Why doesn't she write notes to us?"

Brian shrugged. "I don't know. I thought of that too, but she seems almost too scared to write messages. It took some convincing to even write for her homework."

That made no sense to Jace. He remembered Mrs. Stevens telling him that she could physically talk but never did, and now he learned that she could make personal notes but was too scared to. What was she afraid of? He decided that it was a riddle for another time. "Hey Brian, what do you know about cars?"

"Cars?" Brian adjusted his glasses. "Quite a lot actually. See, I have been thinking about it..." His speech drifted away when Jace put the key fob on the table. "What's this?"

"A project." Jace stood up and walked over to Maya. "Go see what you can do."

"Uh, okay." Brian grabbed the fob and stood up. "Where is it?"

"Out front. You'll know it when you see it." He sat down next to Maya while Brian left the room. He watched her for a moment, again wondering why she wouldn't communicate to them. He contained a laugh when he noticed how terrible her handwriting was. "How's your studying coming along?"

Maya briefly looked up to Jace and answered with a shrug.

"Yeah, I was bored with school too. You want to go to a movie tonight?"

That caught Maya's attention. She looked up with a smile and enthusiastically nodded.

He grinned and gave her a half-hug. "Okay. Finish up your schoolwork, get cleaned up, and then we will—"

"ARE YOU SERIOUS?" Brian's comment through the earpiece was so loud, Jace flinched from the surprise and reflexively took it out of his ear. He took a moment to recompose himself, rubbing his ear with a finger.

Before putting the earpiece back in his ear, Jace finished his thought with Maya. "And we will head out."

Her nods became more enthusiastic, and she turned her attention back to the writing.

Jace stood and walked away from the couch to the back room, still hearing the screams of excitement over the earpiece even though it wasn't in his ear. When the loudness finally lowered, Jace put the piece back in.

Brian seemed more excited about the car than Jace was. "Oh my gosh. Oh my gosh. Oh my—"

"Brian, are you done?"

"Oh. Sorry, Jace. But this is... Oh my gosh!"

"I get it." Jace sighed. "Listen, what can you do with it?"

"I mean, how loaded are you? The base model of the ZTX goes for—"

"Brian! Focus..." Silence for a few heartbeats. "What can you do with it?"

"Okay, okay. Umm... Okay. I can put in a gravity-based GPS that will pinpoint your precise location while giving it an ultra—"

Jace sighed and took out the earpiece. After a few seconds, he brought the communication device to his ear to hear Brian still rambling on. Feeling Brian wasn't going to stop any time soon, Jace decided to put an end to it. He put the earpiece back in.

"...And the HUD would be—"

"Brian, do it."

Brian didn't immediately answer. "Do what?"

"All of it. Everything."

"Everything?"

Jace rolled his eyes. "Yes, everything."

Again, Brian stayed quiet for a long moment. "Okay, Jace. You won't be disappointed."

As Jace brought his hand up to disconnect, he heard Brian repeat, "oh my gosh" over and over again.

———

As the days passed, Jace continued his plotting and planning on his confrontation of the Atmos candidate, making sure the pathing worked out for the chase. And though Brian worked all hours of the day on the car, he always had enough time to help Maya with her schoolwork.

Jace and Brian sat at a sidewalk table for lunch in the city where the job was.

After Jace took a bite of his taco, he decided to talk about his mission with Brian to see if he had any insight. "Hey Brian, does the word 'Atmos' mean anything to you?"

"Atmos?" Brian swallowed his burrito bite and took a drink of his tea. "Isn't that the thing I found?"

"Not helpful."

"No, no. That thing I found when doing all that research for you back at the orphanage. Don't you remember?"

That did sound familiar. Jace thought back to those times and how much he read those files. "Yeah, that's right." Then he remembered the cataclysmic events that the Atmos was suspected of playing a part in. He felt his heart sink while he looked around at the surrounding buildings. If the Atmos creature played a role in that kind of destruction, then everyone here would be in danger. On top of that, Maya and Brian would be in danger too. Jace took a solemn bite of his taco.

"I don't know much else about it, but I do remember those circles."

Jace nodded. "Yeah, you're right." He took a drink of his water to wash down the crunch of his taco. "When I start my hunt, you and Maya get out of the area. Maybe go to the coast for a minivacation. Just to be safe."

Brian stared at Jace for a long moment, running his tongue over his teeth. "Sure thing, Jace."

The two ate in silence for a couple of minutes before Jace spoke again.

"I want to see Brittaney again before the hunt."

"Oh?" Brian took a drink of his tea. "What are you going to tell her? Isn't she brainwashed?"

"She's not brainwashed! She just..." Jace took a moment to compose himself. "I don't know, but something did happen to her. I just want to talk to her once more to see if I can get some answers."

"Sure thing, Jace."

Jace nodded to himself while he stared at his empty plate. "When will you be finished with the car?"

Brian was in the middle of his last bite. "Mm, about that." He chewed and drank the last of his tea. "The car is ready, but I don't ever think I'll be finished. I can work on that thing all the time without finishing it."

"How is Maya's schoolwork?"

"She's a smart girl. She's already caught up and getting ahead of her classes."

"Perfect. I'll leave tomorrow."

———

The drive back to Brittaney's was a sour enjoyment, as he knew what he would find when he confronted her again. Jace had to hand it to Brian; he knew his stuff. The upgrades he worked on in the car were more than he could understand. His favorite upgrade was the night vision, and the interesting heads up display the windshield had. The car's extra buttons, switches, and gizmos that Brian installed were nothing but a mystery to him.

With this visit, Jace figured he would make a different impression on Brittaney. He got a hotel room and some new clothes to look more presentable, replacing his dirty coat and grim clothes for something with a bit more fashion and style. On top of that, he took a hot shower, got a fresh shave, and put some product in his growing hair. The contradictions he had to his new clothes were the fingerless gloves and his harness and holsters, just in case things got hairy somehow, and his old brown backpack. And in case he needed to get a hold of Brian, he had the wrist computer thing and earpiece on.

When he pulled up to Brittaney's, he spotted her car in the driveway, and another vehicle parked in front of the house, which was odd as there were many open spots for the surrounding houses. Perhaps she had company? He parked behind the mystery vehicle and walked up to the pathway through the well-tended grass to the house.

The knock on the door had the dogs bark in reply. And like the last, a whispered command made them go quiet.

An older man, maybe in his 50's and who wore an unbuttoned white shirt with a casual and bright colored shirt underneath, answered the door.

Jace fingered the edge of his tailored coat, feeling good about his appearance, but suspicious of this new guy's presence. "Brittaney, please."

Bright Shirt visibly scanned Jace head to toe. "And you are…?"

"I am someone who isn't in the mood to talk to anyone but Brittaney."

Bright Shirt took a stern and defensive posture, standing straight and crossing his arms. "Well, I'm her father and—"

"Her father?" Jace scoffed. "Well then maybe I am in the mood to talk to someone else." He took a step toward the taller Bright Shirt. "What did you do to Brittaney?"

Bright Shirt's eyes squinted. "It's you, isn't it? Get out of here before I call the cops!"

The familiar voice of Brittaney came from inside the house. "Daddy! Don't!"

The imposter father turned his head to look in the house. "Is this him?" Bright Shirt reached to the side and grabbed a bat. "What did you tell her?"

Again, Jace scoffed. The stance the imposture held was laughable at best—poor balance and awkward positioning for less than powerful strikes. "I could ask you the same thing."

"Get out of here!" Bright Shirt lifted the bat threateningly over his head.

Jace didn't budge. Instead, he replied in a cold and slow tone, eyes narrowed in controlled rage, "What did you do to Brittaney?"

The imposter brought the bat down hard. Or at least his expression looked like the attack came down hard. Jace casually sidestepped the slow downward attack.

Bright Shirt swiped with the sports club in a horizontal arc in a glorious display of pathetic determination. The bat smacked into and bounced off of the doorframe. Jace grabbed the bat and gave a deft but simple twist, disarming the imposter father. He tossed it behind him without a care.

Jace was losing his patience. He took a threatening step forward. "What did you do to Brittaney?"

"Stop!" Brittaney shouted, her rushed clicking footsteps drawing closer to the door.

At the corner of his eye, Jace noticed the two oversized spotted dogs got up and stared at the door, teeth bared.

Bright Shirt held Brittaney back as soon as she got to the door. It looked as if she had just gotten off of work, with some sort of fancy gray suit and skirt with matching heels.

"Stand back, pumpkin. It's time to teach this punk a lesson."

Jace glared hard at Brittaney, and a look of fear overtook her face. "Do you remember who I am?"

With moistened eyes and labored breaths, she nodded her head. "I think so."

"Then you'll know how this will turn out if you don't stop him." Jace returned his attention to the imposter.

"I know how it will turn out!" Bright Shirt brought his arm back for a punch, but Brittaney grabbed onto him to hold him back.

"No!"

Bright Shirt and Brittaney struggled for control of the arm. "Let go!"

"This is...my house!" Brittaney won the match, pulling her weight back to hold the arm into place. "This is my house, and I say who can be on my property."

The imposter glared at Jace. Then he broke free from Brittaney's grasp.

"Sit down, Daddy." After a couple of heartbeats of motionlessness, she repeated more sternly, "Sit down!"

Bright Shirt huffed, continuing his glare for a moment longer. Then he turned and walked to the couch with the dogs.

After the tense moment passed, Brittaney turned to face Jace. "What are you doing here?"

Jace took a half step back to give Brittaney a little bit of personal space. "To talk."

"To ruin my life!"

The two stood in silence for a long moment while Brittaney recomposed herself.

Jace quickly glanced at the inside. The imposter stared back. "It seems like your memory is a lot better today."

"And you don't look like a smelly bum!"

Jace contained a smirk. "Regardless, let's talk."

"Why should I?" Brittaney crossed her arms in defiance.

He gestured to her, then to himself. "Because I'm thinking you know I'm right, but you just don't know why."

"And I suppose you know?"

Jace shook his head. "No. But maybe we can piece together what happened, and figure it out."

Brittaney stared at Jace, taking a moment to herself. Her eyes scanned his appearance, probably noticing his new attire. "Okay, fine."

Jace, feeling better about spending the money on new clothes and the time to look groomed yet ridiculous, peered over her shoulder. Bright Shirt and the Dalmatians stared back. "Privately." He took another step back.

Brittaney paused, sighed, uncrossed her arms, and stepped on the porch, closing the door behind her.

"Mind if we go for a walk?"

It was Brittaney's turn to scoff. "You're kidding, right?"

Jace smirked and started his walk down the pathway toward the sidewalk. He heard another sigh, then she walked up to him, her heels clicking against the concrete with each step.

Brittaney paused once they got to Jace's car. "Whose is this?"

"Mine."

"You're kidding."

Jace grabbed the key fob from his pocket and pushed a button to make the car beep.

She stared at Jace in shock.

"What? You thought I was a bum?"

"Well, you certainly dressed like one."

Jace smirked and turned to continue his walk.

CHAPTER FIFTEEN

THE TWO WALKED FOR A LONG WHILE, WITH JACE AGAIN DOING most of the talking. He talked more about the orphanage and specific events that should have triggered memories. Brittaney would ask a question from time to time but still remained convinced that her life at home was the truth. She did, however, mentioned an incident where she had memory loss in her teenage years. She explained it was from a hit-and-run, but had no real memory of it.

When they stood in front of her house again, Jace called Brian on the com.

Many moments later, Brian answered. "Hey, what's up?"

"How can Brittaney get a hold of me?"

"Just give her your number," Brian answered.

"And what is that?"

The silence from Brian was awkward. Then, as if considering who he was talking to, Brian chuckled. "I'll send it to you. Just tell her to pick up any com device and type that number in. Just like talking to me, you can call her."

Jace's wrist vibrated. "Okay, got it." He flipped his wrist around, showing the file Brian sent. "Here..." He wrote down the digits displayed. "If you want to talk, you let me know. Otherwise..." He handed Brittaney the piece of paper. "I'll stop bugging you, and you can get on with your life."

She took the piece of paper, not saying anything.

"And either you call me or not, it was good to see you." Jace got into his car, taking one last moment to look at Brittaney as she stood on the sidewalk before driving away.

"How did it go?" Brian asked when Jace arrived home.

"Not as well as I had hoped. Her 'daddy' was there to protect her."

"How is that possible? She's like us. She didn't have any parents."

"I know." Jace took a turn at high speeds. "That's what concerns me."

"Alright, I'll look into it."

"No," Jace said sharply. "At least, not yet. We have more important things to do. The mission is coming up, and I need the rest of the prototypes done."

"Yeah, I'm working on it."

"Good. I got a hotel for the night. I'm going to the mountains tomorrow morning, then I'll head back."

———

Jace drove back to the mountains and quickly discovered that his car wasn't well suitable in snow. Though he could drive up the slick path, the bumps in the road and the lack of safety rails had him use other means of travel. So even though he enjoyed the tire screeching high-speed adrenaline rush, Jace found himself once again walking up the mountainside in the snow.

He wanted to bounce some thoughts off of Erica on Brittaney's condition. To his surprise, she wasn't there. Only her assistants were in the medical offices.

To quell his mounting frustrations, Jace went back to the ground floor, took a mission, and left, leaving the babbling morons be in the common room.

———

After stopping by the hotel to meet up with Brian and Maya, Jace drove for a few days to his next job. Finally, he arrived on the outskirts of his target in the middle of the night.

According to the file, local police had asked for assistance in dealing with a small gang that had been abusing their supernatural powers, leaving bodies behind in their wake. And the only way to deal with demons was to leave them rotting on the ground.

He geared up and closed the car door, leaving it behind in an alleyway near his mark. Jace opened his palm to get a view of the map Brian sent him. A few buildings down in the surprisingly well-kept neighborhood was the house the demon gang held up in. He approached the street, keeping to the shadows. He felt around his belt for the flares, then patted his coat pocket, feeling the baseball-sized device Brian had given him - a prototype Fenrir grenade. If the device worked, spotting demons would be a lot easier, and he would feel more comfortable executing monsters knowing that they were just that - monsters.

A pair of young-looking humanoids exited the target building, each with a red and green shirt under their light coats. Red and green, blood money. And according to the file, everyone who sported those colors in the area were demons. And though Jace usually preferred more proof on a demon's identity, the fact that their colors were like a poster child to the job file was enough for him. He almost chucked. Funny how their ties to their gang would be the crosshairs for their demise.

Jace watched them as they approached, seemingly oblivious to his presence. He took out one of his boot knives and looked behind him, grinning at the distraction in the alleyway he inadvertently set up. He retreated into the alley, took cover, and waited to strike.

The duo walked up and paused, looking down the dark lane at the exotic blue car. After talking amongst themselves, they approached the car, one whistling a catcall. The other ran its fingertips over the paint job. Anger built up in Jace's chest. That one needed to die first.

Jace sprang up from his hiding spot, covering the mouth of the one who touched his car with his hand and running the blade between its ribs. The Whistler turned at the noise and gasped. Before it could make another sound, Jace ripped the knife from the demon's heart and threw it at Whistler, sticking deep into the demon's neck. It gurgled and fell on Jace's car before crumbling to the floor. That bastard just had to get in one last insult in before choking on its own blood.

He dragged the bodies into the shadows to get the evidence out of sight, but not before using the red and green shirts to clean the blood off his car and the blade of his knife.

Jace returned to his hiding spot in the street and watched the building. Lights were on in almost every window of the two-story structure. Thumps of some upbeat music and people laughing told Jace they were throwing a party inside. It was a full-on nest in there.

Jace tapped the earpiece. "Brian, you copy?"

"Yeah. I'm here, Jace."

"Are you sure the rear exit is sealed? I can't have any escaping on me."

"Yeah. The building behind it burned down a couple of months ago and blocked off the back door. The permit I found is still in the pre-cleanup stage."

Having that information confirmed made Jace crack a smile. "How many demons were supposed to be in this gang?"

Jace watched as another figure exited the building. It stood outside the doorway on top of the stairs and put a cigarette in its mouth. It snapped its fingers and the cigarette lit up. Another demon.

"Nine total. With those two you took out in the alley, seven are left."

Seven. Not bad. But then he wondered when the file was updated, and if the gang of demons had time to recruit. And based on the music and laughter inside, it sounded like there were more than just seven. He decided not to trust the file. At least not when it came to their numbers.

"Hey, Jace…" Brian sighed. "Are you sure they're demons? I mean, we haven't tested the grenade, and they look like kids and—"

"The file says they're demons." Jace ran across the street, staying low to use the car and trees for cover. "It doesn't matter how old they look. They're monster through-and-through." He put his back against a tree, running his fingertips on the hilt of the knife.

Brian didn't sound convinced. "Yeah, I guess."

Jace peeked around the trunk to get a look at the demon. As soon as it turned away, Jace broke cover and took to the building shadows.

Slowly Jace moved up, taking shelter behind the stairways while watching the movements of the demon. The cigarette embers burned closer to the butt. He was running out of time.

Jace continued to move up just as the creature flicked its cigarette butt into the street. Just as it turned around to go back inside, Jace grabbed the demon's leg. It fell forward, smacking its head against the door. Jace dragged the creature down a few steps and leaped on top of its back. Just as he plunged the blade in the side of its neck, the door opened. A girl screamed.

The jig was up.

When Jace looked up, the girl turned and ran for help. At first glance, he didn't see a red and green piece of cloth, but that didn't mean she was human either.

"That looks as good a place as any." Jace grabbed the baseball-sized object, activated it, and tossed it in the front room. Shouts came from inside as people rushed to investigate. Jace took cover at the side of the door, drew a handgun, and waited. Nothing happened. He peeked his head around the corner just as a small group entered the room. There were quite a bit more than seven people. He glanced at the grenade that cracked open and spewed mist everywhere.

To stop the rush of potential demons, Jace fired a couple of rounds into the wall. "It's not working Brian."

"You forgot the flare."

"Oh yeah." Jace grabbed one of the flares and tossed it into the room. More people screamed and shouted in fear as part of the floor caught fire. A couple of potential demons ran up to him as if to get through, or to attack, but stopped when Jace pointed his gun at them. "Brian?"

"Give it a minute."

A faint lick of blue outlined one of the humanoids. Then another. A couple of heartbeats later, almost everyone in the room had the blue aura. Though barely visible, Brian's design seemed to work.

With their identity confirmed, Jace pulled the trigger, blowing a hole in every single demon that started to glow. Those he didn't shoot screamed and fled in the house, taking cover behind whatever they could find.

Jace slowly entered the house. In each new room, he tossed a flare, shooting every demon he saw, killing everyone who wore that green and red shirt, regardless if they glowed or not. After all, Brian's design only kind of worked, but Jace knew those colors meant demon. Most of them begged for their life in between their sobs, but the only good demon was a dead demon. And those who didn't glow or have that shirt on, Jace let go. If they were a demon, they probably didn't get any mist on them. But Jace had no proof they were inhuman. They would have to be hunted later.

"Jace, this doesn't feel right. They look like kids."

"A baby scorpion is still a scorpion." Jace executed another demon, then moved to another room while reloading his handgun. "It doesn't matter how old they are, they're still poisonous."

"Yeah, but—"

Jace had enough. "Remember that demon at the bank? How it used human blood to power its magic?" He knelt and grabbed one of the corpses. "That fucking thing was younger looking than this demon, and how many people did it kill? How much damage did it cause?" He tossed the body aside and continued his inspection, getting ready to head to the second floor. "Remember what we fight for —humanity."

Brian didn't answer.

After he finished going through the house, Jace walked out and started his way down the sidewalk. Sirens were heard from a distance, closing in fast. "Sounds like the police were able to reclaim this area." Jace turned down the alleyway and got in his car. A police cruiser sped by and came to a screeching halt in front of the house Jace had just exited, weapon drawn.

Jace felt good about helping the police. They would be able to round up those stragglers he released since the biggest threat had been dealt with. He pulled out of the alleyway and drove off, knowing he had saved countless lives that night.

———

After returning to the hotel and saying hello to Maya with a hug, Brian took Jace to the side to have a personal conversation.

Brian looked over Jace's shoulder as if getting a bearing on Maya. "You know I got your back and all, but are you sure this is the right thing?"

Jace shook his head, disapproving of Brian's apparent lack of understanding on why they do what they do. "We've been over this-"

"I know we have, but..." Brian let out a deep sigh.

And though Jace wanted to retort, something in Brian's eye made him relax his stern posture. Brian looked pained and conflicted. His expression was something he saw many times in the military on the men and women who were on the brink of a breakdown. Because of that, Jace decided to stay quiet to let Brian finish.

"They were just kids, you know? That wasn't some sort of gang camp. I looked it up. That was a simple party. They were celebrating getting into the regional dance and theater competition."

Jace shook his head, hearing enough of Brian's rambling. "We're at war, and they glowed blue! I do what I have to for the future of the human race."

"Jace, I'm not a bad guy.

"And you're not. You—"

"No, Jace!" Brian peeked over Jace's shoulder again after a louder than usual repost. He leaned a little closer and spoke quieter but kept his tone stern. "No. I don't care if they're Evolved or not. No more kids." Before Jace could reply, Brian added, "No more, or I'm done."

Jace took a long moment to consider Brian's proposal. Though he could get another support person, he trusted Brian. And Brian helped him take care of Maya. Without him, Jace was dead in the water when it came to accepting jobs. Feeling he had no real options he nodded his approval.

"And you'll only hunt guilty Evolved."

"How am I—"

"Me." Brian adjusted his glasses. "I don't know how you pick your missions, or even if you get to pick them. But if I find out you killed someone who didn't do anything, I'm done."

Again, Jace thought about Brian's words. He was asking a lot, and this would limit his available jobs. And what if he was assigned a mission? It's not like he could turn it down.

"Deal?" Brian held out his hand.

Jace looked at the hand. It couldn't be helped. He needed Brian for his missions, and this would be the only way he would stay. Jace shook his hand.

Brian smiled. "Good. Now give me your guns. I have some work to do on them."

CHAPTER SIXTEEN

NOT HAVING HIS GUNS WITH HIM MADE JACE FEEL RATHER naked, but Brian needed some time to work on the equipment upgrades. Even with that subconscious feeling, Jace didn't mind as it gave him an opportunity to spend some time with Maya. And she was happy to be with him—going on road trips, lying on the grass to cloud watch, walk through the many parks in the city, going to the movies and eating out at restaurants, and visiting some amusement parks. Even though she refused to go on rollercoasters or haunted houses, she loved the shows and the carnival games and gorging on fried foods.

Eventually, Jace figured it was time to get back to work, even if it was an easy job like a ridiculous package delivery. Whatever it was, so long as Brian would approve.

As Jace walked up the snow-covered road toward the mountainside facility, he again wondered why it always snowed, and why it never got more than a few inches deep. Even in the summer, the white specks of frost would fall.

When he entered the great hall of the mountainside structure, Jace paused for a bit as he considered heading down to see Erica. Then he noticed more people in the common room than usual, who mumbled amongst themselves when he entered.

He approached the job board to see what was open. As he sifted through the listings, his eyes eventually landed on a candidate evaluation job. At first, he passed over it, thinking it had to do with standing in a classroom and watching them take a test or something. Then a thought came to mind regarding when he first met Xin. He looked over the details—assess the physical capabilities and internal stability of the candidate. Jace rubbed his chin. Very odd. It seemed to be almost exactly how he and Xin met. Not only that, but he didn't need his hardware to do the job, and Brian would approve. Perfect.

Jace didn't give it a second thought. He accepted the job and went to the elevators to go to the cage where he got his pay, a folder with the job details, an envelope with a wax seal, and a small vial. He stood in the elevator and stared at the blue liquid through the ceiling light, losing himself to a distant memory. When he realized he exited the elevator on ground level instead of Erica's office, Jace caught the subtle scent of vanilla and heard the clicking of heels on the tile floor. He looked around and noticed Erica turn to walk down a hall toward the cafeteria.

After a few seconds of internal debate, Jace put the blue vial in an inside coat pocket and rushed down the corridor to catch up to Erica.

She entered the cafeteria with Jace close behind. The loud ruckus of the overfilled room gave Jace pause, and he lost sight of her in the unusually massive crowd. Figuring she went toward the buffet line, Jace started his way to intercept. He was right. She grabbed a cup of coffee and put it on her tray to get food.

Jace grabbed a tray of his own and stood next to her in line. He choked as he tried to think of something to say. Eventually, he was disappointed when nothing came to mind.

Erica started the conversation for him. "So, you're back. For how long this time?"

He was caught off guard. The conversation came at him when he was totally unprepared. After a moment to recompose himself, Jace grinned at Erica. "I don't know. How long do you want me back?"

Jace caught a smirk on Erica's lips. "I don't suppose you felt any changes." Before Jace could answer, she added, "didn't think so."

"Why do you keep ask—"

"As I said, everyone goes through certain changes, then they're assigned support gear before taking on missions. It is critical to assign the proper support gear as they are prone to conflict with one another."

That confused Jace. Aside from equipment being too big or heavy, how could they conflict? "What does that mean?"

Erica gathered her food and started wandering through the chaotic ocean of chairs and tables. Jace collected his own tray of tater tots and fruit and followed. Finding a table near the back, she sat down with Jace sitting across from her.

She looked at his tray. "Tater tots?"

"And an apple." Jace presented the single healthy thing on his tray as if the achievement of such deserved praise.

"And an apple." Erica took a bite from her salad then she said with her mouth full, "Has anything new happened to you lately?"

"Like I said—"

Erica shook her head, waving her fork at him. "No, no. Different topic." She took a drink from her diet soda to wash down the rabbit foot. "The readings I've been getting from your blood tests are... unique. They've been more irregular these past few months."

"Irregular?"

She took another bite of her salad. "Yeah. I just can't explain what it is or why."

Jace took a moment to think about what changed in his life.

"But with these unusual test results, you not showing any changes, your white cell count being stable, AND you doing all these missions with astounding success..."

"Keeping track of my missions?"

"Well, yeah. Look around you. You've been making a name for yourself."

Jace remembered Xin mentioning something about that the day he got promoted. He subtly glanced to his side to find that people have been watching him. "I heard."

"You're almost like a celebrity."

"Why?" Jace returned his gaze to Erica. "I'm just doing my job."

"True, but you're also flying solo with no support equipment. You have a high kill count that is growing faster than anyone else, and you're surprisingly successful on your missions."

Jace took another bite from his tater tot wondering how Brian's agreement would hurt his infamy in The Order. He also didn't know how much he should tell Erica. She seemed to have taken an interest in his work, but was it because he was going at it solo yet successful, or was it something more? He didn't want her to think less of him if she knew he would be nothing without Brian. Instead, he decided to backtrack the conversation a little. "So this support thing, what is it? Why would I need it?"

"Need? No. Not you. Your performance is off the charts without it."

"You still haven't answered my question."

Erica didn't immediately reply, which was fine because her mouth was again stuffed with dressing-covered leaf clippings.

Jace took out the vial of blue liquid and showed it to Erica. "Do you know what this is?"

Erica's eyes went from the vial to Jace. Finally, she smiled and shook her head while she chuckled. "How do you do it?"

Jace only blinked in confusion as a reply.

"How can you be so damn ignorant yet so successful? You're like a prodigy or something."

"You still haven't answered my question."

Erica smiled again. "Amazing. To your first question, something about you will be heightened after Sir Dunmore finishes his initiation - such as your strength or agility."

"After initiation? You mean..."

"Yep. You getting beat up on day one was all a part of the plan. And you were only submerged for a few days, which is unusual since initiates usually stay at least a week. Maybe that's why..." She trailed off on her words.

Jace once again thought about any real changes he may have noticed after the match with Dunmore. He lightly shook his head. No, everything that he considered strange happened before the incident—his unusual appetite after a fight, his recovery from injuries, the fact that everyone was so damn slow and clumsy. Maybe that was it. Everyone got even slower once he started his first mission.

"And the second question..." Erica pointed at the vial with her fork. "I guess you could call that a high-powered sample of the goo upstairs. Very concentrated and should only be taken in small doses. Once you take the contents orally, it heightens metabolism and increases white blood cell activity. But because it burns a lot of energy, you should eat a bunch of calories shortly after taking it. Many members carry that with them on missions where they know they'll get hurt. Of course, too much too often will cause massive internal damage that even the submersion chamber can't heal."

Jace stared at the vial, feeling like he better understood Xin's intentions when they met in the arena. He put it back in his coat pocket. "And how would I know if I changed?"

"How would you know?" Erica looked up at him incredulously. "I'd like to think you'd notice yourself turning superhuman."

Jace took a moment to think to himself.

"What? Do you think you noticed something?"

"Well, not after Dunmore's initiation. So, no. I guess not."

Erica scoffed. "You are one scary guy." She stood up.

Jace looked up at her. "Wait, where are you going."

"Back to my office. I'll meet you there."

"Wait. What?"

"You heard me, hotshot. Take that apple with you and let's go."

Jace stood and followed Erica while she put the food tray away. The two walked to the elevator and started to ride it down.

He took a bite of his apple. "I'm not injured. Can't get enough of me?"

"Well, you definitely keep me busy."

"So, you can't."

Erica didn't answer. Instead, she smirked and glanced at him, then she exited the elevator and walked over to her office. She grabbed a needle and some vials.

Jace's eyes locked on the blood drawing equipment, and he sat down. "You should have a storm cellar full of my blood by now."

She tied the tourniquet on his arm. "Oh, I do." Erica slid the needle in Jace's arm and started to fill up the vial. "But according to you, I just can't seem to get enough of you."

Jace looked at Erica and grinned, though her focus was currently on the bloodwork. "So, do you take this much blood from others?"

"Nope. Just you." She set aside the filled vial and grabbed another.

"Maybe you're just making excuses for me to see you."

"Well, aren't you modest." She removed the tourniquet with a snap. "I'm just trying to answer the riddle of your bloodwork."

"Are you going to tell me what's wrong with it?"

Erica set the vial next to the other one and removed the needle, pressing gauze in its place. "Short answer—there is magic in it."

Jace had to catch himself as he almost fell out of his seat. Though from what she said or from the blood loss, he couldn't immediately tell. All he knew was he was scared. "Magic? How?"

"Now you know why I'm trying to find out."

A nightmare thought popped into Jace's head. "Am I... am I a demon?"

Erica almost burst out in laughter. "No, you jackass. Not a chance."

"Well, I have killed a lot of demons. Maybe like a...a side effect or something?"

"A side effect? Residual exposure." Erica looked at the desk as if watching an imaginary spot that held her interest. She started to murmur to herself. "Is that even possible?"

"Tell you what, I have a job that doesn't have me dealing with demons. We can compare bloodwork and see how things look."

Erica continued to look at that imaginary whatever for a long moment before nodding. "Okay. Come see me as soon as you get back."

Jace turned to leave but paused. He turned back around. "Hey, do you want to get dinner sometime?"

"Dinner?" Erica scoffed. "The cafeteria isn't exactly fine dining."

"Well, what about time off? You *do* get time off, right?"

"Sometimes."

"Okay, then. How about I meet you somewhere for dinner."

She smiled and shook her head. "You have a hard time taking a hint, solder boy?"

"Yep."

Erica licked her lips and looked away for a moment. "Go do that job and come back for some more bloodwork."

Jace nodded, then left Erica in her lab. He walked out of the building and started his walk down the mountainside.

CHAPTER SEVENTEEN

THE TOWN LOOKED OLD AND RUNDOWN—A DIFFERENT experience than he was used to. There were no holographic billboards, no scanners for "personalized" advertisements, nothing. The only things Jace drove by remotely modern was an electronics store, a car lot, and a hospital that looked like it had some decent technology on the inside.

The map Brian set up in the car led Jace to a shoddy neighborhood. Heads turned and stared at him when he drove by. The attention he got wasn't something he wanted, but it couldn't be helped. When raindrops hit his windshield, Jace gave a sigh of relief. People would go inside, and he could drive by in peace.

By the time the map took Jace to the address from the GPS, it was pouring rain outside. Jace pulled up to an open fence that surrounded an expansive property. He pulled in and slowly drove down the gravel road which had weeds down the middle, but not where the tires ruts were. Wild overgrowth flanked him as he took the last turn that led him to a rather large white two-story house with boarded-up windows and missing or damaged siding. The building itself seemed dilapidated, but Jace did notice some things that seemed out of place.

He considered the front door, which appeared to be strong and secure. And the windows weren't just boarded up, but covered by something on the inside, like newspaper or paint, as if the owner didn't want anyone to be able to see inside. None of the wild overgrowth touched the house, and the gravel appeared to be well-tended to. Then Jace's eyes went toward the red-tiled roof and the damaged gutters. He found it odd that even though the gutters seemed broken and useless, the water never found its way anywhere but the downspouts. Jace knew what this building really was - a lie.

He grabbed his backpack and got out of the car. When he got to the doorway, he ran his fingers through his soaked hair, then opened the door. When he stepped inside, he grinned and shook his head as he stared at a massive pit in the middle of the hollowed-out shell of a structure. All around the walls were seats that went up toward the ceiling to look inward.

A man with a thin mustache wearing a purple suit approached him. He had wild and eccentric hair as if he stood in front of a giant fan, and his hair froze in place from the wind. "You're trespassing."

Jace reached in his coat and produced the envelope.

The man eyed Jace suspiciously, then took the envelope and inspected the wax seal. He looked up to Jace. "What is this?"

Jace didn't answer.

After a moment, the man's attention went back to the envelope, broke the wax seal, and removed a letter. He reached in his fancy purple coat and produced a pair of thin-framed glasses, taking a moment to read the contents. "I see." He folded up the letter, then put it and the glasses away in the inner pocket. "She is expected tonight. I will make sure she goes first."

Jace nodded and walked downstairs toward the arena.

————

One by one, people entered the house and started to fill the seats. As the building became more occupied, the volume of their conversations grew. And though the arena spotlights were still off, Jace laid in the middle of the ring with his hands behind his head, using his backpack as a pillow, and ankles crossed, staring up into the darkness. He thought about the mission and the criteria for the evaluation—combat prowess, calmness, mental stability, maturity, and how they react to winning or losing. The last criteria made Jace wonder if recruiters had lost to candidates before.

He didn't have to wait long as the surrounding lights dimmed. Jace closed his eyes, and the spotlights clicked on.

An announcer spoke over the intercom, "Ladies and gentlemen, thank you for coming…"

Jace took a deep breath and sat up, resting his elbows on his knees.

The announcer continued, "Your champion, Zoey Forest!"

The crowd began to cheer. Jace looked up into the darkened seats, remembering when people gave him ovations like that. Then he saw his mark exit a back room.

A young teenage girl leaped up on the stage. She was thin yet muscular, and her dirty blond hair was tied back in a tail. She rubbed tape-wrapped hands together, then punched her palms. Jace looked for grabbing points if the match turned into a grapple, but her grey top and tight black shorts hardly give any hope. Her ankles were wrapped too, telling Jace that Zoey probably used her feet in her fights as well.

The two stared at each other for a long moment, but Jace recognized the fury in her eyes. Shortly after, he stood up, casually putting on his backpack, then continued to stare at the young girl.

The announcer said the final line before the start of a match. "Fight until knock out or tap out!"

Jace smiled at the memories of him hearing that line. How foolish he was for thinking the arena was all he could live up to be.

The girl called out to him. "You gonna fight?"

That brought Jace out of his reminiscing as the crowd bellowed out, and he looked at the girl, who seemed confused but ready to pounce at any moment. She had a cocky air about her like she couldn't lose, but her obvious rage burned hot. Jace wondered if that's what he looked like when he was her age.

Zoey gestured with her head. "Why do you have a backpack on?"

Jace gave a slight chuckle at the thought. He wondered if his trademark look was his backpack, much like when he gave Xin his nickname when he first met him. He smiled and shook his head. "Glasses…"

"What?"

Jace kept his arms to his side, and he took a step forward. "Don't take this personally."

"Don't you worry. I won't." Zoey started to circle Jace, her small hops guiding the way. Jace casually turned to keep facing his mark, waiting for her to make her move. The first thing he needed to assess: combat prowess.

Jace shifted his weight to defend against a low kick, then bobbed a left jab. She feigned another left, but her real attack was a hard sidekick that was aimed for Jace's ribs, which he sidestepped.

The girl was quick. Much quicker than a lot of the ordinary people he'd met the past few months. But like the bank robber, she wasn't nearly as fast as the blinding hurricane that was Xin, or the many demons he had faced. She appeared to have good balance, and her strikes seemed to be precise and powerful. When she punched or kicked, she still had her defense up, telling Jace she was ready for any counterattack an ordinary opponent would have tried to give. After a series of her attacks hitting nothing but air, Jace felt satisfied in her abilities. It was time to move on to the next part of his assessment: calmness.

Jace stepped to the side when she kicked and swept the leg from under her. She fell to the floor and held her arms up in a defensive position. The crowd cheered loudly at the action, and Jace took a step back, allowing her the time to recover. He looked into her eyes, which glared at him with confusion, but her expression continued to be one of pure rage. Cautiously, she got back to her feet and continued her fighting hops.

After a couple of heartbeats, she let out a jab. Jace grabbed her hand mid-punch and pulled her forward. Her stumbled step was enough loss in balance for Jace to again sweep the legs from under her. She fell once more to the floor. Zoey didn't bother putting up her defenses as she got back to her feet. She came with the familiar combo of a feigned punch with her real attack coming with a kick to the stomach. Jace caught the leg, put a foot behind hers, then pushed her to the ground. She smacked her fists on the mat and stood back up in a growl.

Not very calm. Jace sniffed, deciding it was time to assess the next part of his assignment: mental stability.

Immediately, Jace knew she'd fail that subject. Her attacks started to come in with rage as she gradually lost herself in her anger. Each punch and kick came in at full force as if she threw caution into the wind. Not taking any chances to get hit by any of her furious attacks, Jace started to swat aside and block her attacks instead of just dodging.

Then he started to wonder if this is what Xin saw when he and Jace fought. His methods would have been different, but surely the criteria were the same. If that was the case, no wonder Jace failed the test. Then again, he did have a lot going on at that time, with rescuing Maya being his priority. Maybe if Xin had shown up just a couple of days sooner, the test results would have been different. Could he have passed? And if he did, what would have happened? Then he started to wonder once again what the story was with his glasses. Could he even see with those things on? Even indoors, dim rooms, and in the middle of the night, Xin wore those dark sunglasses.

That's when he realized he still blocked and dodged the fury of Zoey Forest, almost like he had forgotten about her. With her rage taking over, her once well-built defensive stance was overridden with critical openings.

Jace leaped back to gain some distance between his opponent. She had stopped hopping and was on the verge of rushing forward. Jace sniffed and rubbed his nose with his thumb, then rotated his shoulders. After failing her mental stability test, Jace moved on to the next part of his assessment: maturity.

The crowd cheered when Jace started to go on the offensive. Though his attacks were restrained, Jace felt his gloved knuckles land against skin and bone, and his kicks continued to hit behind her knees and in her sides. After a few well-placed hits, Zoey's attacks started to slow down. She looked exhausted like she blew all of her energy in the flurry of fury.

Zoey came on with another round of furious attacks, but Jace knew this test was coming to an end. After a blocked punch, Jace stepped behind Zoey and wrapped his forearm around her neck, pivoting and redirecting the energy into a reverse throw. She flew up and over a few feet before finally landing and rolling on the ground. She came to a stop face down, heaving and panting. Zoey growled and smacked her fist on the mat, as if throwing some sort of temper tantrum.

Not very mature.

Jace had seen enough. He turned and started to walk away, and the crowd began to boo.

Zoey shouted from behind over the roaring jeers, "Wait!"

He stopped and turned around.

"You haven't beaten me yet!" She staggered to her feet, ready to continue the match.

At least she had determination.

Jace smiled, seeing the uncanny similarities between him and Zoey when he was her age. She obviously favored one leg, her guard defended her sides, and her face was bruised and bloodied. Jace turned and continued to walk away.

The crowd's jeers grew louder, but Zoey's vocals impressed Jace once more as her shout was again heard over the boos. "I said stop!"

Jace turned, and her rushing attack stopped in mid-charge a couple of paces away. "You win." He continued his leave and leaped off the stage. "Oh, before I forget." Jace took out the vial and put it on the edge of the arena. "Take this and get something to eat. You'll need it."

Zoey was obviously perplexed as her gaze remained locked onto Jace.

Recognizing the confusion, Jace decided to answer her unspoken question. "I wasn't here for the money. I was here for you." He turned and continued toward the exit, but not before calling over his shoulder, "Don't forget to eat!"

Zoey shouted something behind him, but the roars of the crowd drowned it out.

CHAPTER EIGHTEEN

PEACH SYRUP COULDN'T BE DESCRIBED AS LESS THAN PERFECT ON Jace's waffles. And though he would usually savor each bite, even going so far as an occasional moan of tasty pleasure of the inevitable overeating, he instead sat at the diner booth with a nearly untouched plate of heavenly goodness. He had his head leaning against his hand, and he stared at the holographic Zoey Forest folder on the palm computer device that Brian had put together for him.

Though he understood the reason behind the evaluation of Zoey, the fact that he basically beat on a kid bothered him. And as Jace read through the digital record of Zoey, he couldn't help but see himself in the file, orphaned at a young age, a loner, prone to violence, trouble with authority, etc. It was as if he stared into a mirror of his own past.

As he absentmindedly ran his fork over the cooling and soggy dish, Jace wondered why children were being evaluated in the first place, and how The Order knew about these kids. After all, the Zoey Forest fights took places hundreds of miles away from where he grew up. So how did they know?

That's when his eyes locked onto where she grew up—A Better World Orphanage. An orphanage? There had to be some sort of connection. But what? Could The Order be controlling the orphanages? If so, why? And how would they select these candidates?

Jace sighed and looked at his mushy waffle. Such a waste. He stood up and left the diner to start his path on getting answers.

———

A Better World Orphanage—a massive, open area that boys and girls who lost their families grew up in. It was made up of various single-story buildings with a couple of two-stories thrown into the mix. Jace stood in the rain next to his car as he looked up at the main brick building. At first glance, the general layout was completely different. Jace wondered if he was wrong in his conclusions in the diner, putting pieces together that had nothing to do with one another.

He walked inside, his clothes dripping water from the heavy rains outside. Before he could even pat himself off, a middle-aged woman who sat behind a desk greeted him.

"Welcome to A Better World. Do you have an appointment?"

Jace ran his fingers through his soaked hair, and he looked at the woman. "Yeah. I mean, no. I'm looking for Zoey Forest."

"Zoey?" She seemed a little surprised at the request but Jace didn't miss the recognition in the woman's face.

"Yeah. I think you know exactly who I'm talking about."

"Why do you want to see her? And you do know that I can't let you see any of the children without an appointment."

Jace knew he was being blocked. The Sanctuary for Orphaned Children gave him a similar run-around when he wanted to see Maya. Though he was losing his patience, he decided to give this place one last shot at helping him out with his simple request. He used the most charming voice he could muster. "I'm sure someone who may be willing to adopt a kid here would be allowed to see them. I mean, that *is* what an orphanage does, right?"

"Not without an appointment, I'm not allowed to-"

Jace figured he wasn't much of a charmer, especially in bad moods. He planted his palms on the desk and leaned forward to get a little closer to the receptionist. "Listen, lady, I know what this place is, and I will see Zoey whether you want me to or not."

The woman was taken back. Before she could get through her

stammering, Jace walked past the woman toward the back. She called from behind, "Hey, you're not allowed back there!"

Jace walked through one door, then another, looking around for anyone who might help him. Then he realized he was surrounded by people who would give him information. If Zoey had the same reputation he had, everyone would know her. Jace walked up to a random boy. "Hey kid, have you seen this girl?" Jace opened his hand, and the holographic image of Zoey appeared. "Zoey Forest?"

The boy looked at the image for a moment. "What do you want with her?"

Jace heard the commotion of orderly gathering behind him. Since he was running out of time, he gave the kid some cash.

The boy happily took the bill and turned his head toward a side door. "She's always outside exercising."

"Thanks. And if someone comes looking for me..." He gave the kid another bill. "Tell them I went somewhere else."

The boy smiled and took the money, and Jace walked out the door to the backyard. He stopped and looked around, the rainfall soaking his already wet hair and splashing against his coat. When he didn't immediately see her, Jace started to walk through the rain. He noticed the place had very similar amenities from his orphanage - soccer field, baseball diamond, swimming pool, basketball courts, and more. Then he saw a blurry shape of someone near the back of the property doing situps. It had to be her.

The woman who greeted him called out from behind him. "You can't be back here!"

Jace turned his head. "Then try to stop me. Go get your security if you want. And when you do, why don't you tell your doctor to expect patients. They will need it."

The woman's jaw went slack, but she turned and ran back into the building.

Jace shook his head and approached Zoey. She lay on an elevated plank of wood as to keep out of the mud. He stared at her, wondering if the thick gray and blue shirt and pants would keep her from getting sick.

For a moment, Jace didn't know what to say. What kind of

questions did he want to ask her? Knowing he didn't have any time to waste, he cleared his throat. "Hey."

She ignored him, continuing to do sit-ups.

"Do you normally exercise this much after losing a match?"

That seemed to catch the girl's attention. Zoey turned to face Jace, and her eyes went wide. Her face was bruised up, and she had a swollen lip. "You!" She quickly got to her feet.

Jace felt terrible about giving her those injuries. He thought he pulled his punches, but apparently, he didn't restrain enough. She wouldn't be in such a sorry state if she had just drunk that bottle like he told her. Jace pawed the air. "Calm down. I'm only here to talk."

"Talk? How dare you say that after what you did!"

Jace shrugged in reply. He had a good idea on what the girl was going through, and he briefly thought about his match with Xin.

Zoey eyed him suspiciously for many heartbeats. "Well?"

That's when Jace realized he didn't really know what to say. He looked up at the cloudy sky, the rain hitting his face and dripping down his neck.

"Well?" Zoey repeated, but with a bit of anger and impatience in her tone.

Jace closed his eyes for a moment, hearing the shouts of people behind him. He looked over his shoulder at the half dozen staff running toward them. "I won't have time. Tell you what..." Jace reached in his coat pocket and took out the receipt to the diner he ate at. "If you want to talk, meet me there at noon tomorrow."

She stared at Jace for a long moment, then hesitantly took the receipt.

"And do yourself a favor. Drink that bottle I gave you and get some food. You'll need it."

The orphanage security arrived and began to flank Jace. He turned to face the group, who had their hands on clubs attached to their belts. Armed orderly was something his orphanage didn't have. "Relax. I'm done here." He walked by them and left the orphanage.

———

Jace sat at a window seat in the diner the following day. The rain went from a downpour to a drizzle with a breeze giving a chill air in the town. He didn't eat. Instead, he sat patiently while he waited for the girl to show up sipping on hot chocolate.

Right on time, Zoey walked through the door. She pulled back her hood and shook off the drops from her thin dark jacket. Her eyes scanned the room, finally locking onto Jace. At first, she only glared at him. Then she eyed him cautiously as she started to approach.

Jace noticed the busted lip and bruises on her face were gone. "So you drank that thing I gave you?"

She didn't answer that question. Instead, she sat down and stared him straight in the eye. "Okay, Backpack. What do you want?"

"First off, my name is Jace."

"Hi, Backpack. Now, what do you want?"

Jace smirked at the nickname she gave him, once again reminding him of Xin. However, her defensive posture - arms crossed and leaning back - told Jace he had to be careful on how to ask his questions. He decided to start positive to try to get her to relax. "You're a good fighter."

Zoey scoffed. "Not good enough."

"Is that so? What would you call 'good enough' then?"

She didn't immediately answer, and she diverted her gaze, as if something outside was more demanding of her attention than him.

"Are you hungry? I'm buying."

"What do you want?" She snapped her gaze angrily back to Jace and smacked her palms on the table. "Why are you here? To embarrass me?" Before Jace could answer, she continued, "Who pays for a fight then forfeits when they win?"

"Someone who wasn't there for the money. Like I said, I was there for you."

"What does that even mean?"

"You're a good fighter. Keep that in mind, but I wasn't there just to test your fighting skills."

"To test?" She leaned back in the seat and crossed her arms again.

"Yes."

"What was that drink, anyway?"

It seemed that both of them wanted answers. Jace pawed the air, thinking of an idea. "You have questions. So do I. Let's just take turns so we can each get our answers."

Zoey eyed him for a moment, then nodded.

"That drink was some sort of metabolism thing. I don't understand it myself, but you basically heal faster."

Zoey rubbed her cheek where her black eye used to be.

"And for whatever reason, it makes you really hungry after. I don't know."

After a moment, she nodded and put her hands on the table, visibly relaxing. "You still buying?"

Jace nodded and called the server over.

"Tuna salad sandwich, fries, and a pot of coffee."

The server wrote the order down then looked at Jace's empty mug. "Refill?"

Jace nodded and handed her his cup. She took it and walked off. "Okay, my turn. Do you have any friends?"

Zoey looked as if she wanted to reach over the table and slap him. "What is that supposed to mean?"

"I mean…" Jace sharply exhaled while he tried to think about how to phrase his questions better. "I know you, Zoey. At least, I think I do. I know how you grew up, and why you found yourself fighting for some asshole in an illegal arena."

"You don't know nothing."

"Maybe. Maybe not. That's what I'm trying to find out."

The server returned with Jace's hot chocolate and a pot of coffee, then left the table once more.

Zoey went on the defensive. Jace figured he had to explain himself in order for her to answer his questions.

He blew on his hot chocolate for a bit, then took a sip while he pieced together what he was going to say. "I was a kid when my family was killed. Car accident. On my sixth birthday, I was released from the hospital in the care of an orphanage. When I made my first friend, she vanished. Not adopted. Vanished. And that didn't happen to just her, but every friend I made." He set down his hot chocolate as he continued, "Now you're probably asking yourself, 'what does this have to do with me?' See that's the thing. I'm just trying to find out if I'm making shit up, or if there is something to my friends disappearing."

Zoey just sat back in her chair with her arms crossed staring at him. Jace didn't know how long the two sat in silence, but she finally uncrossed her arms and poured herself a cup of coffee. "No."

"No, what?"

"No, I don't have any friends." She picked up the cup and blew quick breaths over the steaming brew.

The server returned with Zoey's plate of food. "Anything else I can get you?"

Jace raised his hand. "We're good."

"You let me know if you need anything." The server left.

Zoey took a bite out of a french fry. "What were you really doing at the arena last night?"

"Like I said, to test you."

"What does that even mean?"

"My orders were to test you and evaluate your performance physically and mentally."

"Your orders? So what are you? Some sort of cop?"

"Not exactly. And before you ask, I'm not at liberty to tell you anything else about my mission."

Zoey scoffed, then started to eat her sandwich.

It was Jace's turn to ask a question. "So why are you alone?"

She put down her sandwich and sipped at her coffee. "I don't know. My reputation, I guess."

"I don't think that's it. You're a beautiful young woman with incredible physical prowess, and obviously beaming with confidence."

Her chewing slowed, and she stared up at him once more. After a moment, she took another bite from her sandwich.

"Have you been in fights ever since you arrived at the orphanage?"

Zoey nodded while she chewed on her tuna.

"And your first fight was within a couple of days after you first arrived with someone older than you."

Zoey stared up at him in mid-chew.

"And this older girl wanted something from you."

Her attention seemed to be on Jace at that moment. "How did you…"

"And I'm betting that you've tried to make friends, regardless of your so-called reputation. And something happened. Maybe your friends were suddenly 'adopted,' or maybe they just stopped hanging out with you for apparently no reason."

Zoey dropped her sandwich on her plate and leaned back in her seat. "How could you know? Did someone tell you, or you look this up in a file or something?"

"I have a file, but that wasn't in it."

"Then how could you—"

"How about this..." Jace leaned forward, taking a drink from his cooling hot chocolate to moisten his throat. "How about I tell you a little bit about myself, then I'd like to ask a simple question."

Zoey eyed him for a long moment, then she nodded.

From there, Jace told the tales of his arrival to the orphanage. He told her about the fights he kept getting into, and the one person who saved his life - Jessica. He told her how happy he felt during that time just for her to be taken away. Then he explained that the only thing that he knew how to do was fight. He told her about The Pits, and when he got to know Brittaney. With her in his life, he talked about feeling okay with the horrid experience at the orphanage, and him finally finding a friend after so many long and depressing years of being and feeling alone. Then he told Zoey that Brittaney had vanished too. He paused to think about those sad years of his life and stopped his tale there.

Zoey sat across from Jace speechless. She seemed lost in thought as if digesting the tuna salad sandwich and the story she had heard. Finally, she was able to speak. "Are you lying to me? Was this all in that file you told me about?"

Jace shook his head.

Her eyes wandered to the window as she mumbled something to herself that Jace couldn't understand.

"Now my question - how much of that can you relate to?"

Zoey sniffed, her eyes watering up a little bit. She looked back to Jace. "All of it. Every little piece."

"I knew it!" Jace clenched his fist, feeling a sense of victory, but dread at the thought of his life being echoed by others, and not just one place either. He wondered how many children had suffered the same fate as him. The thought made him sick to his stomach. Confirming his suspicions felt as if a heavy weight was removed from his shoulders only to be replaced with a different burden. And his suspicions were pointed at The Order. This was too big for him to tackle all at once. He needed to start small, and the troubled girl across from him would be his first step. "I want you to know something that the orphanage you're staying at may hide from you."

Zoey looked up to him, the redness of her eyes and dilated pupils showed she held back tears.

"You're a strong girl. Don't let the Better World Orphanage drag you down. There is a life beyond that place if you stay strong." Jace patted his chest. "Look at me. You and I lived the same life, and I'm alive."

Zoey's gaze went back to the window. Her breaths were labored, and her voice quivered. "How can you know? I tried to run away, but they always found me."

"Because I've been there. I've lived it. And trust me, this is only one small part of your life. Once you're out, you don't ever have to look back at that place again."

Her gaze returned to Jace, and a tear ran down her cheek.

"From there, you can do whatever you want. Make friends with whoever you want. You'll have the freedom to live your own life away from the violence and the loneliness. Trust me."

Zoey sniffed and dabbed her eyes with a napkin.

"If I could survive, I know you'll survive too."

She nodded and gave a slight smile.

Jace started to really miss Maya at that moment. He had the urge to do all sorts of stuff with her and to fill his sorrows with her playfulness and positivity. Jace put some cash on the table, stood up and put a hand on Zoey's shoulder. "I have to go now, but you take care of yourself. And remember, you're not alone. You're a fighter. Just fight through this, and you'll be okay."

Zoey looked up at him with a tearful smile, then Jace left the diner to return to his little sister.

CHAPTER NINETEEN

His mind swam with the conversation he and Zoey had at the diner, and he wondered how The Order influenced the lives of children in the orphanages. Though the incidents happened regions apart from one another, the coincidences were just too frequent to ignore. It was time for him to return to the Sanctuary for Orphaned Children, but not before spending some time with Maya on the way.

When Jace opened the hotel door late in the evening, he looked around to see Maya on the couch watching something on TV and Brian at the table with his usual papers scattered all over. It seemed that every time he came back from a job, they were at those same spots.

Brian looked up after Jace closed the door. "Hey, you're back."

Maya peeked her hooded head over the couch, then she wasted no time and leaped over the couch and crashed hard into Jace with a hug.

Jace hugged Maya back, picking her up from the ground with a groan. "Hey, Maya. I missed you too."

Brian stood up and walked toward the kitchen. "I have some stuff for you."

"Oh, really?" Jace put Maya down and walked with her to the couch.

"A few things, actually." Brian entered the front room and sat on the seat across from Jace. His eyes looked dark as if he hadn't slept in a long time. "I think you'll be excited."

Jace and Maya sat on the couch. She leaned against him while she continued to watch her show, but Jace wondered what Brian wanted to show him. He had Brian work on a lot of projects, so he couldn't really predict what he had in store. "Hey, Maya, let's make a deal."

Maya sat up and looked at him.

"It's late. If you go to bed now, and if you're all caught up on your schoolwork, let's go to the zoo tomorrow. We can talk and catch up then."

Maya's eyes lit up, but then her expression turned to disapproval. Then she nodded gave Jace another hug, and she got up to head toward the bedrooms.

"Tomorrow morning. Promise."

Maya waved her hand as if dismissing Jace's words.

Once they were alone, Jace looked at Brian. "Okay, what do you have for me?"

Brian grinned. "You're going to love this." He stood up and went to the corner of the room where a duffle bag and a couple of boxes were stacked. He took the smaller top box and put it down in front of Jace, then he sat down once more, smiling all the while.

Jace looked at the box. "What's this?"

"Open it." Brian rubbed his hands together, apparently more excited about the gifts than Jace was.

Jace opened the box to find a bunch of baseball-sized objects with a button on the side. "Is this?"

"Yep!" Brian stood up and grabbed one of the Fenrir grenades from the box. "I think I got it to work! I got the idea from a movie Maya watched. It instantly humidifies the air with the glowing compound, and an electrical current ignites the mixture."

"Is that so?" Jace picked one up and started to inspect it. "This electrical thing, how bright is it? And is it dangerous?"

"Not very bright. And actually, it's not dangerous at all. You could probably hold it in your hand and not get hurt. Maybe a little shock at most."

"Is that so?" Jace rubbed his chin and closely inspected the barely-fist-sized canister. "Range?"

"Maybe twenty or thirty feet. Smaller than the prototype, but they're tinier, and you won't need to carry flares."

"Good job, Brian." Jace put the grenade back in the box.

"Aaaand…" Brian excitedly went back to the corner, grabbed a duffle bag and a larger box, and returned to his seat. He presented the items to Jace and sat back with a grin still on his lips.

"More?"

"Yep!" Again, Brian rubbed his hands. "Bag first."

"Alright, bag first." When he unzipped the bag, he saw some strange robotic-like contraption. "What am I looking at?"

Brian stood up and grabbed the contraption. "The reload harness!" He held it up with pride. "It's smaller, lighter, and easy to operate." He slung it over his shoulders like a backpack. "See, you're always wearing a backpack, so I decided to work the harness with the appearance of a backpack!" He turned around, and Jace saw a row of strange looking ammo strung down his back. Brian went to his chair at the table and put on his coat, then returned and grabbed the second piece to the contraption puzzle. He put it on, showing how it fit nicely over the strap. And it looked exactly like a backpack. "See?"

"And it works?"

"Yep! So you can have your backpack over the jacket, and the jacket over the harness. Then…" Brian reached down and opened the box. He took out one of Jace's shiny hand cannons, but it looked a little different. "You just snap it here and…" Brian reached back and put the butt of the gun in one of the small hidden arms. With a spring snap and a click, he brought the pistol forward and pressed the slide stop. "And you're loaded. Well, not now because these are blanks. But if you have real ammo, you're loaded."

Jace stared at Brian in speechless astonishment. Brian bent and twisted around while Jace stared at him, studying him to see if something stood out that didn't look right. For the most part, it seemed utterly inconspicuous. "Brian, you're a genius." Jace stood up and smacked him in the shoulder. "A damn genius!"

"Here, you try it on." Brian removed everything and handed it over to Jace. Then he showed him the steps in getting everything set up.

After getting the armor, his clothes to cover the armor, the harness, his coat, and the backpack on, Jace stood in the mirror and looked himself over.

"You have three clip-loads worth on your back per side, and more feeding to the harness in the backpack. I also used your holsters and integrated it in the harness."

When Brian handed Jace one of the guns, he immediately noticed the weight difference. They were lighter. Much lighter. "Holsters in the harness?" Jace reached back like he naturally would. Like magic, the gun locked into place. After a click, the spring and snap sounded.

"Oh, and it reloads your guns when you put them away."

Jace shook his head and smiled. "You're a fucking genius." Jace pulled out his gun and looked it over, noticing the modifications it had. "Wait, what's this?"

"Oh, that. You remember the Senator Wells job?"

Jace nodded.

"Well, I used the general concept of that rifle and implemented it into the designs of your desert eagles while retrofitting a lot of it with titanium and crafted up a new chamber and barrel system to counter the recoil and to accommodate the heightened—"

"Damn it, Brian. Bottom line."

"Bottom line?" Brian cleared his throat and adjusted his glasses. "Yes, bottom line. Your guns are now caseless and clipless, have a higher accuracy rate, and more stopping power per round. They are lighter and more durable than your other guns, and the recoil has less of a kick."

"Is that right?" Jace brought up the gun and inspected it. The tribal skull engraving looked the same. And aside from the weight change, it felt the same too. "Like I said, a fucking genius." He put the guns away and sat back on the couch to get a feel for his new hardware. His eyes locked on the first gift, and he reached over and picked up one of the grenades. "This is one of the last pieces of the puzzle."

Brian sat down across from Jace and leaned back to relax. Almost immediately, he yawned and started to shut down. "I think so. Also, you're out of money."

"What?" Jace put the grenade down and looked at Brian. "I have tons in my backpack."

"I mean the budget. You know." Brian lazily pointed to all the boxes. "This stuff is expensive, and retrofitting your car—"

"Okay, I get the point." Jace took out some cash from his backpack and tossed it on the table.

Brian grabbed the cash and put it in his pocket. "What else do you need?"

"Well…" Jace considered that thought for a moment. Though the expenses for his equipment caught him off guard, he was very pleased with the concept and results. "Maybe better armor?"

"Yeah, okay. Just leave it, and I'll take a look at it." And just like that, Brian's head went to the side, and he fell asleep.

———

Maya's eyes went from one exhibit to another, looking amazed at the exotic creatures around her. She ran around, climbing on top of rails and pulling Jace along for the ride. By the time they got back to the hotel, Jace was beat. How in the world could she have so much energy? He figured it probably was the copious amounts of cotton candy.

The day off got his mind away from the conversation with Zoey and allowed him to think about the next steps of the upcoming mission. His plan for the Atmos candidate was coming together, and it was almost time for his hunt. First, he wanted to check a few things.

After a long drive, Jace pulled up to the gates of the Sanctuary for Orphaned Children, once again disgusted at the thought of having to return to that hellish place. He got out of the car and stared up at the third floor, wondering if his hunch was right. He entered the building and saw the bastard Dr. Crisp exit his office to his left with a child screaming from inside the room. Crisp didn't seem to notice him though, as his ever-balding head was buried in a folder. Then, the tall, wide, and bright tropical shirt-wearing Sechen stepped out and closed the door behind him.

Sechen gave his usual great big smile as he spotted Jace, his tan skin making his white teeth seemingly glow. His voice was a little raspy, but still deep and cheerful. "Is that you, Jace?"

Jace approached the door. "Open the door."

Sechen frowned. "I'm sorry, Jace. I can't."

"Sechen, you kind of looked out for me, and you've even done me a few favors. But there were days where I really wanted to deck you."

The frown turned into a smile. "Thanks, Jace."

That comment made Jace pause for a moment. Taking a moment to re-organize his derailed thoughts, he continued. "Since you've always been kind and fair to me, that stopped me from hurting you. But if you don't open that door, I might have to go back on that word."

The two stood silently for a moment. Finally, the big man nodded with a frown and pressed his palm on the lock, opening the door.

Jace walked into the room and looked around. A boy curled in a ball in the corner. He was bruised up and his skin red with apparent rage. Tears streamed down his cheeks, and his fingers dug into his leg.

Jace's memories spiraled far back into the past, seeing himself in that exact spot when he first arrived. "Sechen, go get this kid some juice."

"Jace, I can't—"

Jace turned and glared at Sechen. "I'm not asking."

Sechen nodded and left the room.

Jace closed the door shortly after he was gone, then took a deep breath to calm down a bit. Feeling a bit more relaxed, he turned and approached the boy, stopping a few paces away. "I'd introduce myself, but if you're like how I was, you don't really care." He knelt down and met the boy's angry gaze. "Here is what I'm going to do. I'm going to assume a few things. Afterward, if you'd like to talk to me for a moment, then I'll be here. If not, I'll leave you alone, and you can continue these sessions with that asshole Crisp."

The boy's glare didn't let up.

Jace decided to continue with his plan. "If my guess is right, you're about six or seven years old. Something tragic happened in your life that landed you to this place."

The boy's knuckles started to get color back as his grip lessened on his leg.

"I'm guessing you got into some sort of fight with an older boy, and this boy wanted something from you. I'd say about two days ago?"

That coaxed a nod from the boy.

"If my guess is right, I'd say this happened somewhere near the bathroom. Maybe even inside it."

Again, the boy nodded.

"Do you want to know why I know?"

The boy sniffed, but he seemed to have visibly relaxed. He nodded. "Uh-huh."

Jace stood up. "First, why don't you have a seat." At that moment, Jace couldn't believe what he had just asked. He always hated Dr. Crisp for forcing him to sit on that damn sofa, and here he was suggesting the same thing. "And by the way, I don't work here." Jace sat in the seat where Dr. Crisp always sat, which was remarkably comfortable. "I'm just here to ask someone a few questions, and I thought I could help you. That's all."

The boy hesitantly stood up and approached the couch. The color of his skin slowly returned to normal as he visibly relaxed. He sat down, but his expression spoke of caution.

"The reason I know all of that is because I went through the exact same thing - the loss of my family, the fight, all of it. And recently, I talked with this girl two regions away who went through what we did. And you know what? That's not normal."

The boy looked shocked. "R-really?"

"Really." Jace leaned forward, putting his hands on his knees. "Listen, kid; I'm going to tell you the same thing I told that girl - something is wrong here. And I'm going to find out what it is."

"How... how do I know you're not lying?"

Jace smiled and leaned back in the chair. "See that patched hole in the wall? It's under the window where I found you."

The boy twisted around to look around the sofa.

"I did that."

"You were a kid here too?" The boy sat back on the couch.

Jace nodded. "Yep. And though I can't explain everything, I want you to remember one thing - you are not alone. No matter how you feel, you're not—"

The door slammed open, and Dr. Crisp entered the room. "What the hell are you doing with my patient?"

Jace stood up and glared at Crisp. Sechen and two others walked up behind the short, balding man.

Dr. Crisp pointed to the door. "You are hereby ordered to leave. Now! Before we call the police!"

Jace stared coldly at Crisp. "You know as well as I do that the police have no jurisdiction here." He approached Crisp slowly, who in return took a step back in fear. "There are maybe a dozen staff members in this building. That won't be enough to save you."

Two orderlies Jace had never seen before stepped forward to protect Crisp. Then Sechen came forward.

The middle guy barked an order. "You two go high, I'll go low."

Jace raised a hand to stop the three as they were about to make their move. "Hold on a moment." He glanced at Sechen. "Did you get the juice?"

Sechen presented a juice box and a napkin in his hand. "Yeah, it's right here."

Jace put his arm down, then looked at the two orderlies. "Okay, I'm ready."

The middle orderly gave a semi-crouch as he went in for a lower tackle. Jace sidestepped the slow and clumsy fool, ducking the first orderly's grab. He punched out his knee with a right cross and dug his knuckles into the first orderly's side. Just as the first started to fall forward to the ground, Jace smashed his face with a rising elbow.

When the middle orderly turned to confront him, Jace greeted the guy with a backhand then a left hook across the jaw. With the middle guy stunned, Jace finished him off with a palm to the nose.

The first guy started to get up just as the middle guy fell back in a bloody mess. He tried to take a swing, but Jace caught the punch in midair and kicked his boot deep into the man's side. When he lurched forward, Jace stepped in and spun around, using the momentum of the falling guy to toss him up and over, smashing him on top of the middle guy.

Jace stopped his spin in front of Sechen, who stood motionless and in fear. "Thanks for getting the kid some juice." Jace grabbed the drink and handed it to the boy, who sat with a great big smile while he stared at the heap of bodies. "Remember what I said."

The boy nodded. "I will."

Jace turned to face Sechen once more. "I do believe we are now even." He walked past him to see that Dr. Crisp was gone.

On his way to the stairs, Jace stopped by the first floor physician's office. He cracked open the door. "You still here, Jammaul?"

"Yeah, man," Jammaul called in his usual care-free voice from behind the curtain. "Hey, is that you, Jace?"

"Yep. You're needed in room 1A." He closed the door and started his way up the stairs.

In the distance, he heard Jammaul say, "Aww, man. Come on!"

On the third floor, Jace entered the office of the Warden's receptionist. The lady in red behind the desk looked up just as Jace opened the door to the Warden's main office. She called out in protest, but Jace closed the door and stepped inside. The Warden sat behind his desk in his expensive-looking suit and his shiny scalp. He stared at Jace under his bushy eyebrows, his nose slightly elevated as if to talk down to Jace.

"I heard you decided to pay us another visit. Causing more trouble, I see."

The last time Jace had spoken to the Warden, he was ordered to talk with respect and other nonsense. And to Jace's surprise, he did. That always struck Jace as odd, and he never could understand why.

Jace sat down in the chair opposite the Warden. "Nothing more than what is deserved."

"It's a shame. You had such potential, but it's wasted by boundless insubordination."

To prove a point, Jace leaned back and put his dirty boots on the desk.

"Are you planning on kidnapping another child? Perhaps take your anger out on good, honest people who care for the wellbeing of unfortunate children?"

Jace scoffed but otherwise stayed quiet.

"So do tell me, because my time is so limited for pointless and trivial matters, why are you here?"

After a few heartbeats of silence, Jace removed his boots from the desk, reached in his coat, and took out a small sphere. "For years, I have always wondered something—why couldn't I talk back to you?" He put the sphere on the desk and pushed the button. The shell burst open, a gentle mist shot out in every direction, and with a crackling of electricity, a mild flash of light came from the middle. A moment later, the Warden started to glow blue. "And now I know." In a swift move, Jace pulled out one of his guns and pulled the trigger. The Warden was violently thrown back into his chair and skid into the wall. The hole in his head oozed blood and brain matter as the Warden lurched over, falling lifeless to the floor.

Jace returned the weapon to the holster as the receptionist burst into the room. She screamed in fright and horror while Jace walked up to her. He grabbed the amulet that hung around his neck and showed it to her. "Do you know what this is?"

The receptionist nodded, tears ruining her mascara.

"Good. Now get me everything you have on this place and its business with The Order."

CHAPTER TWENTY

THE SNOW CRUNCHED UNDER HIS BOOT AS JACE WALKED UP TO the bridge over the frozen river. Every breath gave a hint of frost, as the steam and fog escaped his lips. Finally, he laid eyes on the great mountainside structure, but he didn't feel the usual relief as he had in the past. He paused for a bit, thinking about what he had learned from the files the orphanage gave him, then started across the bridge to the great entryway.

With a push, the doors opened. Warmth flooded out of the room, hitting the numb skin. Snow drifted in on the smooth marble floor. The doors slammed shut as Jace entered the building.

Xin stood just beyond the door, hands behind his back. "I have been waiting for you." He lifted his arm to invite Jace to the elevator.

"Yeah?" Jace brushed his fingers through his snow-soaked hair, looking around for others. Surprisingly, he saw nobody, not even in the common room. "Well, I want to talk to you."

Xin's arm went limp to his side. "I heard you paid a visit to your old stomping grounds, and you even called the police. Your friend, Detective Petterson seemed very motivated to have a look around."

"Petterson?" Jace took a step forward. "What did you do to him?"

"Nothing. In fact, we are letting him do his little investigation. But we have more pressing matters." Again, Xin lifted his arm to the elevator.

Jace wondered what Xin's plans were. After a huff, Jace let Xin lead him to the lifts. "What's going on?"

"I am not at liberty to say." Xin pushed a floor button, and they started moving.

When the door opened, Jace entered a dark room with the spotlight in the middle. He shook his head and rolled his eyes. Again with these damn rooms. And to Jace's surprise, Xin stepped into the circle as well. After a sigh, Jace walked up and stood next to Xin.

A man's voice called out from the darkness. "You have returned, Paladin Lieutenant Ghost. Just in time, too."

A woman's voice called out, "We assume you heard about the Atmos candidate?"

Jace nodded. "Xin gave me a letter of some kind."

The first voice said, "We have confirmed this candidate's location. Sir Randen spotted a pattern for the creature. It has been going to that location every Friday and Saturday."

A third voice, a man, spoke. "We will move in on the nightclub in ten days at midnight."

Jace didn't like the sound of that. "Move in, how?"

"Paladin Commander Xin," the woman's voice said. "Please fill your lieutenant in."

Xin bowed. "We have called in many knights and paladins to that region. Once our scouts spot the candidate, we will spray the Fenrir mist over the area and storm the nightclub."

Jace scoffed. "That's a stupid idea."

"Anyone in the way shall be harmlessly tranquilized, and all Evolved shall be taken prisoner for evaluation."

Again, Jace scoffed. "Prisoner? I didn't know we even took prisoners."

Xin half-grinned. "They shall have their uses."

Jace shook his head. "Like I said, that's a stupid idea. It puts the lives of innocents at risk of being caught in a crossfire. And if this bastard is as powerful as you say-"

The third voice boomed, "That is not your concern, Lieutenant."

The first voice continued, "Your orders are to be in that region by next Thursday. Sir Xin will give you the coordinates."

The lights dimmed while the second voice closed with, "That is all."

Jace stood in the dark with only the light of the elevator visible. He saw the silhouette of Xin returning to the lifts. Just as Xin got in, Jace caught up to him. "That's a stupid plan."

"It is not for us to question our orders." Xin handed Jace an envelope. "Eight days. Do not be late." The elevator doors opened, and Xin left.

Though Jace wanted to discuss his findings of the orphanages and their roles in destroying children's lives, the meeting with those three voices took front and center of Jace's thoughts. How could The Order jeopardize so many innocents? Though he understood the importance of the Atmos creature, he wondered at what lengths they'd go to get it. He shook his head in frustration at their plan. Jace decided he would have to make his move before they did.

He didn't waste any time. He decided to take an easy job—sensor placements on a rooftop, much like his very first mission—to take any eyes off of him. Once he went to the cage and got the sensors and the pay for the Zoey Forest mission—another job he questioned but didn't have time to get his answers—he started his walk down the mountainside. He started to think about travel, and the window he had to begin his plan. "Today's Wednesday." The many hours of travel started to go through his mind. Assuming he went straight to the hotel, he would have two days. With that thought, he slightly slowed his pace, realizing he wasn't in the hurry he thought he was.

The crunching of snow behind him had Jace stop and turn around. The limo pulled up next to him, the back window rolling down.

The subtle smell of vanilla coupled with alcohol wafted in Jace's nostrils. Erica. "Do you still get motion sickness?"

The dome light turned on, and Jace had to hold back his surprised reaction. She was dressed up, her hair tied back in a braid, her lips thinly covered in red lipstick, and with low dangling earrings that almost touched her shoulders. She wore a tight blue dress that wrapped around her chest, leaving her neck and shoulders uncovered. A sash was in her lap.

"Do you want a ride?"

Though Jace usually enjoyed the mountainside walks, he figured the ride would speed up his trip. He nodded and opened the door.

Erica slid aside as Jace climbed in. She reached in the minibar and grabbed a bottle of water. She had her own drink though—a dark orange/brown combination. He figured it was some sort of alcohol, which would account for the mixed scent of the car. "Some rather interesting stories have come up about you."

Jace took a sip of water. "Oh yeah? Like what?"

"That you went back to where you grew up just to hunt a monster."

Jace cracked open the window to keep his mind focused on the fresh air. "Yeah. I did that."

Erica held Jace's hand, and she turned it palm up. "What is this thing, anyways? You always have it on."

"Oh, this?" Jace activated the holographic palm thing Brian had given him. "This is something my business partner gave me a long time ago."

She rotated Jace's hand, inspecting the equipment. "This is pretty high tech, especially for you."

"Yeah, well, after my first mission, I figured I needed some sort of map so I didn't get lost again."

Erica gave a single laugh and finished her drink. "I do remember that." She let go of Jace's hand. "So are you on a mission? Are you heading to the airport?"

Jace took a sip of water and shook his head. "Kind of, but I have other things to do. And not the airport."

"Then let me take you to the city. I go dancing after I finish my shift rotation. It's kind of like a 'freedom' thing."

Jace looked surprised at Erica. "Dancing?"

"Yeah. Why not?"

He leaned back and looked at her. "Are you asking me out?"

Erica scoffed. "Get over yourself."

"You're the one who's asking me to go dancing."

She smiled and shook her head.

The two sat in silence for a moment. Jace took another sip of water.

Erica made herself another drink. "So, how did you end up here so early in your life?"

Jace looked at Erica.

She leaned back with her drink. "You're, what? Twenty-one? And you're already an officer. That has to be some sort of record." She grabbed and ate an alcohol-soaked olive, then she tapped the toothpick against her bottom lip. "I didn't even know they let people so young join."

"You can't be much older than me."

Erica shrugged and discarded the toothpick in the trash bin. "You got me there, but I'm not a soldier. I'm just a civilian."

"The head of medical whatever at twenty-one?"

She chuckled. "I'm not quite twenty-one." She took a drink then continued, "I love medicine. Ever since I was a kid, I spent my time reading and learning how to be a doctor—graduated high school at sixteen, got my first degree in medical theory before I was nineteen, then my cellular engineering degree at twenty-one. I've been here ever since."

Even though Jace didn't ask for her history, he found himself listening to her, intrigued by her story. "How long have you been here?"

"Three years." Erica swallowed the rest of her drink and put her glass down. "Been head of the medical department for over a year now." She poured herself another drink. "So what about you?"

"What about me?"

Erica sat back in her seat. "Yes, what about you?"

Jace didn't quite know what to say. He shrugged. "Well, what do you want to know?"

"Um, how about this?" She touched Jace's wrist, and at the device, he had on. "You said your old business partner gave it to you."

Jace looked at the bracer and ring. "Well, I really don't know how to use this thing."

"Okay, then. How about you tell me how you ended up an officer of The Order."

Jace closed his hand and took a sip of his water. Then he looked out the window, taking a moment to breathe in the cold air. "It's hard to explain. I'm still trying to get answers myself." When Erica didn't reply, Jace began to speak, as if talking about what he thought rather than engaging in a conversation. "So many things didn't add up then. So many things don't add up now."

He began to reflect on the strangeness that rose in his life, focusing on his thoughts to straighten out unanswered questions. He wondered if everything went by some plan and if Zoey's life was expected to follow the same path as his own.

Erica's comment snapped Jace out of his thoughts. "Well that's pretty vague." She took a sip of her drink. "In fact, that was an unfulfilling answer."

Jace looked at Erica, his eyes glancing over the near-empty bottle beside her.

She seemed to notice and brought up the booze. "You're right." She pushed a button. "Percival, change in plans. Take us to a bar."

The limo driver replied over a speaker, "Yes, ma'am."

Seeming satisfied, Erica comfortably leaned back and smiled. "There. Problem solved."

Jace grinned and gave a half shrug. "Problem solved."

——————

The limo dropped the two off at a bar in the city. As soon as the limo drove off, Jace and Erica looked up at the night sky after thunder boomed in the darkness. She put the sash on her shoulders and took cover under the bar awning just as raindrops fell to the ground.

They entered the building, a seemingly run-down establishment. Jace scanned the room, from the unused karaoke station in the corner next to the stage to down the bar where a half dozen people sat, then to the billiard tables and the mini balcony above. They took a seat at the bar to order drinks.

After a few minutes of laughing and talking, Erica turned on her barstool to face Jace, drink in hand, and finished her story. "You should have seen Sir Dunemore's face. Sir Ricktor spent the next week in the tank."

Jace couldn't help but laugh. "I've made plenty of jokes about his mustache, and he hasn't tried to hit me. Not since the first day."

Erica shook her head in mid-drink. "Mm, no. He can't lay a finger on you. You're his equal in rank." Though she kept talking to him, Jace noticed her eyes were elsewhere, as if watching something over his shoulder.

"Is something wrong?" Jace turned to see what caught her attention.

"You tell me."

Jace started to scan the room again. "Three people down the bar have been staring, two people in the corner next to the pool tables are talking, and three younger people in the balcony have been laughing and staring."

"Yep." Erica took a mighty swig of her drink, then leaned forward to Jace, the subtle scent of vanilla intoxicating his senses. "Do you think the frat boys in baggy pants on the balcony or the biker gang at the pool tables are underdressed? Or perhaps I'm a little overdressed and getting a lot of attention?"

Jace scanned her head to toe as she ordered another shot.

She gestured to herself. "I'm way overdressed for this place. I bet they think I'm some sort of high-class whore to be in a place like this."

Jace smirked. "You do look good, though."

Erica chugged the rest of her beer and downed her shot, then she smacked the shot glass on the counter. "Do you want to get out of here? Or do you want to wait around for trouble?"

Jace stared at her for a moment, noticing a hint of a slur coming from her lips. He glanced outside a window, noticing the rain had stopped. "Uh, sure. Let's go." He put some cash on the counter and extended his arm, both for manners and because he didn't know if she was going to fall over in her high heels.

"My, is this what a gentleman does?"

"Sure."

She took his arm and Jace led her out of the bar.

Erica's heels clicked against the concrete with each step, but her posture and demeanor told him much about her personality. She seemed high-class and prestigious in her outfit, but the alcohol was really starting to take its toll on her mental state.

Jace gazed at her shoes. "Do you always wear heels?"

She looked down to her two-inch heels in mid-step. "For a short girl like me, I need to stand out."

He wasn't a stranger to looking up at people, being only five and a half feet tall, so he could relate to what she talked about. But with her heels, Erica was barely taller than Jace by maybe an inch. Regardless of him being as short as her, he didn't quite understand what she meant. "So why do you need help standing out?"

"Haven't you seen those...those holo-ads for strip clubs? And makeup? They're all tall and beautiful women." Erica put her hand to her chest, then brought her cupped hand forward. "They're HUGE, while mine are..." Her hand went to her chest. "Mediocre."

The entire time Jace has known Erica, he never imagined her talking about herself in such a fashion, especially when it came to her breast size. "Well, I think you look great."

"Really?" When Erica looked down at her body, she staggered a step. "I'm a short, small-breasted short girl."

Jace gave a slight laugh. "How much have you had to drink?"

"Me?" She almost looked insulted. "Not much. I had those three beers, and that shot... and a shot or two in the back of the limo just before we exited, those three drinks after I picked you up... Oh, and a quick double-shot just before we left."

Jace shook his head. He knew it—she was plastered. And she would probably get more wasted as the night progressed. "Alright then, how do we get out of here?"

Erica looked around. "I dunno. Where are we anyways?"

Jace stopped Erica in their tracks. "You don't know where we are?"

She shook her head. "Nope. I just needed a drink, and this was the first place I found."

"Why didn't the limo stick around?"

"They're not a taxi service. They only drop you off. They have more important things to do than to be yer chauffeur." Erica pointed to Jace's wrist. "Hey, why don't you... Why don't you use that thing? Get a map?"

Though Jace wasn't happy at that reply, he sighed and accepted it for what it was. "I don't know how to. But let's get a room and—"

"A room?" Erica removed her hand from Jace's arm. "Now look here, mister. I've told you before. Don't make me say it again."

Jace smiled at the ridiculousness, then reached his arm out once more. She looked at him, then his arm. She smiled and took it, and they continued their walk in the night.

Erica tapped Jace's arm. "I think yer hiding something."

"Oh yeah? Like what?"

Erica waved the finger. "No, no. Don't tell me. I have a mission to figure it out."

Jace laughed. "I'm sure you will."

She chuckled, then before Jace could do anything, Erica fell to the side and crashed hard into a small waist-high fence in front of a house. Jace reached to grab her. Then the fence gave way, and Erica fell face-first into a damp garden, taking Jace with her in the fall.

Jace felt a sharp sting in his arm as he got to his feet. He patted himself down, then reached out a concerned and helping hand. "Are you okay?"

Her skin looked flushed under the dirt that covered her skin. Pebbles were in her hair, and her dress was covered in dirt. "I'm fine."

She took his hand and started to stand but winced and stumbled when she put some weight on her leg.

Jace glanced down at her ankle, lifting her dress to take a look.

"I think I twisted my ankle." She slightly rotated her leg but grimaced at the action. "Doesn't look broken, though."

"Are you sure?"

Erica gave a forced scoff. "Who do you think yer talking to?" She leaned closer to Jace, inspecting his arm. "What happened?"

A slight breeze sent a chill on his flesh as he noticed a deep gash on his forearm. That's when he noticed a nail protruding from his section of the broken fence.

She tore off a piece of her dress and wrapped Jace's laceration, obviously favoring her uninjured leg, even though she continued to wear her two-inch heels.

"Can you walk?"

Erica looked up to Jace, then to her feet. When she put even a little bit of weight on her leg, she stumbled.

Feeling his arm was patched up decently enough, he picked her up and carried her down the street in his arms.

CHAPTER TWENTY-ONE

ERICA FOUND ANOTHER INJURY ON HER SIDE WHILE JACE carried her in his arms. With her ankle swelling up, her bruising, and her intoxication, there would be no way she could get anywhere without falling over again. Jace figured she needed to rest for the night. And even though the morning would be painful, sobering up with two moderate wounds, Jace didn't really know what else to do besides get a hotel. After thinking about the timeframe once more with his window to go after the Atmos candidate, he would still be on schedule with the lost night.

Jace opened the door to the top floor suite, still carrying Erica in his arms. After entering the suite, since the economy-class rooms were sold out, he closed the door with his foot and made his way to the couch. He set her down, but not before she winced and grimaced a little from the aches and pains. He disconnected his backpack and took it off to stretch, which he kind of regretted when he felt his back muscles crunch in on themselves from carrying Erica for so long.

After tossing his jacket on the backpack, he went to the kitchen to ransack the ice maker. His attention was briefly diverted toward a snack bowl when his stomach growled in a profound hungry protest. After grabbing handfuls of ice, he grabbed a few towels, and returned to Erica, but not before taking a couple of bags of snack-sized chips from the counter and holding them in his mouth. When he was done wrapping up some ice with one towel and handing it to Erica, he gave her one of the bags of chips, then made his way to her ankle, which was swollen and discolored. He put her foot in his lap, gently removed the remarkably resilient high heel, then placed the makeshift ice pack on her ankle.

Erica winced, but she held firm, keeping the chilled towels against her bruising skin. She gestured to Jace. "I didn't even know you had those…those guns on you." She sat up, groaning in pain, and reached a hand out. "Where are you keeping those things?"

Jace put his bag of chips on the coffee table. His stomach growled again, apparently unhappy with his decision to eat a little later. "Lay back down."

Erica lifted her arm, which looked as if it caused her a bit of discomfort, reached to her side, and unzipped her dress. It partially slid down so she could get a look at her wound.

Jace's eyes were inadvertently drawn to the low hanging dress on her chest while his heartbeat just a little faster. It was almost like she went down further than she needed to inspect her injury. He forced his gaze to the side of her chest where dark blue and red bruises on her ribs had formed, which looked nasty and painful.

Erica sighed. "Damn it." She placed the ice pack on her side and held it in place with her arm. Then she looked up to Jace, and though she glared at him with narrowed eyes, he thought he saw something else. "Hey." She nudged him with her injured foot, which made her wince a little in pain. "Focus."

Jace smirked and brought his eyes back to her ankle.

She laid back and groaned.

The two stayed quiet for a long moment while the ice did its work. Finally, she sighed in a little frustration and shuffled a little bit. "Gah, this is going to hurt tomorrow. Can you take me to the room?"

Jace looked up at the door, then to Erica. He carefully moved off of the couch, taking great care not to cause any pain or discomfort, then positioned himself beside Erica. After she wrapped her arm around his shoulders, Jace picked her up and held her in his arms. "Are you okay?"

She smiled and gave a nod that seemed like she was just about to fall asleep, her head resting at the base of his neck.

After getting to the door, he shuffled with his hands to try to turn the knob, finally opening the door with his foot. When he took a step inside the room, he realized his movements made the unzipped section of Erica's dress slip down past her chest. He gulped as one breast was plainly visible, but he couldn't do anything to cover it.

He lifted his head up to make sure he didn't stare. Erica's hand grabbed the back of Jace's head and brought his gaze back, and she kissed him. It started soft, but her passion grew more and more with each passing heartbeat.

Jace walked to the bed and sat her down. She scooted back a little bit but held him as she rubbed his chest. Her hands roamed all over Jace's chest and back, but she then felt the reload harness.

With her grip focused on the confusion that was the device strapped on him, Jace took a step back.

Her blue eyes were filled with lust as she breathed heavily. When she reached back and unbound her blonde hair, she shook her head back and forth, letting it fall freely to the sides of her face that made her look sexy and wild.

Jace took a deep breath to steady his nerves. "Get comfortable while I take this off." He gestured at the harness, which he could easily remove right there if he wanted to.

Erica shifted her weight and let the dress fall down her chest, and she slid it off to let it fall to the ground. She had on thin, black lace panties that were partially see-through. She crawled on the bed and laid down. "Don't keep me waiting."

Jace smiled, then turned and left the room.

He went to the dining table, where he unbuckled his holsters and put his guns on the table. Then he took deep breaths to get his emotions and desires under control. Once he felt his breath steady, he walked to a side closet where he discovered an extra pillow and blanket and tossed the spare bedding on the couch. He sat down and took another moment to relax.

His attempts to control his racing heart failed. A woman as smart and as beautiful as Erica throwing herself at him was a temptation that was difficult to resist.

Then his eyes went to the bag of chips he left on the coffee table. His stomach growled loudly in approval.

After a few minutes had passed, Jace tossed the empty bag of chips back on the table, cleaned and bandaged the cut on his arm, then went to the bedroom. He stood in the doorway, staring. Erica laid on the bed with only her panties on. His heart raced again but was glad she was passed out from the night's events.

He walked over to her and gently pulled the blankets from under her, doing everything he could to make sure she didn't wake up. Next, he put the ice packs against her injuries then laid the blanket over her. He picked up her dress and hung it on the door, then he grabbed his coat and walked back to the door. He stopped to look at her once more, giving a deep sigh as he thought about turning her down. Maybe next time. He shook his head, almost feeling disappointed in himself, turned the light off, and closed the door behind him.

———

Since Jace hardly ever got more than a few hours of sleep a night, he got cleaned up then went out to pick up some supplies. Just before the sun even started to rise, he returned to the hotel, making great efforts in staying as quiet as possible. He put the various store bags down, taking the bottle of pills out of one, got a glass of water, then snuck into the bedroom. Erica was still asleep, and it hardly looked as if she moved at all during the night. He saw her chest go up and down, so she wasn't dead.

Jace set the glass of water and a small bottle of pills on the nightstand, taking a moment to look at Erica while she slept. Her hair slightly covered her face, but he resisted the urge to brush it behind her ear. Feeling everything was in place, Jace snuck out to let her rest, closing the door behind him.

After he put the groceries away, Jace stood patiently at the window and watched the sunrise. When he heard the bedroom door open, Jace turned around.

Erica limped out with her dirty dress on. And though her hair was a tangled mess, she still tied it back. She looked around, taking a moment when she noticed the folded up bedding Jace used on the edge of the couch, then her eyes went to him.

Jace started to walk away from the view to assist, but Erica stopped him with an upraised hand. As she hobbled to the table to sit down, Jace went to the kitchen.

She cleared her throat. "So..."

Jace looked toward her while he grabbed some orange juice from the fridge. She didn't even look up to him.

Erica looked uncomfortable and confused. "I guess last night got a little crazy. Huh?"

Jace poured a small glass of orange juice and sat at the table across from her.

She finally looked up at Jace. "Look, I—"

"You were drunk." He put the orange juice in front of her. "Don't worry. Nothing happened."

Erica stared at Jace for a long moment, then she looked at the bedding on the couch once more. Her gaze went back to him, and she smiled. "Thanks." She pensively drank the juice. "Last night is a little fuzzy, but didn't you hurt your arm?"

"Oh. Yeah, it's nothing."

"No, that's not how I remember it."

"I'm surprised you remember anything."

"Oh, shut up. I think you'll need stitches. Let me see it."

Jace presented the bandaged up limb. She unwound the gauze and inspected the wound.

Her eyes went wide. "What the hell?"

That gave Jace a bit of alarm. He brought his arm back to inspect the cut. It looked fine to him. "What?"

"This!" Erica grabbed the arm and yanked it back toward her. "This is about a four-inch gash that I could have sworn went down to the bone. This looks like it's been healing for at least a week." She put his arm down. "It's starting to scar."

"It's nothing new." Jace reached over and grabbed one of the bags.

"Nothing new? I've never heard of anything like this." She put her chin in her hand as if she started to get lost in thought.

"I've always been like this, even while I was still at the orphanage." Jace placed the bag in front of her. "Here."

"What's this?" She set the glass down and peered in the bag, then she started to take out the change of fresh clothes, some medical supplies for her injuries, sundries, and bath salts and oils. Then she took out the bra and panties, and her eyes went wide.

"That's your size, right?"

She glared hard at Jace with a hint of barely controlled anger. He figured if he had sat any closer, she would have slapped him. She looked back to the undergarments once more.

Jace stood and held out a hand. "Let me help you."

Erica slapped his hand away. "I have had just about enough with your help." She stood straight up, even putting weight on her injured leg. Though Jace knew she tried to hide the pain, he could tell from her eyes that even her defiance wasn't enough to dull the ache. "I have to save some shred of my dignity." She stuffed the bag with everything she took out and stormed off in a limp to the bathroom.

Jace sighed and shook his head, then went toward the kitchen to start on breakfast.

She stayed in the bathroom for over an hour, which gave Jace time to prepare and cook some of the sides. Finally, she came out wearing the white and blue striped shirt, loose-fitting gray blouse, and dark slacks. He figured she wore the undergarments as well. As she limped toward the table to sit down, he noticed the bandage wrapped around her ankle. "It's barely eight in the morning. How did you find the time to do all of this? And what clothing store is open this early?"

Jace finished cooking the pancake and plated it with some scrambled eggs, bacon, and toast. "I don't really sleep much." He poured another glass of orange juice just and put everything in front of Erica before returning to the kitchen.

"Why are you doing this?"

Jace was confused, and he looked at Erica. "Doing what?"

She pointed to the plate in front of her. "This..." Then she gestured to her clothes. "And this. Why are you doing this?"

Jace only smiled in reply and went back to cooking.

Her gaze went back to her plate. "I'll pay you back."

"No need." Jace prepared another plate, poured himself some orange juice, and sat across from Erica.

She stared suspiciously at him. "Are you going to answer me?"

"What?" Jace organized the silverware in front of him. "I don't know. Because I wanted to, I guess."

Erica sighed and shook her head, then turned her attention at eating her food.

———

After escorting Erica to her apartment building in the city, Jace called for a taxi cab to take him back to his car. When it arrived, she kissed him on the cheek and handed him a small card with her phone number on it. As he climbed in the taxicab, she waited out front and watched as the car drove off.

He sat back and closed his eyes, wondering how in the hell his night got sidetracked so hard. His fingers played with the edges of the card, and his thoughts were focused on Erica and that alluring scent of vanilla.

During his drive back to Maya, he still thought about Erica. Was that night a fluke? Should he have taken her up on her offer regardless of her being drunk? He wanted to. That was certain. Jace shook his head, deciding his actions and decisions were for the best. She was drunk, and who knows how awkward their professional relationship would have been every time he visited her to take a dip in the tank? With a reinforcing nod to himself, Jace forced his thoughts on the job at hand - the Atmos candidate.

———

When Jace pulled up to the hotel, he popped open the door and got out. It was a long and exhausting drive. The valet rushed to meet him.

"Good afternoon, sir."

Jace handed him the key fob. "Give it a quick wash." When the valet sat in the driver's seat, Jace held the door open. "And don't go on a joy ride this time."

The valet looked shocked at Jace. "Sir, I don't know what you're..." As Jace glared at the valet, he changed his tone. "Y-Yes, sir."

Jace waited a moment longer, then closed the door. He entered the hotel lobby, where the manager met with him.

"Good afternoon, sir. Is there a problem with one of our valets?"

Jace turned his head back at the door as his car drove off. "Nah. I'm sure he'll take good care of my car." He walked on by and went to the elevator.

Jace entered the hotel room and plopped on the couch. Maya ran from the backroom in her hooded pajamas and leaped over the back of the sofa to land next to him with a hug. Brian, like always, sat at the dining room table working on paperwork and drawings.

"Hey, Jace. Long trip?"

"Yeah." Jace gave Maya a one-armed hug. Even though he was tired, Jace gave Maya a gentle shake. "Hey, are you hungry?"

She nodded.

"Okay, get dressed, and let's go out to eat."

Maya hopped up and bolted to the back room.

Jace stood up and went to Brian. "How's it going?"

Brian put down a notepad with drawings and scribbles of what looked like Jace's armor. "Still working on the revisions."

"The Atmos thing has been pushed up, and we're out of time. We start on Saturday night."

"That's tomorrow. I won't have your armor done."

Jace sat down. "It's okay. I'll just use the one you have now. No choice."

Brian nodded.

"I had a thought. Could you make different types of ammo for the guns and harness?"

"Different how?"

"Well..." Jace took a moment to reflect on some demons and their abilities. "Like if one of them put up some sort of dust shield, I was thinking like an explosive round. Something that could break through the barrier. Also, maybe an armor-piercing one, and an incendiary one?"

"Four types of bullets?" Brian adjusted his glasses, but his expression told Jace he wasn't too keen on the idea. "What about the harness?"

"Well, that would have to be adjusted. Could you make it work?"

"I don't know, Jace. I already have a lot going on, and that's asking a lot more."

"It doesn't have to be done for Saturday's job. I mean for future jobs."

Brian thought to himself for a long moment while he stared at the notepad. "Let me finish this, and I'll see what I can do."

Jace stood up just as Maya returned from the backroom in her hoodie and a skirt with leggings. She had a couple of barrettes in her blonde hair, which made Jace smile.

"But no promises," Brian added.

Jace nodded, then he led Maya out of the room. "And how about some cloud watching afterwards?"

CHAPTER TWENTY-TWO

BEING RUSHED ON A COMPLICATED PLAN WAS NEVER A GOOD thing. And that's precisely what Jace felt - rushed. It couldn't be helped though. In order to save many innocent lives, the schedule needed to be pushed forward. He mentally went over everything, feeling rather confident everything was in order. Or rather, feeling like everything was as good as it was going to get. Jace parked his car in the alleyway next to the club, grabbed his gear, making sure to take the box of tranquilizers Brian got for him, and snuck into the nightclub just before it opened.

He crept around, keeping an eye out for any employees who might spot him while he made his way to the fire system room. When Jace got to the door, he tapped the earpiece and reached in his jacket pocket. "Are you sure this will work?"

"Yeah. First, use the blue striped side. Jace, are you sure about this?"

"Sort of. Besides, this is Plan B." Jace looked at the card and sighed, then slid the card through the slot. "Okay. Now what?"

"Hold on... Okay, slide the card again using the gray strip and type in pound, three, ten, forty-six, asterisk."

"What the hell is a pound?"

Brian audibly sighed over the earpiece. "The number symbol."

"And what about an asterisk?"

Again, Brian sighed. "The star-like button."

Jace slid the card and proceeded to type in the code. "Why not just call it 'number symbol' and 'star symbol'?"

"I don't know, Jace. Let's... just hurry this up."

"Relax." The door cracked open, and Jace slid inside. "I know what I'm doing."

The light flickered for a moment before totally turning on. A lot of red pipes ran up the wall and through the ceiling with a large tank in the middle of the room. He approached the container and looked it over, finally seeing the refill hatch. "This is a big tank. Are you sure this will work?"

"Relax, Jace. I know what I'm doing."

Jace scoffed and climbed up the tank to open the hatch. Once it swung open, Jace took off his backpack and dropped what looked like salt bricks in the container, and then he closed the hatch, sealing it once more. He slid off, reconnecting the backpack to the harness. "Okay, no problems yet."

The door to the room opened, and two bouncers. They were huge, muscle-bound neckless wonders wearing the same black t-shirt and jeans, like they came out some sort of vending machine. There was no place to hide. Jace was caught.

"Hey, what are you doing back here?" one bouncer asked.

"Uh, working?" Jace approached the two, who obviously didn't like Jace's reply. They stood shoulder to shoulder, blocking the door. Jace figured this might be an interesting opportunity, and may solve one of the problems with plan B. "Hey, is the owner in?"

The bouncers crossed their beefy arms in unison. Why do they always cross their arms?

"Mr. Frog won't be in until tonight," The first bouncer said. "Why do you want to see him?"

Jace shrugged. "Because it beats you calling the police."

The first bouncer asked, "And why is that?"

"Because the club is about to open. Right? And wouldn't this 'Mr. Toad' want to know why a short guy like me was in the fire safety room?"

"That's Mr. Frog."

"Mr. Toad. My mistake." The two looked confused and angry at the same time. "But think of it, who knows what I did in here? Think of the fines and lawsuits if a fire broke out and this thing doesn't work. Think of the lives you could possibly save." Jace paused a moment for the two meat sacks to understand his comment fully. "And if he doesn't like what I have to say, you'll probably try to beat the crap out of me THEN you can call the police. How does that sound?"

The two neckless wonders looked at each other for a moment, then they grabbed Jace by the arm and forcefully led him toward the private upstairs booth, which was exactly where he wanted to go in the first place.

Jace stood in the private office in the upper levels of the nightclub accompanied by the two bouncers who stood behind him and the infamous Mr. Frog. Loud rhythmic thuds gently rattled the walls as the music from the nightclub compelled those below to move their bodies on the main dance floor. The floor was partially one-way glass, allowing a full view of the club below, the vast amounts of women dancing on the poles, and the energetic and often exotic and erotic shows that went on.

The entire floor was broken up into many rooms, looking as if it were instead a large and luxurious apartment rather than a business office - indoor spas, comfortable and expensive couches, fireplaces, TV's, massage tables, thin poles that stretch from floor to ceiling, and much more were in the vast and absurd floor. Everything was in loud, pastel colors as if begging to be noticed. The owner of the club was no exception either.

Mr. Frog was a skinny man dressed in a bright green suit, with thin white stripes running down the length of the entire outfit. His shoes were of fine leather, but the visual quality was ruined by the unnatural coloring to match the finely tailored yet desperate silk attire. The tailcoat was unbuttoned, showing a white shirt that almost looked half untucked under straps that went from his pants over his shoulders. Numerous chains dangled from the man—a few actually on his neck, some to his sides, and more than a few that went from one pocket of one piece of clothing to another pocket in a different piece of clothing. Each finger had at least one ring, and he even had some teeth replaced with gold. The hat, which was the same loud color with a white horizontal strip that followed the wide brim, had a purple feather protruding from the top.

Mr. Frog sat on the orange fuzzy couch with his feet up on the coffee table, speaking in slang, as if his vocabulary broke off some parts of certain words. Maybe he was drunk? "So let me get this straight, you asking to have my girls give some fools a private party so you can find somebody? You asking to have my girls go in the back rooms with these fools? To give them a private show? And you don't even know what this mother fucker you're after even look like? *And...*" Mr. Frog sat up straight and glared at Jace. "You asking me to do this for free?" He waved his hand, looking away as if not being able to believe what he had just said. "Psh, get the hell out of here before I lay the smackdown on you."

The plan wasn't quite going smoothly, but Frog's cooperation was crucial for isolating his mark from the innocent civilians. For a moment, Jace considered slapping the guy and forcing him to do what he said. But then who knew how far that incident would escalate, and he couldn't risk his mark fleeing at any signs of trouble.

Frog flicked his wrist toward Jace. "I said git!"

Jace looked up at the two bouncer clones as they flanked them. "So, do you come out of a factory or something?"

One bouncer put a hand on Jace's shoulder. Jace immediately had the urge to have him reconsider that act. "What do you want us to do with him, Mr. Frog?"

Mr. Frog shrugged and waved them away. "I don't care. Beat his ass and toss him to the curb."

So much for the non-violent method.

Jace took a step toward Frog with an upraised hand, stopping the bouncers for a moment. "Quick question—how is your medical insurance?"

The two blinked for a moment, and then one reached out for a grab. Jace whipped his hand around, grabbing one of the guy's thumbs, and twisted it, joints popping with the motion. The bouncer reflexively fell to the side. He reached pathetically for his locked wrist and winced in pain.

Frog gasped from behind Jace, then yelled, "Kick his ass!"

That apparently got the two to snap into action. Even with his wrist painfully locked, the first guy tried to punch Jace while the second bouncer charged in. Because he was apparently so eager to feel more pain, Jace decided to give him exactly what he wanted. He bobbed the punch and leaped to the side, kicking off the second bouncer to push him back a step while positioning himself behind the first. With human reflexes leading the way, the first guy followed the twisting of his wrist while his weight came crumbling down. Jace planted his feet against the first bouncer's ribs and launched him in the air, crashing headfirst through a wall.

After Jace got back to his feet, the second guy lunged at him, throwing a wild right-left combo. A bob and a duck made the slow and clumsy attacks pass by harmlessly. While under the defenses of the barrel of muscle, Jace gave a small combo of his own, landing a quick right backhand and left uppercut in the guy's armpit. He lurched a little to the side and dropped his arm to cradle the injury.

The two were at a standoff for a brief moment, but the second guy continued his quest for pain. He swung at Jace again. Jace, being at least a foot shorter than the bouncer clones, easily ducked the punch, retaliating with another two-hit combo. This time on the bouncer's neck. Immediately, the bouncer visibly heaved and struggled to get a full breath while he held on to his throat.

Jace took a step forward to close the distance. Like a fool, the guy tried to attack again, as if he didn't quite get the fact that he was done for. Jace planted a left-right against the mid-section, then blasted the breath out of the bouncer with a hard right cross.

The fool had his defenses down, and he grabbed his throat and his solar plexus wobbling back and forth. After a few moments, he fell to the ground like a wet noodle.

Jace turned to face Mr. Frog once more, running his hand through his hair. "Room C. That's where I want the targets to be."

Mr. Frog, mouth ajar, stared wide-eyed at Jace. "Man, you need a job?"

The first bouncer leaped through the wall-door he made and growled in anger. Jace turned around to see the man start to grow in size and bulk. Horns sprouted from its head and its skin turned red. Claws pierced through the tips of its fingers, and the already tight shirt burst open from the increased size. The demon snarled, showing long fangs from the elongated mouth and jaw.

Mr. Frog sounded like he tripped over his coffee table at the sight of the beast. "What the hell?"

Jace recognized this type of demon and had battled more than a few on previous jobs. They used little to no magic. And though they were dangerous in human disguises, their real strength was in their devilish form. Fortunately for Jace, he had Brian's armor on, and that would hopefully stop any claw from piercing his body.

He had two problems though. One, the demon's leathery skin was durable and robust, and breaking through its hide would require a larger caliber weapon than Jace had strapped to his back. And if a bullet couldn't punch through the leather, then his fists would be even less effective.

His second problem was the mission. Even if he could blow holes in the demon, the mini-explosions could cause a full-on panic below. And if that happened, he would lose his target.

Regardless, Jace needed a plan.

The demon let out a wide swing, bringing its claws to bear. Jace used his small size to his advantage and ducked, then leaped to the side, both to get some distance away from the creature, and to get Mr. Frog out of its attack range. He even provoked it a little more by throwing a candle at the creature's eye. It whipped its head around and snarled.

The two stood off, staring hard at each other, allowing the thumps of the music below to be consciously heard. Those thumps gave Jace an idea, and he started to bob his head with the beat. He threw a couple of pillows at the creature, who swiped and shredded them in midair. Feathers scattered all over the room and fell lazily to the floor. Jace ducked and dodged another swipe, then leaped back to avoid getting skewered from a razor-toed kick. Jace tossed a book, a computer, and whatever he could grab at the creature, all of which were promptly destroyed.

An overhead chop split a table in two, and another claw ripped out a chunk in the wall. Growling in anger, it picked up and swung a couch like a cushioned club. Jace dodged one couch swing after another, then rolled under it when the demon threw it, all while keeping his head bobbing to the beat from below. It crashed against the outer window making a huge crack up the structure. During the roll, Jace grabbed one of the fallen seat cushions and closed the distance to the creature. He bobbed and leaped to the side to avoid being grabbed. Then the demon opened its maw and tried to bite down. Jace shoved the cushion in the monster's mouth, letting it chew on the pastel-colored fart container.

The demon fought back with wild and deadly swings. Jace bobbed one, then ducked another with a sidestep and a spin. As he spun around, Jace reached behind him and pulled out one of the guns, jammed the barrel against the cushion, then, with a final bob of his head, pulled the trigger. The pillow muffled the typically loud explosion, and the bang was concealed with the thumping beat of the music. Dark ooze dripped from the side of the creature's maw, but no spray of blood was visible, which meant the tough hide that could stop his bullet from punching through the skin also prevented it from making an exit wound. And the power of the gunshot probably melted or scrambled the monster's brain. Smoke came from its mouth, and dark blood trickled out of its nostrils. Its eyes rolled up into its skull, and it fell backward, crashing to the floor.

Jace reached behind him and put the gun back in its holster. He took a few steps toward the horrified Frog. "Whoever I mark, Room C. Get your dancers and bouncers ready."

"W-Who the hell are you?"

Jace didn't answer but put down a small stack of cash on the coffee table, turned and went toward the VIP elevator to return him to the ground floor. All the pieces were in place. All things considered everything was going according to plan. Now, it was time for him to find his target.

CHAPTER TWENTY-THREE

THE ELEVATOR DOORS OPENED, AND JACE STEPPED ONTO THE dance floor. The thumps and beats were louder, and the ambiance was darker, with colors diffused by lights in seemingly random spots. Colored lasers shot into the air, the trail being visible through a gently hidden smoke. Poles stretched from floor to ceiling at the corners of the room where live entertainers, stripped down to leave little to the imagination, rubbed their flesh on the steel in exotic ways for their pay. Each of the dancers reminded Jace of the ever-growing holographic ads he always saw in the cities, where beauty was promoted by unhealthy life habits and soul-crushing stereotypes all for an unrealistic body image.

As he walked toward the bar, Jace remembered that Erica loved to go dancing, and wondered if these were the places she patronized. With her drinking and physical playfulness, it wouldn't surprise him.

Jace tapped his ear after he ordered some ice water. "I'm in place. Everything ready on your end?"

"Just about," Brian replied over the com.

After finishing off his drink, Jace chewed on the lemon wedge.

The bartender leaned in, handing Jace another drink. "I got a message from Mr. Frog. He said to tell you his girls will be ready."

Jace looked around the room, noticing some girls against the wall looking as casual as possible, but their eyes were on him. Getting the participation from the owner meant it was time for the next step.

After a minute, Brian finally spoke again over the earpiece. "Okay, ready."

"Just a gentle mist," Jace said after putting the wedge in the glass.

"Got it."

Though it didn't register to him immediately, Jace started to notice a change in humidity in the room. The bouncing patrons and the various staff members, on the other hand, didn't seem to notice. One thing Jace did note was the absence of the telltale glow.

Jace sat at the bar with a barely touched glass of water in his hands. "I don't see anything. Are you sure it'll work?"

"I'm pretty sure," Brian replied. "It's a pretty diluted formula of the concentrated compound that you gave me. I mathematically calculated the amount needed for—"

"Okay, okay." Jace sipped his water and carefully scanned the room. Perhaps there were no demons on the dance floor. "Diluted, like not as strong? How subtle do you think the glow will be?"

"Very."

Jace nodded, then set his glass down and went toward the dance floor. He dodged heavy breathing, sweating people from every side while he made his way from one side of the room to the other. When he didn't see anything, frustration started to build up in Jace's chest. Just as he was about to bitch Brian out, something strange caught his attention.

Jace approached a guy with a sideways hat and gold necklace dancing with a girl way out of his league. Her lack of eye contact showed that she obviously wasn't enjoying herself too much. He tapped Mc Douche's shoulder to get his attention, and to better inspect the oddity he thought he saw. "Where did you learn how to dance?"

Mc Douche looked at Jace, and there it was—a subtle glow in his eyes. "Practice."

After Mc Douche turned back to his unhappy dance partner, Jace pointed to the guy, then took a few steps back to see the outcome. Not long after, a couple of ladies flanked the guy. They shooed off the girl, who looked offended for whatever reason, and they led him toward the back room.

Jace wondered how he was going to incapacitate the creatures without causing a ruckus. If a single monster did anything, it would put the entire nightclub at risk, and the Atmos candidate would be gone. Not only that but if this thing was indeed a vast source of magical power that could destroy cities with a single word or gesture, then he would have to make sure the demons didn't see or expect his ambush.

When Jace entered Room C, he found Mc Douche in a chair in the middle of the room tied up and blindfolded. The two ladies who escorted him teased him with their touches. Jace almost laughed at how inadvertently effective this idea was. The girls were doing most of the work for him.

Jace gave a silent hush as he entered the room. Knowing Brian would want more of a confirmation on the demon's identity, he reached in his backpack and took out one of the grenades. When it went off, Mc Douche glowed blue. Perfect.

Jace injected the tranquilizer in the creature's neck, knocking it out. He secured the creature in ties and put a better gag in its mouth, then paid the girls for their work. "Get one of the bouncers to set it aside in storage. And make sure this thing stays bound and gagged. It's very dangerous."

After placing the order, the girls went to work while Jace went back to the dance floor for another prey.

Seven more people with glowing eyes were found mingling in the crowd. The girls lured each of them into the back room, where they were tested with Brian's grenade. Of the seven, only four glowed. The ones that glowed were tranquilized and stored in the back. Those who didn't were given a pre-paid good time and taken to another room. Since he didn't know if any of his captives were the Atmos candidate, he took them alive to let The Order sort things out. So long as The Order didn't lay siege to the club and endanger these people, Jace felt good about how his plan unfolded.

Jace stalked around the dance floor, spotting another potential demon with a woman in red—a tall man wearing a dark suit, deeply tanned skin, slicked-back hair, and immaculate features. Maybe too immaculate?

He tapped his shoulder. "Hey."

The guy had an accent, like the end of every word was slightly drawn out. "Yah."

"Do you know how to get to the second floor?"

"How should I know?" The guy turned to continue his dance with Red.

Jace gave the signal and stepped back. Three girls approached the mark, then led him, and Red, to the back room.

"Shit." Jace followed, wondering what he should do about the woman he didn't expect to follow.

When he entered the room, the guy wasn't tied up, but he was blindfolded. He couldn't see Red, figuring she was just around the corner and out of sight, but the three dancers worked their magic on the mark.

When one of the girls noticed him, Jace brought his wrists together and shrugged, as if asking, "What about the hands?"

The dancer gave a slight single-shoulder shrug in reply.

Jace pointed toward where he believed Red was and covered his eyes for a moment.

The dancer nodded her head and seductively walked around the corner.

After a minute, Jace peeked his head around the corner. He had to hand it to the lady—she earned her pay. She sat in the Red's lap, finishing up her blindfold while the other two girls worked on the mark. He grabbed one of the grenades, as well as a tranquilizer, and entered the room as the three girls stepped back.

The mark blindly looked around, as if sensing something was going on. "Girls?"

Jace popped the grenade. The demon glowed blue, but Red was human.

The demon unexpectedly removed its blindfold and stared at Jace. "Oh, it's you."

Jace lunged to stab the demon with the tranquilizer, but the beast kicked himself back off the chair. When it landed on its back, it burst into a dark floating amorphous shape.

The girls screamed. Red took off her blindfold.

The shape, still glowing from Brian's grenade, went through the exit and started its escape through the crowds.

"Shit!" Jace ran out of the room to give chase, noting the path the shape took. "Brian, Plan C!"

"Plan C. Got it!"

Jace pushed and shoved his way through the crowds as the shape went out the main entrance. When Jace reached the outside, he saw the shape morph into a human-sized bird to gain altitude. If it wasn't for the glow, Jace might have lost the shape in the night sky. "Brian?"

"Okay, and...there!"

The streetlamps flickered for a moment. The demon bird smacked into an invisible barrier a few times, then it started to fly down the road while still trying to gain altitude.

Jace ran to the side of the building. "Start the car!"

The door opened, and the car started.

Jace leaped inside and sped off, tires screeching, while he reached up and closed the door.

After fishtailing on the main road, Jace spotted his mark. "There!" The demon bird tried to turn down a street, but the modified posts stopped all traffic going in and out. There were only two ways to go—to Jace and his car, or toward the park.

"Jace, something's wrong."

"Don't tell me that, Brian."

"The GR's automated system detected the glitch and is starting a restart sequence."

Jace swerved to avoid hitting a slow car. "What does that mean?"

"It means the gravity rails will shut down for a moment, and anything and everything can pass through again."

"Damn it." Jace reached behind him and grabbed one of his guns, rolled down the window, then started to fire at the demon bird.

"What are you doing? I thought you wanted to take it alive."

"Yeah." He fired off a few more rounds. "But I can't let this thing get away."

The streetlights flickered.

"Jace, the GR's are down."

Apparently, the bird noticed too, and it turned a corner.

Jace continued his chase but regretted it almost immediately as he sped down the one-way street. He brought his arm back inside just as the driver side mirror exploded from a passing vehicle. The car jerked when he went to the curb. Trash and other things smashed against the grill of the car, and the passenger side scraped against a building.

The creature turned again down a street, back toward the park. When Jace finally reached that road, he pursued his mark.

"Jace, it's getting altitude."

"I can see that." He brought his arm out the window again and fired. The slide of his gun drew back, and Jace tried to reach back to reload the weapon. "Hey, found a flaw in this reload harness." Jace hopped the middle divider to avoid the slow traffic. "I can't reload while sitting down." He tossed the gun to the passenger seat as he dodged an oncoming vehicle.

"I was afraid of that. The arms that come down and-"

"Later, Brian." Jace jumped the middle divider again and reached to grab the second gun. He strained his arm to reach the grip, but he couldn't grasp it.

"Is it me, or is that thing flying a little awkwardly?"

Jace leaned forward to get a better look. It did indeed seem to be a little unbalanced.

"Did you hit it?"

"I don't know, but there's the park." Jace grabbed the wheel with the opposite hand and reached back to get the other holstered weapon, then continued to fire wildly at the creature.

After swerving to avoid getting t-boned, Jace's car smacked the curb that led to the park, violently rocking him back and forth. When he recovered, he drove on the grass that went to the lake. He was out of room, and the monstrous bird flew over the water - something he didn't plan for.

Jace turned and skidded his car sideways as it drew closer to the shore. He took his time to aim at the fading glow of the bird, took a deep breath, and squeezed the trigger on an exhale. The slide of the gun slid back, and the monster bird jerked. Though barely visible, the shape fell to the earth.

He clenched his fist and shook it in victorious excitement. "Got it!" He started to drive around the lake, or he tried to as the tires spun out on the grass. He put more pressure on the accelerator only for him to realize that it made him more stuck.

"Damn it!" Jace grabbed his gear and got out of the car, then started running around the large body of water, the contact lenses adjusting so he could see in the dark.

"Jace, police reports are coming in about you."

"That's nice." Jace holstered his guns, hearing the spring and click of the reload harness while he sprinted around the perimeter of the lake. "How long?"

"I don't know. It sounds like they're still trying to piece everything together."

Jace panted as he arrived at what he believed was the monstrous bird's crash site. As he inspected the area, his suspicions were confirmed with a patch of missing grass, as if something big and heavy crashed into it. He knelt down to inspect the area. As he ran his fingers through the blades of grass, he discovered black patches of some sort of dark moisture were on the tips of his fingers.

"Is that blood?" Brian asked over the com.

"I think so." Jace looked up toward the bordering trees where the blood trail led. "How big are the woods?"

"Umm… Only a couple of acres."

"Only." Jace rubbed his thumb against the blood-covered fingertips. With the thrill of the hunt now upon him, Jace grinned and took out one of his guns.

In controlled breaths, Jace moved swiftly and silently, tracking his prey's movements through the woods. He noticed the blood spots were lessening as he moved on, indicating that the demon got its bleeding under control.

When the blood trail ended, Jace looked around to find any signs of the monster's path. Seeing nothing, he knelt at the last spot the demon blood was seen. Nothing. At least, nothing to work with.

Jace clenched his fist and gritted his teeth. There was no way he lost his prey. He looked around once more, and then he remembered something—the monster turned into a bird and must have taken to the sky.

Just as he looked up, a man-sized shape of a bird swooped down on the attack and smashed into Jace's chest with a deep thud. The hit launched Jace off his feet, flying back, eventually sliding on the grass and losing his grip on his gun in the process. After the hit, the monster returned to the night sky with a screech, the glow from the grenade gone.

Lying flat on his back, Jace grasped his chest in pain. He exhaled, catching his breath after such a brutal hit.

"Holy smokes, Jace. Are you okay?"

After another cough, Jace rolled to his hands and knees, looking down at himself to assess the damage. His shirt and jacket had massive gashes in it, but he didn't see any blood. "Your armor probably saved my life." His eyes went to the night sky. "The damn thing isn't glowing anymore. I can't see it." As he began to rise, he got hit from behind with a glancing blow. He spun in midair, eventually crashing into a bush. The creature again flew away with a screech.

"Get out of there, Jace!"

The hit wasn't as bad as the first, but it still left him a little disorientated. He got to his feet and took a step toward his escape route, but then he stopped for a moment.

"What are you doing? Get out of—"

"Shh!" Jace knelt, keeping his eyes in the sky, but more importantly, his ears open. He took out one of Brian's grenades and held it at the ready.

A flap caught Jace's attention, and he saw the dark shape swooping in for another attack. He threw it at the demon bird and rolled out of the way. The device flashed, and the demon screeched. Jace turned to see the once black demon bird glowing in the night sky and deftly between the trees.

Jace ran to his fallen gun and started his chase through the woods. "Those grenades are saints!" He leaped over a line of foliage stopped to regain his mark. Jace looked around and listened.

Snapping and creaking caught Jace's attention. After a loud crack, he saw a barren, dead tree falling toward him. It was too wide to dodge. All Jace could do was duck. A branch or something smacked his head, and he fell to his back.

When he started to regain his senses, Jace painfully sat up to assess the situation. The bad news was he had lost his gun. The good news was the tree was too large, and the top caught on something to stop it a couple of feet from the ground, which saved his life.

He slowly blinked to try to get his wits around him. Instead of hearing any crisp sounds, the throbbing in his head had him hear a muffled screech.

Jace started to crawl as best as he could from under the tree when the glowing blue shape landed hard on the tree trunk. He looked up at the amorphous monster, who returned his gaze with deep yellow orbs. The two went motionless locking stares for a couple of heartbeats.

The creature reached with a talon. Jace kicked himself out from under the dried trunk, flipping himself back to his feet. The creature screeched in protest then lunged forward. Jace met the attack with a charging leap of his own.

A bladed tentacle-like appendage formed from inside the black shape and slashed at Jace. He lowered his shoulder and pivoted to the side, his jacket suffering a gash in return, and the two collided hard in the air. Instead of passing through the creature, he found a solid corporeal object, which he pushed back against the tree trunk.

The creature didn't seem as dazed like Jace had hoped. After it bounced off the dead tree, it immediately started its attack routine, lashing out with sharp claws, bladed tentacles, and a snapping beak. Even with Jace dodging and bobbing, spinning and weaving, a few glancing blows found their way against Jace's armor.

Before Jace could get any solid footing, the creature grew out yet another set of arm-like appendages, pressing Jace even harder. A slashing limb cut deep into the armor. It felt like it ripped through and slashed into his skin while a thrust pierced through the protective gear just above the shoulder. He was impaled and in trouble.

The demon morphed the blade into a barbed hook, then it started to retract the blade, ripping out flesh and muscle in the process.

Jace screamed in pain as he held onto the barbed appendage. Instead of fighting the pull, Jace went with it, leaping toward the monstrous bird-demon, smashing his knuckle into the its beak. It seemed a little stunned, and the barbed appendage ripped free from Jace's shoulder.

He fell to the ground, rolling as best as he could to get behind the creature, then got to his feet and started to get some distance from the monster. The beast shifted once more, taking the shape of a long, slender bipedal creature with huge fangs and sharp claws.

With no signs of the demon slowing down, Jace was in trouble. He was losing blood, and he had a series of miscellaneous injuries. His thoughts were on escape and survival.

In a single bound, the demon closed the distance, swiping at Jace with its newly formed claws. When Jace tried to leap back to dodge, he smacked his back against the fallen tree.

The monster's other claw came up high and swiped down hard toward Jace. Knowing the tree was slightly elevated from the ground, Jace knelt and leaped backward on his back under the fallen tree. A few large chunks of tree trunk fell to the ground from the slash.

Jace got to his feet as the monster went low to chase him from under the tree. Jace didn't turn to flee like he originally planned. An idea popped in his head, and he charged at the demon. He leaped over a swinging claw and landed on the makeshift bridge to look at the chunk the demon broke away the dead tree trunk. The claw marks were more than a few inches deep, almost half of the diameter. He hoped it would be enough.

Jace leaped as high as he could and pressed down hard against the trunk at the claw mark. Though it cracked and creaked, it didn't budge.

The creature flipped to its back and screeched below him. A claw slashed into Jace's boot, and he felt a sting in his ankle.

Jace leaped again, growling on his descent. He put all of his strength on his landing. The tree snapped in half, and Jace painstakingly fell face-first to the ground, crashing hard on his injured shoulder.

He tried to catch his breath while he winced in pain from his shoulder. When he tried to get up, it hung awkwardly, and the limb began to numb.

Jace got to his feet and turned to face the demon. There it was, pinned under the weight of the dead tree, branches punching through the once amorphous shape. Its high-pitched cries told Jace it was probably in more pain than he was.

He scanned the area, locating his missing gun near the demon's feet. He picked it up and approached the creature, climbing on the dead tree to get a look at its face. It hissed and cried, howled and screeched. When he finally stood on top of the tree, he gazed down at the pathetic creature. It was in the shape of an unremarkable human with no distinguishable features.

Jace observed the monster for many heartbeats as it tried to push the trunk off of it. He found it odd that the demon didn't shape change or turn into that amorphous blob that escaped the nightclub. And an important thing Jace noticed was it didn't use magic.

"Show me," Jace said as he stomped on the trunk. "Show me that destructive power the Atmos has."

Then, he waited, for an earthquake, a lightning bolt, even for a gentle breeze. Nothing.

Feeling he had his answer, Jace brought forth his gun and shot the creature in the head. He didn't stop with one round, but unloaded the entire clip, blowing holes in demon flesh and the ground beneath. When the slide came back, Jace relaxed his arm.

"Brian, I got it." He climbed down the tree, but almost fell from the sudden dizziness and pain that almost overtook him.

A huge exhale came from the earpiece. "Holy smokes, Jace. You'll be the death of me."

Jace holstered the gun, looked back toward the distant lake, and sighed. He grabbed his left shoulder, noticing the computer thing Brian had given him crushed and slashed, cradled his broken arm and limped back to the lake.

The numbness in Jace's arm started to wear off when he finally broke through the forest. His ankle pulsed with agonizing pain, his head ached, and his chest and back were stiff and sore. More than a few occasions, Jace had to stop and rest. Otherwise, he was going to pass out. On top of that, his stomach growled loudly and painfully.

Across the lake were the strobe lights of police cars surrounding his stuck vehicle, and a modern hover vehicle flew around with a spotlight around the area searching for something.

"Brian, what's this?"

"Umm… It looks like they found your car."

He sighed, then continued to limp painfully around the lake.

"Jace, I found a bunch of reports of a car speeding recklessly through the city firing a gun. They say they're looking for a guy on drugs in a stolen car."

"Any injuries or casualties?"

"Not that I found. What are you going to do?"

Jace nodded as he approached the yellow tape that marked the police perimeter. "Talk to them." He ducked under it and started to make his way toward the car when a police officer finally noticed him.

"Hey, hey!" The officer approached Jace with a hand up to stop him. "You're not allowed back here. You…" His voice trailed off as he stopped and stared wide-eyed.

Jace continued to limp forward. "Can you get my car unstuck?"

As if putting two and two together, the officer drew his gun and pointed it at Jace. "Hold it right there!" That got the attention of other police officers, and they followed suit to back up their comrade.

Jace stopped his advance. "Is there a problem, officer?"

"Hands in the air!"

Jace blinked for a moment after a brief moment of dizziness washed over him. He scanned the area, noting approximately a dozen people with their weapons pointed at him. "You should have enough." Jace slowly grabbed the chain around his neck and took out the pendant. "Get my car loose and get me a snack."

CHAPTER TWENTY-FOUR

AFTER BEING INTERVIEWED BY THE LOCAL LAW ENFORCEMENT throughout the night, Jace told them about the nightclub, and the detainees he had in the storage locker. That's when he was informed that someone from The Order already came and took them away. He figured it was that scout that reported Jace's progress, so his job was done.

He got into his car and sat for a long moment, taking in the aches and pains from the fight.

A police officer leaned down to inspect Jace. "Are you okay to drive, sir?"

"The paramedics set my arm and patched up my shoulder. I'll be fine."

"You should let the paramedic take you to the hospital."

"No need." Jace started the car. "I ate that protein bar, remember? I'll be fine. Now close the door for me."

The officer paused for a moment, then pushed the door down. It closed, the mirror connected by a couple of thin wires rattling against the side, and Jace sped off.

Brian spoke over the com. "So you got off scot-free?"

"Yep."

"How? I mean… How? They had you dead-to-rites on all sorts of charges."

"My rank in The Order gives me power over local law enforcement."

"What?"

"Yeah. Hey, program the map thing to take me to the hotel."

"Sure, Jace." After a few taps over the com, the GPS updated. "Hey, if they basically control the police, what else do they control?"

"What do you mean?"

"Like, what about the media?

That gave Jace pause before he repeated, "What do you mean?"

"I mean… hold on. Maya woke up."

"We can talk later."

"Okay, Jace."

Jace tapped his ear and disconnected the com.

———

When Maya first saw Jace, it looked like she almost burst into tears. She ran up and hugged him, which made his numb limbs feel a little warm. He smiled as her hugs always made him feel better. Brian walked in the room, he paused in stunned horror as he stared at Jace. Perhaps he looked worse than he felt.

For the next few days, Maya waited on Jace hand and foot, getting him everything he needed, even when he protested, saying, "I can take care of myself." She wasn't having any of it. And throughout that, Jace had an insatiable appetite, probably since he was sitting around and doing nothing. Because of his painful hunger, he didn't complain at the burnt toast or runny eggs she served him.

During that time, Jace thought about what Brian said. Does The Order control the media? Other problems and inconsistencies came to mind, forming a pool of doubt in his head. The orphanage took Jessica and Brittaney, but The Order controls the orphanage. Did The Order give a command to take his friends? How come they test kids? And why didn't The Order do anything about the Sanctuary of Orphaned Children's gang problem? Were they a part of The Order's plan? It all seemed totally ridiculous. Too many things had to happen for one entity to control everything that happened in his life. Still, a seed of doubt was planted and grew in his mind.

Before the next weekend, the time The Order was to attack the nightclub, Jace felt fit enough to be exercising once more. His shoulder scarred up, and his arm felt like it was back to normal. The hole through his ankle and the deep gash in his scalp were healed too. Jace wondered if being dipped in Erica's goo had anything to do with his rapid recovery. But even with him being up and running again, and though he didn't want to admit it, Maya taking care of him made his spirits sore. The feeling gave him something he lost a long time ago, and she slowly filled that void - family.

Brian had been hard at work on Jace's gear during the week of downtime, fiddling with the reload harness and backpack, downstairs working on the car, and what Jace guessed was another version of protective gear. He even worked around Maya, which didn't please Jace too much. By the time Jace was able to question him, the reload harness looked quite a bit different, and he was eager to show it off.

He held up the harness, his face beaming with pride. "I'm still working on some of the mechanics, but I think I have the multi-ammo function done."

"Really?" Jace sat down opposite of Brian and inspected the contraption.

"Yeah." Brian set the harness down and grabbed the backpack. "You'll have less storage, but the ammo feed will come from the bottom rather than the top." He attached the backpack to the harness and picked up one of the guns and showed Jace the modifications. "I installed a sensor switch that you flick with your thumb. And when you reload your weapon..." He put the butt in the reload port. The backpack made some mechanical noise, but the spring and snap eventually sounded. "It'll detect the setting and load with the appropriate ammo." He pulled back the slide showing his usual ammo.

"What about the ammo already loaded?"

"Ah. See that was a problem." Brian adjusted his glasses and flicked the thumb switch. "I made some modifications to the clip chamber. So when you reload with a different setting..." He put the butt of the gun back on the reload harness. Again, the backpack made some mechanical noise, like metal grinding, then the spring and snap. "It removes the ammo and loads in the new." He pulled back the slide to show a different round in the chamber.

"Brian, you're a genius!" Jace took the gun and brought the harness closer to him. He flicked the switch and swapped the ammo. Though it took longer than he originally wanted, it was still so much quicker than doing it by hand. "How many different ammo types?"

"Well, three so far. I have standard, exploding, and incendiary."

Jace pulled back the slide to look at the third ammo type. "A fucking genius."

"How are you feeling? I mean…" Brian gestured toward the sling.

"Oh, it's fine." Jace looked over his shoulder to check on Maya. She sat in the front room. "I wear it to make her feel better, but I'm good to go." He inspected the gear. "Alright, I have to pack up to do that mission I told you about, then I'm going to report to The Order."

"I still think you should be taking it easy. You looked like hell just last week."

"I know." Jace stood up. "It's an easy mission, but I have until tomorrow afternoon to get those radar things up."

"That's a strange timeline. Why's that?"

Jace shrugged. "Doesn't matter to me. If I take a job, I get it done."

"Oh, and I have this…" Brian pulled out a dark gray long-sleeved shirt with straps dangling around different sections. "Here. Try it one."

The texture felt a lot like scales and chain, and it folded over his hand rather nicely. He stared at the fabric that was no thicker than his own t-shirt, then to Brian for a moment. "It's nice, but not really my style."

"Just put it on."

Giving in to the request, Jace removed the sling and slid the shirt on. At first, it was very loose-fitting, and it draped over his body as if it were three sizes too big. Then it started to tighten, a pinpoint light on the straps blinking in the meantime. Finally, it stopped shrinking, and it felt firm yet snug against Jace's chest and arms. "What the hell is this?"

"Your armor! I've been working on this bad boy for weeks, and this is where most of your deposit last week went to." Brian took out a pair of pants made of the same material. "See, I took the concept of an old chainmail style shirt and combined it with the idea of Kevlar, used the fitting technique you see in many clothing stores, and applied that with the A-06 flex mesh the government wishes that was top secret, then-"

"Wait, wait..." Jace pinched the neck of the shirt, feeling how thin it was. "This is my armor? What kind of protection does it have?"

"Pretty much the same as your other suit. Can probably stop a .45 caliber." Brian snapped back one of the straps, and it released its fitting grip.

"Probably?"

"Yeah, well..." Brian adjusted his glasses. "I haven't really tested it yet."

"You haven't tested it." Jace looked skeptically at the thin meshed gear. "Well, I guess I'll have to test it for you." He headed to the backroom to start his packing, patting Brian on the shoulder as he walked by.

———

After getting his gear rounded up, Jace said his goodbyes to Maya and headed down to the car. The weight on Jace's injured shoulder didn't bother him like he thought it would. He reminded himself to take it easy because he didn't want to see the look on Maya's face when he first entered the hotel again. Perhaps it was time to slow down, and maybe get a place of their own. After all, Maya was still a kid, and she needed a more stable life than going from hotel to hotel.

While he walked through the lobby, Brian ran up to Jace in impatient excitement. "I found her!"

That startled Jace. After the reflexive recoil, he turned around to face Brian and glared at him. The amount of potential "hers" flooded Jace's mind. "Who?"

Brian handed Jace a box. "Here. Since your other PPC broke with that shapeshifter, I got you a new one."

"Who?"

"Well, put it on and find out."

Jace sighed in frustration, then put on the bracer and ring combination. When he flicked on the power and opened his hand, a holographic image of a woman with brown eyes and short, brown hair appeared.

At first, Jace didn't recognize her, but a key detail brought his memory back to years passed—a very bright blouse. "Claire!"

Brian beamed with pride. "Yep! It was tough. Her info was deeply buried."

"W-what..." Jace took a moment to recompose himself and to get his emotions in check. "What about Jessica?"

Brian shook his head. "Still looking."

Jace stared at the holographic image and looked at the information around the picture, noting the location and miscellaneous details of her life and residency. "It's pretty far." He considered her region and started to plan his route: Mission, The Order, Claire. Hopefully, she wouldn't be brainwashed like Brittaney. Seeing enough for now, Jace closed his hand, gave a smiling nod to Brian, and continued his trek down the hotel lobby.

Brian escorted Jace to the car, which was still scratched, dented, and beat up all around. His heart sank at the sight of the damage, but at least Brian reattached the mirrors and noticeably repaired the significant problems.

Jace tossed his bag in the back and got in the car, starting the engine. Brian climbed in the passenger seat. "I uploaded and updated everything to your PPC and GPS. And one more thing..." Brian grabbed a large bag from the backseat and pulled out a metal sensory rod for his mission. "I've been studying these things like crazy during your recovery. I don't know what this thing is, but I haven't seen anything like it before."

Jace eyed the metal object for a moment. "What do you mean?"

"Well..." Brian adjusted his glasses. "I mean, I don't know what this is."

"That's the scanner thing for the job."

"Oh." Brian stared at the device for a moment. "This isn't like any sensor I've ever seen or heard of." Brian returned the device to the bag and put it in the backseat. "See if you can get an extra or something. I'd love to take it apart and study it." He brushed his hands on his shirt as he continued, "I'll let you do your job. Call if you run into trouble." He got out of the car and turned back to face Jace. "And take it easy. I'm sure the A-06 flex mesh will protect you and all, but you're still recovering from your injuries." He shut the door and took a step back to watch while Jace drove off.

———

After a day and a half drive, Jace pulled over to the shoulder of the road at the city limits of his mission target. Throughout the entire trip, his thoughts were mostly about Brittaney and Claire. Like he had done whenever he took a break from his trip, Jace opened his hand to look at the holographic file Brian had made for him about Claire. Worries filled his heart. Worries and fear. He hoped she wouldn't end up like Brittaney.

After a deep, calming breath, Jace closed his hand and focused on the mission, and drove into the city.

Buildings were like fingers of glass and steel reaching for the clouds. Colorful lights from clubs and casinos lit up the strip, large holographic ads plagued the optics, and a lot of aero vehicles flew on the skyway. The sidewalks were packed with patrons as they went about their way, going to bars, restaurants, movies, or whatever else people do on their time off.

Though the job wasn't located in a hostile area like the last one, Jace still had to park his car and walk for a couple of minutes to reach the correct building. It was a nasty-looking thing, like a dead tooth in the mouth filled with white teeth. It was an old three story tall run-down building. A rusted spike fence surrounded it to prevent anyone from entering the property. Not that anyone would. The first floor was sun-bleached green, and each section between levels looked like it had a two-inch lip made of white brick. The second and third floor were made of orange bricks. Near the roof was another lip that spanned the entire perimeter of the building. The doors and windows on the first floor were boarded over with a yellow sign reading, "This property is condemned by the State and Local authorities. Do not enter."

Jace caught a whiff of something strong yet stale, and the scent grew stronger as he got closer to the building. He peeked through a crack in the window. The inside looked gutted, leaving only the main support beams and frayed electrical lines behind. Mold stretched from the rotted floor, over and around the old furniture, and reached up the paint-peeled walls. The buzzing of flies and the scouring of rats caught Jace's attention as they ran freely inside the abandoned space.

The fact that he couldn't just climb the stairs made Jace start to sigh, but the stench made him gag. He covered his nose and mouth and took a few steps away to catch his breath. When he was able to control his gag reflex, Jace inspected the exterior of the building once more. The sun was still rising, but it was almost noon. He was running out of time.

Jace adjusted his fingerless gloves, pulled the straps of his backpack to assure its security, then ran his fingers through his hair. After rocking his shoulders a little bit, Jace leaped off the door frame, giving him just enough height to grip the ledge of the first tier of white bricks to start his climb.

Jace sat in a second-story window frame for a moment for a rest, his feet dangling in the open with a spiked fence below. He briefly studied the surrounding buildings, again wondering why The Order chose this particular structure.

A boy's voice called out from below, "Hey, what are you doing?"

Jace gazed down at the boy, who stared up at him from the sidewalk. "Uh, exercising."

The boy found it wise to stuff a tiny finger in his nasal cavity. "Why?"

"I, uh...like to climb."

Brian spoke over the earpiece. "You say something, Jace?"

Jace pointed at the child. "Not you. Some kid on the street saw me climbing." Jace got to his feet while the child continued to stare. "Stay quiet. I need to focus."

The boy called out from below, "Why?"

Jace didn't answer. He shimmied himself up the window frame and reached up to grab a handhold to the third floor. The brick he held onto slid from the wall, and Jace found himself plummeting toward the street. He reached out and grabbed the bay window frame. It cracked and started to crumble but held firm as it stopped his freefall to the concrete. His feet dangled freely as he took a moment to take control.

Brian gasped over the earpiece.

The boy called out, "Are you okay, mister? I'm going to get my mom!"

"No, don't!" Jace turned to look at the boy, but he had already run off shouting for his mother. "Great." He pulled himself back to the window and sat down, giving his palms a break. "Just great." Jace looked down below at the spiked fence he almost landed on.

Though he was sitting still, Jace felt like he was shifting around, or moving backward. Then he noticed the ledge he sat on had started to collapse. Jace shot his arms out and planted his hands on the window frame just as the bottom fell away. The bricks impacted the concrete, shattering into many pieces.

Suspending himself in midair, Jace took a moment to stabilize his position. He half-heartedly laughed to himself the close call. Even with the A-0-whatever armor on, he could still have impaled himself on that fence or get crushed bones from the fall.

Once his hand and feet were planted on the window frame, he plotted another route to the roof. Getting another path planned, he continued his climb.

Jace heard the shouts of the kid and a woman from around the corner. Since he didn't want any more unwanted attention, Jace recklessly launched himself up, almost accidentally away from the building to reach the roof. Just as he realized he was away from every grip and hold, Jace reached up and grabbed onto the gutter, which creaked and bent under the weight.

"This way, Mommy! Hurry!"

Not taking a moment to make sure the gutter would stay connected to the side, Jace pulled himself up and over the ledge and onto the rooftop.

"There!" the boy exclaimed.

"Where?" a woman asked.

"He was right there. I swear, Ma. I swear!"

"I don't think anyone is there."

"But he was!" The kid's voice grew quieter as they walked away, the boy frantically trying to convince his mother of what he saw.

Jace sighed in relief. "Alright, Brian. I'm up." Jace looked at his achy and torn up fingers, then shook his hands to loosen them up.

"That armor is pretty flexible. Good work. Now, what can you do to help me free-climb?"

"What do you mean 'free-climb'?"

Jace got up and cautiously made his way to the center of the questionably stable rooftop while taking off his backpack. "Weren't you watching through the lenses?"

"Yeah. That was super scary!"

"Free-climb. Like to quickly scale a building without the use of a rope or whatever." Jace started to take out the sensor units from his backpack. "Out-of-the-blue stuff, like I'm chasing something down, or something is chasing me."

"Yeah, yeah, yeah. Umm, I don't know. Let me give it some thought."

He pulled out the metal sensor unit, extended the telescoping pole, planted the node in the middle, then turned it on. "Maybe some sort of retractable claw or something in the gloves." He started on the six smaller sensors, lining them up with the lasers that came out of the center node, doing his best to leap or step over the holes in the rooftop. "And maybe the boots, too." Jace stood up and looked at his work. Everything seemed to be in place. "Plenty of time."

When Jace placed the last device, the central node split in half, then popped up an inch. Lights from each device turned on, looking as if they connected in some sort of pattern.

"That's new." He shrugged, put his backpack on and patted his hands together to brush off the dust. "Mission accomp—"

The floor below him gave out, causing him to crash straight through the rotted rooftop. He tried to grab the roof, but that immediately crumbled. His body jerked when his back hit and broke through a horizontal beam. He crashed through one floor after another until he hit the first floor.

Jace had a moment to regain his wits. That moment didn't last long before that section fell apart too, and he smashed hard into the basement below.

Jace started to roll to his hands and knees, but the building itself began to collapse. A falling brick flew towards Jace's head, almost as if it was aimed, smashed into his face. In a blink of an eye, the loud explosion of a collapsed building went silent, and the early afternoon sky turned pitch black.

———

With how dark it was when he came to, Jace didn't know if his eyes were open, or if there was simply no light. All he knew was that his ears rang loudly, his head pulsed with pain, and he could feel the crust of dried blood on his face. His back was flat on the ground with what felt like rotted wood and soggy drywall trying to pin him down.

With a gasping push, Jace's arms punched through the rubble on top of him. From there, he started to wiggle out of his little hole, finally bursting his face from the rubble tomb he almost found himself in. He gasped and coughed, falling on his back once more to recompose himself and to figure out what happened.

The voice of Brian calling out gradually replaced the ringing in his ears. "Jace! Are you okay? Speak to me!"

"Yeah." Jace gave another cough. "I'm alive."

"What happened?"

"Good question." Jace looked up through the hole he made when he fell—a hole that stretched all the way from the basement and through the roof. The afternoon sky was replaced by a star-covered night. "The damn building decided to show me a short cut to the ground floor. Fucking rooftop gave out, and I took half the building with it. Why the fuck does The Order want a damn sensor thing here anyways?" He coughed again while he stared at the night sky. "How long was I out?"

"Hours. It's the middle of the night. I thought you were dead, Jace."

"No such luck." Jace rolled over and got to his feet. "I can't see shit. Turn on these damn contacts."

The darkness was replaced with the monochromatic shades of black and gray, but at least he had depth.

Jace stretched, trying to assess any injuries he sustained. Though some of his muscles ached and his head pulsed with pain, the only real discomfort he had at that time was a grumbling stomach.

"I'm glad you're okay. I was really worried."

"I'm fine." Jace shook his hands and feet to ward away the numbness. "Well, that shirt you made stopped anything from piercing my skin, so there's that. But I think a damn brick fell on my head."

"The all-mighty Jace, slayer of demons and monsters of every shape and size, fearless and all-powerful, taken down by a single brick."

"Oh, shut it." Jace approached a window and started to rip off some of the wood that blocked his exit.

Brian chuckled over the earpiece. "I'm sorry, I just think it's—"

"I said shut it!" Jace gritted his teeth as he let his anger play out on a particularly stubborn piece of wood. He finally ripped it out with a good chunk of the window frame and tossed it to the side. After climbing through the window, Jace stumbled a bit while he walked across the street, then he sat down to take a moment to recover. After taking a deep breath, he decided to try and lighten the mood, feeling a little guilty for snapping at Brian. "Damn brick got away, too." He gave a strained chuckle.

"You don't let anything get away."

"Yeah. That brick will be the first. It will probably tell his friends. But the next rock thing that threatens me, I'm going to kick the shit out of it." He was about to lay down on his back but noticed the roof of the building he just made an elevator shaft for glowed in a pale white light.

"What is that?"

"I don't know." The glow went from white to yellow, and Jace got to his feet while staring up at the strange phenomena. The light faded. After many heartbeats, Jace sighed. "Well, whatever it was, it's gone n—"

The building exploded! Jace flew through a window behind him, and he tumbled over the furniture inside, finally coming to a stop with a chair and a lamp lying on top of him.

After getting his senses back, Jace slowly rolled over to his hands and knees. The sounds of crashing wood and stone came from across the street. Jace got up and made his way to the newly formed door to see what was going on.

Across the street was a towering, glowing pillar that pulsed back and forth from white to yellow. Around the pillar, large pieces of earth were ripped from the ground and floated around the glow. The stones orbited around the strange beam, smacking into one another. But instead of crashing and crumbling, they molded together, as if they were made of some sort of liquid or putty. The mountainous tower grew taller and taller as the arm-like appendages stretched out into the night sky. Then the bottom of the rocky structure split vertically down the middle, creating a sizeable bipedal-like creature. The white and yellow glow pierced through the cracks of the stone as its arms formed large chunks of rocks at the ends that resembled fists.

It lurched forward, slamming its fists into the ground. A parked car was flattened, and the roadway split and crumbled under the sheer power of the hit. The light inside the monster pulsed with energy as the stone skin flexed. Then it's mighty leg stepped out of the hole the creature created and stood up straight, standing taller than the three-story building next to it.

"Jace, where did that come from?"

The creature let out a mighty roar that sounded like grinding stone that was probably heard miles around, shattering some of the windows in the area.

Jace gulped, feeling the dryness of his throat, and he shook his head. "I don't know, Brian. I don't know."

CHAPTER TWENTY-FIVE

THE ROCK CREATURE SMASHED ITS FIST IN THE GROUND AGAIN, cracking and crumbling the concrete in a deep web of thin canyons.

"Jaaaace," Brian said over the earpiece with more than a little uncertainty in his voice.

Jace didn't answer. All he could do for the moment was stare up at the forty-five-foot monstrosity and listen to his racing heart. He tried to stay calm while he studied it as best as he could while he formulated a plan.

Like he didn't question it just a moment ago, Brian still asked, "Where did that thing come from?"

"I don't know." Jace climbed out the window. "Wait a minute..."

"You got something?"

More pieces to his uncertain puzzle started to come together. "Brian, do you remember that attack on the city when we met up again?"

"Uh, yeah. Kind of."

"Find out as much as you can about this thing, starting with that attack."

"Shouldn't you call for backup somehow?"

"I have a feeling the backup I'd be calling is responsible for this... this thing."

The monster swiped at a building next to it, cleaving it in half. As the top half scattered across the ground, the beast pummeled the rest of the building into rubble.

"I don't know, Jace. What are you going to do?"

"Not a clue. I'm kind of making it up as I go along."

People from the surrounding buildings started to flee from their respective homes to escape the rock creature. Jace considered his situation—this was a new foe, he had no information, the monster had the power to decimate a building with ease, and innocent lives were at risk.

He locked his eyes on the monster and huffed. "It'll have to do." Jace drew his pistols and started to unload on the beast. Each round popped and crumbled a tiny bit of the creature's exterior. It turned it's monstrous rock-like head and stomped toward Jace. The creature was surprisingly fast, but the rock foot crashed just in front of him, his hair blowing back from the wind, with dust and dirt flying in his face.

An overhead chop came down. Jace leaped to the side only for him to roll again to avoid a second slam. Though he wanted to put more holes in the creature, Jace was purely on the defensive.

The creature swept its mighty arm, uprooting everything in its path. Jace put his guns away, getting one of the craziest and stupidest ideas he ever had. He sprinted toward a wall, running from another swipe, then he leaped off the wall and up into the air as high as he could. The fist barely missed Jace as he flew up and over the attacking limb. Jace reached out and grabbed the monster's appendage, landing on the rock arm.

Jace held on tight with both hands, staying in a kneel to maintain a better balance. When the monster paused its movements, Jace sprinted forward, climbing up the forearm to the elbow. Before the creature flailed again, Jace went to his hands and knees to grab onto another handhold. Just in time too, as the arm swatted aside a streetlamp.

Figuring it was a good a time as any, Jace grabbed one of his guns and shot at the creature's elbow. It seemed as if nothing happened. Then a subtle glow pierced through the cracks just as the slide of the gun came back.

The monster boomed a thunderous roar as Jace returned the gun to the reload harness. Jace almost lost his grip when the monster suddenly raised its arm into the air. His heart skipped a beat as the arm jerked to a stop high into the sky, and his eyes went wide as he looked down to the ground some six or seven stories below. Then his eyes went to a multi-story building close by. Perhaps in jumping distance?

The monster lurched forward as it began to bring its fist down like a club. Jace leaped off, hoping to land on the roof or at least through a window. Instead, his back smacked against the wall, and he crashed through some sort of awning or canopy. The impact still hurt and being entangled in the awning cloth prevented him from rolling on impact to absorb the fall.

After finally getting the cloth out of his face, Jace staggered to his feet and began shooting at the beast, hoping to whittle down its stone armor.

The stone beast smashed the front face of the building he leaned against. Leaping out of the wall of falling rubble, Jace looked up and noticed the attention of the monster started to focus elsewhere—a woman holding what looked like a baby still in their apartment.

"Shit!" Jace got back to his feet, flicked the ammo switch on his guns, then reached back to let the harness swap his ammunition. Each second felt like five as the harness continued to click. "Come on..." The monster took another step toward the building. The harness continued to swap the ammo. "Come on, damn it!"

The spring clicked. Jace whipped his gun around and took aim.

The monster brought its arm back to wipe out the building.

Jace pulled the trigger, almost losing the grip on his guns. Each round gave a surprising amount of recoil, and Jace briefly wondered what the kickback would be like if Brian hadn't improved the recoil resistance. When the bullets hit, a booming explosion almost deafened his ears. Huge chunks of the monster blew apart with each high explosive round that hit. By the time the gun slides drew back, the guns smoked and sizzled.

The giant creature paused with the hits as a little bit more light escaped the chest chassis, but only for a moment as the beast followed through with its attack. In the blink of an eye, the entire second story was swept away.

Jace fought back the urge to search the rubble for survivors, but he knew more people would be in serious danger every second the stone monster stood.

He flicked the ammo toggle to the third setting, feeling the spring click just as the first floor of the building was destroyed. He fired at its feet, hoping to either slow it down, get its attention, or both. One round after another hit and red-blue molten liquid sprayed all over the immediate area. Parts of the rock sizzled, but Jace could see some of the stone melt away. Finally, his guns clicked empty.

"Brian, tell me you got something!" Jace alternated the ammo type when he reloaded - explosive rounds in one gun, incendiary in the other. Then he charged the creature.

"I don't know. I'm having a difficult time even finding out how it got in the middle of the city."

Jace shot at the beast at different spots around the abdomen and chest. "Keep looking!" He lifted his arms as the rain of stone and fire fell onto him. He felt a burn on the back of his hand and heard a sizzle as a small piece of molten stone smacked his skin, burning through the fingerless gloves like they were nothing.

The monster turned its attention on Jace and started to approach him. Knowing his attacks hardly seemed to slow the creature down, Jace turned and ran.

He leaped over a little fence and slid across a parked car's hood in a driveway. The monster behind him swatted aside everything in its path, flattening or destroying whatever it touched. When he was far enough away, Jace turned and fired a couple more rounds.

After a few iterations, the slides of his guns drew back. Jace ducked as the monster kicked a car. It spun end over end in midair toward Jace. He fell to the ground to take whatever cover he could just as it crashed behind him. Glass sprayed all over him.

When he looked up at the monster, he saw it picking up a van to hurl toward Jace.

"Stone golem!" Brian exclaimed.

Jace dove to the side, landing hard on the ground when the van landed nearby. When it was clear, Jace didn't waste any time and got to his feet to run away. "What's that?"

"Uhh…" Even with the loud slamming of stone to stone, Jace still heard Brian tapping away on his computer.

Reloading his guns with standard ammo, Jace prepared for another barrage. With no answer coming from Brian, he turned and fired at spots he shot and melted. Though he hoped the bullets would punch through the weakened spots, the stone chest was just too thick.

Jace leaped up and over the thrown van and continued his run as the monster continued its chase.

"Jace, I think I got something. I'm reading something about a core."

"More info." He turned and fired a few more rounds.

"I don't know. This article just talks about some vague method on how to create one. It hints at the core being the source that holds the golem together."

"Maybe that strange light?"

"I don't know. Maybe."

"Good enough for me." Jace skid to a stop and turned to face the charging golem. He shot a few more rounds just to make sure it still went after him and no one else.

The golem uprooted a palm tree and used it like a javelin. Jace's eyes widened, and he dove to the side as it crashed beside him. He rolled over and fired a few more rounds, still hoping to break through the shell. Then dodged a flying boulder.

Jace returned fire as the golem threw another vehicular projectile, then ran to the street just as the golem blew the top half of a nearby building. He sprinted as fast as he could, feeling chunks of wood and stone smack against his arms and legs. "Maybe we should invest in actual grenades. It would make this so much easier."

Jace looked back to see the golem swipe another building and blowing it to bits.

"Hey!" Jace leaped up and waved his arms to try to get the monster's attention.

The golem turned and faced Jace, then swiped another building. This time, it seemed as if used that debris as a weapon.

Jace dove behind a parked car and used it for cover as the pieces of the building rained down on him. A couple of painful bumps and smacks on his hands and head.

He blinked a few times and took a moment to regain his senses.

Then he got up and ran just as an earth-shattering stomp flattened the car he used for cover.

Jace planted a hand on the fallen palm tree to vault over it and continued to gain distance, waiting for a good time to move in. "Can your fire rounds melt rocks?"

"Easily. They're just not active for very long."

That would have to do.

The golem picked up another tree and threw it at Jace. Instead of running away, Jace took a couple of steps to the side and braced himself for the impact of the branches, covering his face with his arms and hands. When it landed, he grabbed on the branches and climbed inside the leafy cover.

After a moment, the golem picked up the tree and waved it back and forth.

Jace leaped out from his cover onto the golem, grabbing at the shoulder. The golem twisted and spun to try to shake Jace off, but he held firm. While his legs whipped around, Jace inspected the chest plate of the creature, seeing the many deep dips and missing chunks. And he was right—the light was escaping from those cracks.

After feeling comfortable with his grip with one hand, Jace grabbed the gun set to incendiary. And though he swung wildly, Jace took his time with his aim, figuring he was low on ammo. He fired at what looked like the weakest point in the golem's chest. It lit up and glowed red with the heat, with parts of it dripping away. Then he fired again at the same spot to the same effect.

The golem leaped into the air, and Jace's face smacked against the stone. He held on tight, knowing if he lost his grip, he'd not survive the fall. Then, for a brief moment, Jace was weightless. A moment of peace. The calm before the storm.

Suddenly, he fell fast and hard. His feet were lifted in the air, but he continued to hang on. He gazed at the fast approaching ground as he clenched the monster and prepared for impact. It landed hard, sending a shockwave of destruction all around it, breaking windows and damaging the general structure of buildings in the immediate area.

The impact was too much, and Jace lost his grip. He fell freely, rolling over a few times as he skid against the incline of some limb, and he crashed hard on his side in a car windshield.

"Jace! Are you okay?"

He rolled, then uncontrollably slid off the hood of the car and onto the driveway. He slowly and painfully sat up, feeling a deep throb in his shoulder, and gasped for many heartbeats before finally choking in some air. "Maybe. I think so."

The crashing of a building caught Jace's attention as the golem continued its wave of destruction.

After catching his breath, Jace slowly got to his feet, favoring his left side. "Where are the damn police? They should have been here by now."

"I think they're forming a perimeter or something. I don't know."

He scoffed, taking one last moment to steady his nerves. He cringed when he saw the creature stomp on a car that drove by. "Okay, let's do this." He charged the golem once more while it took out the second floor of a motel.

Jace ran up the stairs, down the pathway, and leaped back onto the golem with a determined yell. His fingers clenched onto a section of the chest that was partially melted. The sharp glass-like segments cut deep into Jace's fingers, but he held on regardless. His feet dangled freely some thirty feet off the ground.

The moisture of his blood started to run down Jace's arm as he tried to steady himself. When he finally stabilized, Jace pulled out his incendiary gun and let off one round after another until the slide came back. The plasma burst and stuck to the stone, melting it away. A large chunk flew off and smacked onto Jace's shoulder, part of the plasma sticking to Jace's skin. He groaned in pain as the plasma started to eat through the armor and then his flesh, but defiantly fought through the agony.

That gave the monster pause, and it lurched back and roared, a large section of the torso finally melting away to show the bright light underneath. With the break in momentum, Jace put the gun away and started to climb, doing his best to ignore the shredded fingers and the burning skin. Slowly, he lifted himself up, scaling the golem to get to the spotlight on the monster's torso as it began to move. Hand over hand, bloody handprint over bloody handprint, he drew closer.

Before he could make his way toward the hole in its chest, Jace noticed the golem moving toward an apartment building where people stared out of their windows. Those stupid bastards didn't evacuate when the neighboring block was getting bombed.

Fearing for the safety of the innocent dumb asses, Jace quickened his pace, recklessly tossing himself upward to gain momentum and distance. His hand slapped hard against the bottom vicinity, then his bloodied hand shortly after. With a grunt, he pulled himself up and over the brightly shining stone lip. Jace scrambled to get to his knees as the monster charged toward the building.

The sudden shift in balance almost had Jace plummeting down the pulsating cavity. He looked down to the center of the golem, seeing the brightest part of the inside. Not giving it a second thought, Jace grabbed his second gun and pulled the trigger with his bloodied hand. Each round exploded and nearly deafened Jace, and chunks of stone blew into his face. The impact almost blew Jace out of the cavity, but he kept at it, squeezing the trigger for a second shot. Then a third, and a fourth.

Exploding rocks flew at Jace, pummeling his face. The monster lurched and roared over the sound of explosions. A fifth and a sixth, and Jace felt the monster stop its charge and it growled. He fired the seventh and final round in his gun. The golem leaned forward, then back, as if trying to regain its balance. It roared again, the sound and the pressure pushing Jace back against the side of the cavity. Then his footing failed as the cavity crumbled. Rocks and stones came crashing down, dust and debris preventing him from seeing or catching a breath. He felt himself fall and slide with the rest of the rock as the golem finally crumbled, burying Jace inside the stone alive.

CHAPTER TWENTY-SIX

Echoes of a deep, distant voice tried to break through the haze of the unconscious mind. Looking into the pitch black, trying desperately to find any source of light to cling to, a face of a faded memory slowly appeared from the nothingness. It was the face of a woman who had brown eyes and straight black hair that went past her shoulders. The woman smiled, light beaming from behind her making her details turn into a dark silhouette.

It was the second time that night he woke up under a pile of rubble. He groaned in pain, then blinked a few times to try to get his senses back. He heard the muffled sound of high pitch noise sliding to a low pitch noise of alarm and urgency. The sirens were getting closer.

Brian spoke over the earpiece, "Jace! Come on, talk to me!"

Jace gasped, his throat corse and dry. "Wh…what?"

"You're alive! Are you okay?"

Jace shifted and struggled, trying to get an idea on his condition. He felt aches and pains, but nothing too sharp or debilitating. He felt the mesh armor pressing against his skin and silently thanked Brian for once again saving his life. "I think so." He shifted his back, allowing his shoulders more room to move.

"What happened? Everything went quiet all of a sudden, and I couldn't see anything in the cameras."

Jace coughed, visibly expelling dust in his mouth through the low light images from the contact lenses. He grunted as he lifted his arm, sliding the rocks above him. "Yeah, I'm okay." He pushed hard against a slab of stone, slighting lifting it from the ground. With another grunt, Jace shoved it to the side, allowing him access to fresh air once more. He sat up, then surveyed the area.

He was buried in a large pile of rocks that ranged from pebbles to large chunks that were half his size. Many of the pieces looked like concrete, and others with tons of dirt around them. He leaned back on his hands, then took a deep breath.

"I got it. Holy shit, I got it!"

"Holy smokes!"

When Jace climbed out of the rubble, people all around him started to shout in praises of gratitude. After getting to his feet, Jace began to walk toward the side of where the golem last stood, then knelt to pick up his fallen weaponry. Before he was able to stand up again, people from all over the area surrounded him. Jace took it all in stride. He slid both of his guns in their respective holsters, then started to walk through the crowd.

A police hover vehicle landed beside the crowd, and a law officers came out of the sliding doors. They rushed to the scene to get it closed off from the public. Moments later, another hover vehicle arrived at the scene, followed by a few land cruisers. People poured out of their cars and went to work to get a handle on the situation.

Seeing the moment of controlled chaos as an opportunity to leave, Jace slipped away. He climbed in the car and closed the door, sitting in the dark for a long moment to recompose himself. He ached all over. He looked at his hands, and at the deep cuts in his fingers, and rubbed his bloodied and stiff wrists. After taking another moment, Jace let out a deep sigh and put his hands in his lap. Again, he wondered how the monster got there.

"Hey Brian, any thoughts on where the hell that thing came from?"

"I've been going through everything I could on the stone golem. All I know is they are created."

He considered where he was when the monster formed, then a memory of the previous mission he had like this came to mind. The coincidences seemed too consistent. Jace's face grew pale at a thought. He shook his head in disbelief, but he decided he had to be sure. "Brian, look up on how to create a stone golem."

"What? Why?"

"Just do it." Jace leaned forward to unstrap his harness, fighting through the pains in his body.

"Okay. Geez, this thing looks complex. What do you want to know?"

Jace groaned after a particular twist of his back produced a sharp, deep pain in his side. After fighting through the pain, Jace let out a relaxing breath. "Is there a picture or something on how to create one?" He finished removing the harness and tossed it on the passenger seat.

"Yeah. I see a diagram of some circle with some very intricate shapes in the middle. It's really fascinating. It is—"

"Does it have six points?" Jace leaned back against the chair to ease the pain of his body.

"Uh, points? I, uh…I think so. Inside the circle intertwined in the shapes and symbols, I think I see some sort of six-pointed star or something."

Jace's eyes popped, and his heart skipped a beat. "Requires moonlight or darkness?"

"Yeah. Wait. How do you-"

Jace wasn't paying attention at that time. He instead started to consider how coincidental everything seemed. It all seemed too convenient. All of the seemingly random things that came about started to seem not-so-random. The attack on the city just after he put the sensors on the top of the building, and the destruction that ensued shortly after. He considered what Brian had told him about the sensor unit, and how he didn't know what it was, or how it worked. Back then, it seemed odd to Jace. Now, it started to make perfect sense. This was exactly what happened on his first mission.

"I'm reading reports of all of the lives you saved. Way to go! They're calling you a 'mystery hero' and…"

Jace hardly heard what Brian said. He suspected something was wrong, but he never seriously considered his doubting feelings until now. He felt he was born to hunt these things. He trained his entire life to destroy these creatures. Now, he had deep suspicions on The Order using these things they claimed to kill on sight. A sickening bile started to churn in his stomach at the implications. "Why?"

"What? Why what?"

Jace again looked at the deep lacerations in his fingers, and at the caked blood that formed in the seams. With a deep breath, he placed his head against the back of his seat. Claire would have to wait. "Sit back." Jace sat up and started his car. "Get everything packed and ready to go, just in case."

"In case of what?"

Jace reached under his armor, under his shirt, and took out the pendant. He stared at it for a long moment, deep in thought.

"In case of what?" Brian asked again.

"I don't know." He spun the pendant on its chain. "Just in case." He put the pendant back under his shirt, then drove away.

———

It snowed. It always snowed. The once strange phenomena didn't seem so unusual to Jace at that moment. He stared at it as he drove up the mountain road—something he hardly ever did due to the lack of traction from the tires. Even though the strange white flakes had crossed his mind, he always thought it was just the location or something he didn't care to understand. He shook his head at the thought, feeling stupid for not questioning those kinds of things. He looked at his hands once more, noting the scars that were quickly forming on his skin. Even though Erica had told him that there was no magic or whatever in the goo, Jace couldn't help but wonder if the goo was in fact as unnatural as the falling snow.

As he pulled up to the bridge, he wondered how deep the plot went. How far did the corruption go?

He parked the car, geared up, then walked over the bridge toward the circular garden of the great mountain structure. Jace looked at his hands once more, letting the snowfall onto the scabbed wounds on his fingers. He wondered about Erica, and what her role was in this conspiracy.

He walked up the stairs and opened the door. After the initial shock of the hot air, he stood in the entryway, pausing for a long moment to visually scan the few people that were walking around. Everyone seemed normal while they went about their business like nothing had happened. At least until the lurking eyes spotted him.

As the door closed behind him, Jace wondered what his next step should be. He needed answers, but should he confront Erica first? Clenching his fist painfully, he decided that was his next step.

Jace walked into the infirmary and saw Erica working on her glass tablet while talking to a familiar-looking guy in a tight greenish-brown shirt, camouflage pants, and military-grade boots. He had a buzz cut, and a glimmer of something around his neck that Jace figured were dog tags.

Erica glanced toward the door and paused for a moment. The man glanced his way, then asked Erica something Jace couldn't hear. She shook her head, said something in reply, then went back to doing whatever with the man.

Twenty minutes later, Erica and the army man exited the room. He stood nearly a foot taller than Jace, with muscles much larger than his own. He stared down at Jace with a superior look in his eye. Though his face had several old scars, including a sizeable vertical gash just to the side of his left eye that went from his temple to his jaw, the skin-colored facial tattoo caught Jace's attention.

Jace reached a bloodied hand toward Erica's arm. "Let's talk."

That sparked the military man into protective action, and he reached out to grab at Jace, revealing another massive tattoo of a snake and eagle on his right bicep with numbers and letters going under it.

"Don't touch the lady," the man said protectively.

Jace looked at the man's eyes with deadly calm, and again at the tattoo on his left cheek—three thick bars only a little darker than the natural skin tone.

Erica put a hand on the guy's arm. "That'll be all, Roberts. Go up in the elevator to the lobby."

Roberts remained motionless for a moment, then released Jace's arm, eyeing Jace as he walked toward the elevator.

Erica grabbed Jace by the wrists and inspected his hands. "Come on. Let me get you taken care of. We can talk in my office." She released his wrists, then walked toward her office.

His mind focused on his questions to her. He wondered what was going on and why she acted so distant. Was it because of their night at the hotel? Should he bring up her attitude or his revelation since his last mission? Conflicted, Jace relaxed his arms, having his hands fall limp to his side, then followed Erica in her office.

Jace sat in a swivel chair while Erica stood in front of him. Her tightly tied back hair was a little messed up from the long day she probably had, but her alluring scent of vanilla always put Jace at ease.

She started to clean his wounds, removing the layers of dried blood and dead skin. "When was the last time you ate?"

That brought Jace out of his distant contemplation. Was she asking him out on a date? Or did she ask because his stomach wasn't shy on the loud and uncomfortable growl?

Erica smirked and shook her head. "That answers my question."

"Uh, well..." Jace cleared his throat. "I've been thinking a lot about things lately."

"Oh?" Erica lightly pressed a disinfecting swab on the deep gashes in his hand. She looked up at him. "What about?"

He didn't know how to react, nor did he know how to bring up his suspicions. And though topics came to mind, he felt helpless and tongue-tied. Jace gazed into her blue eyes. "Well..." He considered his thoughts for a moment, then decided to do what he came here to do. "How well do you know this place?"

"What? This place?" Her tone had a subtle hint of venom in her voice. "What about it?"

Jace paused for a moment, carefully planning his questions. "Would The Order ever allow the use of magic?"

"What a stupid question." She looked back down at Jace's wounded hands. "Of course they wouldn't."

"And... What about you?"

"Me?" She glared at Jace, then swept her arm in a wide arc. "Look around you, soldier boy. I built this place. I don't need anything like that. Why dabble in things like that when everything you need can be solved by science?"

"What about the goo?"

"What about it?"

"Is that magic?"

Erica scoffed. "I designed and developed it. Aside from the magic of biomolecular chemistry, there is nothing *magic* about it."

"Nothing?"

"Nothing." Erica pressed the point by applying more pressure than required on Jace's hand.

He winced from the sting but was satisfied with the answer.

She eased up on her grip, then reached over and grabbed a bandage to wrap his hand. "What's this about?"

Jace didn't answer. He sat still, staring off at the distant nothing wondering if he was putting pieces together to different puzzles.

"Hey!"

His eyes blinked a couple of times, then looked back at Erica.

"What's this about?"

Jace looked at his bandaged hands.

"They're treated with special crap I developed," Erica explained, anger and impatience in her tone. "Now, what is this about?"

"Something…isn't sitting well with me and I need to figure it out."

"Cryptic as always." Erica turned around and removed the protective gloves from her hands. "You're done here. Go get something to eat. You'll need it."

Jace stood up. "What are your thoughts on magic?"

Erica shook her head in an exaggerated exhale. Her tone and posture were getting more irate. "Look, is this really relevant?"

Jace gave a half-smile and shook his head. "Always saving my ass."

Erica returned Jace's expression with a half-smile of her own.

He turned and left to go to the upper floors.

———

Though Jace trusted Erica and believed she had nothing to do with the strange incidents that have been happening, his concerns and suspicions still needed to be addressed. He swerved around the corners and walked down the halls to make his way to the corner office of his mentor, Xin. He paused when he reached the door and again wondered if he was just paranoid and if he took the smallest things out of proportion. Perhaps they were just coincidences. He blinked a couple of times. "Perhaps not."

As he reached for the handle, the door opened wide. Feint smoke came out of the office as Sir Xin stood in the doorway. "Come in. Sit."

Jace looked baffled for a long moment, then walked in the office.

Xin closed the door behind him, then walked toward his desk chair. "What brings you to me today?"

"Well…" Jace tried to once again find confidence in his suspicions.

Xin sat across from Jace, his hands resting on the armrests.

"I finished a mission, and a monster appeared." Jace paused to study Xin at that comment, but he remained expressionless, his glasses hiding any eye movements that could tell Jace what the strange man thought.

"It appeared right on the building the sensors were placed on."

Again, nothing.

"The last time I did that type of job, the same thing happened." Jace grew more confident as he continued. "Those creatures don't just appear out of nowhere. And the fact that they appeared on the very building the so-called 'sensors' were placed on is more than suspicious."

When Xin didn't say or do anything, Jace continued.

"It requires a great deal of energy, an intricate circle, six points of power, and the dark of night to create such a thing." After many heartbeats of silence, Jace continued, deciding to be frank about his suspicions. "I think the 'sensor' is the power source, the six scan nodes are the points of power, and maybe that thing creates a perfect circle through some mechanical stuff. I think those things were created to make those monsters. Why else would the mission need to be done before nightfall on specific days?"

Xin remained a statue—motionless and expressionless.

The silence and unreadable expression from Xin frustrated Jace. "I want to know what's going on."

"Do you?" Xin finally said.

"Yes. What the hell is going on?"

Xin lifted his hands, putting his fingertips together in a steeple fashion. "You are the youngest person ever to receive the rank of Paladin Lieutenant of The Order. You have a unique talent that separates you far from your peers. Because of your rank, you are allowed to know. Because of your age, I do not think you should know."

Jace bent forward, putting his bandaged palms on the desk. "I just risked my life saving an entire neighborhood, and more! I deserve to know!"

Xin's head ever so slightly moved downward, as if looking at Jace's bandaged hands. "You have defeated the stone golem?"

"Isn't that my job?" Jace stood up straight but paused when he caught a possible slip of the tongue from Xin. He never said it was a stone golem.

Xin's head went back as if to allow him to look at Jace through his dark glasses. "Remarkable. Very well." After a long pause, Xin's hands went back to the armrests. "Fear."

Jace blinked, not quite understanding.

"Fear is what runs this world. Fear is what keeps order. Fear is what creates power.

Try as he might, Jace couldn't hide the shock on his face. His eyes widened, and he subconsciously took a deep breath at the sudden revelation.

Xin stood up, then started to walk around his desk. "I did not expect you to realize that we planted those demons in the cities. I did not expect you to realize the true meaning of those devices. At least not yet."

Jace's eyes lowered in horror. He thought about the lives lost in the first mission and wondered if he had taken part in anything else of the sort. He wondered how many lives he was responsible for destroying when all he wanted to do was save them. Save everyone. That feeling made him feel sick to his stomach.

Xin stopped beside him. "You do not approve?"

His eyes absently shifted back and forth, as if he were scanning the desk. "No." Jace shook his head, then looked up at Xin. "No. That's not how we do things."

"Ah, but it is. We have been planting the seed of fear for a long, long time."

Jace shook his head again. "That's not how I do things."

"But it is," Xin once again correct.

"I won't take part in anything that takes human lives."

"But you have... And you are."

Jace's shoulders slumped at that notion.

Xin continued to walk around Jace, circling him. "Now that you know, it will be much easier to plant the devices, as well as many other missions. Your raw talent will help bring the world peace and order. You will play a major role in the salvation of the human race."

Jace thought about that for a long moment. He always fancied himself the savior of humanity. He always found himself battling demons and saving people at the same time with no regrets. Like The Order, saving humankind was his calling. Or so he thought. He felt his heart sink as his world slowly collapsed around him. He felt himself fall into chaos and confusion.

In the midst of his emotional darkness, Jace saw something—a little girl with brown hair under a hoodie. She ran through the fields across from SOC and pointed upward at the imaginary clouds above. She smiled and bounced through fields. His inner-eye focused on that image and wondered if The Order would sacrifice her for their stupid missions.

Jace lifted his head in renewed determination. His eyes were focused with rage, and he clenched his bandaged fists at his sides. Without taking his eyes off of Xin, he reached up under his shirt, ripped off the pendant he wore around his neck and tossed it on Xin's desk. "I won't be a part of this, not if it sacrifices innocent lives." He started to move past Xin and towards the door.

As Jace exited the room, he walked around the corner to see Erica walking down the hall.

"Be warned, Fallen," Xin called from behind.

Hearing the title "Fallen" gave a pause in Jace's steps.

"Forsake us, and you will not last. Remember, you are being hunted by Evolved. You are well-known to them and will be alone in your life."

Jace took another moment to consider his words, then continued walking.

Erica put her hand on Jace's shoulder, having him turn around. She recoiled at the anger in his eyes. "Fallen? What's going on?"

"I won't have any part of anything that kills innocent people." Jace had to take a deep breath to calm his mounting fury. Without another word, he spun on his heels and left.

"Wait!" Erica called out, but Jace didn't stop.

When Jace returned to the snow, he saw Roberts standing next to the door staring off in the distance.

"Stay away from Erica," Roberts said as Jace started to walk down the stairs.

Jace stopped for a moment, then turned his head. He locked his gaze at Roberts, who stood in a superior fashion on the top step, massive arms crossed. He noticed that Roberts' tattoo wasn't so much three lines, but letters. He was too far away, from the skin toned ink for Jace to make out what it read. Jace was going to put the man in his place, but he remembered that he was no longer welcome. He was a Fallen—an outcast from The Order.

His eyes lowered in fury and shame, then he turned and continued to walk down the stairs. He didn't feel like fighting anyways. He didn't feel like much. All he wanted to do was see Maya again, relax, and center himself once more. He needed to figure out his next step.

CHAPTER TWENTY-SEVEN

JACE TOLD BRIAN A SUMMARY OF WHAT HAD HAPPENED AFTER HE got back to the hotel. Though the news bummed and shocked Brian, Jace was glad that they didn't need to leave as quickly as he had feared. Having to pack up an emergency kit put Brian on edge, and Jace's non-urgent arrival was just what he needed to calm his nerves.

Jace spent the next week with Maya. And though his hands and many bruises all around his body were basically healed, he was in a melancholy state, which Maya always was able to break. She was always able to brighten his moods in the past, no matter how foul, and she always made him feel whole. Not this time, though. He felt empty. Lost. He felt like he didn't have any form of direction in his life.

Maya ran past Jace as he sat on the couch in the living room, then stopped in front of a window and stared at a bird that landed on the balcony. She turned and pressed her hands against the glass as if to get a closer look at the animal. A smile crept onto Jace's lips as he watched her stare in awe and curiosity. The bird flew away with Maya's gaze never leaving the bird until it was out of sight.

Jace decided he needed to get out of his emotional slump. He had money. He had Maya. He also knew where two out of three of his childhood friends were. It wasn't that bad, Jace decided. He pushed himself off the couch to get to his feet. "What do you want to do today?"

Maya turned around, her hood falling off her head. She shrugged, an eyebrow following the motions of her shoulders.

"Yeah, me neither." Jace walked up beside Maya, and the two stared outside. He noticed a lot of people walking around that day. More people than usual. He considered that for a moment. "Is there an event going on today? Maybe a festival?"

She replied with a shrug.

"Come on." He turned around. "Let's go find out."

Maya bounded off into her room as Jace went to put on his boots.

———

The two walked around for hours. They asked nearby patrons, but they found nothing. No special event or anything Jace could think of was around to warrant such foot traffic. Eventually, they stopped for lunch, going to a pizza place they often frequented ever since they started staying at the hotel.

Jace put the pizza pan on the table, then sat in the booth across from Maya. Her face beamed with joy at the steamy goodness of melted cheese. Immediately, she reached over to grab a slice, quickly putting it on her plate, then shook her hand to cool off the minor burns she inflicted on her fingertips.

"Relax." Jace put a napkin in his lap. "It's not going anywhere." After a moment, Jace too reached over to grab a slice. After putting it on his plate, Jace shook his hand to cool off the burns.

Maya smiled and covered a silent laugh with her hand.

Jace's face twisted in mock anger. He grabbed the napkin from his lap and tossed it across the table. It gently hit Maya's face, covering her eyes. While she was blinded, Jace swiped the food from her plate and hid it out of sight. She yanked the napkin free from her face, then looked down to discover her missing pizza. Jace diverted his gaze, pretending nothing had happened.

She tossed the napkin back at Jace and stood up.

"What?" Jace caught the falling napkin.

Maya pointed to the table in front of her.

"Oh, you want a salad?"

Maya crossed her arms, and her lips blew out in a stern pout. She plopped heavily on the booth chair, then reached over and grabbed another slice of pizza placing it on her plate. She took a sip of the drink she had through her straw when a loud crash of what sounded like aluminum startled her. Maya whipped her head to the side. The distraction allowed Jace to finish his ploy. With a quick gesture, he put the hidden piece of pizza on her plate before she looked back, returning to the same pose and posture he had been before her attention was diverted. She turned to face to Jace, then back down at the now two slices of pizza she had in front of her. She looked back to Jace, who continued to look away as if nothing had happened. Her face mimicked Jace's mock anger expression, then she threw her napkin at Jace.

Jace caught the napkin in midair, then looked at Maya, who smiled. Jace too smiled and gave a light laugh. The two continue to eat their meal in a playful and warm manner.

"Hey, can I ask you something?" Jace asked after the two finished their lunch.

Maya looked up to Jace, then nodded.

"Why don't we learn sign language together? We could have conversations and…"

Maya frantically shook her head side to side.

Jace found it odd that her expression was one of horror like the idea terrified her. "Okay, how about writing down what you—"

Again, Maya shook her head with the same expression. He noticed her eyes moisten, and her cheeks turn pale.

Jace got up and sat next to her. He put his arm around her shoulders and hugged her, comforting his sister. "Forget I said anything. How about some ice cream?"

———

The next day, Jace checked out of their hotel. The manager was sad to see them leave but was happy for their patronage. Like The Order, the military, and the orphanage, it was time to move on.

Jace packed up the trunk of the car. "Go make sure you got

everything." He placed his equipment bag down to the side, then grabbed some of the blankets the three had accumulated over the course of their travels.

Maya had a little teddy bear backpack on, and her hoodie covered her head. She nodded, then scampered past Brian, who walked out of the hotel with a box of goods left over from their stay.

Brian approached Jace, who still put things in the trunk. "Hey, Jace, I've been meaning to talk to you."

Jace stood up straight, grabbing the box from Brian. "What's up?"

Brian looked away and scratched the back of his neck. "After everything that happened, I'm not feeling right... About what we did."

"We still saved countless lives. If you weren't with me, I'd have died a long time ago, and who knows how many people would have been killed by that stone golem?"

"So what are you going to do?"

Jace put a box in the trunk and scooted it aside. "I don't really know, but I don't want any part of anything that involves killing innocent people."

"The Order isn't exactly innocent. Would you shoot them?"

Jace opened his mouth to reply but found himself temporarily speechless. He cleared his throat, regaining his lost voice. "I don't know, man." Jace ran his fingers through his hair. "Look, I don't even know where to go from here."

The two stood silently for a moment.

Brian smiled and adjusted his glasses. "Relax. Take some time off. We all know you deserve it."

After a moment's pause, Jace nodded his head, looking back up at Brian. "Yeah, I need to get my shit straight."

Again, Brian and Jace stood silent for a moment, then shook hands.

Brian smiled. "Keep in touch."

"Yeah, I will."

The two started to separate when Maya hopped out from the building. Brian walked up to Maya to talk to her for a bit.

Jace smiled at the loving notion, then reached over to put his backpack in the trunk. His hands moved up to the trunk handle when the corner of his eyes caught something that demanded his attention.

His eyes peered over to the other side of the street, and at two suspicious people who stood facing the hotel. He paused for a moment, then patted himself down, as if to look for something. After giving a frustrated rolling of the head, and the arms falling to his side in anger, he grabbed his equipment bag, took his backpack out, then closed the trunk. He walked up to Brian and Maya, who started their goodbye hug.

"Hey," Jace said in a clear, upraised tone. "I forgot something in the hotel room. Help me find it."

Brian and Maya looked at Jace, both with confused expressions on their faces. Jace stayed motionless but moved his eyes towards his bag and backpack.

Brian's eyes widened in understanding. "Sure." He took Maya's hand, and the three started to walk back into the lobby. Without saying a word, and walking calmly and casual, the three stood in front of the elevator as it opened up. The three got in, then pushed the button to their floor.

Once the doors closed, Jace pushed the emergency stop button, dropped everything and frantically took off his jacket.

Brian knelt down and started opening the bag. "What's going on?"

"Something doesn't feel right." Jace grabbed the mesh armor from Brian's hand.

"Like what?" Brian handed Jace the gun harness.

"I don't know. Maybe it's nothing. Maybe not." He finished donning the harness, then put on his jacket. Brian opened the large, silver case from the bag. Jace reached inside and grabbed his guns, then put them in their holsters. "Either way, I want to be prepared."

"Here. Last two." Brian handed Jace the last of the Fenrir grenades. Jace took them and placed them in their respective pockets. Then, Brian zipped up the bag, grabbed the handle, then stood up and grabbed Maya's hand.

"What kind of ammo?" Jace asked.

"Standard in all three. You might have a belt or two of special ammo in the backpack."

"And in the guns?"

"Normal."

Jace nodded, pushed the resume button on the elevator, and he glanced at Maya, who stared up at him scared and confused.

The doors to the elevator opened. Jace's eyes widened, then he pushed his back against Brian and Maya, pressing them against the elevator wall. Half a dozen large three-foot spears of ice flew into the elevator, embedding themselves in the wall narrowly missing Brian.

Brian gasped in fear. "Holy smokes!"

The three didn't have much room on the one side. Jace had to get to the other side for better cover. "Stay here."

"Wh-what?"

Jace grabbed his guns and went low, dropped to a knee and shot a few rounds blindly. As another spear of ice flew toward him, Jace rolled over his shoulder to the other side of the elevator.

Jace looked over to Brian and Maya. "Barriers."

"Holy smokes, holy smokes!" Brian kept his back as far against the wall as possible. He held Maya, trembled in fear covering her mouth with both of her hands, to his side in the corner of the elevator.

Jace met with Maya's gaze. "Hey, are you okay?"

Brian gasped. "I'll be fine."

Jace glared at Brian. "Not you!"

A ball of ice flew into the elevator and smacked against the back wall, exploding on impact. Brian turned and protected Maya, using his body as a shield. He grunted in pain when the shards hit him. Jace simply held up his hands to protect his face, the armor protecting him from the exploding ice.

Figuring they were sitting ducks, Jace knew he had to move to a new location. "Wait here." He saw Maya's eyes peek from over Brian's protective shoulder. Jace gave a reassuring smile. "Don't worry. I won't let anything happen to you."

Maya, wide-eyed and scared, continued to cover her mouth and nodded in reply.

Jace held up his guns, then spun out of the elevator, using it for both distraction and defense. He looked down both sides of the flanking halls, and in the main entryway to the hotel room while firing another blind shot at an attacker before getting to cover.

To Jace's side, he saw someone come from around the corner. Purple and green bolts of pulsating energy shot from the flanker's fingertips, spiraling in midair down the hallway. Jace leaped on to and off the wall. He reached up and, with his guns still in his hands, grabbed the dangling light fixture by the very tips of his fingers. The bolts spiraled by, narrowly missing Jace. They slammed into the floor and walls, exploding on impact, leaving baseball-sized holes behind.

He released his grip, twisting and rotating his body, and firing off four rounds at the flanking opponent. He landed in a kneel as the bullets ripped through the attacker. Blood splattered against the walls, and it fell to the floor lifeless.

Before Jace could stand, the first attacker came from behind and blasted Jace in the back with some form of frost attack. Jace felt the cold bite at his skin, but it seemed the mesh armor absorbed most of the shock. Jace turned around just as he saw a seven-foot-tall, four-armed ice monster grab him in a tight hug. He grimaced as the hold grew tighter and tighter. The beast was too strong for him to break free.

Desperate, he did his best to angle his wrists downward, then squeezed the trigger. One after another, Jace's bullets shot from the hand cannons. Each round dug into the monster's foot. Then, a large crack went from the broken foot and to the ankles. The ice shattered, and the beast lumbered forward. Holding Jace, they both crashed hard to the ground. The impact blew the he breath from Jace's lungs.

He struggled to keep his focus as the ice beast sat up. It roared, as Jace worked to free an arm from the pin. It opened its sharp-toothed maw and went in for a killing bite. Barely able to keep his composure, Jace freed one of his arms free from the hulking grasp, jammed the barrel of the gun inside the mouth of the monster, then pulled the trigger. The slide came back as the back of its head exploded. The beast fell into an icy powder, covering Jace in snow.

Something heavy collapsed on Jace. He pushed it aside and saw the body of a dead human-looking attacker, the back of its head missing. The beast must have been some sort of bonding or mutation spell or something, but he didn't have the time to contemplate that mystery.

Jace rolled over, coughed a couple of times, then reached back to reload his guns. He looked around, gasping for air. No one was around. "Brian, you and Maya alright?"

"We're okay," Jace heard Brian reply.

"Hang tight." Jace slowly went to his feet. He turned around and saw someone run around the corner. Jace brought up his guns and put them against their forehead. "Don't move." Jace stared hard into the man's eyes.

The man quivered in fear, not taking his eyes off of Jace. "I—"

"Don't even talk!" Jace pressed the barrel a little harder against the man's skull, making him shut up. Jace put away the second gun and grabbed one of the Fenrir grenades. His gaze never left the man's fearful eyes as they tried to move to follow Jace's actions. When the gaze made their way to the corpse behind, the man shook in fear. The grenade went off and covered the area in a fine mist. The man didn't glow.

Jace took a step back, removing the gun from the man's skull. "Get out of here. Use the stairs."

The man's breath quivered in fear, and he took a few cautious steps to get past Jace, then he ran down the hall.

Slowly and cautiously, Jace made his way back to the elevator. When he got inside, he looked at the two who were huddled in the corner. "Does the elevator work?"

Brian looked around as if he were inspecting the device. "I'm not sure."

Jace heard footsteps down the hall. The doorway exploded, electricity sparking between the door studs. "Push it!" Jace grabbed the second gun and leaned out to fire a couple of rounds into the hallway. He didn't even see if the shots hit, as they were meant to slow the pursuit. He leaned back against the wall with both his guns pointed at the door. The sliding doors finally closed just as figures got into view.

The elevator lights flickered as Jace took off his backpack and knelt down next to the bag. "Reload the harness." He grabbed an explosive ammo belt and handed it to Brian. "One is empty."

Brian grabbed the ammo belt and quickly started to reload the harness. "What's happening?"

"Apparently, my reputation precedes me." He handed an incidniary belt to Brian, then manually loaded the missing rounds from his guns.

Brian slapped Jace's shoulder. "So they're here for you?"

"Probably." Jace, trying to ignore the guilt of putting Brian and Maya in danger, stood up and re-equipped himself. "I was warned that this might happen." Jace slightly tilted his head as a thought came to him.

Brian stared at Jace questionably. "What?"

"If The Order uses golems to destroy a city block, who says this isn't their doing too?" Jace looked over and saw Maya gripping Brian tightly, hiding as best as she could behind him. She still covered her mouth. He knelt and smiled. "Don't worry. I won't let anything hurt you."

The elevator bell dinged as the lift came to a shaky stop.

"Get against the wall." Jace stood and moved to the elevator corner. "Whatever you do, don't let Maya see anything."

The doors slid open. Nothing. Jace lifted his hand up to his lips, and silently shushed, indicating for the two to stay quiet. He knelt, put his gun toward the ground, then slightly moved it into the doorway. He looked at the reflection in the polished weapon, and at the half-dozen people standing in the entryway of the hotel. Jace tucked that gun under his arm, then grabbed the last of the grenades. He primed it and tossed it into the lobby. It exploded, making the air very humid.

As the grenade popped, Jace sprang into action. He leaped out of the elevator, sliding on the slick marble floor. As he slid the few feet, he fired a few rounds from each gun at any glowing target he saw. One shot hit one in the head, which was violently thrown back in an explosion of blood. The second and third round missed. The fourth hit the leg of a glowing target, blasting a hole in the bone.

Jace used his remaining momentum to roll to his knees, and he took cover behind the desk as a burst of flame blew out from the side of his shelter. Then, water started to fall from the sky. Jace looked up, wondering if it was the sprinkler system. His face contorted in confusion when he saw a dark cloud form above him, and he felt a strange breeze carry papers off the desk.

Not fully understanding what was going on with the strange cloud, Jace put his focus on what he did know. He quickly stood up, his guns pointing at the remaining foes. They were scattering, with one on the floor dead, and another next to him holding his leg and screaming in pain. Jace got his beads on a single target who ran for cover behind a large structure pillar. His guns fired again and again, each shot barely missing its mark. Jace reached back and reloaded his weapons with the regular rounds.

Then, the cloud acted.

Lightning shot out from above, striking the puddle of water below Jace. The electrical shock stung, making him uncontrollably jerk. He fell to a knee, trying to catch his breath. The blast hurt, but his thick boots, and maybe even the mesh armor from Brian, possibly saved his life.

The strange cloud vanished.

He was about to rise but saw someone come out from their cover. Jace met the target by blowing a hole in its chest. That's when he noticed his fingers were numb and tingly. Probably from that electrical strike.

Then his guns focused on the structure pillar and unloaded. Hole after hole was blown into the structure until Jace saw a body fall lifeless to the floor.

Jace slowly stood up, reloading his now empty guns with explosive and incendiary rounds, then started to move toward the walls of the building.

"Uh, Jaaaace!" Brian shouted.

Before he could answer, he saw a ball of fire hurled toward him. Jace fired the explosive round into the wall. The explosion that came from the wall slightly dissipated the ball of flames, but it didn't stop it. Jace was engulfed, but only briefly. He was blown off his feet, sliding back until he hit the back wall. Being soaked from the strange indoor rain, Jace didn't get burned too badly.

The fifth and last of the glowing targets stepped out from their cover. It waved its arms, and a yellow and blue outline of a man-sized rectangle appeared. Then the two things vanished.

"Jace!" Brian shouted again.

On the ground, Jace worked on regaining his composure. He tilted his head to see what was going on, but a glowing demon stood before him. With one arm, the demon picked Jace up by the neck and slammed him against the wall.

The numbed fingers and sudden hit made Jace lose his grip on his guns. He felt his back slam against the wall again. He lifted his legs up and wrapped them around the slender arm that held him in the air. Jace felt another slam against the wall, then a mighty arcing swing that brought Jace fast toward the ground.

Using that momentum, Jace grabbed the wrist on the way down, then used the armlock as a pivot, bending the demon's elbow just as Jace hit. The sudden and awkward shift in balance brought the demon forward a step, but that was enough to have Jace flip it over, head over heels. Jace grabbed the arm tightly, then pulled, straightening his legs.

The demon said something in a strange language, then the demon's arm grew. Muscles bulged, and the demon's clothes tore away. Its skin turned reddish yellow, and the fingers turned into claws.

Jace released his armbar and rolled to his feet. He watched the transformation of the fifth glowing target as a long, spiked tail sprouted from its backbone. Four tentacles sprouted out from the back, large slashing spears at the end of each. The eyes of the snout-nosed beast sunk into the skull, turning black. The legs grew, the feet enlarging, forcing the monster to stand on the balls of its clawed feet.

"Jaaaaaace!" Brian said more urgently.

"I'm okay," Jace called out as he reached down to grab his guns, the numb in his fingers gone. He rolled backward as one tentacle after another launched themselves up and over, punching holes in the ground where he once stood. The tentacles, stretching beyond their plausible means, ripped deep into the ground. Jace turned and ran, the tiled floor tearing apart under the lifting power of the monster. He sidestepped to take cover behind the blown apart pillar as a massive chunk of floor flew past him, crashing hard into the wall.

The pillar split in two as one of the tentacles cleaved through it. Jace leaped forward in a roll when more ungodly limbs punched through the stone pillar in an attempt to grab him.

He rolled to his feet, then fired his guns at the monster. Each shot hit its mark as the beast didn't make any attempt to dodge the attacks. The impact of the exploding rounds caused a lot of smoke and blew away the nearby walls.

As if not even concerned from the bullets hitting it, the monster took a deep breath, then unleashed a green moisture from its mouth.

Jace leaped hard to the side to avoid the cloud. He slid on the ground, crashing into and breaking a potted plant.

The smell of the acid burning the building was atrocious. The demon who was shot in the leg screamed in agony, then fell silent, and the sickening smell of burnt flesh filled the room soon after. Then he saw the walls and support columns starting to smoke and bubble, making Jace question the remaining integrity of the building.

A movement to the side had Jace look at the sixth target. He saw a man with a rifle, but he wasn't glowing. The man quickly stood up, about to point his gun as Jace. Being that he was human, Jace couldn't shoot him. So he pushed aside the plant on top of him and threw one of his guns at the guy. The chrome smashed his nose, which tossed him backward. The man instinctively pulled the trigger of his automatic rifle, firing wildly into the wall.

Jace felt the punch of three bullets hit him—one on his right leg, one on his abdomen, and one in his left shoulder. He stumbled to his feet, took a step forward, and unleashed a flying kick that smacked square into the man's chest. The man flew back into the wall and bounced off. Jace grabbed the back of the guy's neck and swung him into the air in a reverse throw, slamming him hard into the ground. Jace finished him off with quick shots to the temple with the butt of his remaining gun.

Jace knelt and felt his body, patting where the bullets hit. The areas stung, and would probably heavily bruise, but he didn't see any blood on the hit marks or his hands.

"Jace!" Brian shouted.

"I'm fine!" Jace leaned over and saw the monster lumbering toward the elevator. "Look out!" Jace stood up, grabbing the gun he threw at the now unconscious man and ran headlong into the melting room. After a few strides, Jace stepped on a partially melted chair to a table and leaped high into the air, pointed the gun, then fired as fast as he could at the back of the demon. His knees hit the back of the monster, and the sudden impact made it fall forward into the elevator.

Keeping his focus on the monster, Jace reached his arms over the creature's neck. "Go!" He squeezed hard, trying to cut off the oxygen of the beast as it went to its knees.

"But Jace—"

"Now, damn it!"

Hearing the running footsteps of the two fleeing the elevator, Jace looked at the control panel and kicked it hard. He saw the elevator light flicker, then the door closed, sealing the two inside the lift, then the slight shift in momentum as the elevator began to rise.

Jace put the gun to the monster's head, then pulled the trigger. The slid came back, but the bullet didn't finish the job. In a wild and desperate rage, Jace started to hit the monster with the butt of his now empty gun, all while trying to close his arm tighter around the monster's throat.

A tentacle wrapped around his entire torso, and it started to pull him away. Though Jace tried to keep his grip, it was no use. He wasn't strong enough. His arm slipped from the monster's neck, and he found himself being lifted off of the ground.

The elevator stopped moving, and the door opened. Denying whatever anatomical physics the creature may have had, it turned and morphed itself to face Jace. It took a step forward, tentacles tightening, the monster's gaze seemed as if pleased of its pending victory.

Jace noticed he was just outside the elevator. Then he looked at the monster while weakly lifting his left-hand gun. His hand was swatted up in a futile manner, but that was Jace's intent. With the high explosive gun pointed at the main cables, he fired a round. The explosion snapped the cable, and the elevator fell freely. Jace landed on his feet, then lunged himself against the wall as to not be drug down with the monster. The corner caught the tentacles as Jace was pulled toward the falling elevator. He stared down the vast shaft as the tentacles loosened, letting him catch his breath. Jace gasped and rolled behind the wall again just as the elevator crashed. The building shook, and a plume of dust and debris flew upward, blowing out of the open doorway.

With a series of coughs, Jace shook himself free from the dismembered tentacles, then grabbed his guns. He stood up, reached back to reload, then started to walk down the hall toward the fire stairs.

Jace opened the door to the first floor and cautiously walked out into the lobby. Many small fires started up, the clutter from the elevator making it challenging to get to the doorway.

Seeing that the way was clear, Jace leaped over the desk, put a gun away, then picked up the unconscious human attacker. He made his way out of the hotel lobby to the street, where Jace couldn't help but notice the lack of sirens or emergency vehicles.

Brian pulled the car up with screeching tires to the lobby entrance. He got out of the car as Jace put the man down.

"Jace, there is something you need to know."

Jace looked up at Brian in alarm. Negative thoughts and images came to his mind. If Maya was hurt, he would physically tear every monster from limb to limb with his bare hands. "Is Maya okay?" He ran to the car and opened the door.

"Yes, but…"

Jace stopped in his tracks. There she was, as beautiful as always, even with the tears in her eyes and dirty face. Her hoodie was ripped and dusty, and she held on tight to her teddy bear backpack. Her skin glowed blue.

"W…what?" Jace took a step backward, then fell on his rear when he tripped over the curb.

"The mist from the grenade," Brian tried to explain, but Jace wasn't having any of it. His world came to a screeching halt. He wanted to see her, to see past the glow to his little sister. He tried to see the sweet little girl he called his family. But he couldn't. All he saw was the blue aura in the passenger seat of the car, and at the monster before him. All he saw was a murderer and a killer. All he saw was the destruction of humanity, and the enemy he swore to kill.

With grim determination, Jace slowly stood up, staring at the haze in front of him. Moisture dripped from his eyes as his instincts told him to do the job, the one thing he built his entire life around. He heard the slowed and muffled shouts of Brian as Jace reached back behind him to grab the handgrips of the loaded guns. He pulled them out, staring intensely at the demon. His face twisted with rage, and his heart pumped in anger, but his mind was drowning in confusion. The rhetoric of The Order's training and their subtle brainwashing echoed in his mind. They were abominations. Heathens. Demons. Monsters. They were the destructors of the world, and they needed to be stopped.

Jace gripped his guns. There was so much moisture in his eyes that he couldn't see the details of his beloved sister anymore. All he saw was the blue glow. Jace tightly gripped the guns that hung down at his side. Then, with the purest and undiluted anger, as his body uncontrollably convulsed with rage, Jace let out a primal, agonizing scream. He gasped for breath as he fell to his knees, and let out a second shout, dropping the guns to the ground. He bent forward, his fists pounding the ground. He struggled for breath, and he felt himself get lightheaded.

Brian slowly and cautiously walked up next to Jace.

"Get her out of here," Jace said between gasped breaths, tears soaking the concrete.

"But—"

"NOW!" Jace's hands clenched, his nails clawing at the concrete.

Brian didn't move but stared down at Jace as his entire world crashed down on him.

Tears dripped down from his face, splashing on the back of Jace's hands. His voice quivered. "Please."

Jace heard the heavy breathing from Brian, and an emotional sniff as if to hold back tears. After a few moments, Brian finally moved, closing the car doors and sped off.

EPILOGUE

HE WANDERED AIMLESSLY FOR MILES. FOR DAYS. WEEKS. Months. The only times he slept was when he collapsed from pure exhaustion or passed out from the overconsumption of alcohol. He was like a zombie—dead on the inside but living on the outside. He didn't know where he was, nor did he care.

Facial hair took the uncleaned face, and his hair, greasy and unkempt, went down to his mid-back. His boots were worn down to the sole, and his clothes, stained and dirty beyond repair, were ripped and torn. His rugged and worn backpack was one of the few things he had that was still in working condition. The mesh under his clothes stuck to his skin in an awkward manner. The constant shifting of the mesh rubbed his sunburnt skin raw. What was once a finely fit piece of armor now hung loosely over his limbs. He didn't eat. Didn't sleep. The only thing he had was a paper bag and a half-drained bottle inside.

Every day was a blur, and every night was a distant memory destined to be forgotten. Every breath felt like it was forced. Every morning was greeted by a large swig of potent alcohol, and the only thing he consumed was hard liquor.

One day, Jace found himself waking on some lakeside beach with the sun high into the sky. He violently thrashed his head back to pound it against the sand, wishing he never woke up. It hit with a deep thud. Slowly, he sat up, gripped the bottle of booze by the neck, and lifted it upward toward his parched and dry lips. He stopped though when nothing came out, and he tilted the bottle upside down. It was bone dry.

Jace yelled in rage, then quickly stood up, and threw the bottle as hard as he could into the water, hearing the splash and watching the ripples from the lake make their way towards the shore.

He panted in anger, and he gritted his teeth, then he threw a couple of stones that lay nearby into the lake. When he ran out of ammunition, he spat at the water, as if trying to deny it admittance to the shore. Feeling he was out of options, he turned on his heels and walked toward the buildings nearby.

———

After the bartender cut him off, Jace reached over the bar to grab a bottle. The bouncer grabbed him and pushed him away, only for Jace to fall from his stool while still clinging to the bottle of booze. After being picked up, the bouncer tried to pry the bottle from Jace's fingers, but he couldn't get it out. Even after a few hits that gave Jace a black eye and a bloody nose and lip, he still held firm. Finally, he was dragged out of the bar by two people, then one guy held him while the other guy repeatedly punched Jace. He knew he could defend himself, but he let the beating happen.

That was a common occurrence and happened in almost every place of civilization he went to. He relished the pain. He wanted to feel something, even if it was just the pain. But he was so numb, even that wasn't helping him.

After the beating, Jace staggered to his feet, the alcohol making the floor rock back and forth. He didn't shout in defiance, nor raise his hand to wipe the blood from his nose and lip. He just turned and walked away, drinking the bottle of booze along the way.

———

Jace lost track of how many days he wandered the town. Time had lost all meaning.

When he awoke one early morning, he found it too difficult to move. His muscles ached, and his head pulsed with pain, his insides hurt, and he felt weak and sick. He tried to look around but found his neck paralyzed or something. All he could see was the grass he was on in front of some house. Jace let out a resigned sigh, then slowly closed his eyes. He knew this was it—the end. He didn't care, though. He wanted his pain and sorrow to flow freely from his being and wanted his soul to leave this accursed life. To move on into whatever came next.

The distant sound of footsteps on the grass was the only thing Jace could focus on. Then, the distant yet familiar voice broke through the midst of pain and despair. The voice, so different yet so familiar, had Jace try to open his eyes. He looked up to see a fuzzy image of a woman standing before him.

A woman's voice broke through the wall of pain. "Is that you, Jace?"

THE END

———

Don't miss out on your next favorite book!
Join the Melange Books mailing list at
www.melange-books.com/mail.html

THANK YOU FOR READING

Did you enjoy this book?

We invite you to leave a review at the website of your choice, such as Goodreads, Amazon, Barnes & Noble, etc.

DID YOU KNOW THAT LEAVING A REVIEW...

- Helps other readers find books they may enjoy.
- Gives you a chance to let your voice be heard.
- Gives authors recognition for their hard work.
- Doesn't have to be long. A sentence or two about why you liked the book will do.

ABOUT THE AUTHOR

J. P. Edgar is an American author who was born in Sacramento, California in 1980. He went to college to obtain his Associates Degree in Information Technology, and then got his Bachelor's Degree in 2010 in Game Design. A man of many faces, J. P. Edgar is a musician, a technical artist, a game designer, and a computer programmer. Now, he is working on the Bloodlines of Atmos series, expanding his web of talents to the art of story writing.

www.jpedgar.com

ALSO BY J. P. EDGAR

Bloodlines of Atmos, The Story of Jace, Book 1 - Sanctuary